Winter Horror Days

Winter Horror Days

Edited by

David Lucarelli

Omnium Gatherum
Los Angeles

Winter Horror Days
Edited by David Lucarelli
Cover Design Kate Jonez

Anthology Copyright © 2015
Individual stories copyright by individual authors.
"The Christmas Spirit" appeared in *Haunted Holidays: 3 Short Tales of Terror*, Nov 2014. "Dread of Winter, Dreams of Summer" originally printed in *Necon eBooks Flash Fiction Anthology* 2011, Apr 2012; *Tales of Death and Magic*, June 2014. "Krampus Comes to Town" first appeared in *Fearworms*, 2014. "And Eight Rabid Pigs" first appeared under the title "Satan Claus" in *Alternate Outlaws*, 1995

ISBN-13: 978-0692595756
ISBN-10: 0692595759

First Edition

Table of Contents

"Now I remember those old woman's words,
Who in my wealth would tell me winter's tales,
And speak of spirits and ghosts that glide by night."

—Christopher Marlowe (1589)

Introduction

It's always struck me as a little strange that we celebrate Halloween and tell ghost stories at the time of fall harvest. I mean, sure, if you know where to look, there are signs that death is coming. There is a chill in the air. The leaves have started to fall from the trees. But there's still plenty of time to get that flu shot. Plenty of time to check the heater and stock up on food. Death is still far away. It's coming, but certainly not for us.

But it's in the dead of winter, when the days are at their shortest and the light is at its most fleeting, that death is no longer a mere abstraction.

We know on some level the holidays we have to get us through this time are based on lies. That "peace on earth and good will toward men" is only a small aspect of humanity's potential; that history has shown us—time and again—we are more than capable of great atrocities. That the evergreen tree you put in your house is just as mortal as you and I, as evidenced by the pine needles it has consistently spit out since the day you brought it home. The Hanukah miracle that you celebrate symbolically by lighting one more candle each night? Best to blow out all the candles after the children have gone to bed, lest the cat knocks the menorah off the table in the middle of the night and burns us all alive.

The wonder of the first snowfall has been replaced with dread. We should go to the grocery store one more time, but the roads are getting icy. Death is closer now. We dare not tempt it.

Time passes. Now death is not only at our door, it has entered our house. We are snowed in. That flu we got is not going away. We've lost power. We can only hope and pray we have enough food and blankets. The specter of death sits at our table and it does not want to leave empty handed.

If only we had some stories to help us deal with *this* time of the year, when we are locked in struggle with such malevolent forces. Well, now we do. Use them wisely.

These are the *Winter Horror Days*.

—David Blake Lucarelli

The Christmas Spirit

By Lisa Morton

"Merry Christmas, sweetheart."

Ray handed her a small package wrapped simply in tissue paper with a length of hemp cord wound around it.

Elise looked up in surprise; the clock on the mantel read just after four. "Why so early?" She regretted the words as soon as she said them; she knew Ray would think she was refusing the gift. She tried to recover with a smile as she reached for the present.

He handed it over. "Just open it."

She did, with an odd knot of dread in her stomach. Things hadn't been good between them for a while, ever since the fertility experts had been unable to help them conceive. Elise had inherited Great Aunt Priscilla's house a month ago, and they'd decided to get out of the city, leave London and spend the holiday at the old country place before they put it on the market. It was an isolated cottage, situated near a peat bog in the Yorkshire countryside. Aunt Priscilla hadn't actually lived in it for years, having forsaken the isolation for the relative comforts of the city. It'd taken them six hours to negotiate the holiday traffic coming up from London, and the place was a slight letdown—neither old enough to be romantic and intriguing, nor nice enough to bring a decent price.

"Dear God," Ray had said as he'd pulled their bags from the car, his feet crunching on ice and gravel, "someone actually lived out here?"

The inside was dusty and dim, with just enough

furniture left behind to make it function as a residence. Elise had brought a few Christmas decorations along, but the strings of twinkling lights and fragrant green wreaths did little to enliven the gloom.

That arrival had been two days ago. They'd quarreled and retreated to silence since; today, the 24th, Ray had spent most of the day in the village while Elise had puttered in the kitchen with a roast and Christmas pudding. Now she tried to act happy as she unwrapped the gift, but she was imagining it as something sarcastic and cruel—a baby name book, perhaps.

It *was* a book, an old hardback bound in plain green cloth. She opened it and read the title page:

The Christmas Spirit
By
Mrs. H. Warren
Privately Printed by the Author
1895

"I found it in the antique store in the village," Ray said. "The proprietor thought the author might have lived around here."

Elise flipped forward a few pages, looking for a clue about why Ray had bought this, but she found only a first chapter about a young widow spending Christmas with an eccentric aunt. She looked up at Ray, trying to seem merely curious.

"Remember last week, we were talking about how people once read ghost stories to each other on Christmas Eve? I thought maybe we could read this aloud tonight. Might be fun."

"Oh, yes—of course." Elise closed the book and saw the author's name in gilt on the spine—Mrs. H. Warren. There was something vaguely familiar about the name, but she couldn't place it. "I wonder who she was, and why she had this privately printed..."

Ray laughed as he headed for the kitchen, going for the wine. "She probably wasn't good enough to sell to a real publisher. Nowadays she'd just put her self-published e-book online."

"Probably."

By the time Ray came back with a glass of Merlot, Elise had read the first two pages. "Actually, it's not bad."

He sipped the red wine, settled into the worn old green couch before the hearth, and said, "Read it to me."

"Now? Shouldn't we do it after dinner, when it's dark?"

Ray shrugged. After eight years of marriage, Elise knew that gesture meant he wasn't happy, but he didn't think it was worth fighting over. She relented. "Tell you what: Pour me a glass of that, and I'll start reading."

Smiling, Ray rose, heading to the kitchen.

The smell of the roasting meat filled the house, a small fire glowed from the hearth, and Elise tried to feel comfortable in the house, but she couldn't. She remembered visiting it once as a child. That had been in June, but even then the house had been chilly, and there was something Elise could only describe as "oppressive" about its atmosphere. Her Great Aunt Priscilla had lived here then, surrounded by frilly pieces of the past—ceramic dog figures, tatted doilies, ruffled pillows, framed photographs of other people's children—but Elise wondered if all the manufactured cheeriness had been her aunt's attempt at covering up the essential gloom of the house.

There'd been something else on that visit, something Elise had never confessed to her skeptical husband: She'd been playing outside, alone, in a small out-building that served as a combination storage shed/garage. She'd felt an odd sensation, like a chill without a cold temperature, and had turned to see a man watching her. He was inside the garage, in the farthest, darkest corner. Even shadowed as he was, she saw quite plainly his old-fashioned suit, his handsome face, his large hands. "Hello," she said.

He didn't answer.

"Do you know my aunt?"

He continued to stare.

Eight-year-old Elise felt another chill, and turned to race back to the house. She bounded into the kitchen, where her mother and aunt were preparing tea. "Aunty Priscilla, who's that man in the garage?"

"What man, dear?"

"He wouldn't tell me his name, but he's wearing very old clothes, like something from a black and white movie."

Priscilla, already a pale, older woman, had gone completely white. Elise's mum had noticed, grabbing at Priscilla's arm in concern. "Are you all right? What is it?"

"Oh, it's..." Priscilla shook her head before continuing, "...there's no one there, dear. Just a pile of old cans with some towels draped over them. You're not the first one to see something there."

"But I *did* see a man." Elise turned to her mother. "Mummy, there *is* a man out there, come see—"

Mum had cast a quick look at Priscilla, whose expression remained carefully blank. "I'll be right back."

Priscilla just nodded.

Elise led her mother across the yard to the outbuilding. She raised her hand to point. "He's back—"

She broke off as she realized they were alone. No man in an antiquated suit; just what Priscilla had described, a stack of containers and cleaning cloths.

"There, darling, you see? Aunty Priscilla was right. There's no one there."

Elise hadn't openly protested, but she knew what she'd seen. A man.

Or...something that was not a man.

That'd been nearly thirty years ago. Not long after that, Priscilla had moved and the house had been forgotten, until a few weeks ago when Elise had been shocked to find that Priscilla had died with no other kin and had left her estate to her grand-niece. There wasn't much—a small bank account, some old belongings, a family album that Elise found fascinating—and Elise doubted the old cottage would be worth much. Unless it could save her marriage.

She heard footsteps overhead, and wondered why Ray had gone upstairs. Perhaps he'd forgotten something—

Ray returned from the kitchen, extending a full glass to her. She took it, puzzled. "Were you just upstairs?"

"No. Why?"

"Odd. I heard footsteps."

Ray set the rest of the wine bottle on the table near the couch and resumed his seat there. "Ooh, that sounds like the beginning of the ghost story right there."

"Hardly." Elise sipped her wine, then picked up Mrs. Warren's book. "This was written in 1895, so don't expect CGI effects."

"Just read."

Elise cleared her throat and began. "Chapter One..."

The Christmas Spirit
By
Mrs. H. Warren
Chapter One

At twenty-three, I was too young to be a widow, or at least that's what everyone told me.

But accidents don't care who's too young or too old; they're impartial when it comes to age. Otherwise, my Henry would still be alive, instead of moldering in a grave at the age of twenty-four.

"A freak accident", they called it. No one could have fore-seen the machinery blowing apart in quite so spectacular a fashion at the exact instant that the factory foreman—Henry—was walking past. A plate-sized cog wheel caught him in the head. They said the machinery could never have been expected to do that, that it was really quite safe. They told me it had been instantaneous, that he hadn't suffered.

I, on the other hand, certainly had.

Henry and I had been married for two years. At the time we were wed, I had no family to speak of except dear old Aunt Vanessa; Henry, on the other hand, had family, but despised them all and invited none of them to the wedding. Until we could start our own family, we were really all each other had.

But we hadn't been blessed with children yet. We'd bought a lovely little place just outside Manchester; it had enough room for the son and daughter we hoped for. We clung to the notion that my own mother had had me late in her life—she'd been in her thirties—so perhaps ours would simply arrive later.

Then my world was taken from me. Henry was dead. There would be no children.

He'd left me with enough money to survive on for the immediate future, but when he died it was two weeks before Christmas, and I was quite naturally devastated, to the point where Aunt Vanessa feared I might attempt something foolish. She wrote me letters daily, urging me to join her for Christmas. "Dearest Jane," the letters would say, "you know how I care for you and worry about your future, because you're really all I have left." She even suggested that I might consider a permanent move.

I wasn't ready yet to give up our little Manchester home, but the idea of spending Christmas alone also held no appeal to me, so on the 21st of December I wrote her back to tell her I was coming. It took me a day to make arrangements, and I was off.

The train north was decent, but finding transportation from the station to Auntie's cottage proved more difficult— Carlton Abbey, the village where I disembarked, had no regular cab service. I finally found a man who agreed to drive me out in his open hay wagon, but because it was now late in the day, we'd have to wait until tomorrow morning.

"Nobody goes out that way towards dark," he muttered, in the thick local accent.

Luckily the village inn had a room to let; it was clean and quite tolerable. The bartender's wife was a kindly middle-aged woman named Sarah who had broad hips and vivid red cheeks. She brought me a bowl of savory stew once my bags had been taken upstairs and surprised me by asking if she could sit with me and talk for a few minutes. "Of course," I answered.

She pulled out one of the sturdy pub chairs and addressed me with a serious tone. "I don't mean to pry, miss, but...how much do you know about that old house and your aunt?"

The question surprised me. "Not much about the house, and only a little more about Aunt Vanessa."

"Have you visited these parts before?"

I shook my head. "No. I've only met my aunt a few times, and those were always when she visited my family. We never came to see her."

Sarah thought for a moment, and then said, "The house is not right."

"Whatever do you mean? Is it unsafe?"

"In a manner of speaking. And your aunt—she's not a bad sort, but there are things about her you don't know."

"Such as...?"

Sarah caught her husband watching her from behind the bar as he polished glasses with a towel. She lowered her eyes, pulling away from the table. "It's not my place to say more. Just...be cautious, miss."

She left, returning to the kitchen. After a few moments her husband followed, and I heard a muffled conversation occur between them.

I finished the excellent stew and returned to my upstairs room without seeing them again. The bed was comfortable enough, the fireplace kept the temperature at an adequate level, but sleep eluded me. I kept going over Sarah's words in my head. Something was wrong with the house? And my aunt apparently possessed—what, disturbing qualities she'd kept hidden from the rest of her family?

I would find out the answers to these questions soon enough.

~

Elise lowered the book. "And that's the end of Chapter One."

Smirking, Ray said, "I think I've seen this movie before. It's not exactly wildly original, is it?"

"It does feel a bit like a Hammer horror movie. Still, I like its earnest tone. Shall I keep going?"

Ray poured himself another glass of wine, and Elise realized he was already drunk. "Why not? Let's hear all about Aunty."

Elise returned to the book. "Chapter Two..."

~

The next morning—the 23rd—dawned chilly and gray. Outside, snow was falling; it had already piled up against the sides of Carlton Abbey's few buildings. I wondered if my trip to the house would be delayed, but Mr. Murphy, the wagon driver, appeared at the inn at exactly 8 a.m. He handed me a rough woolen blanket. "Here, miss—you'll need that for the trip."

We loaded my bags onto his buckboard wagon. The two horses drawing the contraption stamped in the cold, their breath coming in cloudy snorts. Finally we took our places on the open driver's bench, tugging hats and cuffs and blankets into place. Mr. Murphy gave the reins a little flip, and off we went.

It's possible that, at some point in my life, I've been colder, but if so I have no memory of it. I wondered if we wouldn't have been better off in a sleigh, but the snow hadn't built up much yet and the simple but tough wagon served fine. Mr. Murphy wasn't a loquacious companion, but I did learn that he made this trip once a week, bringing food and supplies to my aunt. Occasionally he brought her into the village so she could tend to various matters, but I was the first visitor he'd brought out to her.

The trip took about an hour. By the time we passed the peat bog and the cottage appeared behind a whitened hedge, I wondered if I might have frostbite. I was moving stiffly as I stepped down from the wagon and heard a voice from the house: "Oh my dear, my Jane, come inside at once!"

I hadn't seen my Aunt in twenty years, and my memories of her were colored by childhood's perceptions. I remembered her as a small, neat, very pretty woman with a sweeping mass of dark hair. Now she was mostly silver-haired, prematurely bent and slightly pudgy. The lines of her face were still clear and striking, though, and she moved easily, without the stiffness I was currently conveying. She rushed out, took my arm, and led me into the cottage. Mr. Murphy followed behind with my bags.

Aunt Vanessa took me into her parlor and gave me the seat of honor closest to the fireplace, which was currently blazing. I let her remove the heavy blanket and my outer wraps, and hand me a cup of steaming tea. Seeing me settled, she went outside again with Murphy. They returned a few moments later with several boxes of supplies. Mr. Murphy hastily gulped a cup down, accepted payment, doffed his hat once, and then turned to go. "Merry Christmas to you and your family, Mr. Murphy," she called after him.

When he was gone she closed the door behind him before joining me in the parlor. "Now, darling Jane, tell me how you are."

"Thawing," I said, my teeth still chattering.

We chatted amiably for a bit, about the dreadful weather, and my train trip, and the world outside Carlton Abbey. Finally I seemed to have reached room temperature, and Aunt Vanessa showed me to my room. Mr. Murphy had already carried my bags there.

It was charming, with a large, fluffy bed, a small fireplace, dresser, basin, mirror, rocker, window seat. The decorations were warm and comforting. Aunt Vanessa suggested I take a rest before supper, and I agreed. I'd slept little at the inn; now that I was here and warm again, I was surprisingly drowsy. I lay down on the bed, thinking merely to test it, and drifted off almost instantly.

I awoke when someone came into the room.

I was half-asleep when I heard the footsteps. Thinking it was my aunt peeking in to check on me, I opted for a few more minutes of sleep and didn't open my eyes. But then I had the sensation of someone standing over me, and so I did force myself awake. I looked up to see that the light in the room had dimmed—the fire had gone out, the light spilling in through the window was less—and it took a few seconds for me to make out anything. Then I saw: A silhouetted figure at the foot of the bed. A large figure, with broad shoulders. A man, in other words.

I tried to call out, but couldn't seem to move, to even force sounds from my throat. My limbs were equally unresponsive, my heart hammered but uselessly. I was paralyzed.

He stood there for some time, not moving, not speaking. I couldn't make out his face or any particulars about him.

I finally closed my eyes, tightly, as if I could somehow make him vanish by refusing to see him. Almost immediately, I felt something in the room change—it lightened again, a crushing sense of essential *wrongness* gone. I opened my eyes.

He was gone.

I took a few moments to collect myself—to let my heartbeat return to its usual pace—before I rose and left the room behind. I found my aunt in the kitchen, sipping tea and writing in a journal which she closed as I entered. "Ah, there you are. Did you nap well, dear?"

"Aunt Vanessa, who is the man I saw in my room?"

Her polite smile disappeared instantly; her shoulders slumped; she set the tea cup down, rattling it in the saucer. "Oh. Oh dear. I'd hoped this wouldn't happen..."

"That what wouldn't happen?" I sat down across from her and poured myself a cup of tea from the pot in the center of the table.

"That you wouldn't meet Joe."

"Who's Joe?"

"Our ghost, dear."

I set the cup down and stared at her, incredulous. "Ghost? But surely..."

"Oh, please, dear Jane, don't tell me there are no such things, or that you don't believe in them." She stood, pumped more water into the tea kettle, and hung it over the kitchen fire.

"Aunty, do you mean to say that you think your house is *haunted*?"

She returned, sat across from me, and fixed me with a resolute stare. "I don't *think* it, dear—I *know* it. Joe, you see, is a man named Joseph Hood, and he died here under rather tragic circumstances thirty-six years ago." She broke off as her eyes took on a distant look, then she continued. "In fact it will be exactly thirty-six years ago tomorrow."

"He died on Christmas Eve?"

Aunt Vanessa nodded. "He was intoxicated. He came into the living room, dropped something near the hearth, tried to reach for it but tripped and fell into the fire."

I realized she was referring to the same hearth I'd warmed myself before just a short time earlier, and I shuddered. "How horrible."

"They said he at least didn't suffer—he knocked himself out when he fell."

"Who was he? Did you know him?"

My aunt looked away, and I had the distinct sense that she was covering something up, or being less than completely forthcoming. "Yes. He...worked for me. Just a local fellow. I was the one who found him, in fact."

The way she choked up on the last bit seemed authentic, and I had a rush of sympathy for her. I stood and moved behind her so I could rest my hands on her shoulders in an empathetic way. "Oh, Aunt Vanessa, I'm so sorry."

She reached up and patted my hands with hers. "It's really quite all right, dear—it was such a long time ago. And frankly, having Joe around since has frequently been... well, interesting."

I resumed my seat and decided to humor her. "What does he do?"

"Oh, he's quite harmless. He might slam a cabinet door, or knock on a wall. He must be quite impressed with you—I don't actually see him all that often."

After that, we talked about other things. I told Vanessa about my life with Henry, and she told me about her family growing up. They were an intriguing group of people, this part of my family I didn't know at all—a collection of eccentrics that included a tea trader who'd sold opium in China, a madwoman who'd died in an asylum, and a professional street mummer.

We chattered away through the late afternoon, past sunset, and well into the night. Finally Aunt Vanessa yawned and said she needed to seek the solace of her bed. I was initially uncomfortable with the thought of returning to my room, but I soon convinced myself that whatever trick of light and shadow I'd seen couldn't possibly exist at night, and so I retired as well, taking a book with me. I stoked the little fire and slid under the blankets, convinced that sleep would elude me...but after an hour of wading through the sadly-dull book, my eyes became heavy and I slid into a deep and dreamless slumber.

~

Elise lowered the book and looked around the house. Ray poured more wine for both of them. "Was that the end of the chapter?"

"Yes," Elise said, distractedly. After a few seconds, she added, "You know what's odd? The house in this book could be the very one we're in."

Ray followed her gaze around the room. "True, but I would imagine that most of the old country houses were built like this."

"I suppose so...still..."

Ray smiled. "It's more fun to believe it's the *same* house, is that it?"

"You caught me."

He laughed and toasted her. "Please continue. This is so much more entertaining than watching another Fanny Cradock re-run on the telly."

Elise—who loved cooking shows—shot her husband a vicious look before raising the book again. "Chapter Three..."

~

I awoke in the morning surprisingly refreshed and happy to be where I was. Yesterday's storm had passed, and the day was bright, with just the occasional puffy white cloud scudding past the sun.

Aunt Vanessa and I spent the day like two old sisters, nattering about in the kitchen preparing foods for a Christmas dinner that could have fed ten. We fixed goose and mincemeat and puddings and popcorn; we even made a wassail bowl, although there were only two of us and we had no intentions of going wassailing come evening. The lovely scent of the wassail—cider, cinnamon, nutmeg—mixed with the other food smells to fill the house with a cheerful holiday scent.

Day passed into evening. We laid out our merry feast and indulged ourselves. We were soon both quite besotted from the wassail. I'd never been much for drink; even a small amount went straight to my head. By midnight we were both reeling and stumbling as we wished each other a Merry Christmas and made our way to our rooms.

I undressed and crawled beneath the covers, warm from the drink and the food and the pleasant evening. The little fire began to die down as I headed into sleep.

At some point in the night I became aware of a dream I was having. I was still disoriented from the wassail, and unsure where I was. I felt another in bed beside me, felt the firm muscles of a man, and thought I must be dreaming of Henry. It would only be later on that I would realize how odd it was—if not close to impossible—to be so self-aware during a dream that you *knew* you were dreaming.

I shan't describe the dream in detail here, for it progressed in an extremely intimate fashion. Suffice to say I was ecstatic to give myself over to it, to have my Henry for one more evening. Even though he was somewhat rougher, more impassioned, than I recalled him having ever been, I considered this dream of Henry to be the most cherished Christmas gift imaginable.

A terrible headache awoke me in the morning, the after-effects of my wassail consumption. For a few seconds, I felt only the grinding pain in my temples, ears, and just above my teeth. Then I realized I was unclothed beneath the blankets, although I'd gone to bed in my usual proper nightgown, which lay discarded on the floor beside the bed. Increasingly alarmed, I drew back the covers, and saw small red splotches dotting the white linen. I looked down at myself, and saw the blood had come from crescent-shaped marks on my shoulders and bosom. They were unquestionably bite marks, and their pain was a large part of my headache.

I bit back a scream and leapt from the bed. That was when I saw it—red marks dabbed on the pillow that had just been beneath my head, marks that formed seven letters. The letters read:

LOVE JOE

I did cry out then, not so much a scream as a sort of prolonged sob. It was enough to rouse my aunt, who proceeded to bang against my door, calling my name. She asked me why I'd locked the door, and I realized I *hadn't*. I went to it and turned the lock, and she entered.

When she saw me, she gasped loudly. She was asking what happened when she saw the bed—or, more specifically, the pillow.

Her expression went cold, and she said, "You need to leave here. Today. NOW."

I didn't argue. I requested only the time it would take for me to attend to my wounds and gather my things.

She waited for me in the living room. When I came in, struggling with my bags, she told me to leave them, that she'd have them sent later. She had a neighbor less than a quarter-mile distant who had a horse and carriage; he could take me back to the village.

She offered no kind word of sympathy, no apology or explanation. Nor did I ask for any.

Together, we walked out into the chilly Christmas morn. It was overcast again, though not snowing yet. Our breath came out in opaque puffs as we trudged along the lane. We finally reached her neighbors, the Lees. They were a family of five, simple farmers with generous dispositions, who rushed to my side in concern when Aunty told them I'd fallen ill and needed immediate transportation to the village. They agreed instantly; the father, George, went out to hitch the horses to their carriage.

Aunt Vanessa gave me a rather cool embrace, muttered something about being sorry our Christmas had ended so poorly, and then left.

Once she was gone, I asked George's wife Annie who Joe Hood was. She gaped for a second, and then bade me sit down as she made a hot cup of tea for me. She sat beside me as I sipped the good, strong tea, and she told me the story of Joe.

"You may believe your aunt to be a lifelong spinster, but the truth of the matter is that she was married once—to Joe Hood. She was twenty, and although you might not know it now, she was considered a beauty among the local folk. She wasn't rich, but she'd been left enough money to live comfortably for the rest of her life.

"Because of all that she had any number of suitors, but only one caught her fancy: Joseph Hood was a young man who'd come up from the south—some said he'd been run off after a scandal with a society lady—and he was very comely. He saw an easy life with your aunt, so he wooed her. They were married just three months after they met, and Joe moved into the cottage with your aunt.

"That's when she found out what kind of man Joe Hood really was: He drank, he cursed if asked to work, but worst of all, he chased after every young lady in the county—including myself. I wanted nothing to do with him, but there were others who gave in to his tender words and caresses.

"Vanessa was hardly blind; she saw how Joe flirted with all the others, and it turned out she possessed something of a temper. They'd have terrible fights, and Joe would take off for the village pub again on their one horse.

"Well, on the first Christmas Eve after they were married, Joe came home late from the pub, drunk as usual. Later on the story was that he'd fallen in front of the hearth, hit his head, didn't even know as he was burned alive. But there were many of us who thought otherwise: That your aunt had surely had enough, hit him on the head with something like an andiron, and put him in the fire to concoct that story.

"It worked, too—they couldn't prove a thing against her. Plus, Joe was hardly well liked hereabouts, so the constabulary didn't exactly exert much effort on proving he'd been murdered."

I felt a chill despite the hot tea. My aunt was a murderess? And the crime had taken place in a house I'd been invited to share for the rest of my life? "The house…"

Annie reached out and touched my hand for support. "Did something happen to you there?"

I nodded, ashamed to admit the full truth. "Last night…I was—attacked."

Annie exhaled sharply before saying, "Your aunt was wrong to invite you, and on the very night of the murder, no less. She must have thought she could control him, or that he was weak—"

George entered then, saying he had the carriage ready; he told me he'd come back later in the day with my bags. I thanked the two of them for the great kindness they'd shown me.

Now that I look back on it, I think I can say in all truthfulness that I owe my life—or whatever is left of it—to them.

~

Elise looked up from the book, dazed. "My God. Well, I suppose we know now why she had to self-publish this. Sex with a ghost simply wasn't done in 1895."

Ray, who had already broken open a second bottle, laughed and added, "I'm still not clear on whether we're supposed to take this as fact or fiction."

"Oh, Ray, surely..." Elise broke off. She'd been about to say, "It *must* be fiction," but then she realized she wasn't so sure. A memoir about hysteria, perhaps? Wasn't the spiritualist movement in full swing when this written? Perhaps Mrs. Warren had been more deeply influenced by all the stories of ghostly contact than she'd been aware of.

Ray gestured at the book. "Is there more?"

Elise flipped through it. "One more chapter. The rest of the pages are blank—I guess to give it enough heft for the binder."

"Well, let's finish it out, then."

Elise turned the page. "Chapter Four..."

~

George was as good as his word, and arrived later on Christmas Day with my two bags. There was no train back to Manchester until the 27th, so I spent a quiet Boxing Day in the pub, letting Annie tend gently to my injuries.

A day later I was home again, determined to put it all out of my mind.

A month later I found employment working for an elderly solicitor. The work involved mainly writing letters and keeping accounts, and my employer was benevolent and thoughtful.

In March, I was finally sure: I was with child.

I sat up late into the nights, working out timelines: It

could be Henry's. We'd been together as man and wife the night before he'd died. I tried over and over to tell myself that was the only logical explanation. Of *course* it was Henry's.

But the pregnancy became increasingly difficult. I knew, of course, about morning sicknesses and the usual little traumas, but that was nothing like what I was going through. Everything, even water, made me violently ill. I was constantly besieged by excruciating abdominal pains. Blood trickled frequently from my womb, staining my undergarments.

My employer not only gave me time away from the job, but provided the best medical care. The doctors were puzzled; they'd never seen such a condition. They asked me if there was any history of problematic pregnancy in my family. I told them I knew very little about my family.

I never confessed what I knew about the father.

At five months, I looked (and felt) ready to burst. I was completely bed-ridden by then, and I'd taken to biting a rolled piece of cloth to prevent shrieking in agony.

Finally, one night in early June, the pain peaked. It was midnight, and I was alone in my bed chambers. I felt a shudder take me, a great deal of warm fluid gushed from between my legs, and the sensation of ten-thousand glass shards piercing me caused me to (thankfully) lose consciousness.

I awoke several hours later, weak but at last out of pain. I struggled to a sitting position, looked down and saw—

I shall never describe what I saw, what had passed from my body as I'd lain unconscious. I was too spent to move, so I waited. The doctor who arrived to check on me in the morning saw the dead thing on the bed and promptly sicked up his breakfast. After, he assured me that he would dispose of it in fire and tell no one what he'd seen.

I was four weeks recovering. Thanks to the careful attentions of my doctors, I did regain my strength. I returned to my work and to my life.

That was some time ago now. I've done my best to put the whole experience behind me, but I've been unable to. I still bear semi-circular scars on the upper part of my body, and I will never conceive again. There've been men who've shown me attention, but I've fled in terror from them. I've never heard from my aunt, although the lovely Lees have corresponded with me throughout the years, bless them. We never speak of Vanessa or of that Christmas.

I know that as much as I try to forget, the rest of my life will be spent re-living that terrible night I spent in the house by the bog, a house where a sprightly yellow paint job and pillows quaintly embroidered with nature scenes couldn't hide a hideous crime and the undying nightmare it had spawned.

~

Elise closed the book and set it on the table beside the couch. Neither she nor Ray spoke for several seconds.

At last Elise said, "My God."

Ray could only shake his head and gulp wine.

Elise looked down—and her eyes widened at what she saw. "Ray..." She pointed at something beside him on the couch. He picked it up.

It was an ancient satin couch pillow, its sheen faded but still in good condition, hand-embroidered with an image of birds flying over snowy trees.

"This is the house."

Ray picked up the pillow and squinted at it before tossing it aside. "Coincidence..."

"The yellow paint job? The bog? The pillows? Ray, this is *the* house. The one in the story. I'm sure of it."

"That's it—no more ghost stories for you, my darling—"

Elise abruptly stood and went to one of her bags. She'd brought Aunt Priscilla's old family album with her, since she'd thought going through it in her aunt's old home might be a nice small tribute. She found the old, velvet-covered album, stuffed so full of pictures that it bulged out, and carried it back to the light by the hearth. She'd remembered something she'd seen in there, tucked in among all the photos of distant relatives she didn't know—

There. It was a large photo, showing around two-dozen people, dressed in the fashion of the 1930s, three lines on a short flight of steps. There was writing on the back—"*Family Reunion 1935*"—followed by names.

The third name from the right in the top row was "Aunt Jane".

Elise flipped the photo over and peered at the named woman. She was in her sixties, with short gray hair and a flower-print dress. Her expression was the oddest among the group: She seemed to be trying to smile, with a slight tilt to her lips, but her eyes were serious.

Elise showed the writing on the back of the photo to Ray. "There, I knew it: Ray, she's a relative."

Peering at the writing, then the photo, Ray asked (slurring his words), "Who is?"

"Jane—Mrs. H. Warren. The woman who wrote this book."

Ray hiccoughed as he tossed the photo aside. "Don't be absurd, Elise. I'm sure every family in England has an Aunt Jane."

"But I'm sure I've seen mentions of "Warren" in Priscilla's things, too. We could probably track down the deed history of this cottage to be sure."

"And then what?" Ray staggered to his feet and threw an arm out at the hearth, in an overly-dramatic gesture. "Ladies and gentlemen, step right up and see where the ghost was murdered? Shall we charge a pound a ticket, sell souvenir shirts?"

This happened more often than not when they were together: They drank too much until the alcohol led to a fight. Elise hadn't wanted to argue on Christmas Eve, but now there was no escaping it. "Why don't you want to acknowledge that it's at least a possibility? Didn't you say that the man who sold you the book said it was written by a woman who'd lived around here? It's not exactly a heavily-populated region, is it?"

Ray raised his arms over his head. Wiggling his fingers, he began to utter a ghostly wail.

Elise was done. She stormed out of the room, heading down a short hall to the first room she found with a locking door. She entered, flipped a light switch, slammed the door, turned the lock. Outside, she heard Ray continue to utter his ridiculous moans. She regretted having left her phone outside; she could've at least plugged in the earbuds and drowned him out with music. Not Christmas carols, though; she'd had enough of the holiday.

He finally went silent, and she waited. Would he come knocking on the door, drunkenly taunting her? She didn't expect an apology, or even an offer at compromise. That wasn't Ray's style.

She turned to examine the room. It had a soft bed, a fireplace, a small dresser, a rocking chair. The bed covers were only slightly dusty. She pulled them back and saw that the bed was made beneath and seemed surprisingly clean. Outside the room, full night had fallen; she had no idea what time it was.

She turned on a bedside lamp, turned off the overhead, removed her shoes, and fell into the bed. The room spun; she'd had too much wine. She knew the sensation would pass soon, so she waited.

While she waited, she thought about the story. She was sure Jane Warren was family, and that this was the house. At that thought, her heart skipped a beat.

Because if this was the house, then this bedroom...

She started to sit up, but the room whirled around harder. She was afraid she'd be sick, so she forced herself back down. Besides, if she came out of the room now, what would Ray say? He'd surely launch into a fresh round of mockery. No, she wouldn't give him the pleasure.

She waited. The spinning slowed. Time passed. Her thoughts grew muddled. The temperature dropped as night set in; she pulled the musty blankets up over herself, enjoying the warmth they brought.

And sleep arrived.

~

At some point she was dimly aware that he'd entered the room and settled into the bed beside her. He'd come to apologize after all. He'd realized that he'd been wrong.

He reached for her. His touch was cold. Had he been outside? She wanted to ask him, but she couldn't speak. She was incapable of movement.

His frigid hand pulled her shoulder, hard.

Elise knew, then: The door was still locked. It wasn't Ray.

She struggled against whatever force held her, but it was immovable. Weight settled around her. The bed springs creaked.

No.

She wouldn't let this happen.

Elise gathered every ounce of will power she possessed, forced her mouth open...and screamed.

The power holding her evaporated. She was alone in the bed.

She leapt from it and stumbled up. She heard Ray outside, running to her door, calling her name. She reached the lock, twisted it. The door flew open and Ray stumbled in. "Elise—!"

"Ray." She embraced him, the fight forgotten. She didn't know if they could save their marriage, but right then she knew he was human and real and that she wanted to try.

She hung onto him, looking over his shoulder, wondering if Joe even knew he'd lost, or who exactly had defeated him. Elise didn't believe—*couldn't* believe—that *The Christmas Spirit* had come to her by happenstance.

"Thank you, Jane," she whispered to the woman who had just given her the best Christmas gift of her life.

In the Dead of Winter

By K. A. Opperman

In the darkest dead of winter,
On the longest night of the year,
See the Yuletide fires of our long-dead sires
On the haunted hill appear.

In the barren dead of winter,
When the boughs are bare of leaf,
See the mistletoe on the gray oaks grow
Like a plague with no relief.

In the frozen dead of winter,
When the snow has whitened all,
See the Wild Hunt ride through the woodland wide
With a Horned God riding tall.

In the very dead of winter,
Turn your heart toward cheer and song—
For the dark was old ere the light unrolled,
And the night is very long.

Mother Night

By Elise Forier Edie

He remembered this: slipping in a pool of blood and melted ice, black in the moonlight. Someone—*Robert? Adam?*—managed to croak out a word before his insides pumped from his throat. "Run," he'd said, while gobbets of gore dribbled and plopped, making the same soft sounds as loads of snow slipping off tree branches.

A little girl in pink pajamas, tiny amongst the fir trees across the clearing, reached out her hands and screamed. *Sylvie.* Between them, a churned soup of snow and death rippled, and upon it a mad carnival twirled: nets of veins and pulsing organs, shining sheets of slick fat, all of it waltzing, and whirling to the clink of falling icicles, and everywhere the dark smell of fresh meat.

Sylvie. He slipped again, fell to his knees. Ice water soaked his jeans. He crawled forward on his hands and knees, through pools of blood and water. He would make it go away. He was sorry about this. *For her. For her.*

He reached out a hand, reached for Sylvie, but a woman of sparkling light and frost grabbed his fingers. Her eyes were silver, remote as moons. She pulled him away, pulled him into the dance. He expected his own stomach to crawl up his throat, for his insides to pour on his chest and patter to the ground, like Robert's, like Adam's. But she kissed him instead. She filled his mouth with her tongue. He kissed her back. *God.*

He danced and somewhere, and very far away, he heard a little girl crying.

2.

He remembered this: sunlight. He tore at his clothes. The woman held out a cup of sweet, cold water. Willow leaves—*wasn't it winter?*—rippled in her hair; she placed a mouth-sized piece of cake on his lips—*hadn't someone died? Hadn't there been blood? Robert's?*—the taste of honey flooded his mouth—*Sylvie.* Music drifted through the air like milkweed puffs. *Sylvie.*

The woman kissed him again. He tongued tart apples and sweet syrup. They made love. When his heartbeat finally slowed, and his bedazzled eyes focused, he feasted on nectar and fruit. Afterwards, he married her.

Later on, he would sometimes remember that his wife's tail, fluffy like a squirrel's, was unusual, even frightening; that her back, opening to a smooth, cedar-scented hollow, like a salad bowl, was somehow wrong. But at night, when she curled around him, soft and lithe, he nestled in her tail as if it were a scented fur throw, tickling his naked skin. And when they lay belly to belly, he could slip his hands inside the hollow gourd of her back, rub his fingers on smooth wood, and lose himself in sensual novelty, forget all about how she didn't have a heart, or a soul, or even give a shit about anyone or anything. Neither did he. Neither did he.

3.

A child tapped his shoulder.

He said automatically, "Daddy's busy right now."

She poked him. "You have to come away. Mama needs you."

He opened his eyes. Found he lay in a moss-softened copse. Feathery ferns rustled by his face; a small waterfall misted the air with tinkling, cool drops.

The child knelt beside him. She wore no clothes and her hair was dark as a midnight storm.

Jesus. He sat up. For the first time in—*how long?*—he felt self-conscious, a naked man in a forest of watchful silence. He blinked at the child. She was familiar and not.

"How'd you get here? Where're your folks?" He peered over her shoulder. *Where was anyone?*

"Sylvie needs you," she said.

Sylvie. A warmth, tinged with fear, spread through his chest. *Sylvie! Jesus! When was the last time he'd seen her?* His heart clutched. *The clearing! The blood!*

"Where the hell is she?" He stood, his nakedness forgotten. "Where is Sylvie?"

"In the cold place," the child said. "Where you left her."

Thick pools of blood steamed in the snow between them, and the little girl in pink pajamas screamed, Sylvie screamed. Robert and Adam were dead and dancing madly. How long? How long ago? He clenched his fists. He couldn't catch his breath. He couldn't catch—

"How long have I been here?" he asked.

"Twenty years," the child said.

Twenty years. Twenty years! He sank into the ferns. The waterfall, beside him, babbled on. He looked at his hands. *This skin, looking the same as it ever had, this skin, for twenty years . . .*

"Am I allowed to go back?" he whispered.

"Do you want to?"

Around him, beauty hummed and twined. Come nightfall, the leaves would twinkle with waltzing lights, flowers would open in shining, starlike clusters, the air would smell of marzipan. His wife would appear and embrace him with her soft arms and tail. *There would be honey cakes, sweet water, hot sex, cold snow, steaming blood. Sylvie. Sylvie.*

"Do you know the way?" he asked

"I know all ways between worlds. But you will pay a price, if you go."

A price. He glanced around at the world he'd sold his soul for.

"I'll pay it. Whatever it is," he said. He almost laughed, even as his heart quivered, like a fawn's tail.

4.

He remembered this: Before the blood-letting, it had been beautiful, in the clearing at the top of the hill. They had roasted a pig in the ground. Robert had made the agreed upon concoction, a little mead, a little fly agaric. It tasted vile, but it went down fine with heathen prayers and a mouthful of clean, powdery snow. Afterwards, ice-covered branches spiraled to the sky. Snowflakes tumbled between them, like cold little butterflies. Adam said something about the Dean really shitting his pants if he knew they were conducting this kind of research. Robert began singing selections of the prayers in Old Icelandic. That's when ladies made of spun silver, naked and lovely, danced into the clearing, music floating like smoke in between them. Breasts, shoulders, proud pudenda, all sparkling, dusted with iridescence.

He remembered gratitude burned a warm star in his chest. He had helped make this magic happen. He had drunk and eaten and sung and called creatures from another world. The Dean, would indeed, shit his pants. Ha! He fumbled for a notebook in his pocket, to write it all down, exactly as it happened. He imagined the book contract he would get for this. He heard Adam laughing in wonder, saw Robert wipe tears from his eyes.

It was true. It was true. A little mead and a little mushroom.

Christ. Before the murder started, it had been so beautiful.

5.

Unborn children carried messages between realms. He had read that somewhere, in another life, when he'd read everything he could about the Fae.

This child glimmered and glowed, leading him along a path that wended through spindly trees and fat shadows. She looked like Sylvie, except her eyes were black where they should be blue, and her hair brown, where it should be gold. The sturdy body was the same though, long in the waist, the feet with a second toe shooting by the big one. Her face, clean and heartbreaking, shined like a lamp in the thickening dark. *Her face. Across the clearing. Screaming.*

"You're Sylvie's child?" he asked.

"I was."

"My granddaughter?"

"I suppose."

"Miscarriage?" The child didn't answer. "Was it a miscarriage that brought you here?"

"Because of you," the child said. "Sylvie wants no children." Grave and ghostly, she held aside a branch. Beyond, through an opening in the trees, he saw the path that led to swirling winter, and deep snow. "You go on alone into the mortal realms. I am dead and cannot follow."

He knelt and touched his granddaughter's face. She would have been beautiful, he thought, had she lived. But Sylvie had rejected her, and now he would never show her the books he'd written, the framed diplomas and awards he'd acquired. He would never tell her tales of the *Huldrafolk*. But maybe now she knew them all anyway.

"Thank you for coming to get me," he said.

"You'd better go. You wife is coming."

Still, he hesitated. "What's my name? It's been a long time."

"You are Dr. Jericho Jones."

There we go. His mind grabbed at blinking memories, like a boy catching fireflies. He nodded, stood and prepared to step into the cold. Wind slapped his face through a slit in an invisible curtain. Tiny slivers of snow misted his skin.

Sylvie, I'm coming. I'm coming to save you. He stepped forward.

Too late. Lithe arms embraced his chest, and a soft, squirrel tail tickled and twitched on his skin.

His faery wife whispered, "Whither goest thou, my love?"

6.

In his other life, his real life, Jericho Jones had written books. Been awarded tenure. Won the Chicago Folklore Prize for his examination of Volkskunde.

He had written an article about *huldra*, published in *The Folklore Historian*. It related similarities and differences between the Scandinavian and German versions, and their relation to current Icelandic tales. In most of the old stories, the huldra were beautiful, resembling women, but formed like wooden bowls, or Russian nesting dolls, hollow, except for long tails that brushed the snow. In the stories, they usually fucked men to death, although sometimes, in rare cases, they let their mortal husbands go back home. These men inevitably returned to a world they did not recognize, time having ebbed and flowed differently in the faery world.

He fought his wife's embrace, but she just laughed as she said, "Wouldst thou leave without saying "fare thee well" my love?"

The world streaked, the wind roared.

"I required a hundred years of your service, Jericho. Wast that not our bargain?"

She hugged him close. Her breasts were soft. His mind slipped into sunlight, into honey cakes. He gritted his teeth against it.

Come on. Come on, man. Once upon a time, he told himself, *you had a book-lined office at the University of North Carolina, Greenville. You were the foremost expert on Scandinavian folklore, outside of Sweden. You favored jeans and long hair and a Harley motorcycle. Your students loved you. You had two grad assistants, named Adam and Robert. And you had Sylvie.*

"My daughter needs me." He ground out. "I have to go to her. Tell me what you want, I'll pay. Whatever you require. Just let me go."

His wife's silver eyes glowed. He braced himself. Her

face was lovely. But her anger was like a giant fist splintering his bones.

7.

He fell over, appalled at his weakness, appalled at the pain, how the icy wind drove right through his skin to his core. *Jesus, Jesus.* Snow filled his nose, his mouth. *Jesus, Jesus.* Was that thin fluttering in his chest his heart trying to beat? *Help.* He pictured a tattered flag, rippling in a feeble breeze. Tried to raise his head. Couldn't. His faery wife had put her tiny foot on his skull.

"So shalt thou take the years owed, Jericho Jones," she said. "So shalt thou carry them on thy back until death."

He tried to say, "Fuck off," but only weak little breaths whuffed into the snow.

"Thine own kin shall not know thee. Thine own flesh will repel thee. And still shalt thou live."

He waited for another blow, because curses always came in threes.

"In the end, thou wilt not know thine own self, so old will thou be. Snow will fall. Snow on snow, in the deep midwinter of thy life. Snow 'til thy mind be like snow. As is now, so wast it long ago."

He clenched his jaw. But there was only quiet, filled with snowfall.

His wife had gone. He was alone in the Pigsah Forest. It was Yule Eve. It was the 21st century. He was freezing to death and he couldn't move.

He thought, *Sylvie will never know I came back, if don't get going. My daughter needs me.*

He raised his head, chin wobbling. His jaw dropped; his diaphragm kicked into gear. *There you go.* Lungs filled. *There you go.* So cold. *Never mind. Get up, get up, Jericho. Somewhere there's a road. Get on it. Even if you die there, someone will find you. Out here, in the middle of nowhere, you don't have a chance. Move. Move.*

He got up, inch by inch, trembling. He put one foot in

front of the other. Everything looked filmy and blurred, whirling white and blobs of black. *Was he blind now? Had his faery wife made him blind? Was that the price he paid?* He heard a rattling noise and realized it was his breath, wheezing in his chest. *What had she done to him? Why couldn't he breathe right? What had she done?*

8.

He remembered this: At age thirty, Jericho Jones became an Associate Professor of Folklore and Anthropology at UNC Greenville. The tenure award had felt like the final polish on a high octane, 76 horsepower life, one that had rocketed him right out of his hillbilly roots and into a bona fide ivory tower, hushed, prestigious, exclusive, charmed. He took twice yearly trips to Iceland. He wrote with authority about trolls and *huldra* and Pine Tree Mary. All the stories his ma, hell his whole hillbilly family, had sneered at, all the excursions he had taken as a lad into the woods, searching for elves, for doorways into world, all of it had paid off. He edited annotated collections of oral histories and fairy tales. He published a lavishly illustrated, bestselling children's book, a Rip van Winkle story from Sweden, about a charcoal burner and his otherworldly bride.

Visiting his ma in Asheville for Thanksgiving vacation that year, he brought with him a twenty-pound turkey, a freshwater pearl necklace and a signed copy of his book. But she just eyed the title and wrinkled her nose. She said, "Jericho. Ain't right just telling them old stories. You'd be better off studying the Bible, hadn't you?"

He said, "The Bible's just another fairy tale, Ma," and laughed at her shocked expression.

He didn't bow his head for grace. He just started filling his plate while she was ripping into the "Bless us our Lord." Later, while everyone else exclaimed admiringly over cousin Zeke's enlistment in the Marines, Jericho hiked the quiet, frosty trails he'd loved as a boy, leaving his anger piled in the snowdrifts behind him.

9.

Lights, then brighter lights in his filmy eyes, then a terrified voice saying, "Oh, my God. Oh, my God. Call an ambulance. Holy shit. What happened to this guy? What's he doing out here?"

A blanket scraped Jericho's skin. A bottle banged on his teeth. He tried to speak, tried to speak. Failed to speak. Failed to say, "Sylvie." *Failed.* Everything slid, except the conversation, the one he couldn't join, fading in and out, as hands jostled him into the back of a vehicle. *Failing.*

"Better head to Transylvania Hospital over in Brevard. Jesus Christ, this guy—"

"Call an ambulance."

"—think they have an ICU. In Brevard, that is."

"Fucking hear me? Call an ambulance. I am not letting this old dude die in my Jeep."

Old?

"Well, I can't get a signal out here, genius. So keep driving to Brevard."

"What's he doing in the middle of the woods? You think someone left him there?"

"You think he walked? Come on. This guy's like a hundred and ten."

The hell. I am no such thing. Fifty-five, maybe sixty, tops. I was thirty-five when she took me.

"Leaving some sick, old grandpa naked in the middle of the woods at Christmas. That is some cold shit, man."

Twenty years have gone by. My granddaughter said. It would follow—

"He could have Alzheimer's, though."

Oh, for God's sake. I was kidnapped by faeries.

"My aunt had it. She used to walk around the neighborhood in her underwear, scare the shit out of little kids. She'd be thinking she was having a picnic, or going to the church, or who the hell knew, right? We tied her up, man. Had to. It was sad as shit."

Unless. Oh, God. She said I owed her eighty years. She

said I would carry them on my back. She wouldn't, she wouldn't, would she? Make me old? Pile eighty years on me and send me back that way?

He tried to tell them. Make them understand. *I've been kidnapped by faeries. If I'm old it's only because they made me that way. The stories. The charcoal burners.*

"Is he dying in my fucking Jeep?"

"I don't know. Jesus."

"Make him stop that."

"He's trying to talk. Hold on. Hold on. I got a signal."

"Oh, God. Dial 9-1-1. Tell 'em we'll meet 'em on the highway. Please God, please don't let this old dude die or crap my Jeep. Puh-lease. I will do anything."

Sylvie won't recognize me if I'm a hundred and fifty years old. She won't know I came back.

"Hello? Fuck, yeah, it's an emergency. Someone dumped some poor old guy naked in the Pigsah woods and we're pretty sure he's dying. Like, now."

She said, my wife said, my own kin will not recognize me. Jesus. What else? What else did she say? Winter in my mind. My flesh. Winter.

10.

He remembered this: A stupid, but very comely Anthro grad student seduced him and turned up pregnant a few months later. He had not wanted a wife, though his ma rejoiced. He had certainly not wanted Sylvie, but she shot into Jericho's world anyway, blazing, red faced, one fist waving furiously. She was still half inside her mother, still being born, when she yelled like a fire alarm. The doctor gave her the highest Apgar score a kid could get. Healthy? She was off the charts.

The unreasoned love she pulled from him was both a surprise and a delight. Sylvie puked, and he about shattered into a million joyful pieces. She snored on his chest, his heart beat in tandem with hers, swift, strong, fear mixed with love, its own shining pulse.

He remembered this: Holding her on his lap, a little warm weight, fine, blond curls soft under his chin. He remembered the smell of her, like flowers, when he, and Robert (bearded, stout), plus Adam (bespectacled, brilliant), first got serious about fusing alcohol with psychotropic substances and guided hallucination, to induce visions of other worlds.

...What about fly agaric? Adam had a habit of patting his mouth whenever he got excited.

The mushroom? It's poisonous, right? Robert ate peanuts by the handful.

Only in large quantities. It's still a common entheogen in Asia. Sylvie had fallen asleep and he kept his voice low.

Really?

He could have headed this off. He could have stopped this silly idea cold. Instead he added, *And I think they take it with vodka at wedding ceremonies in Lithuania. The Lapps are supposed to ingest it, too.*

Robert talked around a mouthful of peanuts, his beard spattered with husks and crumbs. *So we try the right combination of fungus and alcohol and we see fairies? That sounds crazy dangerous, really y'all—*

There might be a book in it. For all of us. Shared publication.

Silence. They soaked that in, like he knew they would. Sylvie snorted and sank deeper into his chest, warm, sweet.

Robert joked. *I thought Carlos Castaneda already cornered that market.*

Adam said, *Does this mean we can we retire from the world, millionaires, with multiple wives, too?*

He could have headed it off. But it didn't. Mostly because he knew how much his mother would hate the idea. *Please. Castaneda was probably a fraud, as we all know. But we would document everything, and publishing a series of monographs—*

Finding Wonderland: The Entheogenic Properties of Fly Agaric—

The Faery Secret: Fly Agaric and Visions of Wonderland

Exactly. What could go wrong?

What indeed?

Sylvie was only three when the fairies took him.

Had she known enough to understand what had happened? Had she understood why her father left her alone in the woods?

11.

Rubber gloved hands grabbed the underside of his arm, a needle poked. His tongue felt like a strip of beef jerky, crusty and disgusting in his dry mouth.

"Gah..."

He tried to speak again. His throat clicked as he swallowed. "Sssss..." Saliva bubbled in the corners of his mouth. *Jesus Christ what kind of a shell of a man had she made him?* "Syl. Vie." There! He'd said it. "Sylvie."

The rubber-sheathed hands shifted. A calm, female voice asked, "Sir, do you know what day it is?"

He rallied. "Christmas. Eve?"

The woman's grip tightened. "Good," she said. "Do you know where you are?"

"Hospital." *God, it cost him to talk. Each word was a grunt.*

"And your name?"

"Want Sylvie."

"Your name is what?"

"I want Sylvie."

"All right. Who's Sylvie, sir?"

He started crying. He didn't mean to, but the tears just came. *Sylvie. Sylvie. I'm sorry. I've been gone so long. I forgot all about you. But I'm here. I'm here, now. You're safe.*

His tears burned his frozen old cheeks like rivers of fire. He welcomed them. He welcomed them.

12.

He remembered this: He absolutely had not meant to take Sylvie with him. He had meant to leave her with her mother. But the stupid bitch had run off to Dallas with some construction worker, or cowboy, or something, and Jericho was left with the child on the very weekend he and Adam and Robert had set aside for their fly agaric experiment. He had paid a nonrefundable deposit on a remote cabin in the Pigsah forest. The mushrooms and alcohol had been purchased. The date had been chosen—Mother Night, at Asatru holiday at Yuletide, when the veil between worlds was said to be as thin as spider silk. He had been looking forward to it, their "Carlos Castaneda tribute party," as Adam called it.

He decided he would take her with him. What was the harm? He told himself the child would sleep through the worst of the Yuletide excesses. She would enjoy a mini winter camping trip. They'd return to civilization, go to her granny's for a dutiful, Jesus-filled Christmas afterwards.

He remembered tucking Sylvie in a bunk, with a Little Mermaid coloring book and a stuffed toy. He kissed her and told her to sleep tight. He only had a moment's misgiving, before he shut the door and headed to the bonfire Adam had built in the yard.

Everything went fine at first. They ingested the mushroom tea, chased it with more mead. Robert had researched pagan rituals and poured honey on the snow. Adam had memorized heathen prayers. Jericho helped roll a Yule log in the flames. He smelled burning cedar and snow-soaked pine. He leapt over the fire; they all did. A shower of orange sparks lit the night, hissed in the snow. He laughed until his sides ached. The mushrooms kicked in. His jaw tensed; blood glowed; the trees around him became hands cupping the sky, giant white swords piercing cold, trails of color and light, shooting into the Milky Way.

When he heard music, like distant silver chimes tinkling on the winter air, he was certain it was a simple auditory hallucination. But the laughter around him died. Adam's glasses reflected the fire as he began looking around. Robert grew very still. Then they looked at one another, because there could be no mistake. They all heard it. Beyond the sound of crackling flames was a haunting melody, floating from the top of a nearby hill.

His heartbeat accelerated. Robert blinked. Adam patted his mouth, patted his wide smile. *What? What? Had they done this? Had they really done this?*

As a body, they turned and started hiking, heading toward the music. They exchanged triumphant smiles. Jericho thought, *Carlos Castaneda can bite my bag.* Because this was no hallucination, not if they all shared it. *Jesus Christ. Real magic, real magic was afoot.* He was like a boy again, hiking in the pines. He was like a boy again, looking in the woods for magic. Only now it was here. *It was here. They had conjured it, and it was real as bell songs, real as church.*

Of course, Jericho didn't know Sylvie had heard the music too. But she had, and followed behind him.

13.

"Yeah, that's Jericho. My fuckin' God. It's a wonder he's still alive, ain't it?"

He opened his eyes, and found his ma staring down at him in his hospital bed, her lips pursed in disapproval. Instead of her customary neat apron and housedress, she wore some sloppy-as-shit running suit with stripes. She'd put on weight, a roll of fat jiggled around her hips, and her arms looked wobbly with extra flesh. But her voice was the same, husky and sweet. That hadn't changed in twenty years.

"Where'd they find him?" She sounded weary as hell, like her long lost son showing up after two decades was nothing to write home about.

Jesus God, she'd always been a cold bitch, but this was taking things a little far, wasn't it?

"Up in the State Park," someone said, a female, a nurse probably.

"Yeah, okay. God. Every week it's the same damn thing." His ma sat down in a chair next to his hospital bed, and stared at the ropes and tubes connecting him to various machines and pouches of fluid. "Guess I'm gonna have to start tying him up, huh? Hate to think on that but Jesus, it's cold out there. Mid-fucking-winter, man. How long before he's stabilized enough to move?"

"We'll probably need to keep him here a few days."

"Fantastic. Just put it on my bill." His mother laughed with no humor. Purple bags sagged under her eyes. A nest of crusty cold sores oozed next to her mouth. She'd pierced her ears, ten or twelve times it looked like, and glistening rings climbed up painful-looking holes in the cartilage to the very top.

Weird thing for a widow in Asheville to do. Ma was always such a Jesus freak, going on about the sanctity of the body or God knows what, he thought, *but a lot can change in two decades.*

Ma and the medical person were discussing treatment options, or transfer, or Medicaid, or all three. He couldn't figure it, and he didn't care. There was only one thing he wanted to know.

He licked his lips. Tried speaking. "Syl. Vie."

Ma turned, and said, "Yeah?"

"Sylvie."

"I heard you."

"Where? Is she?"

His mother rolled her eyes. Took a deep breath. Let it out. She said, "Oh for God's sake, Dad. I'm right here."

What the...

Bright anger surged through him, galvanizing the sagging muscles, bringing a surge of strength to his flagging heart.

How dare she? How dare his own mother play with him like this? Oh, the bitch. Oh, the raving bitch. How dare she? How dare this old nag pretend to be Sylvie? Twenty years had gone by, and Sylvie wouldn't be a day over twenty three...

He bucked and kicked, enraged to find his hands and feet in restraints.

How dare she? How dare she? He had forsaken paradise. He had broken a faery bargain. Sylvie was lost in the snow. She had aborted her child. She was alone in the world. And this woman—this fucking woman—could not keep him from her. He would not let her. Where the hell was Sylvie?

14.

He remembered this: At the top of the hill, in the magical clearing, ladies danced, *huldra* ladies, with no backs and long tails. The tails brushed the snow in hieroglyphics. The hollow backs swayed, filled with secret shadows.

Adam and Robert were bold. They staggered into the clearing right away and the silvery women turned. Jericho watched as a lady took each man by the hand. Robert bit his lips, his feet stumbling. Adam pretended to know what he was doing, smiling a little. They danced, a sort of *pavane*, with elements in common with a traditional *bygdedans*. Jericho hung back, fumbled in his jacket for a notebook. *Someone needs to record this.* He grabbed a pen with thick fingers, thumbed through the pages, trying to find one not already damp with snow.

Adam made a sound. Jericho looked up and saw the scene had changed. Where there had been silver butterfly snowflakes, and the music of bells, now there was only blood, black under the moon. Robert still held a faery-woman in his arms, but gore now poured from his screaming lips, like lava from a volcano. Clots, organs cascaded steaming over his chin, neck and chest.

The pen dropped. Robert's jiggling belly was like a shelf, holding a pile of hot offal before it finally dripped in a thick waterfall to the ground. Adam's receding jaw allowed everything inside him to dribble over his front, until his legs were adorned with his circulatory system, net-like and pulsing. And still the cascade continued, making long trailing skirts, and streamers. And still the men danced, puppets of blood. His students oozed and vomited and twisted and turned, until they were completely inside out. Ropy intestines, glistening fat, swayed and shined like raiment. The clearing went dark with bloody hieroglyphics, and the clean smell of snow was replaced by iron and carnage.

Across the clearing, a little girl in pink pajamas, tiny amongst the fir trees, reached out her hands. She was crying as he staggered towards her. Between them, a churned soup of snow and death rippled, and a mad carnival twirled; everywhere was the sickening smell of fresh meat.

He slipped, fell to his knees. Icy blood soaked his jeans. He crawled forward on his hands and knees, through pools of thickening blood. He would make it go away. *For her, at least. For her.*

He reached out a hand. He reached. He reached.

15.

Something stabbed his arm. They spoke around him like he was a piece of meat, lying on a table. His anger bubbled, even as coolness spread from the crook in his elbow, and a sweet, familiar lassitude swept through his body. Voices wove in and out of his dreams.

He lay in a copse of ferns and waterfalls.

"...I hear when they're lost to the world like this, they might be seeing anything. Elves and princesses and their own past. Can you believe the man was a university professor, one of the youngest at UNC to ever get tenure...?"

A woman with a tail and no back touched him.

"And now he wanders around naked. My granny said her ma did the same thing, even bit people sometimes..."

Thine own flesh will repel thee.

"...I think he feels bad because of what happened when

I was a kid...?"

Sunlight filtered and he smelled marzipan.

"...took me up to the woods, gobbled a bunch of drugs with his grad students, freaked out, had to go to the hospital and get his stomach pumped, I don't know what. It was a long time ago. But I was all alone in this cabin up in Pigsah for days, scared shitless. His students didn't remember me, and he sure didn't..."

He tongued tart apples and sweet syrup.

"Of course they took me away from him. I went to live with my granny in Asheville. But I think he keeps wanting to go back and find me, you know. In his mind, I'm still a little girl, and he, well, he's got the Alzheimer's after all. Doesn't even know the dang year..."

Somewhere in the woods Sylvie wept and wept and called his name.

"...I never did get the right kind of insurance. So it's just me trying to take care of him. Whoo-hoo..."

Unborn children carry messages between worlds. Sylvie. Sylvie. I saw your child. She came to find me. She would have been beautiful. I came to save you...

"...I'll tell you what. I won't saddle no one else with this shit. It's supposed to be genetic, right? So I ain't having no kids. The line stops here....hell, he doesn't even know he's got it, look at him, the bastard...he probably thinks he's teaching a class right now, or something..."

Around him, beauty hummed and twined. Come nightfall, the leaves would twinkle with waltzing lights; flowers would open in shining, starlike clusters; the air would smell of almonds. His wife would appear and embrace him with her soft arms. There would be honey cakes, sweet water, hot sex, cold snow, steaming blood. Sylvie. Sylvie.

Sylvie leaned over and touched his shoulder.

"I'm right here, Daddy. You hungry? You want some applesauce?"

The Eve Sirens

By Lauren Candia

When we arrived in Onyx, it was March, and the wind was unforgiving. As we were unloading the moving truck, the woman who lives a few houses down from ours, Maggie, showed up to introduce herself. She was an older woman, her face leathered from too much sun, but made less severe by the sweatshirt with neon kittens she wore with jeans. I liked her well enough, but we weren't really looking for a friendly neighborhood. We just wanted some space to breathe, which is how we chose the small, desert town to begin with. I appreciated her effort though.

My husband, Drew, was at work and Maggie and I were having a cup of coffee in my kitchen. That day she had on her Minnesota Vikings T-shirt which was at odds with the light-catching rings I kept stealing glances at. "Did you notice the siren at the beginning of this street?" she asked.

I had to say that I didn't. It blended in with telephone poles and the smattering of other unattractive structures that I would just as soon not give a second glance to.

"It's kind of like our own emergency broadcast system," she continued. "We don't think of too many things as an emergency out here. It's pretty quiet. We do hear the siren at least once a year though."

"What do you consider an emergency?" I asked, thinking perhaps floods or high winds were the largest concern.

"You can hear the siren every year on Christmas Eve."

"Christmas Eve is an emergency?"

"Here, it is." Her eyes were fixed on me, chin doubled from the downward tilt of her head.

I sipped my coffee, wondering whether she was going to make me ask the obvious question, but she elaborated on her own.

"Onyx is a lonely place. We're far away from the rest of the world. We're far away from each other. For the most part, everyone is okay keeping to themselves. That's why we like it here. But we do have one tradition. If you want to keep living here, you better adopt it too."

There was an awkward pause before I prompted her along.

"Okay. What is it?" I said, trying to hide my annoyance. I wanted her to just spit it out, whatever it was.

"On Christmas Eve, when the sun goes down, the siren will go off. When that happens, you can't open the door for any reason until the sun comes up on Christmas morning."

I shifted in my seat.

"It sounds strange," she continued, perhaps a little more self-aware than I gave her credit for, "but it's real important. A lot of people just leave, actually. Go see their family or just take a trip. Some of us really don't have that luxury though."

"I'm sorry, but why can't you open the door?"

"The Sirens."

"The siren goes off...and then what?"

"*The Sirens* come," she said, leaning toward me. "I don't know what they are. There's no one around that could tell you."

She was making eye contact with me, her eyebrows severe and scrunched. I don't know what kind of impression I was giving off, but I think she knew that I wasn't buying her warning. She put down her coffee cup with a deep inhale through her nose as if channeling the patience to deal with her misbehaved student.

"They come to each door on Christmas Eve and they want to come in. Never let them in. In fact, do your best to make it seem like you're not even there. Black out the windows. Turn off the lights. Don't light the fireplace." Maggie picked up her mug by the handle and motioned it toward me. "I've never seen The Sirens, but I've seen what happens when someone new comes around and doesn't take us seriously."

Maggie took a sip of coffee and studied my face again. I hoped I'd managed to keep my appearance neutral in the face of possibly sitting across from an insane woman. In the interest of getting her out, I stopped nursing my cup, took longer gulps, and thought of what I could say to cut the visit short.

"You'll see. I want you to follow my advice. Maybe you won't. Either way, you'll see."

Months later, when December came, I found black cloths neatly folded on my front doorstep. I hadn't spoken to Maggie since the awkward exchange between us, but I knew she had left them there. I hid them away in our linen closet, and Drew and I prepared to ignore everything she'd said. Driving through our neighborhood the day of Christmas Eve though, it was hard to ignore the blacked out windows and the way it seemed like time stood still on our little street. It was unsettling in a way I couldn't quite pinpoint.

After a quiet dinner with Drew, I looked outside and saw our newest neighbor, Edith. I never spoke to her. Her son once caught me as I was taking groceries out of my car. He gave me his business card and asked me to call him if there was ever something he needed to know. He was clearly worried about his mother living alone out here. She had lace curtains and I could clearly see her sitting in her dining room with every light on, sipping from a mug. She had arrived in September, and by the looks of it, had harbored the same skepticism that Drew and I had about this Christmas Eve tradition. The more I looked though, the more uneasy I became about how odd her house looked against the backdrop of inactive houses and a dimming sun. I couldn't say exactly why, but I could not get it out of my head that Maggie might have been telling the truth.

As I covered the last of our windows with the cloths, the sky was almost purple. Edith's was still the only home with the lights on—a beacon against the oncoming night sky. Even when the siren went off, I still wasn't sure that I wasn't being silly. The long wailing sounded throughout our small town. The alarm was so old, it choked through its opening sequence.

And then there was silence.

I switched off our porch light and stood by the window lost in thought. Drew must have noticed my anxiety because I felt his hand on my back.

"Why don't you just sit on the couch? I'll make us some tea," he said.

Hours passed with Drew and I cuddled next to each other telling our own version of Christmas stories. Drew recounted the time his father took him and his brother to cut down a living tree for Christmas. They left empty-handed after a frustrating couple of hours of nonstop bickering. I told the story about the chocolate Labrador I had when I was growing up. She ate an entire bag of brown sugar that my sister and I left on the counter while we were baking and vomited it all up back up on the rug. We wondered if we'd made the right choice by moving here, so far away from the people we knew. It had grown cold in our living room with no fire to keep us warm. The small heater we bought wasn't making much of a difference against the biting desert temperatures.

We were fighting to stay awake when a noise seeped through the walls and caused us both to sit up. It was far away, but unmistakable.

Singing.

Drew and I looked at each other.

I took out my phone to look at the time. It was late.

"It's just carolers, Dot," Drew said.

I shushed him and tried to listen more closely. The more I listened, the more I felt like I had made the right decision by blacking out the windows, but I felt I needed to do more. Drew threw up his hands at the precautions I was taking, but nothing was deterring me from lighting our collection of candles and turning off the rest of the lights in the house. I sat back down next to him and thought I might just relax some when Edith crept forward in my mind. I wondered if she, too, decided to adhere to Onyx tradition in the end.

I whispered to Drew, "I'm just going to look through the peep hole to see if Edith has her lights out at least."

He nodded, but the flame from the candle highlighted the wrinkles in his face, which told me he didn't like it.

I was careful on my way to the door, testing each step for creaks before putting down my full weight. I gently put my hands on the wood and leaned until my cheek was right next to the door and my eye was level with the peephole. I could see only darkness outside. Edith had at least shut the lights off. I relaxed into the door as the relief swept over me.

In my quiet celebration, I hadn't noticed how close the singing had gotten. It sounded as close as the next house over. I pressed my ear to the door and tried to make out the words. It was a familiar melody and listening to it caused a swelling inside my chest. I was serene standing at the door wrapped in that sound that took over my senses. The feeling was what I imagine I must have felt like in the womb, being so small and weightless, so safe and surrounded by warmth.

I opened my eyes to see the goose flesh on my arms telling a different story.

The Sirens were on my doorstep.

I didn't want to move, each floorboard seeming too willing to betray me. As they continued to sing their carol, curiosity overtook me. I looked through the lens.

The moon cast just enough light to give each one a glow. I saw three figures, but their faces remained a mystery.

I pressed my ear to the door again.

Myrrh is mine, its bitter perfume
Breathes of life of gathering gloom
Sorrowing, sighing, bleeding, dying
Sealed in the stone-cold tomb.

The high falsetto of their voices pierced through me, the music becoming part of my system. I was aware of the blood in my veins, pushing their message through the rest of my body. I felt it in my bones, my muscles. I knew now how sailors could be called into jagged rocks against their better judgment.

My hand had somehow crept down to the doorknob.

I yanked it away like it was a flame on a stove so close to blistering the flesh. My heart stopped for a beat.

As I exhaled, I relaxed again into the same calm that I had been in before. My fingers cradling the frame, I let myself get lost again in their harmony. It was like being wrapped in a cocoon that fit snuggly and kept me blissfully unaware of my vulnerability.

I found so much comfort in the voices of The Sirens that the inability to breathe barely registered until my body began to react reflexively. The fight for oxygen woke me from my dream-like state.

A heaviness pressed down on me and it took me a moment to realize Drew had come to stand behind me. He must have succumbed the same way I had. Most of his weight was on me and I flailed enough to stir him out of his trance. When he realized what he was doing, he moved away, but not without losing some balance and taking an uncontrolled step backward to where the floor was weak. It whined in protest.

We froze. We listened for any indication that we had been detected.

The singing had stopped and there was complete silence all around us.

I made myself brave and looked outside through the peephole again. I let go of the breath I was holding when I saw that there was no one on the other side of the door.

The Sirens began another song at the house next to ours. Drew and I would be okay, but there were still five houses left on this street before The Sirens got to Edith's front door. I wanted to believe the dark house was a sign that Edith would stay sound asleep through The Siren's calling, but I knew differently. I took out my phone.

"What are you doing?" Drew asked.

I ignored his question and found the number I was looking for.

Maggie answered in a hushed voice, "Everything okay, Dot?"

"Yes," I said, mimicking her voice. "I'm just worried. Did you have the same conversation with Edith that you had with me?"

"I wish I could say I did, but she didn't really give me a chance. I put cloths on her doorstep with a note the same day I did yours."

"The Sirens already passed my house. Does that mean I can maybe go over to Edith's and see if everything is okay?"

"Do not leave the house. Don't even try. No matter what," she said, her voice edged with severity.

I stayed quiet for a moment. "Thank you for the cloths, Maggie. Merry Christmas."

I know she tried to say something back to me, but I hung up before I could hear it.

Drew pulled me closer to him, and I burrowed into the crook of his arm where it was warm.

"I saw them," I said.

I waited for something encouraging, some line of questioning, but Drew didn't say anything.

"There were three. Three glowing children at our door just now."

I needed him to say something. "I'm scared," I said.

"Don't think about it," he said, and kissed the top of my head.

"Aren't you afraid?" I said, putting some distance between us but taking care to keep my voice low.

"I just don't know what's going to happen."

The singing started at Edith's house. At this point, I knew every part of it and I closed my eyes and waited for the end. Just when I thought perhaps I was overreacting, a scream erupted from the house across from us. It was desperate and animalistic. Eventually the screaming stopped. It felt like forever, but was probably just a minute or two. I hid my face in the space between Drew's arm and the couch. When I brought myself upright, Drew was leaning on the arm of the couch, stone still with his hand covering his eyes.

The singing did not continue onto the next house. The disruption of the ritual made me feel uneasy, as if it were an omen of disruptions to come. I tried to sit still, but I couldn't deal with not knowing what happened.

I rose to my feet and went to the window in the same cautious method I used before. Drew told me to come back to the couch, but I didn't listen. Before he could stop me, I drew aside the black curtain. I saw the house across from us with the front door wide open. There was a light coming from within. It was weak, but just bright enough to illuminate something lying in a pile on the porch.

I put my face closer to the glass and squinted trying to make sense of the odd shape on the ground.

It was a mistake. Even just the small candle on our coffee table was enough to attract attention. The three figures came into my line of vision. They sang again, but the voices were somehow changed. Instead of feeling the calm and comfort that I felt before, I was overwhelmed with a fear that rooted me in place. Their bloated, ashen faces moved closer until my knees gave out.

Drew scooped me up from the floor and carried me back to the couch. He asked me questions, but I couldn't respond. We stayed frozen in place even after the candle burned out and we were engulfed in the blackness.

Drew patted me on the shoulder and rubbed my back. "The sun is up," he said.

He waited for a response that I couldn't give him. So he rubbed my back once more and got up from the couch. He stretched and started moving in the direction of the door.

I tried to stop him. I didn't want him to leave, but my body was so stiff and slow, I stumbled and fell.

He came back to help me.

"I'm just going to see what's going on out there."

I held onto his arm, squeezing it as if everything would fall apart if I let go. I couldn't tell him this though. I couldn't open my mouth to tell him how important it was for him to not leave me here alone.

"Do you want to come with me?" he asked.

I nodded because it was all I could do.

When we stepped outside, a few neighbors were already across the street, clustered around the porch. I couldn't see anything except for Edith's wide open door. I thought about staying back and just letting Drew go on alone. It didn't seem right though. The fight or flight reflexes within me wanted to run in any other direction except forward, but together Drew and I joined our neighbors at Edith's front door.

There was nothing left of Edith but a pile of shredded clothes and flayed open skin, not even recognizable as human. The Sirens had taken the bones and the flesh and sucked the fluids dry, leaving just the hide to crust over with blood.

Maggie emerged from her home with what must have been Edith's phone and address book. None of us had made eye contact with each other, but we all looked up at her. Her face was set in a frown. Her nose was red and her eyes glistened. She looked startled at first. Perhaps she was the first to find Edith and didn't know others would come. She looked at each one of us. My face went hot when her eyes landed on mine.

"Will someone call the coroner?" she asked, her voice hoarse.

A man I recognized only by face volunteered.

"I'm going to see if she has family," Maggie said.

I thought about the son's business card sitting in the small kitchen drawer where I kept addresses and coupons, but I didn't say anything.

She stepped around the body and the group of people around the porch parted to let her through to carry on her business.

We all stood there not uttering a word. We barely looked at each other. I felt disgust with myself for failing Edith. I don't know if I could have stopped this from happening. I stood on her doorstep, steeping in my shame and I imagine that others did the same. This gathering here would forever in my mind define our connection to each other. One by one we left, wordless and stricken.

When I turned around, I saw the handprints on the outside of my window. I went inside for a sponge. I wiped the windows many times throughout the day. The smudges were gone, but in my mind, there wasn't enough I could do to make the window clean again.

Christmas '78

By David Ghilardi

I saw the fat clown
Sitting behind the wheel
In his old station wagon.
Sweating upon cracked vinyl
He licked his chops
A wolf dressed as comic sheep.

I ran among the falling flakes
Leaping with young rabbit strides,
Breaking in my new running shoes,
Early delight before Christmas Day '78.

I crossed Irving Park road between the
Red and green lights.
My young haunches caught the clown's
Hooded lupine gaze.

Our eyes locked as I leapt in my new shoes.
Me, Happy to run free.
He, happy to see me.
My lithe body easily bounded thru frigid air.
The fat clown's eyes followed me like prey
As I exhaled the cold refreshing air.

He had murdered more than three dozen
Young men such as I.
He had attacked two fellow students
    in my high school.
But that was yet to be known.
Revealed,
As was the location
Of his buried den of bodies.

Like frozen hares,
Those gelid bodies
Were hours away from being found
Stacked under his crawl space tucked away
In the cold earth.

During our impromptu meeting,
We never broke our stares.
His head swiveled as I appeared across his menu.
Even as the light turned green,
The fat clown longed for me.

He reached over and unlocked his car door.
His white gloved hand flicked up the metal tab.
Clouds of white puffed as I ran past cold with sweat.
My heart skipped a beat,
As my spine shuddered without knowing why.

John Wayne Gacy desired new gifts,
Taking
Whatever he wanted.
Until his lustful hands were cuffed away,
Chained like the monster he was revealed to be.
The wolf leashed at last.

It was Christmas '78
And I ran home to unwrap
My gifts under our tree.
John Wayne Gacy drove to his
Dark home filled with buried guests,
Having wrapped his gifts long ago.

In the cheerful reflection of Merry Chicago lights,
That year
And into January '79
There were cold shadows of darkness.
Reminding all that
Even in the city,
The wolf is never far from the door.

Crying Wolf

By Kate Maruyama

The Christmas lights came out and the dread seeped in. Dread of this party, this holiday, this change in my parents that made them snarling, bitter, snippy winter versions of themselves. Dread from how this party ruined everything for me forever only four short years before.

Knees killing me from fifty-two trips up and down the stairs to the attic, still burping yesterday's Thanksgiving dinner, I stood out front on the yesterday-muddy-newly-frozen front lawn where my dad knelt amidst the cardboard boxes and storage bins full of Christmas crap. His curses came out in puffs of steam as he untangled a condor-sized nest of Christmas lights. "Every fucking year, and who exactly is this for anymore anyway? We've already impressed everyone. You kids don't like any of these people, I don't like any of these people, and yet they keep coming around so she can show off the damn house. Who the hell puts this many windows in a New England house? Didn't they know it would be fucking cold?"

Mid-century modern, sloping ceilings, sharp angles and all windows, our house was cold in the winter, hot in the summer, and leaky in the rain. It was supposedly a "dream house." This was 1979, after all.

Somehow, being around Dad's pissed-off crabbiness was better than being inside with mom's insanity. Pick your disagreeable parent.

"Aha!" Dad found the source of one snare and at least

ten feet of lights came untangled. This was a temporary victory. More struggles and victories lay ahead in the month leading up to the party.

That awful question I managed to keep tamped down the rest of the year bobbed to the surface. It came with the smell of the attic dust, the nip in the air, the tone of my mother's voice that hummed with anxiety as she made lists—of chores, of guests, of hors d'ouevres, of music. Here it was, in all of its furious rage: *Did they believe me? Did they believe me and still let this man come to their house, drink eggnog, laugh loudly, tip ash onto their precious designer furniture and leer at their daughter?*

And the horrible thing my mother hissed at me which lay, tamped down with those questions, but sprang up like a Jack-in-the-Box from the cardboard on the lawn: "Do not repeat a word of this to anyone. The Regniers are a respected family in our social set and I will not have you ruining their good name with your vivid imagination."

It's one thing if they didn't believe me. If they thought I had just made up a story. I made up stories a lot: an imaginary friend from the next street over, a birthday party to invite a cute boy to (he showed up to the door, gift in hand on an ordinary Saturday,) a pet dog that came by only when my family was out. But if they *did* believe me and allowed this monster into their house year after year, then I really, truly, with Teddy off at college, had no one in my corner.

I was ten when it happened. Now I was in my first year of high school. Moving on, right?

"Holly, grab the other end will you?"

The great irony of my life is that I'm named after a Christmas bush.

When I was littler, before that bad time, I loved this party. The ladies would come with their big fur coats, the men with their jackets, leather or cashmere, camel hair, and Teddy and I had the job of greeting them at the door, taking their coats—so heavy!—smelling of perfume and smoke and cologne—and putting them in the TV room downstairs. Mom would put snacks in there for us and we'd watch The Movie Channel or Home Box Office and eat pigs in a blanket, veggie tray, piles of cheese cubes, stuffed mushrooms, and—only two apiece!—clams casino. We'd giggle and get "drunk" on water, make castanets with our clamshells, and be extremely silly. Even if we were at our worst that week, arguing with each other, hating each other, Teddy and I would relax and be sibs again.

And then that winter. Mr. Regnier. But it was stupid. And I shouldn't have worn those boots. They were too grownup for me. And Teddy shouldn't have gone to bed early. And my skirt wasn't supposed to be that short, I just grew. And my tights had holes in them so Mom told me to leave them off. And I shouldn't have been alone in that room with the coats. And I shouldn't have let him come in. There was a moment there, before he closed the door, I could have screamed and someone would have heard me. Why didn't I scream?

No one heard me with the door closed, the holiday music playing, muffled by the coats.

Dad squinted up at the house, like he did every year, as if figuring out how to hang the lights for the first time. "We'll need the ladder."

"I got it."

Anything to not stand around. My feet were cold. It was that time of year Converse are just not warm enough and cold seeps in through the thin rubber soles. I ran out back to the shed. It smelled like snow, a little early for that. The shed was on the edge of the woods. A jungle in the summer, the woods were now bare trees that looked fewer in their sparseness. The Zawisas' white clapboard house was clearly visible the next lot away. Smoke trickled out of the chimney. They were probably having a lazy fireside Thanksgiving recovery. Leftovers and movies. Not for us.

I threw open the shed door and left it wide for the light. The ladder was trapped behind our folding chairs. Typical.

The shed was a mess, a last-ditch repository for things my mom was throwing out. She was always throwing things out to "preserve the lines of the house." Or, in her less charitable moods, "to get this shit out of here, we don't live in a fucking Goodwill!" The way we appeared to society and how we actually were grew more and more different with every year that passed. As time went on it felt like we were tap dancing harder and faster to keep up Mom's idea of appearances. I didn't know how much longer we could last.

I moved some stuff around. Bright plastic saucers (red for Teddy, blue for me) from when we were little, our giant well-worn, slightly frayed toboggan, my ice skates from third grade, bright white and perfect. They had fit for exactly two weeks, but I adored them. My dad made sure to save anything that meant anything to us. This was the only place on our property where the real family was visible.

At last I reached the ladder and pulled on it, but it wouldn't give. I yanked harder. Something thunked at the bottom of the shed. A sledgehammer handle had wedged itself between the bottom rung and the support. I tugged. I hated this feeling—when things were too big or too heavy or too tangled. It made me feel helpless. Like too many coats and not being able to move. One extra-hard heave and my own grunt mixed with a growl of some sort from behind the shed.

I stopped moving. My breathing was loud from the struggle with the hammer and the ladder. I listened.

The next growl was deeper. It was too large a voice for the neighbor's dogs, all of whom I knew by name. This rumble came from a bigger, broader space and was interrupted by the smacking of large jaws, a huge tongue. The animal growled with more determination. I whispered, "Daddy," but as soon as I heard myself, I realized how useless that was.

I grabbed a gardening fork, reached out toward the edge of the door and peeked out. Nothing there. But there was the distinct and terrifying warmth and closeness of something so large it muffled the openness of the sound outside the shed. Wilder and thicker than a doggy smell, a dense animal musk pricked my nose. Under the bottom of the door, only two feet from where I stood, enormous, mud covered, hairy, silver paws paced. Less like a dog than a bear. But dog-shaped. Enormous.

I reached out toward the door, hoping to grab its edge to pull it closed but it was just beyond my fingertips.

I leaned farther.

The growl sharpened and the beastie, wolf? Giant dog? Turned. It crouched low.

For a moment there was no movement, no animal noise.

A branch cracked somewhere out in the woods.

A cold clump of dirt hit me in the face as the huge hind legs kicked up chunks of half-frozen mud.

Something scrambled in the leaves—*wrestled*? The scuffling noise stopped. Then started further away. Stopped. Started again, barely audible and was gone.

I listened for three too-noisy breaths before poking my head out of the shed. The fork still clutched in my hands, Blinking, I stepped on shaking legs out into the light and peeked around the door. As naked as the woods were, there was nothing to be seen. But there, in the dirt, unmistakable, deep gouges where claws had dug out large chunks of dirt.

A power and beauty and closeness swelled me with excitement that drowned out any fears or worry.

Forgetting the ladder, I ran around front, skidding in some just-thawing mud at the corner of the house to tell Dad. While I was gone, he had strung the lights along the ground mirroring the front roofline of the house. He was holding a broken reindeer in his hands, its head cracked off and hanging sideways by one piece of flimsy plastic. He looked at it helplessly.

"Dad! Dad! There was a thing in the woods. A wolf or a coyote or something."

"Maybe that's what killed Donder." He looked at me and

shifted from crabby to angry. "Where's the damn ladder?"

"Dad, it was huge!"

"I told you to bring me the ladder!"

"I think it was a wolf."

His anger subsided into that empty-eyed disappointment that always, always killed me. It was worse than mad. He had given up hope for me. He sighed and said, "Is it this time of year or something?"

My stomach flopped. I don't know why I expected him to believe me. Stupid.

"Something about this time of year and you just start making stuff up. I don't have time for another one of your stories, Holly. Remember Bigfoot?"

Granted, I was eleven when that happened. And it was only a year after the worst thing happened. And maybe someone had been casing the house out in the woods. But that dark, black feeling filled my flopped stomach and any excitement I felt leaked out of me. The darkness clouded out the crisp sunlight and flooded my mind with the nasty feeling I'd been keeping at bay. The combination suffocated me.

"No. I saw it." The tears in my voice made me sound little again.

He looked at me a long, patient moment and breathed out. He looked away when he muttered, "Maybe it was a neighbor's dog or something."

Not only did he not believe me, he didn't believe what he'd just said. He didn't believe there was anything there at all.

The tears on my cheeks were cold and I refused to let him see them. I muttered, "Bathroom break," and trudged up to the house, ignoring my mother's cursing over the state of the china cabinet as I ran upstairs to recover myself enough to deal with the rest of the chores.

~

Four weeks passed. Exams were a great distractor. I was

nose-deep in Algebra, English and History and, while I did linger over the Roman statue of Romulus and Remus suckling their wolf mother, most thoughts of the beast had subsided. I had always loved wolves. *Wild Kingdom*, stuffed animals. I talked myself into thinking that I did make it up.

Last exam done, I was off for break.

At home the mood was frenetic, frantic, uncertain. I resolved to keep my head down and move forward until it was over. I had gotten through other Christmases, I could get through this one.

But then came the call from Teddy. He wouldn't be home in time for the party this year. He had a late project keeping him until the 21st.

"I'm sorry, Holls, I so wanted to make it. I'm just stuck."

"I understand." It came off more pissy than I wanted it to.

"Just stay away from the Creep, okay?"

I never told Teddy what happened. I just told him that Mr. Regnier was creepy. It had become a routine with us, ducking him for the entire party. Teddy ran recon and we slipped from room to room avoiding "Regnier's laser gaze." The game became such a part of tradition that Teddy never questioned it. Part of me wanted to tell him about the whole thing, have someone to share this with. Now that he was grown and off to college, he could handle it. And he'd believe me.

"I'll do my best." I didn't taper the disappointment in my voice, which was probably unfair.

"Take care of yourself, Holls. You can always beg off sick if you want."

"Bye."

When I hung up, I lay on my bedroom floor looking out the window upside down. Only empty branches were visible against the gray, gray sky. The bleakness made me want to dig a hole under the mud and disappear until spring. I would be safe as a toad, asleep in the cold mud, and when I woke up, it would be over.

At the party the year before, Teddy's senior year of high school, we snuck drinks. He tried to bring me into the den to drink them, but I insisted on my room. We giggled, escaping upstairs with our horrible concoctions made of dribbles from various near-empty bottles and soda and drank until we were silly and drowsy. He passed out on my floor. It was late enough in the evening that Mom didn't notice, but I remember having the sleepy thought that I'd like Teddy to sleep face down on my floor every night. I'd be safe.

Mom insisted I wear a dress, so at the very last minute I changed into a floor-length (cover everything!) black velvet dress I'd worn at Halloween. Morticia Addams.

"Good God, you look like a dirge."

I pulled back my long black hair to expose my Christmas ornament earrings and waggled a hand with sparkly green nail polish. She sighed. "Oh, all right. I need your help."

Mom only ever cared about what people thought of her. On my better days, I tried to comfort myself that this was just how she was. She couldn't help it. Her mother had raised her to please others, and this was her primary concern. Getting the stuffed mushrooms out of the oven before they burned rated higher than her daughter's peculiar outfit. The presentational beauty of her house rated higher than her family's daily comfort. Protecting her neighbor's reputation was more important than what he may or may not have done to her daughter in the den.

The guests started arriving at 6:30. It was the family hour. Neighbors with small children came to ooh and ah over the twelve foot tree, to stuff their faces on Mom's famous clams (no Teddy to save them for; I didn't care) crab puffs, stuffed mushrooms and cheese. I had to admit that I did like seeing some of the people again. Mrs. Randall, who taught writing at the local library on her days off lit up when she saw me and reminded me of a story I'd written in fourth grade about leprechauns. Mr. Bix from my Dad's work greeted me warmly and shook my hand like I was a person.

"My goodness, how you've grown!" was the most common nicety.

I said, "Thank you," took their coats and moved them along.

The doorbell rang and I opened it without thinking. I should have thought and looked out the window first. I should have known by the sound of the ring itself. Stupid. I opened it and there he was. It was too late to move.

Teddy had always been there to take creepy Mr. Regnier's coat. That had been our routine for the past three years. But he wasn't here now. And I wasn't watchful enough. I had let down my guard, and there in the doorway was that bespectacled, bearded smile, and I was trapped. It was too late to retreat and pretend a bathroom run or a food run or to somehow disappear.

He was right there. More of his beard hairs had turned gray, but his cologne was the same, and his smell brought it all back, and my stomach burned, and I tried very hard not to blush, which would only cause more trouble. It was my job to do nothing that would bring on his advances. I was older now, I could handle this.

And that common line took a turn as he said, "My! How you've grown."

He leaned in to kiss my cheek and I ducked back. Narrow miss. He held his smile in an injured way and handed me his coat. He then took a gentle, but firm hold of my elbow with those horrible, fleshy hands that were hot through my velvet sleeve as he said, "Merry Christmas, Holly-hock. I will catch up with you later in the evening, I'm sure."

And he turned to the room. "Patricia!" and glided over to make his big entrance.

Catch...you...later in the evening.

And no Teddy.

I could feign a stomach ache and go off to my room.

I could start madly making out with some random

stranger. That Zawisa boy had only two years on me and was kind of cute. Surely he'd defend my honor.

I stood fuming and stunned. My stomach was a rock and the Creep's coat in my hands smelled of whiskey and smoke and of...him. I threw it on the ground behind the door. The front door was still open. The cold air seeping in might have been the only thing keeping me conscious. I leaned forward to close it and saw that the snow had dusted the sidewalk. I stepped out front to breathe the cologne-free air for a moment. Footsteps varying in time of arrival were distinguishable by how much they'd filled in with the swiftly falling snow. Perpendicular to the arrival foot-prints, parallel to the front door was a line of non-human tracks. Very large dog tracks. Dog tracks so large that they would rival a bear's.

The wolves were at the door.

Wolf.

I knew it was a wolf like I knew the white stuff on the ground was snow, like I knew each strand of lights held 50 bulbs.

"Close the door!" The holler came from inside with a burst of grownup laughter. I stepped back in and closed it. I went straight to the liquor cabinet and poured a shot of something brown into a shot glass which I downed before I recognized that it was scotch.

Only when I had done it, did I turn to see if anyone had seen me. People stood around in groups, talking, laughing. In a far corner Mr. Regnier's rounded glasses glinted and a conspiratorial smile opened up his beard exposing those nicotine-yellowy teeth.

I turned and slunk up the stairwell, pausing on the landing to view the room from above. To catch a breath above.

The snow was falling thickly outside now, lit up by the outdoor lights which were pointed at the house, an archi-tectural feature that struck me as ridiculously vain. Our living room with its ellipsed wall of windows resembled a snow globe. I squinted at the tree and the people and imagined shaking the whole thing to swirl the colorful snow inside: the people frozen in their last pose, cocktail in hand, paper plate with napkin clutched in the other, mouths open talking, smoking or laughing, up against the ceiling and settling again to the floor.

I looked out the window past the crowd and saw the wolf. In full this time. Shoulders broad, fur bristled at its neck, head low, its ears back. Despite our distance and the glass, I heard its breath, its powerful heartbeat, the pad of its paws and slight scrape of its claws as it paced the deck, staring through the window, scanning the room. Its yellow eyes locked on mine.

I slunk down the stairs and slid along the wall. I could no longer find the Creep, which unsettled me and should have scared me. Somehow, I knew that if I got outside, I'd be okay.

I was just at the door when I felt his hot hand on mine, sticky with sweat. "Holly-hock."

I yanked my hand away and looked around for my parents, but they had disappeared.

Outside. Get outside.

"I'm busy, Mr. Regnier."

The Regniers are a respected family in our social set.

"But where are you going?"

Do not repeat a word.

I didn't answer, but pulled the door open and stepped outside. The wolf's tracks were thick on the edge of the balcony. I walked to the rail and looked over. It was a she-wolf. I knew this. I knew it by the thing shifting in my chest, the feeling of helplessness being pushed aside by something else.

The white on the grass was undisturbed. I wondered where she had gone. I looked back in at the party, so perfect behind its glass, glowing with lights, laughter, colorful holiday clothing. The snow fell so fast and heavy now that I felt I could hear it if I trained my ears. I breathed in, the cold air tickling my nostrils, sharpening in my lungs. The flakes melted on my skin, but not on my dress where it began to grow thicker. It could white me out, make me invisible, safe for the night. I couldn't see the Zawisa's house, only the white of the snow, the black edge of the wood.

"Holly-hock!"

He called in a flirtatious way and all of my instincts to run were pushed back—the thing shifting in my chest had become a control I hadn't felt before. I turned to face him. He was a small man. I guess I had grown as much as they said this summer. His tweed jacket sported leather elbow patches. His mustard yellow shirt and orange tie was out of style. He looked so stupid, so insignificant. I didn't know how he'd haunted me for the past three years, what my parents saw in him. I hated that this disgusting little creature had held such sway over my nightmares.

"What do you want?"

"I just want to talk."

"Are you kidding? Go away."

I knew she was at my back again, I felt her pacing under the deck.

"You look so lovely in your gown."

I pushed myself off the rail and clutched my hands into fists. I was ready.

Her claws made a hollow sound as she padded up the deck stairs. I didn't know how something so heavy could make so little noise.

"I just wondered if you remember how special that day was. How what we shared was so lovely." Is this all he had to say about what he had done to me? *Lovely.*

He walked toward me, hand out as if I were a cat who would bolt. He moved slowly. I stood my ground.

"Your brother told me to stay away, but..." he looked around him, the light from the porch revealing that he was shiny with sweat, "I don't see him anywhere do you?"

Teddy. My resolve weakened and I took a step back.

But he had reached me. His hand touched my arm and

slid up to my shoulder, then my neck and he grasped my head gently, pushing his fingers into my hair.

Teddy wasn't here. It was only me. And her.

There was nothing to say. Nothing to do but step aside.

His finger yanked one of my hairs as I tore my head from his hand.

The strength of the pounce was light, was not this wolf's full ability, but she knocked him to the deck where his head hit with a satisfying thunk.

His scream was short, cut off by the animal's powerful jaws. The ridge along her back was gray against her fur which was yellow against the white snow. The sound of snapping sinew, a slurping and shaking, she broke his neck. Too quickly, I thought. But soon it was done and she gripped his wrist in her jaws and pulled him across the porch. Despite her size, this was a doggy move.

I should have screamed, but it wasn't in me. This was right.

I breathed in, the air cool and empowering. I shook my shoulders, scattering the snow. I snapped my fingers and she was at my side. Taking one backward glance at the Creep's startled face, glasses askew, carnage at his throat, I opened the back door and stepped inside.

It didn't take long for the voices nearest me to quiet as I crossed the room, her huge form padding behind me. The quiet spread throughout the room and aside from some scattered, "Oh!s," the only sound was Frank Sinatra's "Mistletoe and Holly" blasted from the in-house speaker Hi-Fi system.

My mother stepped forward, her mouth open. My father moved through a crowd of stunned guests and said, "Holls?"

"See, Daddy, it was a wolf."

I went toward the front door and stepped over Mr. Regnier's coat before walking out into the snowy darkness, running my hands through the warmth of her bristle as she fell in step at my side.

Cursed by Saint Basil

By Kate Jonez

Frost crept in around the edges of the plate glass window and encroached on the Christmas scenes painted with tempera. The scent of chili bubbling in an old steel pot hung thick in the air. The sizzle of hamburgs and homefries piled in the corner of the grill, the sound of Nick yelling at Vassily to go faster, even though at four in the afternoon there was no need because there were only two customers, regulars sitting at their regular tables with the winter sun glinting off their well-oiled hair, sipping thick coffee that wasn't on the menu and cursing the fact they couldn't smoke inside anymore. These sights sounds and smells were as warm as an old winter coat, as familiar as home.

Nyla hadn't realized how much she'd missed the diner where she'd worked all through high school. At SUNY Plattsburg she'd never given a thought to her old job or even to her old friends. She'd been too busy with classes and research and all of the obligations that were part of her new life at school. But she did miss them. A little. Enough to come and wish Nick and Eleni a Merry Christmas and take a peek at the new baby. It wasn't so bad to be home after all.

She stepped past the silver Christmas tree with the porcelain angels and blown glass sailing ships and slid into the employees' booth in the corner. She shrugged out of her quilted coat and stuffed her gloves in her pocket. Pushed up against the wall, a wooden bowl filled with water held a wooden cross with fresh basil wrapped around it. When she was a kid, her mother used a cross just like that to sprinkle their house on the days between Christmas and Epiphany. That was the one time of year that the hobgoblins, or Kallikantzaros in Greek, rose from their underground lair and roamed the streets. Sprinkling was supposed to keep them out of the house. The basil was in honor of Saint Basil who was almost but not quite as jolly as Santa Claus. It was a dumb superstition. No one really believed people born during this time of year were actually going to turn into hobgoblins. Except maybe Eleni and Nick. They were a little backward. She'd never seen the sprinkling cross in a restaurant before. Odd.

From habit she grabbed a knife, fork and spoon from the gray plastic bin and rolled them in a red cloth napkin.

Eleni grinned at her like they were best friends. "Coffee?" she called out from behind the counter.

"Sure," Nyla said. She and Eleni were friends but not best friends. They didn't have enough in common even though they were both Greek. Nyla never for a second thought of herself as anything other than American. Not really. Eleni lived her life just like she had back in the mountain village in Greece.

Christmas carols played through the single speaker over the swinging door to the kitchen. Nyla was getting pretty tired of hearing them, but she liked this particular version of "Agia Nyhta."

Eleni had had her baby although Nyla had to look close to make sure. Eleni was on the heavy side even when she wasn't pregnant. And this was her second. She was way too young to be married to Nick who would be ready to retire in a decade, if retiring was a thing Greek men even did. Eleni looked so much older than twenty-two. Mostly it was the frumpy clothes she always wore. If she tried a little harder she might actually be cute. Nyla thought how it might be fun to take Eleni shopping. But Nick would never go for that. Men from Akrata, the ones from the mountains anyway, wanted their wives to be good cooks and mothers. Their girlfriends were supposed to be pretty. Poor Eleni. She could have gone to college and had a good life but she decided on the traditional path. Good for her. Someone had to make the babies. It sure wasn't going to be Nyla.

"You don't have to do that." Eleni took a roll of silverware from Nyla. "You don't even work here anymore."

"You had your baby! Boy or a girl?

"Boy." Something in Eleni's voice hitched just the tiniest bit. Did she not want to talk about this? Most new mothers would have had the pictures out already.

The thought that the baby might have been disabled popped into Nyla's head. Why else would Eleni be so reticent. Mountain people had some weird ideas about children. Oh no. Were they hiding the child? Was the whole town, the Greek contingent anyway, complicit in hiding the baby away? That is not the way disability was dealt with in America. Nyla would just have to be make them understand.

"Sophie must be so excited to have a little brother," Nyla returned Eleni's squeeze on the shoulder and pressed her cheek against hers.

"Yep," Eleni's eyes darted to the left then hovered in the middle as though she was fascinated by the ornaments on the Christmas tree. She tucked her hair behind her ears with a twitch of her wrist.

Was she lying? Everything Nyla had learned so far in her Psychology classes seemed to point in that direction. Eleni wouldn't make eye contact. Why would she lie about whether Sylvie liked the baby? What four-year-old wouldn't be thrilled to have a new baby in the house? Probably they hadn't even introduced Sylvie to the new baby. She'd just have to learn that her little brother was different from the other kids. It would be her job to make sure he was accepted.

"You look great!"

Eleni slid into the booth across from Nyla and rolled her eyes.

Up close Eleni didn't actually look all that good. Her skin was sallow and the circles under her eyes looked like the bruises Nyla got once when she was got too close to her brother's game and got whacked in the head with a hockey stick. When she leaned down to take a sip of coffee, Eleni's hair fell forward. Patches of bare scalp she'd obviously tried to hide were exposed.

Nick was a jerk sometimes but he wouldn't hit Eleni. Nyla looked through the window into the kitchen. She caught his eye, and he waved at her. Something was a little off with him too. He looked bleary-eyed like he'd been living on coffee and cigarettes for a week. Still he wouldn't give Eleni a black eye. Nyla'd known Petra for years, Nick's first wife. Petra had trained Nyla as a waitress. She was a mean one. Always finding fault and complaining. Nyla had been happy for Nick when his horrible wife left him for a man with more money. Someone who could buy her real pearls instead of the fake ones she always wore and let her have acrylic nails as long as she liked. Nick and Petra fought constantly, but he never once hit her. She'd have known if he had, Petra would have broadcast *that* to the world.

"Did you have a good Christmas?" Nyla asked.

"Oh yes, cooking was hard because I was so..." She made a gesture to indicate a pregnant belly.

"Wait. What?" Nyla glanced down at the wooden cross in the bowl of water. "When did you have the baby?"

"Two days after." Eleni looked deep into Nyla's eyes as if the words meant more than they seemed and she was trying to see if Nyla understood.

"You had the baby," Nyla counted on her fingers, "three days ago?"

Eleni nodded.

"What are you doing here?"

"I need to work. Nicky doesn't have anyone else."

"But you have a newborn."

Eleni snapped her head in a perfunctory nod and

pushed her lips into a thin line as though she had made a decision and wasn't going to be persuaded otherwise.

Something tightened in Nyla's stomach. Sometimes women got depressed after giving birth. Especially if the child wasn't perfect. Someone like Eleni wouldn't know how to treat depression.

"You found a sitter for Sophie and the new baby? Good for you. You probably needed the break." Christmas was the hardest time of year for women who went the traditional route. All the cleaning and cooking. It must be exhausting. Although coming to work at the diner didn't really sound like much of a getaway.

"Sophie is with my mother."

"The *children* are with your mother, you mean." Nyla grabbed a blue packet from the sugar container and tore it in half. She poured the extra sweetness into her lukewarm coffee more to have something to do with her hands. Like a cloud had moved in front of the sun, the mood in the diner darkened.

Something was wrong, Nyla's instincts told her. She had excellent instincts her high school counselor had said, which is why she decided to major in psychology. She wished she was a little farther along in her studies but she was confident that her instincts would help her fill in the gaps. If Eleni needed her help she would definitely get it.

"Who's with the baby?" Nyla asked.

"It was born three days after Christmas and nine days before Epiphany."

"Who's with the baby, Eleni? Where is the baby?"

"It is..." Eleni lowered her head. Her hair fell forward exposing a patch of bare scalp. "Cursed by Saint Basil." The words escaped from her like air from a balloon. One tear then another dripped onto the shiny table.

Stupid old wives tales. No one could believe them, not here in the States. Newborn babies don't have the brain capacity to display mania. They can't harm their siblings or their parents. They are just babies. It doesn't matter if they're born when hobgoblins are supposedly running free. They are helpless little things. Eleni needed help. Psychiatric help. This was not the way to deal with a disabled child.

"You can't leave a newborn alone," Nyla whispered. "You can't do that. Tell me you didn't do that."

Eleni stared into Nyla's face, her mouth open but unable to say a word. Little by little she crumpled until her head fell to the table and sobs wracked her body.

"You'll go to prison." Nyla thrust her arms into her coat sleeves and jumped to her feet. She grabbed Eleni's arm and dragged her out of the booth and yanked her toward the door. "You can't leave a baby alone."

"What is happening here?" Nick stormed through the swinging door slamming it into the wall. Splotches of sauce and grease stained the apron pulled tight across his belly.

"Eleni and I are going to check on the baby." Nyla tried to make her voice sound strong.

The old men at the booth by the window averted their eyes and studied the contents of their cups, reading the grounds, staring far into the future.

Nick's eyes flared with anger. Nyla shrank away from him.

"No. Leave that child be." Nick paced toward the women, arms raised as though he were going to squeeze them in an enormous bear hug.

"I'll call the police." Nyla held up her phone with her finger poised to dial. Maybe her knowledge of psychology wasn't enough to help Eleni and Nick. She didn't get to co-dependence and enabling until next semester.

Nick's arms deflated incrementally until they were in a position of surrender as if he were envisioning the police stepping through the door.

"You are going to take me to see the baby and that is my final word." Nyla considered stomping her foot for emphasis, but the moment had passed.

Eleni looked up at her husband with a tentative,

pleading expression.

She was so weak. Nyla was never going to defer to her husband like that when she got married.

Nick studied Nyla for an instant. He smiled, just a little, like he was glad to have someone competent in charge for a change.

Of course he would feel that way. Nyla was almost family. If anyone could make this right, she could.

"Go then." Nick snapped his head forward in assent. He wiped his hands on his apron and turned toward the kitchen.

Eleni threaded her arm through Nyla's and gripped her harder than was necessary. She pulled Nyla toward the swinging door.

"Where are we going?" Nyla asked.

"The cellar." Eleni kicked open the door like they both had done a hundred times when carrying a full tray.

"The baby is in the cellar?" Nyla couldn't decide which was worse. Leaving a baby in a house by itself or keeping it in a dank cellar with the root vegetables and rats. "Why Eleni?"

"I don't know what else to do." Eleni dragged Nyla through the steamy kitchen until they stood in front of a scarred wooden door with a padlock. Vassily turned away from the grill to stare. Nick barked a command for him to keep his eyes on his work.

"You need help, Eleni." Nyla said. "I can find you a counselor, a doctor. Everything will be okay." She was sure of it. Nyla put a hand on her friend's shoulder. There were so many great treatments for depression or whatever it was that was wrong with Eleni.

Eleni didn't respond.

"Let's just make sure the baby is okay. Did you burn his feet until the toenails turned black?" Stupid, stupid barbaric rituals like this had no place in the modern world.

Eleni's face trembled like she was going to cry. "It didn't do any good."

"Oh no, Eleni." Nyla imagined herself in court as the expert witness explaining how her friend was mentally ill and not responsible for falling prey to the superstitions from the barbaric poverty-stricken mountain country. She didn't know, Nyla would explain, that we have better ways to deal with a disabled child. Nyla felt sure she could save her friend. Keep her out of prison at least if not a mental health facility. There were worse places.

Nyla watched as Eleni fished the key out that hung on a string around her neck. She inserted it in the padlock and turned, then lifted the lock from the hasp. Eleni gripped the door knob and pushed the door open. Damp cold air tinged with the green smell of sprouted potatoes rushed over them.

There were worse places.

"You go." Eleni said.

Nyla hesitated a moment. She drew in a deep breath and listened. She didn't hear anything. Not a cry or a murmur. She braced herself against the specter of the newborn dead from the burns to his feet. Stupid, stupid ignorant peasants.

Tears welled in Nyla's eyes. She was a professional. Almost. She could do this. She had to do this. She pulled the string swaying in the drafty air. Feeble light spilled into the basement.

"Nyla," Eleni whispered.

Nyla turned.

Eleni pushed the wooden cross with the basil into her hands. Regret and sorrow twisted her features. Of course she was sorry. Eleni wasn't an evil person. Nyla made a mental note to emphasize that when she testified as an expert in court.

As soon as Nyla took the cross, Eleni backed into the kitchen. She slammed the door.

Nyla stuffed the stupid cross in her pocket and braced herself. Ignorant superstition. Each stair creaked like a crying baby as she stepped on it, which only emphasized the absence of the actual baby's cries. As she reached the bottom, the sprouted roots and dirt smell intensified and mingled with the oily, moldy smell found only in roughly finished rooms baffled from the outside world by a blanket of snow. She stepped into the basement afraid to open her eyes. Afraid to witness the horror that was just a blink away.

The seconds ticked by. Nyla forced her eyes open. They fell on a shelf with industrial-sized cans of soup, corn, carrots, shortening. She turned. Bins of potatoes, onions. Bags of rice, flour, barley.

The motor in a chest freezer whirred. Nyla jumped so hard she nearly wet herself. Her heart pounded. The earthy damp surrounded her, closed in on her. She struggled to catch her breath.

Where was the baby? Nyla's eyes fell on the smooth expanse of the freezer.

Her heart skipped a beat. Her throat tightened. They wouldn't. Eleni would never...

With tiny shuffling steps, Nyla approached the freezer. She placed her hand on the cold top. Hesitated. I won't tell them in court where I found the baby—unless they ask. I'll talk about post-partum depression and how successful the new SSRI drug treatments could be and how family counseling... Eleni might not get life in prison. She might not get the death penalty.

Maybe she deserved it. Maybe she deserved it even if she were mentally ill. Nyla slid her hand into place to open the freezer. Who could do something so horrible to a baby?

Just as she worked up her nerve to open the freezer, she turned her head ever so slightly and caught sight of a basket on the floor right in front of the dryer by stacks of laundered aprons. Nyla's breath came out in one big gush. The heat from the dryer might have kept him warm.

She rushed to the basket. Looked inside.

Nyla's senses narrowed. All the damp and smells and whirring and humming faded into a distant backdrop.

He was tiny but perfect.

Nyla fell to her knees.

He clutched his little fists to his chest. His legs lay perfectly posed like a sleeping baby in in a Renaissance painting.

Was he sleeping? Please, please, please be sleeping.

His tiny toenails were gray, black in some places, but he didn't look seriously burned. No blistering, no swelling, no peeling skin. His little blue eye lids were closed. His lips, lavender pink and bow shaped were impossibly small and still. Wisps of black hair covered his baby head and curled around his face.

Nyla reached out. She moved as slowly as she could. In the moments before she touched him hope lived. It swelled in the basement like a living entity. Throbbing like a beating heart.

She touched the baby's toe. He was cool to the touch but not otherworldly cold as she suspected a dead body would be. Nyla pinched his little thigh gently and wiggled.

The baby didn't kick or turn or make sucking movements in his sleep like other babies. He didn't move at all. Nyla leaned close to see if she could see his chest rise and fall.

An unfathomable sadness washed over her. The cold, damp earthy smell, the smell of the grave, rushed in.

She slid her hands under the cool flesh that was once the embodiment of joy and potential and scooped the baby up. He flopped against her chest. His top-heavy head with the soft black curls rested against her cheek. She held him against her. Wrapped her coat around him and wept as she rocked him back and forth like he was never rocked in his tiny life.

When the baby stirred, Nyla was rocking too hard to notice right away. By the time she realized he was squirming in her arms, she didn't have time to fully process her joy before the baby unclenched its fists and plunged its claws into her belly.

The pain seared like no pain she'd ever felt, burning in her intestines, raging in her chest. She tried to push the thing off but it clung to her digging in deeper and nestling in the cavity it carved out.

Nyla opened her mouth to scream. Before the sound came out, the baby's blue eyelids fluttered open. It locked Nyla in its gaze, piercing her with its red hobgoblin eyes. It opened wide and clamped its fangs around her windpipe.

As the room faded to gray then to black and the intense pain finally gave way to a merciful numbness, Nyla realized she should have listened to her instincts.

She knew all along Eleni wasn't an evil woman.

Witch Sisters

By Sean Patrick Traver

"What'll it be?" The bartender wore a black apron and kept a rag tossed over his shoulder. His bald head reflected the soft overhead lighting. I wanted to call him Lloyd, though the odds didn't favor that actually being his name.

The hotel bar had long since turned seedy, and the piped-in Christmas music didn't help. I ordered a whisky, and probably-not-Lloyd poured it from a dusty bottle he plucked from the mirror-backed shelves behind him. I took a sip, nodded approval, and turned around on my stool to survey the rest of tonight's attendees.

They were mostly bearded academic types. The lounge was awash in tweed. I was about twenty years younger than the average amongst this gaggle of aging nerds. They looked more like old-school Dungeons & Dragons fans than the last preservers of all-but-extinct heretical sects—though there was probably a lot of room for crossover between the two camps.

"So. What's your brand?" a woman beside me asked.

I hadn't seen her sit down. It was like she'd materialized. The sight of her (stunning, to say the least) drove all coherent thought from my head. "Brand?"

She smiled an indulgent Mona Lisa smile, as you do when someone fails to pick up on a joke. "Denomination," she clarified.

"Oh, that." I only held one prelacy, myself, but it was a good one, as far as I knew. Coveted. Suitable for trading.

"Um, Old Roman Gnostic Succession."

"Through Linus of Antioch?"

"No, the second line, down from Zephyrinus the Rude."

I could tell she was impressed. "The schismatic lineage. Interesting. It's nice to meet you, Your Excellency."

"Yeah, you too…" I trailed off, waiting for her to supply her name.

"Kate."

"Kate, I'm Kevin." Bishop Kevin, of Burbank. First of his name.

"Officially speaking, the second line of the ORGS died out during the Spanish Inquisition, you know."

"You a theologian?"

"Something like that."

"Well, Zephyrinus stole his consecration from Sixtus VII when Constantine was Emperor of Rome," I said, paraphrasing the story as it was told to me. "Threatened to burn down his house if he wouldn't perform the laying on of hands. Makes his nickname seem like kind of an understatement, doesn't it? Anyway, the Church denounced him and all his successors, but he fled north through what are now Spain and France and continued the line, despite the threat of execution with a ticket to hell that faced everyone he consecrated. Most of the lines he started were stamped out, but Hippolyto Bartolomeo traveled to Ireland around 1550, where he touched Eoin of Cork, and that branch got passed on in secret. The first American Bishop was made in 1915. Irving Crampton, of Yonkers."

"And now it's come down to you."

I shrugged. After two thousand years, all the way from Saint Peter—a direct line of apostolic succession. The privileges of the office, which not even the Holy Church could revoke, included the power to order an exorcism.

"Yeah," I said.

"Mind if I ask how? I mean, you're not a priest, are you?"

No, not a priest. Not even Catholic. Half-Jewish on my dad's side, and not sure I believed in anything beyond chemistry, physics, and math, though I suppose I once had. Maybe.

Kate was waiting for an answer, so I decided to be honest. "I won it in a card game," I said.

"Are you shitting me?"

Oops. She seemed genuinely angered. Maybe a coat of varnish would've spruced up the truth, but she had me too flustered to apply it. That pale red hair. Those sapphire eyes.

"You idiots never know what you have," she muttered darkly, into her glass of dark red wine.

"I didn't place the bet. I just won it." I couldn't find a way not to sound defensive.

Kate's genial attitude bounced back into place when she looked at me. Her comment had popped out; I don't think she really meant for me to hear it, or respond. "What did you think you were winning?"

"Credibility. The title comes in handy in my, um...line of work."

"What line of work needs a Gnostic Bishop?"

How to explain this? My usual pitch was loaded with new-age woo, and I would've felt foolish reciting it to a scholar, especially a sexy one. "Well, I clean houses," I said.

"You wear a French maid outfit?"

"I charge extra for that. No, I mean houses that won't sell because of their history. Commercial properties too. Any place where somebody died, especially by violence."

"You're a ghostbuster."

"Who you gonna call?" I handed her a business card. It read *Esoteric Services*, along with my name and phone number. "No proton packs or marshmallow men, though. Not in my experience."

"Tell me about your experience," Kate said, after glancing at the card with what might've been amusement. She took a sip of wine.

My experience? Failing as an actor in my twenties, drifting into real estate in my thirties and failing at that too.

Somewhere in between I met Jentri, a girl who worked at a bookstore called the Psychic Eye in Sherman Oaks, and fell in with her drum-circle of neopagan friends. I would've followed Jentri anywhere. When she married her tattoo artist and moved to Cambodia I was devastated. My sales record at work, which was never going to put my face on a bus-bench ad anyway, dwindled until I was saddled with nothing but the hopeless listings nobody else in the office would touch. A North Hollywood bungalow where three prostitutes were strangled. A Pacoima liquor store where the elderly proprietor was shot during a robbery. A Valley Village condominium where a woman slashed her wrists and wasn't found until she'd been partially eaten by her pair of ravenous cats.

Rather than starve myself (maybe inspired by those damn cats), I bought some smudge sticks, a singing bowl, and a copy of the Tibetan Book of the Dead. I may never have been Olivier on stage or screen, but I put on a good enough show to move that condo. And I've been refining the act ever since. Turns out every realtor in the city runs across a murder house now and then. Los Angeles can be a violent place. Nervous buyers are more apt to bite if their agent can assure them that a bargain with a bad aura has been spiritually sanitized for their protection. So I come in to do a little voodoo. The work suits me. There's theater in it, and a lot less paperwork than in sales. I think it gives people peace of mind.

But there's competition. There's always competition, even for things no sane person should want to do. My closest rivals these days are a rabid Baptist bible-beater from Santa Clarita and a Shinto mystic who shoos troublesome *oni* out of Asian homes. What keeps me ahead of the pack is the authority of my credentials. Two hundred and sixty dudes between Peter the Rock, buddy of Christ, and me. The idea of that old apostolic magic under my control turns me into Father Damien stepping forth from a fog-shrouded night, in a client's imagination. Cue the tubular bells.

My appearance at this shindig tonight was made in the name of continuing education, so to speak. To maintain my professional edge. They only held these parties on the winter solstice of the fifth year of each decade, and at them ancient consecrations were hotly traded, or so I understood. The attendees belonged to groups with names like the Anchorites of the Blind Cathar or the Illuminates of Thanateros, and they played at various styles of ceremonial magic, mostly as a kind of psychodrama or performance art. I'd wangled an invitation from the same gambling-addicted garage alchemist who passed the succession on to me in the first place. Once you're imbued with the Holy Midichlorians there's no cure for it (as even the Church will confirm), so I could pass the lineage on again with no loss to myself. I was here to see if my consecration might be parlayed into something even more impressive for my résumé, as a string of titles after my name would look a lot better than one.

Before I could relay a less self-effacing version of this tale to Kate, the event's organizer bustled into the bar with a hotel security guard in tow.

"There she is," Frater Aloysius told the blue-uniformed guard, stepping in front of Kate and pointing right into her face. "That one."

"I'm sorry," the uncomfortable guard said to her. "But this's a private party. You gonna have to go."

"Really?" I said to Aloysius, whom I'd met only an hour before. His real name was Donald Peterson, and he looked more like the stockbroker he was from nine to five than an Archbishop of the Ecclesia Gnostica Catholica—a sect founded by the infamous occultist Aleister Crowley. "What the hell?"

"Sister Katherine knows why she's not welcome," Aloysius said.

Sister Katherine?

"It's all right, Kevin," Kate said, fingering my lapel. "I don't mean to trample on anybody's boundaries."

She stood up and let the abashed rent-a-cop lead her away, sparing me one last glance over her shoulder. Archbishop Donald muttered something and wandered away before I could press him for an explanation.

It was only when I went to drop a tip on the bar for probably-not-Lloyd that I realized Kate had slipped a room key-card into my breast pocket.

~

The elevator bell dinged and I stepped out into a deserted upstairs hall.

The number on the key-card was 333. I wasn't sure what I thought I was doing, but curiosity has killed cooler cats than me. I wanted to know what the deal was with "sister" Kate.

The door to room 333 opened before I could knock or try the card, as if someone had been waiting and watching through the peephole. A woman who wasn't Kate looked me up and down, critically. She was older than young but not quite middle-aged, with a burst of frowsy brown hair. "This your man?" she said, thrusting a smartphone into my face.

"That's him," a jerky digital image of Kate confirmed from the screen. A tiny window in its corner showed me my own baffled expression.

"Then we're on our way," the phone-holder said, before pocketing the device.

A second, younger woman stood up from where she'd been sitting on the edge of the bed. She wore a habit over her long blonde hair, like a nun. Sisters. "Kevin," she said. "I'm Agnes. That's Maggie. Please come in."

"I...think I'll pass," I said, already backing away. Preparing to run, if I had to. I thought things might get weird, but I wasn't prepared for this sort of weird. Whatever sort of weird this was.

"You can't leave yet," a third woman said from behind me. I whirled. This one was iron-haired, stout as a stump.

She had the thick forearms of a butcher or a blacksmith, and a pirate's grin. "Not without meeting the Mother Superior. And that'd be me."

Before I could retort, Mother Superior placed the business end of a handheld Taser against my torso and zapped me like a bug on a hot summer night.

~

When I came to, I was being dragged into a service elevator. I grunted and moaned but couldn't make any coherent noise, as someone had slapped a strip of duct tape across my mouth while I was out. My hands were also taped in front of me. The Mother Superior dragged me by my legs. I caught glimpses of the ones called Maggie and Agnes when I squirmed and thrashed around. They looked nervous, pale and drawn. Only Mother Superior seemed to be having fun.

She hauled me to my feet when she saw I was awake and shoved me out into the chilly night through an employees' entrance at the back of the hotel.

Kate had a van waiting in the alley. Agnes and Maggie hustled me into the big compartment, and Kate slid the panel door closed. She hopped into the front seat and started the engine. I also heard what sounded like a motorcycle cough to life and roar away a moment before we did.

"Mww mwaa wmmmf?" I tried to say. Maggie ripped the duct tape away (along with any plans I might ever have had to grow a mustache) and I bellowed in pain. "What the *fuck*?" I repeated. "Since when do nuns go around kidnapping people?"

"We're not nuns," Kate said from the front seat.

"Not anymore," Maggie contributed.

"I can't imagine what you might've done to get kicked out."

"We didn't get kicked out." Agnes, the youngest, had taken a seat on the opposite side of the rocking van and was watching me. "We left."

"Over philosophical differences," Maggie said. Her explanations didn't include a lot of information, I noticed.

"I'm sorry we had to do it like this," Kate said, glancing back over her shoulder. "It wasn't the plan. But our timetable got moved up."

"Oh, well, that's all right then, kidnapping and assault, if you're in a hurry."

"Don't be a snot," Maggie chided. I got the impression she might've had some experience teaching small children.

"We need what you have, Kevin, and we meant to ask nicely. But now that's not an option." Kate kept her eyes on the road. That motorcycle flashed its red taillight at us from up ahead, and Kate hung a left to follow it.

"What, do you mean my consecration? Hell, I'll consecrate all of you. I'll do it right now. Cut me loose." I held out my tape-tied wrists.

Agnes shook her head. "It doesn't work that way."

"Not that we don't appreciate the offer." Maggie favored me with a quick smile. "But that's how we lost Sister Delphina."

"Who's Sister Delphina?"

"The fifth who left the convent with us," Agnes said. "She was consecrated, same as you. We paid good money for it. That's how we pissed off Archbishop Aloysius at the last swap meet and got eighty-sixed. But it didn't take."

"How could you tell?"

"Because she died." Agnes glared at me like I was the biggest idiot she'd met all week.

"When we called on it," Kate said, "it wasn't there."

"We thought it was a load of old sexist crap, that the succession could only be passed through men," Maggie said. "But apparently there's something to it."

"Some magic is gendered, whether we like it or not." Agnes didn't look like she liked it at all. She shrugged. "Women have different mysteries."

"What magic? What are you talking about?"

"The Rite of Exorcism." Maggie didn't tack on *duh*,

though her expression conveyed it.

"You know it takes a bishop to order an exorcism," Kate said, and I nodded. That piece of ecclesiastical trivia was the cornerstone of my shtick. "Well, that isn't just bureaucratic bullshit."

"The bishop *empowers* the ritual with the current that's transmigrated down to him," Agnes elucidated. "And for some reason this current only clings to the Y chromosome."

"But why?"

"How the hell am I supposed to know?" Agnes snapped. "It hasn't exactly been subject to scientific rigor, has it? It's just the way it is."

"But without that current, the rite's like a flashlight with no battery," Kate said. "Pretty much useless."

"Are you telling me you want me to perform an exorcism? I can't. I don't know how. Not a real official one."

"Not perform. Just order. We'll take it from there."

"Can I do it by Skype?"

She shook her head, easing the van to a stop. "Gotta be on site for this one."

"Speaking of," Maggie said.

Agnes grinned. "We're here."

~

We piled out of the van. Maggie and Agnes flanked me on either side. Kate slipped out of the driver's seat, and Mother Superior dismounted her motorcycle like it was a low-slung horse.

We were somewhere in the foothills, at the base of a sloping drive. Downtown's clump of towers thrust up out of a sea of lights some miles to the south. The driveway before us was blocked by a black iron gate. Old stone buildings loomed above the tree-line, further up the hill. The quiet up here was almost primeval. The glittering city at our backs might have been nothing more than a painted scrim.

"Where are we?" I asked.

"Our convent," Maggie said.

"Our *former* convent," Agnes amended. "Before we got kicked out."

"I thought you said you weren't kicked out."

"Kicked out of the building," Kate said. "Off the property, after seventy years, because the Dioceses wanted to sell. Twenty-three million they got for it. We severed ties with the Church after that."

"Because you got nothing out of the deal?"

"Near enough to it," Mother Superior growled. "But that's not why we left."

"The Church wasn't prepared to confront the threat it allowed to fester here," Agnes said, looking around like she was scenting the air.

"We tried, all up and down the chain of command, official as could be," Maggie said while Kate inspected the lock on the gate in the glare of the van's headlights. "But we never could find a bishop to order the ceremony. Not in this day and age."

Mother Superior, who'd been rummaging through a toolbox in the back of the van, came up with a huge adjustable wrench, fit for Thor's plumber. "We finally had to take matters into our own hands," she said to me before nudging Kate aside and hammering the brass padlock off its hasp with one decisive blow from the wrench. The old bird had a gift for making creative use of tools.

The gate yawned open, creaking on its rusted hinges.

"Come on," Kate said, and we all hustled up the steep driveway, past old rows of olive trees. There seemed to be several acres worth of property, and several buildings sprawling around a central garden. Long galleries with gothic arches connected them, just like a proper abbey. It was an unusual space for the mostly residential neighborhood, and I thought it looked familiar. I meant to ask what had happened, what sort of threat had festered here, as Agnes put it, but instead I blurted:

"Hey, isn't this the old convent Jenny Tempest tried to

buy? The singer?"

The story had made a bit of a viral splash. *Pop Princess Uproots Nuns From Seventy-Year-Old Los Feliz Convent.* I was in the habit of scanning the real estate pages for unusual listings, and that one had stood out, not least for the Twitter-storm of public outrage that attended it.

"The very same," the Mother Superior said. Agnes, who was closest in age to Jenny Tempest's demographic, rolled her eyes.

"That was when we bought a consecration for Sister Delphina," Kate said, "and tried to do the job ourselves. Before the sale went through, because we wouldn't be here to keep the thing contained after that."

"The thing?" I hesitated to ask.

"An incubus," Agnes said. "A malevolent sexual energy."

"I was here when it came in," Mother Superior said. "On the back of a disturbed novice, whose family hadn't treated her well. I was nineteen. The thing went through the girls like a fever. Drove three to suicide and one more to murder and madness before the old Mother Superior—this is two MSs back, now—got some old books together and figured a way to drive it out of the girls and into the walls. She couldn't cast it back to where it came from and didn't dare turn it loose on the world, but she did drive it down into the foundation stones, and we've kept it bottled there ever since."

"How?" I said.

"Wards. Rituals. Hexes." Agnes shrugged. "From a dozen traditions, Christian and pagan alike. Whatever we had to do."

"While the Dioceses dicked around about whether to send a proper exorcist, to clean house for real." Maggie frowned. "Which of course they never did. Scared of the publicity."

"After Delphina died trying to perform the ceremony, the best we could do was ball the sale up in red tape," Kate said. "Lawsuits. Challenges over the title to the property.

Five years, we've managed to keep people out of here. The thing needs minds to move through and emotions to feed on, so if the buildings stay empty, it's pretty much trapped. But that was only ever meant to be a temporary measure."

"Like a Band-Aid on a severed artery," Agnes said, and Kate shot her a look, like this had been a matter of some contention.

We reached the top of the long drive. Kate raised a hand, signaling us to hold back at the tree line while the sisters scoped out the situation. There were lights on in the nearest building, across a broad lawn. Lights, and muffled, thumping dance music.

"We got some bad news tonight," Kate said. "And now we can't wait any longer."

"Let me guess," I said. "The escrow closed."

Twenty-three million was a lot of money. The Church was bound to collect eventually.

"Of course nobody bothered to tell us anything about it. We had to see it like this." Maggie held up her phone to show me a video from the paparazzi website TMZ. It showed a laughing pop goddess and a clutch of glamorous friends lugging a fresh-cut Christmas tree and bags of newly-purchased trimmings across the lawn, before a burly private security guard in a black suit stepped in front of the lens. The footage might've been taken that very afternoon.

"Jenny Tempest is in there right now," Kate confirmed. "In there with *it*."

~

The scene inside the former convent was something Hieronymus Bosch might've appreciated. Three nearly naked young women ran at me the moment we came through the door (a fantasy, under other circumstances), but Mother Superior zapped one with her Taser and the other two shied away, hissing at us like angry possums.

Jenny Tempest's guests were screwing in the corners,

on the countertops and the carpets. Like they'd all gotten into some high-octane molly. There was little new furniture, as of yet—this seemed like an impromptu pre-Christmas housewarming, judging by the strings of tacked-up tinsel, with a few uninvited party crashers thrown in. The frantic fornicators made themselves comfortable wherever they could. Some were bleeding. More than a few weren't moving. Maybe they'd passed out from exertion, or maybe their hearts had exploded in their chests. The entity driving their behavior wouldn't care. A DJ in the corner kept spinning records, and I could see a woman's blonde head bobbing up and down behind his turntable.

We made our way across the main hall like a knot of soldiers pressing through the jungle and emerged into the large courtyard at the center of the complex. At the center of the courtyard was a dark-bottomed swimming pool. That was an odd accoutrement for a nunnery, but this place had been a devout oil baron's private home before he donated it to the Church in the late 1940s, if I remembered the article I'd read. The water in the pool looked as black as oil in the cold December moonlight.

There were fewer revelers out here. The main attraction was Jenny Tempest herself, twirling to the music as if lost in a private dream.

Kate again raised a hand as a silent order to halt, and Jenny looked up at us. Or rather, something else looked up at us through her. It flashed her perfect teeth in a vicious grin and started toward us, holding out her arms.

"Greetings and salutations," the singer said in a distinctly male voice, one that bore no resemblance to her own. The possessed pop star stepped onto the black water and tiptoed out to the center of the pool. Delicate ripples rolled away from the balls of her feet. She bowed theatrically, showing off with a casual miracle. She nodded to each of the women in turn.

"Sister Mary-Katherine. Sister Mary-Margaret. Pretty Sister Agnes. And of course Sister Imelda, the new Mother

Superior. You were never pretty, but we remember when you were young."

"Fuck you, Charlie," Mother Superior shot back.

Jenny Tempest's dangerous grin only widened. "Pity about Sister Delphina."

"Don't you say her name," Agnes snarled.

"Delphina, Delphina, Delphina," Jenny taunted. "What are you gonna do about it?"

"What Del meant to do," Maggie said. "Before you killed her."

"Promises, promises." The entity inside Jenny yawned. "We've heard them all. Like the bleating of goats or the baying of dogs. Your threats mean no more to us. Especially now that so much has changed."

Jenny did a little twirl, on the surface of the water out in the middle of the pool. The entity showing off its prize.

"To think," it said to the ex-nuns, "we once coveted the likes of you. Your stale passions. Your stunted needs, all bottled up between these walls until they went flat and rancid. Little did we know. The name of this new horse we ride is known across the world. All the world, can you imagine? Her image incites the lust of billions, and every act of devotion now nourishes us. Not even the gods can know what we might do with such numbers in our thrall. You will not stop us, little sisters. You cannot. Now run for your lives, before we take them from you."

"You ready, Kevin?" Kate asked.

"What do you need from me?"

Jenny's entourage had quit fucking and crept out of the house behind us, I noticed. They were streaked with various fluids, and they eyed us like a pack of mad dogs waiting to lunge. Agnes, Maggie, and the Mother Superior spread out, as if readying a defense.

"Just say the word."

"Yeah, okay," I said, ordering my first genuine exorcism with a total lack of pomp and poetry. "Yes. Fuck yes, let's do this thing!"

Everything went a little sideways, at that point. Some colossal force crackled through me, and I think I might have screamed. Above became below, below became above, and I was somehow the lynchpin that joined the realms together.

The sisters were transfigured too, though they didn't look any different. Not on the surface, though some light within them all seemed to glow brighter. They each made a series of arcane hand gestures and recited words under their breath. Then Mother Superior stomped the earth, causing a seismic wave that broke the pool's smooth surface into peaks and troughs. Jenny Tempest danced to keep her footing. Agnes drew in a huge breath and blew it back out, her lungs joining in with a sudden gust of wind to knock Jenny over backwards. A dozen traditions, Agnes had said. Kosher and otherwise. The sisters had learned their new crafts well. Maggie darted forward and spit into the pool, breaking the surface tension so that the waters parted when the singer fell, and closed over her with a splash.

Each of the empowered women had an elemental role to play. Earth, air, water, fire—and I was the quintessence that bound them. The ancient influence I'd inherited almost by accident blossomed outward, encompassing us all. I was the engine that drove the ritual. A lightning rod at the heart of a storm. I could see why that pack of theological LARPers back at the hotel got together to pass these lines of succession on. Even after being stolen, sold, traded, divorced from all authority and given away to the totally unsuitable, that old-time magic *worked*.

Jenny was up again in an instant, bursting from the depths to roar and sputter with rage.

Kate plucked the Mother Superior's stun gun from her belt as she stepped forward to do her part. She ripped off a strip of duct tape with her teeth, slapped it down over the Taser's trigger button, and casually lobbed the crackling apparatus into the pool.

A bright blue flash; an electric pop. Jenny Tempest convulsed, then went limp and sank back under the water's surface, trailing bubbles. The shock swatted the entity right out of her. It coalesced in front of Kate, bodiless and roiling, even as Maggie and Agnes hurried to the edge of the frigid pool. They reached in and each grabbed one of Jenny's arms, then hauled her lolling form out of the water and onto the flagstone deck, together.

The star's naked party guests ringed around us—Kate, Mother Superior, and myself. The spirit before us was like a scale-model storm, blowing and cracking. Its anger sounded like the howling of hurricane winds, or the buzzing of a billion flies.

Kate raised one hand, like a crossing guard signaling for traffic to stop. "I name you, Incubus," she said, "and I cast you out."

You cannot. The words occurred inside my head, independent of my ears. *We were old when your kind was born, already waiting when you arrived.*

"Back to the deadlands. Back to the shrieking realms. I cast you out of this world and command you never to return."

You cannot! The non-voice took on a hysterical edge. *You must not! We will share our strength! You will be a queen amongst your kind!*

I felt as though I were splitting open, and that pressurized reality was jutting through the gap that had been me.

"In the infinite names of the all-that-is, I banish you!" Kate thundered. "I compel you to depart and condemn you to remain beyond the veil until the seas boil and the mountains fall. I repudiate you in the names of my sisters, you son of a bitch!"

She looked monumental, in that moment—like the embodiment of something far more than human. Like an allegory carved in marble. The entity clawed at my psyche as it poured through the portal I had become, draining away into some non-place beyond imagination, under the force of Sister Mary-Katherine's will.

And then it was gone. The portal in my head sucked itself shut and my brain fell back into place. My legs felt loose and I sat down hard, like a toddler just learning to walk.

Jenny Tempest, lying by the pool, coughed up a gout of chlorinated water. Agnes and Maggie, who'd started performing CPR at some point, sat back and seemed to wilt with relief. The rest of the guests looked like they just woke up, which I suppose they had.

Kate turned around and looked at me, weary but smiling. Mother Superior hoisted me to my feet by the back of my shirt, and only then did she bother to cut the tape that still bound my wrists together. I flexed my hands to get the blood flowing.

"Did we do it?" I croaked, still feeing shaky. "Did we get it done?"

"We did it," Kate said, brushing a lock of red hair back from her face. "We got it done. Thank you for the assist, Your Excellency."

~

We bugged out before the cops were called. Several people needed medical attention after their Incubus-driven orgy, including Jenny Tempest herself, but we left knowing everybody would survive.

The sisters left me off in front of a Norm's restaurant on La Cienega, just after dawn. The windows had candy canes and drifts of fake snow painted into the corners, in honor of the season. The smells of fresh coffee and frying bacon were almost intoxicating after the longest and strangest night of my life.

Maggie hugged me before climbing back into the van. Kate and Agnes each shook my hand, and the Mother Superior slapped me on the shoulder almost hard enough to send me sprawling.

I wanted to ask them what they meant to do now, but I

could tell they didn't know. Their task was finished, their duty discharged. They could go their separate ways, if they wanted. Move on to new lives. But I didn't think they would. They were still sisters, if not exactly nuns anymore.

And I somehow doubted I'd seen the last of them. Sooner or later they'd need the old magic I carried around, despite my general unworthiness. And when they did, I'd have it waiting.

Mother Superior kick-started her Harley and pulled away, out of the diner's parking lot, with the white van following after. The old bird shot me a two-fingered peace sign as she roared up the street on her bike, reminding me of Peter Fonda in *Easy Rider*.

I turned around and went inside to get some pancakes.

A Ghost Hunter's Guide to Christmas Yet to Come

By Kevin Wetmore

Stave 1: This House Is Haunted

The fog and darkness thickened. He hurried through the murky London streets, moving with more speed than others may have thought possible for a man of his age and profession. He swept from melancholy dinner in his usual melancholy tavern to the gloomy suite of rooms in the dreary old house in which he lived. The fog and frost so hung about the black old gateway of the house that it seemed a malevolent shade directed them.

Later, unnerved by the incident with the door knocker and the apparition which appeared in his chambers, he set to bed determined not to let supernatural manifestations frighten him. He sank into a deep, dark slumber.

Still later, by candlelight, he sat bolt up in bed, the dream still clinging to him. He looked about. Foggier yet, and colder! Piercing, searching, biting cold in his bed chamber. He did not believe in the supernatural. He did not believe in the survival of the human personality after death. What he had seen was most likely the result of indigestion—a bit of bad beef. There was more of gravy than the grave here, he told himself.

Enough was enough. Scrooge was a professional man. When he needed services, he brought in professionals as astute as himself. He threw on his clothes and greatcoat and launched himself again into the streets of London, heading to a small home in Southwark where Scrooge was landlord, knowing the man who lived in it had a strange hobby. This man and his fellow occult enthusiasts would put an end to this nonsense!

Stave 2: The Mission

Scrooge used the handle of his cane to pound upon the door of the Cratchit home.

"Cratchit!" he called out. "Open up! We must discuss a preternatural affair this very night over a bowl of smoking bishop, Bob! Make up the fires, for I require your services."

The door creaked open and a bleary-eyed Bob looked out in a combination of surprise and wariness at his boss. "Mr. Scrooge. This is highly unusual. My family is sleeping and it is Christmas Eve, sir!"

Emily Cratchit pushed the door open. Cratchit's wife was dressed out but poorly in a twice-turned gown, but brave in ribbons, which are cheap and make a goodly show for sixpence. She rose into Mr. Scrooge's face and cried out, "This is a Christian home, our family's home, no thanks to you, you odious, stingy, hard, unfeeling man! How dare you..."

She was unable to complete her thought as Scrooge pushed past her into the family home. "Silence, harpy," he called as he moved past her. "There are spirits in my home and I have heard you people deal with the like. I wish to hire you to clear my home of the supernatural."

"Surely, Mr. Scrooge, you appreciate how unusual the request is. Or at least, sir, you know the timing is, perhaps, odd." The door was closed and the embers of the fire still gave off some heat, but Bob could not help shivering.

"I know nothing of the sort. I only know that you need to investigate survival after death and the existence of spirits the one place where it has yet to be refuted—my house!"

"And investigate it we shall, sir, but," Bob swallowed

hard and glanced through the window at the clock tower of St. Dismal's, visible from two streets away, "it is half an hour to Christmas. You have already given me the day off, sir.

"That was before the spirit of my demised partner entered into my chambers this very evening! The situation is dire."

Emily started at the statement.

Bob, in spite of himself, grew interested. "You saw him?"

"He entered my chambers, dressed as he did in life, wrapped in chains and the weights he had forged in life."

"Wait!" Bob exclaimed. "Are you saying you saw a full-bodied apparition of the late Mr. Marley, sir?"

"Indeed, nimwit! That is what I have been telling you." Scrooge was beside himself. He despised the fact he had to deal with such incompetents. Yet, he needed their "expertise," ridiculous though it was.

In exasperation Scrooge barked, "If you can investigate and clear my home of spirits, you, Bob, may have Boxing Day off as well and I will give each member of your team half a crown."

As Scrooge waited outside, they moved quickly. Bob reached in the high cabinets above the carving board in the kitchen. He removed strange and unique items and placed them in a black leather valise. "We can leave the children with your sister. Take them over as soon as you wake and dress them. I will assemble the team."

"And Tim?" Emily stopped gathering her items and asked without looking at him, her unhappiness in her voice only.

"Tim is part of the team."

She put down her bag and gave her husband a hard stare. "He is but a lad."

"He is but the most powerful physical medium we know." He took her in his arms. "In many ways it may seem that the Almighty has given our youngest a hard lot in life. But

He lightens His burdens with His gifts. Tim may be a cripple, but he manifests spirits like no one since the late John Dee."

"He needs his rest. You know his constitution is weak."

Bob sighed. "I do. But I also know with his help we can carry out this investigation and have enough money for a proper doctor to care for him. Half a crown each for the three of us will ensure Tim gets the medicine he needs. Let us tend to Mr. Scrooge's spirits so that in turn we may tend to Tiny Tim's body."

Emily sighed, but there was steel in her voice as she said, "I fear this is a devil's bargain, Mr. Cratchit. Mr. Scrooge may be worse than the spirits his home allegedly hosts." She smiled mischievously, adding, "But a client is a client and a case is a case. Let's see what Mr. Scrooge has summoned from beyond the grave."

Stave 3: The Team Assembles and Investigates

They were met outside Scrooge's residence by the rest of the team, summoned by Peter, Bob and Emily's eldest who then joined his siblings at Emily's sister's home.

"Who is this lot of rapscallions, Cratchit? Trying to pick a man's pocket by padding the roster of investigators?"

"Mr. Scrooge!" Emily responded with equal bluntness. "These *gentlemen* are the other members of the Southwark Investigative Society of Events of a Paranormal or Supernatural Nature. Each is an expert in his field as you are in yours and shall be treated with the dignity due to gentlemen of expertise or we shall all return to our beds this instant and you may deal with your apparitions by yourself!"

She was pleased to see that Scrooge seemed as if he could not decide whether he was more offended by her outburst or terrified at the prospect of being left alone this night.

Bob intervened before Scrooge could resolve his feelings either way. "Mr. Scrooge, sir, allow me to introduce these august gentlemen."

He gestured to the first, a round-faced, clean-shaven, portly gentleman wearing spectacles and a twill over-coat. "This is Mr. Samuel Pickwick, our expert on all manner of devices and equipment for the detection of the preternatural."

Pickwick acknowledged Scrooge over his spectacles with a kindly, knowing smile, "A genuine pleasure, Mr. Scrooge. Mr. Cratchit here assures me we have a corker tonight!"

Emily could have sworn Scrooge mumbled something about "humbug" under his breath.

Bob continued. "This gentleman," he gestured indicating a tall, thin, black-haired fellow wearing a dashing suit with a revolver visible sticking out of his belt, "is Mr. Nathaniel Winkle, our security expert. It is he who will protect us from elements other than the unearthly."

Winkle doffed his cap and made to bow, rather ineptly knocking the firearm from his belt. It fell to the ground and he reacted as if he feared it might discharge. When it did not he retrieved it, brushed off the snow, returned it to his belt and nodded sagely at Scrooge as if he had intended precisely those actions all along.

"To Mr. Winkle's right, the gentleman in the red hat is Mr. Augustus Snodgrass."

Snodgrass simply stared at Scrooge, who returned his glare, and then nodded. He was also tall and thin, and the same age as Winkle, but he wore a bright red fez, which distinguished him.

"Mr. Snodgrass is our "sensitive," and will oversee the séance," Bob said, then leaned closer to Scrooge and whispered, "Don't call him a psychic." Returning upright to face the group he continued, "Mr. Snodgrass is a mental medium. He can speak with the spirits, but exhibits no physical phenomena. That is left to our physical medium, young Master Timothy here."

Bob tussled Tim's hair through his cloth cap.

The boy, wobbling on a single misshaped crutch, managed to look pleased, embarrassed and exhausted all at once. "It's pleasing to God, sir, that I might use His gifts to help others."

Standing behind the group was a globe of a fellow, gray, greasy and corpulent.

"This," indicated Bob, pointing past the others, "is Mr. Tracy Tupman, He is our agent of last resort."

Mr. Tupman stood with a black ox-leather portmanteau. In the hands of a regular sized gentleman, the case should have seemed overwhelming, but for Mr. Tupman it seemed no more than a hand-held carrying case. Mr. Tupman acknowledged nothing and no one. His moustache seemed to quiver for a second, but he made no notice of Scrooge or even the others.

"Yes, yes," dismissed Scrooge. "I do not particularly care who you are or what you do, so long as you rid my home of these spirits!"

Pickwick smiled benevolently, Winkle placed his hand on his weapon and tried to look reassuring, Snodgrass adjusted his fez, and Tupman ignored them all.

"Mr. Scrooge?" Emily gestured at the door. "Will you do the honors?" Turning to the other members of the team, she said, "You all know what to do. This one is by the book. Mr. Snodgrass and Mr. Pickwick, set up immediately. Winkle, secure the building. I shall interview Mr. Scrooge and Timmy, dear, please rest until it is time."

Nothing more needed to be said—they were professional paranormal investigators.

They climbed the stairs in the dark and entered Scrooge's rooms, immediately separating to their tasks.

Mr. Tupman sat in Scrooge's own chair, its oaken legs creaking under his weight. He did not speak or move, but stared at nothing, occasionally brushing a piece of imaginary dust off of his portmanteau. Scrooge took umbrage with this, but Tupman paid him no mind. Instead, Emily patted the chair next to her where she sat with diary and quill. Dipping her pen in the inkwell she'd set up, she called him over.

Initially he had resisted, insisting that he had already told them everything they need to know. Emily, however, insisted they proceed by the book. All witnesses to phenomena must be interviewed thoroughly. She was pleased to see Scrooge settle down and answer her questions, however begrudgingly.

"The disturbances were primarily in the bedroom, but there have been other incidents as well," Scrooge said, growing more peevish with each question. "Why can you not leave me alone and just drive the spirits from my home?"

Ignoring his outburst she simply asked, "*Other incidents* such as?"

"The doorknocker on the front door turned into the face of Marley."

"Did it indeed?" This was exciting! She knew Bob would be delighted with such phenomena. "When? How often?"

"Only once, last night when I arrived home."

"Bob!" she called.

"Yes, pet?" came the answer from the other room.

"We may have a case here of either induced hallucination or a full blown transmutation of physical matter!"

"Where?" he called.

"Front door. Knocker manifested signs," she called back.

"On it." Mr. Pickwick passed them on his way from the bedroom to the front door. He pulled goggles down over his portly face without removing his spectacles. He smiled benevolently at Scrooge and pumped a bladder connected to the goggles as he moved past. A moment later he called from the front door.

"PK reading is off the chart. Something happened here, Emily. No doubt. No doubt at all."

Emily Cratchit looked up from her notes. "Now, if I heard you correctly, Mr. Scrooge, you said the full form apparition of your former partner threatened you with three more entities haunting you this very night?"

In spite of himself, Scrooge shuddered. "He said he had sat by me invisible since his death. He then told me to expect the first spirit when the bell tolled one this night, the second on the next night at the same hour. The third upon the next night when the last stroke of twelve has ceased to vibrate. I cannot sit by and allow myself to be continually haunted."

Ignoring him, Emily wrote the last of her notes and called her husband.

"Mr. Scrooge has confirmed multiple spirits in this location. I suggest we send him on his way whilst we investigate."

"Nonsense," cried Scrooge. "These are my chambers and I shall not be driven from them!"

"It is your right," Emily said, "as master of these chambers to be present as we investigate. But, I should warn you we will be manifesting all the spirits at once. You might be happier at another locale during the paranormal activity."

"Humbug!" said Scrooge, but rose, threw on his coat and cloak against the cold, and retrieved his walking stick. "Mr. Cratchit, I shall be at the office. I trust you will fetch me when all this is over?" It was not a question.

Scrooge turned, his heavy step down the stairs audible to one and all in his chambers. He opened the door and screamed.

All but Tupman, who remained indifferent in Scrooge's favorite chair, raced down the stairs and ran to the front door where Scrooge had fallen to his knees. Winkle had drawn his revolver, and Pickwick lowered his glasses to look over them out into the night. Emily reached for Bob's hand as Tim came down the stairs last, remaining a few steps up to see over the heads of the adults.

The air was filled with phantoms, wandering hither and thither in restless haste, moaning as they went. Every one of them wore chains like Marley's Ghost; some few were linked together; none were free. Scrooge cried out that he had known many in their lives. He had been quite familiar with one old ghost, in a white waistcoat, who had a monstrous iron safe attached to its ankle. He cried piteously at being unable to assist a wretched woman with an infant. The misery with them all was, clearly, that they sought to interfere for good in human matters and had lost the power forever. Whether these creatures faded into mist, or mist enshrouded them, he could not tell. But they and their spirit voices faded together; and the night became as it had been when they arrived at his chambers.

"It would seem the spirits do not desire Mr. Scrooge to leave the premises," Bob remarked rather calmly considering the situation.

"Indeed," concurred Snodgrass, removing his spectacles to clean them with his handkerchief, as they had steamed up in his run through the house and down the stairs. "It would seem this is no mere haunting but rather a targeted obsession."

"Agreed," replied Emily. The others all nodded.

"What?" gasped Scrooge from the ground to which he had fallen.

Snodgrass cleared his throat, removed his fez, showing his receding hairline, and closed his eyes. "The spirits are targeting you, Mr. Scrooge. They have a grievance against you and are determined to see their malevolence carried out to your detriment. It doesn't take a mental medium such as myself to know that. Have you wronged any in your life?"

Emily Cratchit snorted behind her hand.

"I am a businessman who conducts himself ethically. I am certain there are some who would think I have wronged them, but I assure you, I have always conducted myself according to the letters of my contracts and the law. I ask for no quarter and expect to give no quarter."

"We do not have time for this," Bob cut off his diatribe. "Snodgrass, you and Tim are to hold a séance in the bedchamber in ten minutes. Prepare yourself and let Tim know to do the same."

Snodgrass nodded and slipped up the stairs.

"Mr. Scrooge, we shall keep you in a chair in the sitting room by the fire. Mr. Winkle shall stand guard over you and see no harm comes to you."

"I am paying you to rid my home of spirits. I shall remain front and center while you attend to them," demanded Scrooge.

"Mr. Scrooge. You know not what you ask. We have a mental medium, Mr. Snodgrass, and a physical medium, my son Tim, who will be manifesting the very spirits you feared earlier tonight." Emily took him by the arm and led him up the darkened stairs. "Besides, we ask that our clients not be present for the actual moment of confrontation with the spirits. We must not risk any harm to your person."

"Humbug," said Scrooge. "But perhaps I shall sit in the sitting room with this gentleman," he nodded towards Winkle, "and the rotund gentlemen to ensure they do not rob me whilst you stop the haunting."

"Whilst the bedroom should be kept unlit, perhaps we could turn up the gas jets in the sitting room, hall and foyer. Of what use is darkness here," Emily asked.

"I like it," responded Scrooge. "It is economical. I do, however, have some candle stubs in a box in the cabinet next to the entry way into the kitchen. Fetch them and light them where you will." And with that he turned and went to the darkened sitting room and stared into the dying embers of the fire. Tupman joined him in doing the same.

Stave 4: The Séance and the Spirits of Christmas

Ms. Cratchit mumbled curses under her breath as she set up the candle stubs throughout the rooms.

Tiny Tim came out of the bedroom, his crutch thumping loudly on the hardwood floor, then muffled as he crossed the carpet to stop in front of Scrooge.

"What do you want," Scrooge asked, halfway between

contempt and indifference.

"Mr. Scrooge, the spirits of the unquiet dead surround us always, walking around like regular people. They do not see each other and we do not see them. They only see what they want to see. Many of them do not know they are dead. If Jacob Marley fell into this category, we will let him know he is dead and encourage him to move on into the light. You're helping us do a good thing, Mr. Scrooge."

"Humbug, boy. Go bother someone else. See if you can get that fleshy, quiet lump to say or do anything." He pointed his walking stick in the direction of Tupman who exhaled very slowly.

Emily guided Tim back into the bedroom. Scrooge's bed had been pushed to the corner. A table had been set up. Tiny Tim went and sat on one side, Augustus Snodgrass sat opposite him, his fez now off. Mr. Cratchit sat between them on one side, book and quill at hand. Opposite him was an open seat for Emily. Before she could sit, Pickwick gasped.

He held a device consisting of a box with a spindle mounted upon it and a wax cylinder on the spindle. Mounted opposite was a metallic cone descending into a needle which touched the surface of the cylinder. "Did you get something on the W.V.P.?" Bob asked anxiously.

"What's that?" demanded Scrooge entering from the other room.

Bob called back, "We're engaging in scientific investigation of these phenomena, Mr. Scrooge. Mr. Pickwick has invented a recording device employing wax cylinders. Sometimes the spirits speak through the ether and our human ears cannot comprehend. Mr. Pickwick believes (and has some evidence) that if we ask questions of the ether whilst recording on a wax cylinder, we can sometimes receive replies on the wax inaudible to the human ear. He calls it "Wax Voice Phenomena" or W.V.P. for short."

"And in this case," Pickwick continued quickly, like a clever schoolboy describing his trick on the teacher, "there has been a very clear response. Whilst you were all setting up, I asked a series of questions and received a response on the cylinder that I did not hear with my own ears while asking. Listen."

With that he began to crank the cylinder. His voice, scratchy, came forth from the cone. "I am speaking to the entities in this place. Is there someone there?" and there followed a pause of a few seconds, silence while he waited for a response. "Why are you in this place?" Another pause. "Why are you haunting Mr. Scrooge?"

Scrooge had risen from his chair and stood in the doorway to his bedchamber. The others sat breathless, straining to hear.

From the cone, almost inaudible, almost incomprehensible, a quiet voice that seemed to say, "I cannot rest. I cannot stay. I cannot linger anywhere..."

All of them gasped and Scrooge nearly fell. "It is the voice of Marley," he whispered.

The cone continued. "What do you want?" came the voice of Pickwick, and in the pause which followed, a voice seemed to say, "I am here tonight to warn you that you have yet a chance and hope of escaping my fate." With that, the recording ended and the group sat quiet.

"Well," said Bob, quietly, finally, "it would appear you are telling the truth, Mr. Scrooge. This place is haunted by spirits that mean you no good."

"What must I do?" begged Scrooge. "Cratchit...Bob, assure me that I yet may change these shadows you have shown me. Can you dismiss these paranormal beings from my chambers?"

"We shall do our utmost," said Emily Cratchit. "In the meantime, Mr. Scrooge, stay in your seat in the sitting room by the fire under the watchful eye of Mr. Winkle."

"What of the other gentleman, that Mr. Tupman? What service does he perform? At half a crown I expect him to actively work to remove any and all entities from my domicile."

"I assure you," replied Emily with an edge to her voice, "Mr. Tupman is here in the event that Mr. Snodgrass and Tim are unable to convince the entities to leave of their own accord. Now to the sitting room, Mr. Scrooge. Each second's delay is another second the spirits are still coming for you."

Scrooge hightailed it back to his seat and fell in with a quiet "harrumph," and stared at the embers.

"Now," said Emily, "let us begin. Snodgrass, you first, then Tim. All hands on the table. Pickwick, record everything that happens on the cylinders. This might just be the greatest haunting we have ever encountered."

For a moment the room was still; the only sound the breathing of the five living present in the room and the slow crank of the wax cylinder. Snodgrass relaxed, moving his shoulders while keeping his hands on the table. Snodgrass's head fell to his chest. His head slowly rolled up. His eyes were shut, but he moved his head as if looking around the room.

"Where is Scrooge?" he asked, his voice somehow simultaneously sounding like a child and a very old man.

Bob ignored the question and instead asked, "Who are you?"

Snodgrass's closed eyes turned to him. "I am the Ghost of Christmas Past."

Bob and Emily looked at each other.

"Long past?" Emily asked.

"No. Scrooge's past. I know the sadness that lurks in him through years of rejection."

With that, Snodgrass screamed and threw his head back, his hands remaining miraculously on the table.

His voice was suddenly booming and deep, "Come in, and know me better, man!" He then looked around the table with his eyes still closed, a look of confusion on his face. "Where is Scrooge?"

More confidently this time, Emily asked, "Who are you?"

"Look upon me!" the possessed Snodgrass returned. "You have never seen the like of me before!"

"Who are you?" Emily commanded.

"My life upon this globe is very brief," said the spirit cheerfully. "It ends tonight. I am the ghost of..." Snodgrass's head collapsed upon his chest.

Tim, Bob and Emily looked at one another. Tim moved closer to his mother.

As if a wave had washed over them, the room was filled with solemn dread. Every fiber of their beings screamed to leave and leave now. Every sad, lonely moment of their lives returned simultaneously leaving all in the room lost, lonely and on the verge of flight.

Snodgrass's head shot up, his eyes opened. They were pitch black. He pointed a finger in the direction of Scrooge in the next room and let out an unearthly shriek, then collapsed.

"What in the name of all that is holy was that?" cried Scrooge.

Bob, visibly shaken, said, "There are powerful entities in this place, Mr. Scrooge. Perhaps your chambers lie atop a druid burial site, or some sort of atrocity occurred here many years ago. There are many spirits and they are clearly malevolent and they have fixated upon you."

"Cleanse them, Bob. Exorcise them, as you gave your word!" Scrooge trembled. Emily wondered absently if this was the first time Mr. Scrooge had truly known mortal terror.

Before another word could be spoken, Emily grabbed Bob's hand. "If what you say is true," she whispered, "Tim cannot do this. It might kill him."

A cough from the table next to her called their attention to the frail boy "God has blessed us, every one, mother," he said in a sickly voice. "Mr. Snodgrass has used his gifts to make manifest the evil in this place. Can I do any less? I think it might please God that we help Mr. Scrooge, and perhaps, by helping him, we might change his heart."

Emily sighed, her heart deeply conflicted. Pride for the generous and kind son battled with fear that his heart, which was too big in all senses of the word, might give out as a result of this night's deeds. She did not object any further.

"I wonder if I might trouble someone for a glass of brandy," came the voice of Snodgrass as he pulled his head up off the table and placed the fez back on it. Winkle came in from the other room and handed him a flask which he pulled from his coat pocket, almost dropping it in the process. Snodgrass took two pulls and handed it back. Winkle took a pull himself, smacked his lips and screwed the cap back on. Realizing that the others were all staring at him, he strode from the room and took his position behind Mr. Scrooge again.

"I caution you all," Emily said in a loud voice so that even Scrooge could hear, "we have entered the most dangerous part of the séance. Young Tim here is a physical medium. Whereas Mr. Snodgrass is a mental medium and the spirits can only speak through him, they can manifest physically through Tiny Tim. Be very careful from this moment on. What Tim manifests can hurt us."

Tim breathed deeply and dropped his tiny head. His chest rose and fell three times and then stopped. For a moment, no one moved. No one breathed. He coughed once. Twice.

Then his head shot back, his mouth opened wide and smoky grayish pink ectoplasm billowed forth, a viscous miasma condensing above the lad and beginning to take shape next to him. Even Pickwick, who was used to such phenomena, drew a sharp breath through his teeth and pulled back from the smoke.

At first it was hard to determine the form it was manifesting, and then Emily began to see patterns in the manifestation. It was a face. It was not in impenetrable shadow as the other objects in the room were, but had a dismal light about it, like a bad lobster in a dark cellar. It was not angry or ferocious, but looked at them with ghostly spectacles turned up on its ghostly forehead. The hair was curiously stirred, as if by breath or hot air; and, though the eyes were wide open, they were perfectly motionless. That, and its livid color, made it horrible; but its horror seemed to be in spite of the face and beyond its control, rather than a part or its own expression.

Bob looked it in the empty eyes and asked respectfully, "Dreadful apparition, why do you trouble Scrooge?"

It spoke. "How it is that I appear before you in a shape that you can see, I may not tell. In life I was Scrooge's partner, Jacob Marley. As one first yet final act of kindness, I have returned from the grave to offer him a chance and hope, a chance and hope of my procuring. I have been allowed to let three spirits visit Scrooge so that he may yet avoid the incessant torture of remorse." Tim groaned loudly and Emily grew worried, but the ectoplasm continued to flow from his mouth, feeding the shape of the spirit.

"Spirit," commanded Emily in a smooth voice, "by your own admission, you have come to this place to haunt Scrooge. You are seven years gone. You have been walking the face of the earth as a spirit for seven long years, Jacob Marley. Go into the light."

Again the specter raised a cry, and shook its chain and wrung its shadowy hands at them. "I have come with a warning from beyond. Just as I walk the earth, Scrooge is condemned to do so as well after death. Unless he speaks with the other spirits he cannot hope to shun the path I tread."

"Go into the light, Jacob Marley," Emily repeated, her eyes closed. "There is peace and serenity in the light."

With this Tiny Tim began to spasm, the ectoplasmic form of Jacob Marley began to collapse. Some of the spirit material returned to the mouth of Tiny Tim, some dissipated into the air, some fell to the ground. Tiny Tim coughed so violently his hands came up off the table to his mouth. Emily ran to him and took him in her arms, shooting an angry gaze at Bob.

Snodgrass also collapsed again and then lifted himself up off the table. The contact had been broken.

"Well?" demanded Scrooge, entering from the other room. "Have they left?"

"Perhaps..." began Bob.

"No," came a small voice. Tim lifted his head up, out of his mother's embrace. "The spirits are still here. Such misery. Such malevolence. They are filled with remorse and regret, anger and hatred. So much is directed towards you, Mr. Scrooge. I pity them." With that he let out a stream of wet coughs. "But I fear them more. There is a grave presence here, worse than all the rest. I saw it, standing by Scrooge while Mr. Marley manifested through me. It was shrouded in a deep black garment, which concealed its head, its face, its form, and left nothing of it visible save one outstretched hand. But for this it would have been difficult to detach its figure from the night, and separate it from the darkness by which it was surrounded. This ghost brings nothing but death."

The room fell silent.

"It is as I feared," said Bob with sad finality. "Let us make our final notes and then pack up all our equipment and remove ourselves from the premises."

"Surely you will not leave me alone with the spirits," cried Scrooge, running first to Bob, then to Emily and Tim. "Not on Christmas? We had a deal. We had a deal, Cratchit." He pointed his finger at Bob as if accusing him in court. "If you do not help me you shall be unemployed and forcibly removed to the street. Your family shall not have a home."

Emily gently released Tim and stood up. "Mr. Scrooge, we would do no such thing. You are going to leave with us. I told you if the spirits would not leave of their own accord, Mr. Tupman would be called in to resolve the situation."

As the others gathered up their equipment and moved Scrooge's bed back into position, Bob and Scrooge went into the sitting room. The corpulent Mr. Tupman looked up at them.

"Mr. Tupman, the dwelling is yours. Please prepare the device."

Tupman lifted his enormous girth out of the stuffed chair, its legs still protesting every second. He set down the black ox-leather portmanteau, undid the latches and opened it. The case had held an enormous black metallic device with buttons and wires hanging from it.

"Mr. Tupman works with electromagnetic devices. It is his belief that spirit energy is nothing more than unfocused electromagnetic energy, and he has built a device that dissipates the electromagnetic energy into the ether so that the spirits are cleansed from the location. We are now going to start this device in your sitting room.

As the others carried out the bags and boxes of equipment, Tupman made several adjustments on the device and then placed a large magnet into a side opening. The device began humming loudly and Scrooge began to develop a headache.

Bob winced as well. "Come, sir. Leave with us now and return here at sunrise. Your house will be free of spirits." And with that, they left into the dark Christmas Eve, Bob carrying Tiny Tim on his back as Emily led the others into the night.

Stave 5: The End of It

Scrooge spent the night in a chair at his counting house and returned with the rise of the sun over the snowy London cityscape, his neck and back stiff and his limbs cold.

He unlocked the door with his key, delighted to see neither knocker nor knob turn into Marley. He trudged up the stairs and entered his chambers. The device in the portmanteau was no longer emitting any sounds. It stood silent and cold, a sentinel against a no longer relevant threat.

He went through the chambers. The bed was his own, the room was his own. Best and happiest of all, the Time before him was his own. He no longer needed fear the vengeance of Christmas spirits, or whatever humbug it was.

Indeed, he began to think, it might well have been humbug. In the stone cold sober light of morning, the more the events of the night before seemed phantasmagorical. Who was to say they were not caused by the Cratchits themselves? They certainly seemed to know what to do in every situation and the haunting only stopped on account of them. Perhaps they *were* the cause of it. The more he thought about it, the more Scrooge was willing to believe the Cratchits were behind the entire thing.

Well, he laughed to himself, let Bob Cratchit enjoy Christmas and Boxing Day. He shall return to work on the twenty-seventh to find the metropolitan police waiting for him, and he and his wife and son shall be charged with fraud. Let's see if time in prison changes their lying ways.

Scrooge had no further intercourse with spirits, and was glad on it 'til his dying day.

Black Coal

By David Blake Lucarelli

Gary Grabowski had always been a pain in the ass. He wore cheap suits with loud ties and enough bad cologne to choke an elephant just to keep up appearances that he wasn't on the take. But the thing that would forever solidify Gary Grabowski as a colossal pain in the ass to Daniel Richardson was that Gary had even managed to time his death in such a way as to be maximally annoying.

The company Christmas party was in one week. Dan wouldn't even have time to meet the new union rep until the party itself, let alone commence the usual wining and dining that would ultimately and inevitably end up with him as deep in Dan's pocket as ol' Gary had been. Dan had tried to put out feelers to the union to size up the new guy, but so far he hadn't gotten much.

Younger. That figured.

Dan pictured some snot nosed kid fresh out of grad school full of ideals and piss and vinegar about how he was gonna solve the plight of the working man. Well, that wouldn't last either.

First, he'd meet a few of the folks he was setting out to save and come to realize that they barely deserved to be gainfully employed, let alone redeemed. Then, if he had a family, it wouldn't take long for him to do the math: how much he'd need to afford a decent sized home on the good side of town, save for retirement, and send the kid or kids to college. That wasn't gonna happen on his union salary, not without some significant enhancements that only Dan would be in the position to provide.

Then again, it would probably be better if Dan had the chance to give the new guy some idea of what to expect at the annual Christmas party.

Ah well, no sense in worrying about the new kid getting his feathers ruffled, thought Dan.

However their initial meeting at the party went down, Dan knew what he had to do, and he was as smooth as the scotch he poured himself for a night cap at getting it done. *Besides*, the thought occurred to him, *Jessica was going to be there*, and that meant he was due for a little fun.

"Is that your first one?" said his wife Mary from across the room as she glanced up from her laptop. She had an eyebrow cocked as if she knew it wasn't.

"Third," lied Dan. It was his fifth. "What do you care? It helps me think."

"And what are you thinking about?"

Jessica, he thought. "Business," he answered. Dan walked over to his wife and put his hands on her shoulders. "What are you reading?"

"An article. Some scholars now think that Jesus may have been born in a cave instead of a manger."

"That's not what they taught us."

"Obviously, but if they're right...born in a cave, reborn in a cave. It does have a nice symmetry to it," she said.

"It was a tomb. He was resurrected from his tomb on the third day."

Mary turned around to face her husband. "Once the altar boy, always the altar boy," she said.

Dan knelt before her and put a hand on each leg. "Of course, all men are born in a cave." As he spoke, he slid his hands closer to her crotch. "And we spend the rest of our lives trying to get back in."

Mary's hands met his before they reached their destination. "Go to sleep Dan," she said, "You're drunk."

Dan woke up the next morning with a hangover. He rolled over to find his wife had already risen. Squinting out the window he saw the snowfall had blanketed the driveway and his car overnight. The sight made his eyes ache. There was too much bright white for him to take in.

As Dan attacked the snow in the driveway with a shovel he noticed two words carved in the snow on the front and back windshields of his black Range Rover. On the front it read, *GUILTY*. On the back, *CONFESS*.

Dan stood for a moment, perplexed and pondering. *Kids,* he thought.

He eyed the foot prints captured in the snow.

Boots. Big feet for kids. Ah well, teenagers then.

He continued to shovel, and a chill ran down his spine. *Maybe Jessica had a jealous lover, maybe some environmentalist was "taking a stand." It wouldn't be the first time. Maybe...*

He looked at the words again. *GUILTY. CONFESS. Hell,* he thought, *you're going to have to be more specific than that.*

~

Dan spotted Bradley Blumenfeld immediately from across the room amid the gaudy Christmas decorations and semi-drunk party guests. In a room full of suits, dress shirts and low slung party dresses, he certainly stood out. Not so much as a collar on the kid, or a drink in his hand. He might have his work cut out for him. But then he saw Jessica with her pouty red lips, and tight sweater, and thought, *the kid will keep.*

"Merry Christmas, Jessica," said Dan. "It's good to see you."

"Hello Dan," she purred, "Did you get me anything? I've been a *very* good girl."

He gingerly took her hand to pull her off of the main floor of the party as he spoke, "Well then, why don't you come with me and I'll show you what good girls get?"

Jessica glanced around before letting Dan lead her down the hall. Dan tried the doors of each office in the dimly lit hallway until he found one that wasn't locked. *Perfect.* Dan grabbed her by the arm pulled her inside. He shut the door behind him, and locked it.

"Does anybody else know about us?" he said.

"Oww, you're hurting me," she said.

"Does *anybody else* know?"

"No, of course not. Do you think I'm stupid?"

Dan relaxed his grip. He pulled out a small black jewelry box from the inside pocket of his leather jacket.

"Is that for me?" Jessica cooed.

She opened it to reveal the silver choker inside. "Oh Dan, I love it," she said with just a little too much enthusiasm to sound completely sincere. "What can I ever do to repay you?"

Dan put his hands on her shoulders and guided her head below the desk where he now sat. He felt the warm wet sensation of her mouth and tongue around his member.

"That's it baby, just...watch the teeth," said Dan.

And as he went into his private ecstasy Dan thought to himself, *Yeah, that's the way you do it. Like a man. That's what punks like Gary Grabowski and Bradley Blumenfeld would never understand. It was just like mining. You go inside, you get what you want, and you move on.*

Dan convulsed slightly, gripping the chair as Jessica finished her work.

"I'll go out first," said Jessica.

"Yeah, you do that," said Dan, still off in his own little world. Dan zipped himself up and walked to the restroom. He combed his hair and straightened his shirt. He checked the time on his phone. *Shit. 10:00 p.m.* Later than he had thought.

The festivities were about to begin in earnest and he'd be missed if he wasn't back in the main room for the party soon. Mr. Vanderbilt had already started making the annual company toast. Dan deftly grabbed a glass of champagne and made a bee line to be next to him.

"May 2016 bring a safe, happy and mutually prosperous partnership between the hardworking members of the UMW and your humble management."

Dan grimaced. The old man was really laying it on thick this year.

"Now, as you all know 2015 has been a lean year in terms of the mine's yield, but with the more advanced techniques afforded to us by the latest technologies I am confident that 2016 will be much more productive. In lieu of Christmas bonuses this year, I've made charitable contributions in the names of each of our workers. And now for our traditional gift exchange. Daniel, if you'd be so kind as to do the honors."

Mr. Vanderbilt handed him a small green gift box wrapped with a red bow.

Dan knew what was in it. It was the same thing every year. The question was, did Bradley Blumenfeld know, and how was he going to take it?

Bradley Blumenfeld took the present that Dan extended to him and opened it revealing a large oblong lump of black coal laying in white cotton. The smile on his face died a quick death, and the room became silent except for the Christmas carols that droned on in the background. All eyes were on the kid.

Bradley stared at the black rock in the box.

Dan cleared his throat.

"*Ahem*," he said, "it's, you know...it's a gag gift."

Bradley's eyes met Dan's for the first time.

"It's not funny," he said.

This wasn't going well.

Mr. Vanderbilt stepped in, "It's just that...you fellows are always giving us these rocks, and Christmas is the one time of year we like to return the favor."

"It's an insult," said Bradley. "You want to truly honor the workers, who sweat and bleed for you? They aren't even invited to this party. *In lieu of lean times?*" Bradley extended his hand in the direction of the lavish buffet table. "The company posted record profits this year. You yourself received a record bonus. And now you get to take the tax write-off from your contributions to charity in the workers' names."

"Mr. Blumenfeld," sputtered Vanderbilt, "I did not invite you into the halls of my company to listen to your insults and accusations."

"No," said Bradley, "you did it to make sure we know our place. To remind us what side our bread is buttered on. To let us know that if we aren't good boys and girls who blindly take what you see fit to give us, we get nothing."

Dan knew he had to step in before security escorted Blumenfeld out.

"Hah, it's all right Mr. Vanderbilt," said Dan, "I think our new friend here has just had one too many to drink. Why don't you come with me Bradley and I'll get you into a nice cab?" Dan put his hands on Bradley's shoulders.

"Get your hands off me," said Bradley Blumenfeld. "I don't drink. I'm leaving, but not before I return the favor."

Bradley Blumenfeld handed Mr. Vanderbilt a small rectangular wrapped package. Mr. Vanderbilt dutifully opened it to reveal a first edition copy of *The Jungle,* Upton Sinclair's tribute to the working man's plight. Mr. Vanderbilt pursed his lips and eyed it with disdain. Bradley Blumenfeld marched off toward the elevators by himself.

"Well," said Dan to Mr. Vanderbilt, "Ho, ho, ho."

"We're gonna have our hands full with that one, Daniel. You're really gonna have to earn your keep to turn him into something we can work with."

"Ah, don't worry Mr. Vanderbilt, that's why they call me *The Nutcracker*. Some are tougher than others, but they all crack eventually." said Dan with as much bravado and confidence as he could muster.

"Don't bullshit me boy," said Mr. Vanderbilt with a fierceness in his tone he'd never directed at Dan before. "That dip-shit is in a position to cause us real fucking problems. The last thing I need to take to our stock hold-ers is a strike or even the fucking threat of one. You deal with him. You get him in line or so help me God I will find someone who will."

"Yes sir, Mr. Vanderbilt. Consider it done."

The party returned to nervous laughter and drunken revelry. They knew better than to discuss what had just happened while still there.

Dan took the elevator down to the ground floor. The office lobby was empty. He stepped outside and paused to take in the night air. A gust of winter wind hit him and he broke into a cold sweat. If Blumenfeld really was a true believer, he might have to start looking for another line of work, even if he did know where the bodies were buried at Vanderbilt Consolidated Mines.

Bradley Blumenfeld stood across the parking lot from him, watching.

Their eyes met.

Blumenfeld burst out in laughter.

"What the hell's so funny?" said Dan.

"Oh, come on! That was quite show I put on, no?" said Bradley.

"You scared old man Vanderbilt shitless," said Dan. "Were you trying to give him a heart attack?"

"I was doing what any good negotiator does. I was draw-ing a line in the sand. Or, the snow," he held his gloved hand up to catch some of the descending snow flurries.

"So why are you letting me in on your little charade?" asked Dan.

"Because there's a special bond between us now," said Bradley. "Your boss expects I'll be unreasonable, so he'll bend that much more during negotiations, and you get to be the hero when we finally make a deal on the new con-tract. It's a win-win."

"That's a dangerous game you played up there," said Dan.

"What's business except war without casualties?" said

Bradley extending his hand to shake.

"Okay then," said Dan, "we're in this together."

"I'll see you in two weeks."

"Two weeks?"

"For the annual inspection."

Dan frowned.

"Don't worry, you still have plenty of time to whip the place into shape. Good night. Drive safe."

The kid's a pretty good actor, thought Dan as he started to walk back to his car. *But the question is, was he acting upstairs, or just now? And shit! Was it time for the inspection already?* There was nothing he looked forward to less than going into the mine with the State Inspector and the union rep and trying to put a smiling face on every safety code violation the two of them could dredge up. It had been about as much fun as a root canal with the old union rep, and *he* knew how to play ball. *Blumenfeld? The kid was still a wild card.*

Dan froze as he approached his car. The snowfall had covered it during the party. But written on the windshields in the same writing as before were the words *GUILTY* and *CONFESS*. He looked at the snow around his car but it was densely packed with a myriad of footprints. *Somebody's watching me,* he thought. *Somebody's playing games.*

~

The day of the inspection came and Dan seriously thought about calling in sick. But that would just delay the inevitable. Better to get it over with. At least he had been able to pull some strings to ensure that the state inspector wouldn't be there. Not too hard really. The coal companies had successfully lobbied to cut their department's budget to bare bone levels. They simply didn't have the manpower to inspect half the mines on an annual basis. If both he and Bradley signed off, the inspector wouldn't show up for at least another year. Of course, getting Bradley to sign off was going to be another matter, but he'd cross that bridge too.

It was bright and sunny but somehow still bitter cold outside when Dan got out of his Range Rover and made his way to the mine entrance. He walked underneath the Christmas lights that were strung all across the outside arch, and thought of the volatile party two weeks ago. Strange, he hadn't heard from Jessica since then. She was usually good for at least a text or two between their rendezvous. By the time he put on his hard hat and safety vest, Blumenfeld was already waiting for him in the head car of the tram.

"Let's do this," said Dan.

"Aren't we waiting for the state inspector?" asked Bradley.

"He can't make it. We sign off. That buys us another year."

"And if we don't?"

"Then you and I get to spend a little more time together in the hole."

"Hop on," said Bradley.

Dan entered the car and took a seat.

"Aren't we waiting for the driver?" said Dan.

"No need. My family have been working the mines for three generations. It's in my blood."

The tram lurched to life and began its slow decent along the tracks.

Dan held onto the sides tightly with one hand and gripped his hard hat with the other. He glanced behind him as the last sunlight became a tiny pin prick and then faded entirely. The lanterns that lined the shaft took over with their sickly yellow glow. They came to a cross roads. To the right was where Dan would have directed the tour: a tunnel that led to a relatively dry vein, but one that was well re-enforced, not too deep. Bradley backed the mine car up and went left. The track took a sharp dip and Dan lost his stomach.

"Hey, what's the hurry?" said Dan in at tone he hoped sounded somewhat jovial.

"I thought you might want to get this over with quickly," replied Bradley.

"Are you sure you want to go down this way?" asked Dan. "It's a dead end."

"It's where the newest mining is being done, isn't it?" asked Bradley.

"Yeah."

"Then that's where I want to go."

They pressed on winding deeper and deeper. The air grew stale. Dan loathed going into the mine ever since he had been caught in a partial cave-in during an inspection. In hindsight, it hadn't amounted to much. He'd had to suck on his Self-Contained Self-Rescue device or SCSR for a few minutes while the smoke dissipated and the shaft was cleared. But the memory of that experience still gnawed at him: to go in an instant from being safe and in control to being trapped and completely at the mercy of others. Dan shuddered as if it had happened yesterday.

The deeper down they went the more cut off from the world they were, the longer it would take to get help if something did go wrong. And the truth was the drill bits they used for rescues weren't designed to go as deep as they mined now. The coal that had been close to the surface was long gone. Like a drug addict, they had to go deeper and deeper below to find fresh untapped veins.

Finally, they came to the end of the line. The breaks squealed as the tram ground slowly to a halt.

"You've been awful quiet," said Dan. "Does that mean everything looks up to code?"

"I haven't seen anything I didn't already know." Bradley stood up. "C'mon, let's go."

"Go? Go where?"

"Tunnel Six."

Dan ran the tunnel numbers in his mind. *No. Not Tunnel Six!*

"That tunnel's being retreat mined."

"So?" said Bradley.

So retreat mining is the most dangerous thing we do down here. When the vast majority of the vein had been tapped, they pulled the pillars in reverse order to get what little coal was left around them. Every pillar pulled put more stress on the remaining ones. It was an imprecise method at best, and the more pillars they pulled the more dangerous it became. *Bradley had to know that.*

"It's just...we don't usually go down this far on foot. It's—"

"It's what? Not safe? Not up to code?"

"No, it's just...I like to leave it to the trained professionals when it comes to—"

"Look, do you want me to sign off on the mine or don't you?"

"Of course I do."

"Then I need to see this. Up close. That's why they call it an inspection. We walk to the end of Tunnel Six, and you'll be sipping a scotch by lunch."

Dan could taste that scotch on his lips.

"Yeah, okay. Sounds good."

The two men started on foot for a few minutes following the signs to Tunnel Six.

Dan glanced behind him at the increasingly distant tram and shuddered for a second time when the yellow lamps on the walls flickered for a moment. They came to a vertical ladder.

Tunnel Six.

Bradley shined his flashlight into the crevices. He took notes on a clipboard. Dan tried but failed to see what he was writing. Both men descended the ladder and continued around a long curve.

A slow deep rumbling sound erupted from everywhere and nowhere at once. The steel supports groaned and the timber creaked, as coal dust kicked up into the air and small tiny pebbles fell to the floor.

"Jesus," muttered Dan to himself, "did you hear that?"

"It's settling. It just means the patient is still alive," said Bradley.

"We should go."

Bradley looked over the schematic he held in his hands. "The tunnel extends only another twenty meters that way."

"Okay," said Dan, realizing that for once, he wasn't in a position to argue. They walked on taking cautious and deliberate steps. It occurred to him that they hadn't seen another worker since they entered the mine.

"Where is everybody?" asked Dan.

"I told them to take a long lunch," replied Bradley. "After all, this is like Christmas, right? It only comes once a year."

The ground shook beneath them with a violent jerk that knocked both of them against the walls.

"Are you okay?" asked Bradley.

"Yes, but I have to insist we go back now."

Bradley paused. Finally, he nodded his consent. "Lead the way."

The two men did an about face and began to retrace their steps. The ladder was just in sight when a third and more powerful tremor hit.

They reached out to the walls to maintain their balance and Dan heard the distinct sound of metal bending. Both men tried to keep walking toward the ladder, but they were jolted from side to side. The air became thick with coal dust. They were walking blind.

A sickening snap followed immediately by a thunderous crash made Dan's heart stop

The lights flickered again, and then went out for good.

Bradley pointed his flashlight where the ladder should have been. Slowly, the dust settled to reveal there was now a wall of dirt and coal between themselves and the only way out. God only knew how thick it was.

Dan collapsed against the wall in shock. He coughed hard to clear his lungs and tried to catch his breath. Anger welled up inside him. This was all Blumenfeld's fault.

"Fuck! This is unbelievable. We're trapped! Goddamn it!" shouted Dan.

"Are you hurt?" asked Bradley.

"No."

"Then calm down."

"How the fuck can you be so calm?" snapped Dan.

"It could be worse."

"Really? Tell me, how the fuck could it be worse?"

"It could have happened with a full crew down here."

"Yeah. Okay," said Dan, unclear as to what Bradley was driving at.

"It's a matter of mathematics. The more men, the quicker the oxygen runs out. Two men, we should have all the time in the world."

"Great! How about we radio someone, and get them started on getting us the fuck outta here?"

"Ahh, that. Well, the thing is...I'm afraid I left my radio in the mine car."

"Are you fucking for real? Do you want to die down here?"

Dan checked his cell phone. *No reception. Of course.*

"Don't worry, I'm trained in safety. And the boys will be back from lunch in a couple of hours. They'll realize something's wrong."

"You have a lot of faith in *the boys.*"

"A lot more than I have in *you* about right now. Are you sure this is what you do for a living?"

"Look," said Dan pointing his palms toward Bradley, "if we're going to be stuck down here for a while, could you lose the attitude?"

"Okay. But you'll have to pardon me for a moment," said Bradley as he got up and wandered back down Tunnel Six.

"Where are you going?"

"There should be an emergency kit about ten yards back." He shined his flashlight on the walls ahead as he walked and Dan followed. "I'm also trying to eyeball the rough diameter of the space we have. The gas monitors will tell us if and when we need to use the SCSRs. It looks like the ventilation shafts have been compromised but if we stay close to them that's where the best air is."

"Alright Bradley, you know your shit."

The beam of the flashlight settled on a large metal box sandwiched between an oak barrel and a pile of old tools. On it, in bright orange letters were the words FOR EMERGENCY USE ONLY. Bradley opened the latch, removed the gas monitor from the metal box and turned it on. He studied the monitor carefully.

"We're in luck, the air's not too bad yet."

"Yeah, I'm feeling *really* lucky."

"Are you hungry?"

"Not at all," said Dan.

Bradley nodded. "Best to conserve it all anyway, just in case. Maybe later."

He tossed Dan a flashlight from the metal box.

"Put this on now," said Bradley handing him a self-contained self-rescue device about the size of a large canteen. "If the flashlights go out you won't have to search for it in the dark."

"Thanks," said Dan pulling the strap over his neck. He sat down, and let out a long sigh.

Bradley sat down across from him. "So...know any good jokes?"

They both laughed heartily. Dan took a deep breath and thought, *the instinct to survive, that's the great equalizer. Everyone's your best friend until the plane lands.*

"You know," said Bradley, "you could have met me before."

"How?" asked Dan.

"I was at Gary Grabowski's funeral."

"Oh, that, yeah... I meant to. I really should have gone. It's just, it was right around Christmas, and I had some shopping to do and...you know how it is." Dan scanned Bradley's face for sympathy but found none.

"Even Old Man Vanderbilt sent flowers," said Bradley.

"Nice ones?"

"He didn't break the bank."

"Did you know Gary?"

"I did. It was sad. Like any funeral, when a man dies for no reason."

"I just realized, I don't even know...how did he die?"

"Black lung," said Bradley.

"No kidding? I thought that shit was over with."

"Hey," said Bradley, all air of congeniality gone. "Don't do that. It's just us here. You *really* expect me to believe you don't know black lung's come back to these mines with a vengeance? You got something you want to get off your chest, Dan? Now would be the time to confess."

Confess, thought Dan. Was that word coincidence, or something else?

Of course he knew. The deeper they dug the more toxic the particulates in the air became. The company had their way of covering that up, one that Dan himself had helped put into place with a series of well-placed bribes at the highest levels. They had rigged the system so that they could provide their own carefully selected air samples to prove to the insurance companies that whatever disease the miners were dying from it had nothing to do with them. It was perfect. Zero exposure for the company. But Bradley spoke as if he already knew what Dan's reply would be.

Dan sighed. "Yeah, I know."

"You *more* than know. They couldn't have done it without you. You were the key to making it happen."

"Listen, I don't make the rules around here."

"No," said Bradley, "you just do the dirty work."

"I just did what I was—" Before Dan had a chance to complete his reply they were interrupted by a buzzing sound that came from the gas monitor. Bradley turned his attention to it.

"Time for the SCSRs. Put the flat end of the tube between your teeth and gums, and when you have a tight fit pull this cord on the side to start the flow of oxygen."

Dan did as he was instructed. "Don't worry if the bag underneath doesn't fully inflate. It's not supposed to. This is the newest model."

Dan took a deep breath. The initial burst of air felt shockingly cool to his lungs, but with each additional breath, it grew warmer.

"If you need to communicate, use this," said Bradley handing him a pen and pad of paper from the metal box.

Bradley put on his own SCSR. Both men sat facing each other in silence.

Dan contemplated the weird bug-like figure that now sat before him: Bradley in his yellow hard hat, puffy orange vest, with a black tube protruding from his mouth leading to a bulge on his abdomen. *Is that what I look like? Is that what I've been reduced to?*

Time passed. Dan played solitaire on his phone. 68 percent power left. He noted the time. It had been an hour since the cave in. After a while, Bradley stood up and walked behind Dan. He was writing something on his pad. He handed it to Dan. It read, "Try to stand up."

Slowly, Dan got to his feet, but something felt very wrong. His center of balance was off. He had to struggle to keep his legs from buckling beneath him. He was dizzy. Light headed. In a panic he pulled the tube out of his mouth. "Whoa," he said, "what the fuck? There's something wrong with my SCSR!"

Bradley pulled out his tube as well.

"You're starting to feel the effects of the limited oxygen, aren't you?"

"Huh? What do you mean?"

"The oxygen in your tank is spent. It was almost empty to begin with. Useless now."

"What are you talking about?"

"I put a hole in the bag."

"What? Are you fucking kidding me? You're crazy! You sonofa—"

Out of the corner of his eye Dan saw the head of a shovel

coming straight at him. Contact. The sharpest stinging pain Dan had ever known seared through his body. Then blackness.

~

Things were hazy now. The ache in his head throbbed in time with his heartbeat. He could sense the large swollen lump met a gash in his scalp where the edge of the shovel had dug into the side of his head. His could feel the tightness of his skin where his face was crusted with his own dried blood. Bradley had perched one of the flashlights on a rock so that it shone directly in his eyes forcing him to squint. He tried to move and found his hands were tied behind his back and his feet were bound. His mouth was covered in duct tape.

"You're back," said Bradley.

Dan stared at him.

"I would have told you my secret earlier but you were becoming belligerent and I really felt it was important that you know why you are going to die."

Dan made guttural sounds in protest. Bradley waited until he stopped.

"Are you done?" Bradley had all the air of a condescending teacher losing his patience with an unruly student. "First of all, nobody can hear you. Second, I told the crew to take the rest of the day off. Third, I planted enough dynamite in the mine to bring down the whole shaft. Nobody's coming for us, and even if they did, they could never get to us in time." Bradley paced back and forth in front of Dan as he spoke. "I know. You're thinking, *he's not right in the head.* But how did I became this way? That really comes down to you, Dan."

Sweat dripped down Dan's face. He saw blurry lines and floaters out of the corners of his eyes.

"You're starting to really feel it now, aren't you? The air down here is thick with contaminants. Nitrogen and carbon dioxide. Black damp they call it. "

Dan squirmed.

"I suggest you conserve your energy and listen, because, frankly, neither of us has much time left. Blumenfeld was my mother's maiden name. My father left her for a little gold digger. Broke her heart, but then, dying men do strange things, don't they? See this little gold digger—or should I say *coal* digger—dumped his ass when she got a hold of a bigger fish who could buy her better presents." Bradley pulled the sliver choker Dan had given Jessica out of the metal box and clamped it around Dan's neck. Dan flinched.

"It's a little tight, but I think it suits you."

Bradley used his shovel to pry the lid off the large wooden barrel. The stench of rotten meat flooded the chamber. Dan felt his throat constrict involuntarily and tried not to retch.

Bradley put his hand into the barrel and started to lift something up and out.

Dan felt the blood drain from his face.

"You remember Jessica, don't you?"

It was her! He began lifting Jessica's corpse up by its long yellow hair as a sluice of discolored liquid ran out over the rim. Her slimy wet pale white skin seemed to glow even as her cold, unseeing eyes bored into him. Death had turned her once beautiful face into something cruel and wraith-like. Dan's head begin to spin as Bradley freed her lifeless body from the barrel and lay it at his feet. He struggled as Bradley undid his belt and pulled his pants and underwear down to his ankles.

"Perhaps you're more used to seeing her like this," said Bradley as he placed Jessica's head on his lap, and adjusted her gaping mouth onto his flaccid penis.

Tears rolled down Dan's face.

"Don't cry," said Bradley with mock concern. "How is she? A little cold I'll bet. If you feel some movement down there that would be the maggots."

Dan made whimpering sounds though his nose.

"Don't worry, this will all be over soon. You see, we're both dead men. I could have lived another six months, maybe, but with this *thing* growing inside me every day..." Bradley pointed to the side of his head. "No, this is much better. See those particulates that cause black lung? They also cause brain tumors in children. That was the legacy I inherited from my father thanks to you, Dan."

Bradley stood directly in front of him now.

"I was with my father at the very end. He weighed less than ninety pounds when he died. Do you know how black lung kills you? It's like a tiny screw slowly tightening around your throat. Every day, every minute, it gets harder and harder to catch your breath."

Dan looked at Bradley's eyes. They held a manic intensity.

"Eventually, you have to choose between starving to death because you can't stop breathing long enough to swallow, and suffocating because you can't get enough oxygen into your lungs while you eat."

Bradley retrieved another object from the metal box. Dan strained in the light to make it out.

"I've got something for you now. This is gonna hurt a little bit."

Bradley tore off the duct tape.

Dan howled in pain.

Dan eyed the oblong piece of coal in Bradley's hand, the same one he had been given at the Christmas party. Bradley pulled down Dan's lower jaw and started to shove the large black lump into his mouth. With one hand he pushed it down his throat while holding tight onto Dan's nose with the other.

"Open wide," said Bradley. "It's a gag gift."

Dan felt his lips tear and his teeth crack and tasted the salt of his own blood as the inside of his cheeks and tongue were cut into by the unforgiving rock. As he choked and gasped desperately, Bradley forced the rock farther and farther inside.

Dan writhed and convulsed as tears poured down his

face. He looked to the side and stared wide-eyed in disbelief at the scene their shadows cast against the wall: a priest giving benediction and an altar boy receiving his final communion.

Pâtisserie du Diable

By Eric J. Guignard

You revelers, *défenseurs* and *fêtards* of the feast day Epiphany, lovers of sweet cake, heed my caution, consider this narrative, beware *La Galette Des Rois*, for it is not what you think!

My alarm may sound Impossible! *C'est fantastique!* Absurd, even! But it is so, and nothing further from fiction, and no less than the very ruination of your eternal soul! For what I am to tell you speaks to the infernal, the demonic, and though I am named a fabulist, this is no sensational tale told for thrill, but a forewarning of the most ominous stripe.

La fève, la fève! It is not the sweet charm of childhood delight, *ce n'est pas* the beloved *célébration* of our baby savior, but instead the insidious cunning of *Le Diable* meant to deceive us innocent mortals!

Take heed! Beware! *Méfiez-vous La Galette!*

...Ah, sacré bleu, but you know not yet what I speak, you so unmoved to believe in the dark, the fiendish manipulations that shape this realm, our very world in which we live, you so bound in belief of what you are taught, a skeptic of the spectral, you cannot yet understand... *Non, non, non,* I see I must explain from the beginning...

My name is Henri Hébert, and I was at the time of these events a librarian at *Université Paris Diderot*. There I met and briefly loved a young woman, though the brevity of that romance is through no fault of our own; I would once have wanted to wed and spend all my days anon with her, picnicking on the banks of La Marne, dining at the quaint cafés along Rue Saint-Honoré, strolling the food court at *Le Marché des Enfants Rouges,* sampling tastes of the Japanese, the Moroccan, the Greek, even tasteless *plats de Américains.* For Émilie DuPaquet was, like myself, a lover of all cuisines.

None other have I met whom I bonded with so completely by way of smelling, seeing, tasting, hearing, feeling; Food culture engages all the senses, and Émilie and I accessed the globe together by way of the spoon.

For so goes the code of the gourmand, the same as it is all over: *What do you wish to eat today? Kashmiri lamb-chops from Mongolia? Sicily's shiitake scallopine? Alecha and honey stew, a specialty from Mali?*

"I wish for foie gras parfait from Singapore," and it is so!

"I wish for cheese pirozhki from Russia," and it is so! For there is no food devised which cannot be found plentiful in glorious Paris.

So Émilie and I discovered *amour* through *à manger,* let us say, and I have never been happier. But of our epicurean delights, none other was greater than discovering new tastes at an afore-unknown noshery, in which we'd patronize for several days, partaking of each house specialty, until growing weary and anxious for the next grand esculent experience. By way of this routine, oft we'd let fate guide us to new alchemies of flavors, taking indiscriminate trolleys to distant sweeps of the city, traipsing their obscure lanes, sauntering the cobblestone paths that seemed to lead backward in time as much as they led farther from the glare of *La Ville-Lumiére...*

Thus Woe! Here is where fate led us astray that day, for this is where the dreadfulness of my tale comes to bear, and I urge you to listen with utmost assiduity!

It was winter holiday, you see, and the *Université* closed, so Émilie and I had much time to enjoy the eateries.

New Year's was three days past, and the city reawakening to a fresh course of *bons vivants* and buffet-dreams. The "Twelfth Day of Christmas" was soon coming, another cry for the passions of overindulgence, as if we needed such pretext. Though puddings and pies and sweets are all part of the Christmas holiday, it is Epiphany which is the culmination of confection with the celebratory *La Galette Des Rois*, or Three Kings' Cake, served in great and delicious solemnity merely once a year on the first Sunday after the year's inception.

"We must find the perfect *La Galette Des Rois*," Émilie announced in her joyous sweet voice. Everything was joyous and sweet with Émilie, oh, Émilie. "Epiphany is in three days' time, and we are to attend the Bellerose sunset soiree."

So even in light snow, as it were, no difficulty prevented our traversing the city. We left by trolley on a glum, gray dawn, not unlike most all Parisian daybreaks, not unlike the morn I remember last. It was our stomachs that led us forward that day rather than any notion of cold or discomfort.

"There is *Pain de Rêves* on Rue Saint-Maur," I suggested, weaving my fingers through Émilie's. Émilie was always warm, and even with gloves I could feel her pleasant heat.

"*Non*, they are too stingy with their zest of orange."

"Perhaps *Sucre Amour* on Rue Bonaparte?"

She rolled her eyes. "It's sinful, the glut of vanilla in their frangipane."

"It does not have to be frangipane. We can find *La Galette* instead with brioche or *pâte feuilletée*."

"I thought you argued *pâte feuilletée* to be vulgar?"

"*Oui*, but not for the *La Galette Des Rois*."

"Anyway, it must be frangipane. That is civilized tradition."

We sidelined to breakfast at *Café de Triomphe* on Rue du Foin, well known for their heterogeneity of fare, which

Émilie and I decided to put fully to the test.

"*Bonjour, monsieur et mademoiselle,*" the waiter greeted us. "What do you wish for this morning? We have Scottish salmon on bialy rolls, and sticky Breton kouign amann. Our pistachio and butterscotch quiche is unprecedented."

"I wish for," Émilie said before a dramatic pause; she had such a flair for ordering! "Bread."

"Bread?" the waiter repeated with not unnoticeable disdain in his tone.

"*Oui,* bread. Two slices of your *pain perdu,* toasted golden, no more, spread with caramel-mango sauce. And I wish for a cup of pumpkin soup topped with chestnut shavings, so hot my tongue should tingle. Do you boil black-rice porridge in coconut milk?"

"*Oui, mademoiselle,* of course."

"A side, but served only in a demitasse cup. I wish also for two organic eggs poached soft in a ramekin with sautéed chanterelles, a touch of green garlic, and a glut of blackberries. Do you have that all?"

The waiter tipped his head to her, sharp as a salute. "*Bien sûr.*"

"Add an apéritif of *fromage blanc.* And for drink your finest Kir Royale in a flute, and filtered coffee."

"*Ça sera fait!* And for you, *monsieur?*"

I ordered a dish of salted kippers in bourbon butter, scones of Tamworth pork and maple syrup, *oeufs à la coque* in pear cream, *viennoiserie,* and semolina pancakes cooked with chickpeas and lemon, which I had long wished to try mixed with spicy plantain and Ghanaian beef, though the fusion turned out not to suit me well, and by consequence, perhaps, saved me, at least briefly.

"When I was a *fille,*" Émilie said after some time, sipping at her soup, "We'd get three wishes for Epiphany, one for each of the three magi who presented gifts to baby Jesus. One wish a day, always for sweet stuffs, leading up to the day of His revelation as the Christ child, and then on that day, we would eat the celebratory cake itself at sunset."

"*Moi aussi*, when I was young, we too followed that tradition of wish-a-day. But *ma famille* held to stricter principle, and instead of deserts we received religious gifts: a vial of frankincense for the wise man, Melchior, then a belt of gold cloth for Caspar, and lastly a thorny branch dipped in myrrh for the wisest of the three, Balthazar."

"*Ça alors*! A thorny branch for children?"

"And *mon père* would beat us with it if we tried to sneak a bite too early from *La Galette Des Rois*!"

She laughed immensely. "It still would not have held me back!"

We were into our third course when Émilie tapped the side of her head thoughtfully. Her nails still showed festive polish for the holidays, red and green and white, and each color brought out a different facet of appearance: full cheeks rosy like great pomegranates; bright eyes radiant as sprig of mint under mist; teeth bleached radiant as the iced crème atop gelatin cakes...*ah, Émilie, ah, Émilie!*

"If I should find the figurine—*la fève*—hidden in my slice of the cake," she said, "I will expect to be treated by tradition as queen for the day."

"I've never gotten *la fève*," I confessed, which was true. Always a sibling discovered the small plastic person in their own slice. Only one toy charm is hidden in each cake, and year after year I'd watch someone else exclaim they'd received the figurine by luck, and I'd have to honor them as "king or queen for the day."

Émilie patted my face. "You, *mon cher*, are quite simply deprived."

"I read once," I replied in sudden recollection, "that the wise man, Balthazar, was really the Devil in disguise, and that was his greatest trick, presenting himself as patron to *enfant* Jesus. The gift he gave was deceit, and when we celebrate Epiphany, we unwittingly also celebrate *Le Diable*."

"How did you come to that?"

"Because of the crown you wear, if you find *la fève* in

your slice of cake."

"The crown is for Jesus, *fou de vous!*"

"*Oui*, but Balthazar anointed Jesus in myrrh oil, and said He would wear it until the end of days. Chance what He had on His head at crucifixion?"

"The myrrh?"

"A crown of thorns, or more precisely thorny branches wove from a myrrha tree. Thus the devil is upon us from birth until death."

"I don't like that."

I shrugged. "It is only something I once read."

"You'll make yourself ill, ingesting such wild things."

"*C'est la vie*, and I am filled!"

With that, we left the café to continue by foot, our search for a suitable *La Galette Des Rois*. Probing along the blocks between Rue de Turenne and Rue du Parc Royal for *pâtisseries*, we attempted first a favorite, *Pain de l'Arc en Ciel de Miel,* and then the highly-recommended *Mon Cher Croissant*, and even the famous *Pâte en Pâte*, in which there is a three month backlog of orders by aficionados of all sugar cake tastes. Yet no *La Galette* was found suitable by Émilie.

"Is it so much to ask," she complained, "that the glaze be made from apricot preserves and not marmalade or jelly?"

So we ambled farther on, while disputing the merits of boiled burenwurst over smoked waldviertler. Yet now in hindsight we ambled carelessly too far, entering unsavory locales, past industrial parks minded by graffiti; following stone row homes, boarded over with plywood planks; crossing lots empty but for refuse and strange weeds; trekking further even than the Liquor & Cheese shoppes with their painted plastic signs of half-nude women sipping spirits in the windows, searching, still searching for the perfect *La Galette Des Rois*.

It was after some distance my stomach began to give complaint from breakfast, that most vexing dismay of any dining connoisseur. Though the sights and smells of exquisite fare may still be found intoxicating, the consideration of any foodstuffs actually finding their way down my gullet caused anxious consternation.

I told Émilie as such, and in sympathy she felt resigned to settle for a cake of *pâte feuilletée* instead, and thereafter soon to homeward retreat. But then! *Quelle malchance!* We were taken unawares by a startling vortex of smells, a tempest of buttery paste, sweet fruit crèmes, burnt crusts of sugar, soft toffees, caramel dreams! A bakery air seemed to fill us entirely with lusts for warm yeast and cinnamon swirls like an ocean that overwhelms you, filling your airwaves and lungs until you drown in it, and the currents take your body and drag you where they will.

So were we seemingly dragged to a certain shoppe some blocks away, one with no name but of that which it signified: *Pâtisserie.*

"*Mon dieu,*" Émilie breathed as we entered, "I have never seen such confections."

Indeed, there displayed creations of all shapes and sizes: macaroons as large as cake platters; meringue truffles colorful and rich as Egyptian jewels; towering cocoa cakes lavished in spearmint and iced rum; strawberry arnaud atop Italian Cassata; cannolis wound round Swiss butter rocha...

"*Bonjour, monsieur et mademoiselle,*" a great hairless man behind the counter greeted us. "What do you wish for this morning? Cinnamon peach chiffon à la crème? Pastry of salted pecan with a dash of raspberry compote?"

"Tell me you have *La Galette Des Rois* with frangipane," Émilie said, "and I shall be simply delirious with pleasure."

"*Oui, mademoiselle, oui*! Our specialty, I will make *La Galette* exclusively and exquisitely just for you."

"*Glorieux!* Please wrap it in a double box, I do not trust this weather."

"*Non, non, non,* they are prepared over the course of three days in advance, only for the *célébration* of Epiphany. You must come back, so is fresh, indefectible, a gift worthy of any hallowed king or queen."

"Very well," Émilie said. "So long as it's ready before sunset that night."

"Of course, I have many, many orders dependent upon that hour." The baker smiled at her, an expression that in some way suggested as much treachery as it did of mirth. "Meanwhile, perhaps you may wish for something else to enjoy at present?"

"How can I resist? *Un instant* to decide..."

As they spoke, something from my innards rumbled foul as any wharfside profanity. I cleared my throat to cover the impropriety.

The man, thinking I sought his attention, turned to me. "And for you, *monsieur*, what do you wish?"

My insides, however, were twisting in despicably uncivil ways, and regardless how enticing the pâtisserie's displays appeared, I thought only to reach my apartment's bed, and *toilette* perhaps, post-haste.

"Nothing for me, *merci*."

The man frowned as if I'd insulted his livelihood. "But we have apple butterscotch tart with brandy coulis, and plum-macerated cherries in lemon mousse!"

Suddenly the senses I'd relished so much in overindulgence turned horribly ungovernable, and I faltered under the disharmony of scents, realizing I would not make it safely back to my own apartment; the need struck emphatically of an urgent and immediate need to eliminate.

"*Pardonnez-moi*," I said to Émilie and dashed outdoors. Even in the seeming mesmeric wind which had taken us to that *Pâtisserie*, I'd noticed a public *toilette* we'd passed on the street prior, and I made my way there with swift abandon.

Sometime later I returned to the pastry shoppe, feeling bearably relieved, though still with a sense of declining constitution. Émilie was waiting for me outside the door, while other customers entered and left, none exiting without purchase.

As I neared, I noted Émilie seemed somehow "off," as

if her normal great warmth had cooled a degree, though I granted the waning as to effect of my own senses suffering malaise.

"Feeling better?" she asked in a low tone.

"*Un peu,*" I replied, appropriately abashed. "Did you get what you wished for?"

"*Oui,*" Émilie replied, then paused as if searching for the right words, a difficulty she did not normally ever encounter. She held up a crumpled paper bag, perhaps for inspiration, then with a note of guilt continued, "Gingerbread soufflé, topped by cappuccino-and-frankincense pudding. I ate it while you were gone. Do you know what the man charged me for it?"

"*Non,*" I said, as clearly I'd not been present.

"One hair."

"A hair? From your beautiful head?"

"That he plucked himself. One hair..."

"*C'est étrange.*"

"Quite..." but she promptly shrugged it off. "They wish to set trends, you know these avant-garde shoppes."

"I suppose," I replied, as my bowels begged off discussing the matter any further. "*Chez soi.*"

Émilie lived not far from me, and she saw me to my door with a perfunctory kiss and parting wish that I'd feel better soon. I wished so too, but it was not to be.

For the following day found me in bed with an exhaustion from both ends of my digestive tract. I telephoned Émilie, and she shared to me the queerest experience. She'd awoken that morning with an incessant craving, which would not ease until she'd returned to the *Pâtisserie* from the day prior.

"That great hairless baker asked what I wished for, and my eyes fell upon the champagne truffles wrapped in gold leaf."

"Sounds *délicieuse.*"

"It was. But the cost, I profess, was as bizarre as yesterday's."

"*Qu'est-ce que?*"

"The clipping of a nail."

I sucked in a breath. Though feeling weak myself, I perceived she too sounded weaker, short-winded.

"I do not like this," I admitted. "I don't want you returning there. Something is not right with that shoppe."

Émilie agreed, and again wished me good health. She reminded me I must be fully recuperated for the Bellerose sunset soiree, which was to be the following evening.

And so the day passed, and my spirits and health did recuperate, and I slept well, and by following morning felt, if not fully hale, at least passably able to confront a buffet.

I telephoned Émilie to inquire her availability for brunch. The phone rang several times before she answered, and it was as if I'd woken her from a deep sleep. Her voice sounded thick, viscous, slow to push out words.

Now it was she who did not feel well. She suggested, "Perhaps it was too rich..."

"*Ce qui était?*"

Émilie admitted another irresistible craving earlier in the morning, which led to her return to that vulgar *Pâtisserie*. "I wished for the honey ricciarelli rosettes with licorice myrrh sprinkle..."

"And the cost?" I asked, my teeth clenched as if to shuck oysters by mastication alone.

A pause. A stutter. "A drop of blood..."

"The gall is too much! Émilie, you must not return there!"

"But I must...my cake will be ready tonight, *La Galette Des Rois*...it is being prepared just for me...it will be ready at five, in time for the Bellerose sunset soiree."

"I will pick it up for you. I do not want you to go back!"

Émilie agreed, and said she was returning to bed. Hopefully she'd feel better, rested and recuperated, and would meet me at the soiree in late afternoon.

As I felt better, I left my apartment to make a day of errands and trivialities. By mid-afternoon, I took a trolley to Rue du Foin and from there set out on foot, realizing I could not recall *exactement* where the pastry shoppe was located; it already seemed like a bit of dream how I'd been taken there... I wandered the broken streets for an hour that brought vague reminisce of my previous visit with Émilie, and then, as I saw the public *toilette* that had before saved me, I was once again taken unawares by the scents of cinnamon swirls and buttery paste, which promptly drew me to the *Pâtisserie* in no less a deadly manner than the nectar secretions that lure insects to climb inside some carnivorous plant.

"*Bonjour, monsieur,*" the great hairless man behind the counter greeted me upon entrance. "What do you wish for this morning? Perhaps another *La Galette Des Rois*, like your lady friend?"

"You remember me?" I was surely surprised at this, as the shoppe seemed to have no shortage of patrons.

"I remember all my customers."

"Very well, but I've come only for *La Galette* you prepared for Émilie DuPaquet."

"*C'est ici,*" he said, waving an arm at the counter. A plain pink box was there, where none had been the moment prior.

"I do not like your shoppe's prices," I felt compelled to admit. "What do you use the hair and blood for? An *éclair spécial*?"

"Never ask a chef what goes into the cake," he replied with a smile that, like before, seemed equally as treacherous as jolly. "Just eat."

"And you are a chef who spices with nail clippings?"

"Here, I am the Master Chef...and all will soon call me Master."

Truly, his answer unnerved me.

He continued, "Perhaps I could bake a *La Galette Des Rois* personalized to your tastes? I'm sure we can arrange the prices more to your liking. Three wishes, Henri; you will be surprised at how *satisfying* they are."

Never mind that he knew my name, I was taken aback, unsure if he was mocking or insane. "*Non*, I will eat nothing here."

"Is it not confections you wish for, the sweet stuff of life? Perhaps something more *substantial*? Wealth, power, adoration?"

"You are mad, *cinglé*!"

"Do you wish to hold your lovely Émilie once again?"

"Of course I should wish that!"

"And it is done. Two more wishes, and *La Galette Des Rois* is yours."

"I will report you to the Minister of Health!"

"Ah, something else instead of *La Galette*? After all, *la fève* can be placed in any of our creations."

"What does *la fève* have to do...?"

"Our charms make wishes come true. Wish for something else, Henri, and I will bake it for you."

I was once a much calmer personality than at present, believe me! But that day I'd had enough, and I called forth a wish of the most heinous offense that this "Master Chef" should take a certain body part of himself and insert it into a sensitive orifice, which under normal circumstances should be quite impossible to perform.

Though not for him!

The great hairless man uttered a bit of a shriek, then a growl, and before my eyes he took off his flour-stained apron, pulled down malt-flecked trousers, and proceeded to engage in that which I'd wished—

A contortionist could not have been more flexible, *mon dieu!* In panic, I took the cake and ran, wondering at the absurdity of what I'd just witnessed.

Soon thereafter, as the sun began to wane beyond the glinting Parisian skyline, I arrived at the Bellerose sunset soiree.

Adélaïde Bellerose greeted me with grandiose airs, two kisses upon each cheek, and a heavily-perfumed tour of the estate, leading me from the vast ball room to its lavish dining counters.

"*Mon cher*, it's such a delight to have you arrive. You cannot imagine how dull the conversation has kept on." There were a dozen or so men and women, grazing at the long buffet, staring mindlessly off into space, engaging in small talk that seemed forced, as if expected rather than enjoyed, but for a few who spoke animatedly of chocolate crumpets and plum pudding Christstollen, which could be found without parallel at only one shoppe. Otherwise, there was no *joie de vie* in the room.

Adélaïde continued, "They are drugged, unless they speak of some chichi *Pâtisserie* and the wonderful delectations it affords. Oh, *Pâtisserie* this, *Pâtisserie* that, but no mention of bisques, no remark of tartare or pickled shallot, no insinuation to bouillabaisse, only the confections, and here I am a diabetic!"

At the time, her comment barely registered, for then I saw Émilie bearing a small plate of praline lemon tarts, a daub of yellow crumb at her mouth.

I approached, and my hand slid in caress down her arm. She felt spongy, flaccid, cold in a way—not chilly, but rather like a pork tenderloin that has been set on the counter for too long. "You made it," I said, and then realizing the full asininity of the obvious, added, "It's lovely to see you."

"And you, Henri," she replied blankly. Her voice carried no emotion, and I wondered at her strange way, wondered perhaps if she were still ill.

I kissed her, and there was no reaction. She tasted sour, like overripe cheese. "Are you feeling well?"

Her response was a soft grunt of disinterest, and she sucked absentmindedly at the lemon curd sticking to her fingers.

Her entire presence seemed of one who has been brainwashed or—dare I say, *impossiblement!*—not even her at all... Truly, Émilie looked "formed" somehow, sculpted, as if in replica, though like all copies they can never be as precise as the original. Her mindlessness, her dispassion, the pallor of her skin like cold butter, were of someone else, some*thing* else, a creation one reads about only in old narratives, beings brought forth from inanimacy and controlled like a golem... But I chided myself as Émilie had been right; I'd make myself ill ingesting such wild fancies. Surely this was *mon amour*, a real person that existed and stood before me, simply out-of-sorts, merely weary from a harsh malady.

I changed topic. "You would never believe what just occurred to me at that *Pâtisserie*."

Her eyes suddenly lit up. "The *Pâtisserie*! Oh, you must go, Henri. *Il est très extraordinaire! Très, très extraordinaire!*"

"What—? *Extraordinaire*, the man who takes your blood for a ricciarelli rosette?"

"The *Pâtisserie*, everyone is going! All the chic! The *Pâtisserie* is *la meilleure*! Exquisite! They have bitter cherry cheesecake puffs, and green tea sorbet in tuile cups, and vanilla ganache biscotti with candied cranberry chips. You can wish for anything, Henri, but who would not wish most for the sweetmeats, their blueberry custard beignets, and Turkish baklava and—"

So Émilie went on, raving for some time; I thought to speak over her, question her wits, but Adélaïde Bellerose made the sunset announcement that it was time for *La Galette Des Rois*.

"Though I cannot partake but a nibble," Adélaïde declared, "I hope all else will enjoy *La Galette* that Henri and Émilie were so kind to provide. It has been sliced into equal shares for you present, to celebrate the magi who brought gifts to the manger on this eve so many centuries ago. Each gift, like each year, is greater than the last, and so this cake, like our future, must be evermore splendid! *Bon appétit!*"

I eyed Émilie warily as I cut into my slice. There was something terribly wrong with her, something illness alone could not explain...

I ate.

My senses, as they'd turned already to high alert, shrieked suddenly in my brain: *Délicieuse!* The chilled pastry bread hinted with ginger spice, the frangipane was the dream of almonds, the dusting of sugar so delicate, so cultivated. I'd never savored such crust, such crème; the whipped egg yolk could be no less than a convergence of artistic euphoria and culinary transcendence!

The second mouthful was entirely rapturous as the first, but upon chewing halfway through I bit into something hard, which most certainly did not belong in that master work. The taste of warm plastic leeched across the scintillation of vanilla and nutmeg, while my tongue lolled over rigid features.

I withdrew from my mouth a small plastic figurine... It took a moment to understand, but then I recognized *la fève!* For the first time in my life I'd received the toy charm of *La Galette Des Rois.*

Though I was not in any celebratory mood, it nonetheless caused a smile that I would finally be "king for the day." I turned to Émilie, as the charm brought certain entitlements, when it struck me: *How could the cake be served chilled, yet the charm within be warm?*

I looked down at the small plastic person in hand. It was the natural resemblance of any young woman, though the expression on her face showed not the usual smug smile of a fabricated doll, but rather a frown of much distress. And upon closer scrutiny, I shuddered with recognition...for she had full cheeks rosy like great pomegranates; bright eyes radiant as sprig of mint under mist; teeth bleached radiant as the iced crème atop gelatin cakes. And the toy was warm, warm as Émilie was always warm, even now in her plasticized, miniature scale...

As the enormity struck, I turned back upon the Émilie standing before me, and saw her in a new light: She had full, rosy cheeks to be sure, but the blush was like red jam bleeding through a colander, and her mint eyes were wilted, and the bleached teeth in sugary decay... She truly *was* some sort of golem, a thing born of dough and marzipan, with apricot glaze for skin and cinnamon icing hair, and when I looked about I saw Émilie was not alone. None human were there but myself and diabetic Adélaïde, and all around us they spoke with hints of zest and whiffs of crème...

Three days and three wishes; Three gifts for Émilie, one each of the magi—count them! The frankincense in her gingerbread soufflé; The gold leaf from her champagne truffles; The myrrh sprinkles in her honey ricciarelli rosettes...

It is Balthazar, the Devil in disguise, don't you see! *Sur mon honneur!* Heed this horror, and beware *La Galette Des Rois*! Beware the *Pâtisserie!*

I myself did not fully understand until I escaped the Bellerose sunset soiree and fled to the *Université* library to research further... It's the root word of Balthazar that is key: *Baal.* The title of "Lord" in the Semitic languages, referencing Baal Hadad, god of fire and punishment! *Oui,* this very same Baal, oft depicted with horns, cloven feet, and a three-pronged trident...it is he who gave the gift of deceit, he who grants the wishes, and by his ways do we continue to be ensnared!

Now of Émilie, poor sweet Émilie...if my toffee eyes could weep when I dream of her crying my name, the tears would surely be peppermint. For I made my own third wish, you see, and what did it matter? The giver of deception always gets the last crumb!

I admit the wish was not for my love to be returned; it was not for all the *Pâtisserie's* wickedness to be undone; it was not even for you, *cher* reader, to believe this tale...

Oh, but the taste of *La Galette Des Rois!*

Dread of Winter Dreams of Summer

By Janet Joyce Holden

They fought through the summer, the young priest and the creature of light. He chased her from the church, and when harvest arrived he proclaimed victory; he thought he had won, and that the grace of God had prevailed. But when the nights grew short she invaded his dreams until he became weak with fever and soaked in longing.

He kept silent, and hid the struggle from his congregation—the endless hours kneeling before the altar, praying for strength, and the sleepless nights when he tossed and turned and became tangled in her web of persuasion.

Afraid for the souls of his flock, that she was some kind of demon, he cried out, "You'll never take them. If I fail, others will come."

"You don't understand," she replied. "I came here for you."

By the time the first flurries of snow arrived, she had broken him. He left everything behind—the Church, his people, his life—and on his way up the mountainside he saw a magical man sitting on a rock.

Already numb with cold, he gasped, "Help me."

Winter's shrug bore an apology of sorts. "Alas, I am too busy, and she needs a companion."

At the mountain's summit, Summer stood waiting, and watched as he undressed. She took him in her arms and laid him down upon a litter of human bones. "Here we rest, until spring."

Snowflakes were already falling on his unadorned skin. "But I'll die."

"I know," she said. "And next year, I will find another."

The Sun

By Robin Morris

Ethan woke to silence, screams ringing in his ears. He didn't understand where he was, why everything was wrong. His eyes couldn't make sense of what they saw.

His head hurt.

In front of him was the driver's seat, with hair rising up to the roof. The seatbelt held him suspended above the back seat. Below. He was upside down. His booster seat was loose, hanging with him.

Up was down. The hair curled on the roof of the car. Mom's hair.

"Mom?"

She didn't answer. Ethan wriggled, trying to understand. He remembered screams. They were driving to see Grandma. They would celebrate Christmas, then stay for a while so Grandma could help with the baby.

The car slid on a patch of ice, onto the steep downward slope. Mom screamed. Ethan screamed. Then silence.

The baby made a noise. Ethan turned his head. He saw his new brother in the backward-facing car seat. Little Daniel was awake, his bright eyes looking around and taking in the situation.

"Mom?" Ethan said, louder. Nothing.

It was cold. The engine was dead. There was a little light coming through the windows. The headlights shined on a tangle of snowy branches.

Ethan felt for the buckle. It was tight and didn't want to

let go. He shifted, putting his feet on the seat back in front of him and taking some of his weight off the seatbelt.

The buckle came undone. Ethan hadn't thought about what would happen. He fell toward the roof of the car. The booster seat fell on top of him, clonking his head. The pain in his skull doubled and he became dizzy.

Daniel made a bubbly baby noise. If he had been more than a few days old, Ethan would have thought he was laughing at his big brother.

When the dizziness passed, Ethan oriented himself to kneel on the roof. Now the car, the baby, and Mom were upside down. Daniel started to cry. Ethan crawled to the other side of the car and fumbled with the straps on the car seat, finally figuring out how to undo them. His brother fell into his arms. Ethan had to turn him right side up, which did not stop his crying.

It was not easy to back toward the door with a baby in his hands. The booster seat got in his way so he had to hold Daniel in one arm, pick up the seat in the other, and throw it away from him. He hated that seat. He was eight and a half. He didn't need it.

He felt for the door handle. When he opened the door snow fell in, accompanied by freezing wind.

He saw his knit hat and grabbed it as he backed out into the snow, which was several inches deep. He crawled backward into the cold. He managed to stand, putting one hand on the cold metal of the car.

It was late in the day and the light would vanish soon. Daniel wore a warm onesie and a little hat of his own, but that wouldn't protect him from the cold and wind for long. Ethan tucked the baby into his jacket and pulled up the zipper. The baby snuffled and his crying ended with a sneeze.

Ethan was able to put his hat on, which helped his ears a little. He turned to look at the world. Snow covered everything, up to his knees. It fell in large fluffy flakes, coming down fast, with no sign of stopping.

The driver's window was shattered. Ethan reached in

and shook his mom's shoulder. "Mom." He moved a little more forward. The airbag lay, deflated, between Mom and the steering wheel. A broken branch had come through the windshield. He followed it with his eyes.

The branch ended in Mom's face. Mouth, nose, and eyes were punched into her head. A little bit of jawbone was visible. The fading light hid as much as it showed. Ethan pulled away, sitting back in the snow.

He cried. Sobs filled his body, threatening to shake him apart.

He didn't know how much time passed. He was jolted into awareness when the headlights went out. He saw that the world was even darker. Sunset was near. He realized he was freezing, even though he wore a winter jacket and boots. His ears burned with cold, despite his hat. He kept his hands in his jacket pockets to keep them warm.

Mom's phone. He could call 911. Mom had a thing that held it on the dashboard with a suction cup. It connected to the car somehow so she could talk without picking it up. He didn't know how to do that but it should work on its own.

He had to feel around the branch that had erased Mom's face. Past the steering wheel. He found the phone and pulled the whole suction cup thing toward himself.

The phone was shattered. The screen remained black no matter what buttons he pushed. With a wail, he threw it down.

Holding the baby under his jacket with one arm, Ethan stepped away from the car. Silence fell, the soft silence that accompanies fallen snow.

He knew that if he waited in the car he and Daniel would freeze to death. He moved away from the side of the car, taking each step carefully because the snow covered everything.

Light appeared in the trees. Daniel looked up. A sleigh with tiny lights on it was in the woods. Reindeer were harnessed to it. Santa Claus sat in the sleigh, beard and red suit and everything.

Ethan was way too old to believe in Santa, but seeing him made it hard to hold onto his disbelief. Santa waved, picked up the reins, and made the reindeer move. The sleigh pulled away, heading deeper into the snowy woods.

"Hey!" Ethan shouted. Santa and the sleigh disappeared and appeared as they passed behind trees, then vanished for good.

The baby started crying again. He was probably hungry. Ethan realized he was too. He walked forward, as quickly as he could, with branches and rocks on the ground, covered by snow, making it hard to find a solid next step.

Even if Santa was really real after all, why was he here now? Christmas Eve was a few days away. Tonight was what Mom called the Winter Solstice, the shortest day of the year. She showed him a book about it. People have been having parties on the Solstice for thousands of years, the book said. In the really old days they thought they had to give something to the gods, so the sun would come back and spring would happen. There were drawings of some of the gods.

Even if the Santa he saw was fake, like in a mall, he was a grownup. He would help. He would call for help or take Ethan to Grandma's in his sleigh. The wind blew harder as he walked forward. He pulled the baby closer, trying to keep them both warm. Daniel cried a little bit, on and off, under Ethan's jacket.

He got to where Santa was before. Or where he thought Santa was. There should be tracks, from the sleigh's runners. The snow lay as smooth there as everywhere else.

He looked back. He could barely see the car now. It was a snow-covered lump. Mom was in there, turning to ice. He hoped she couldn't feel it.

There was a bright light. Ethan turned and saw a man standing about as far away as Santa had been before. His head radiated light. No, not his head, a circle behind his head. He had long hair and a beard. He waved and gestured for Ethan to come toward him.

Ethan moved. As strange as the figure was, he did look familiar. Not like anyone he had ever met, but like a picture in a book. Mom told him about this man. She didn't believe in him any more than in Santa Claus, but she said Ethan should know about this man, that Christmas was named for him.

The figure turned and walked away, his light fading into the woods. Ethan went toward where he had been. Why were these strange grownups doing this? Where did they want him to go?

Ethan's feet began to feel the cold. His toes felt like ice. Every step was hard; he had to avoid stepping on a fallen branch or uneven ground. Daniel wiggled under his jacket, emitting an occasional burble but no longer crying.

Hunger twisted Ethan's guts.

He looked up and saw a woman, wearing a long dress that touched the ground. She had long blond hair, in two braids. In one hand she held some string or something, attached to a thing that hung down. It was spinning. She glowed, her light filling the forest.

Instead of walking away, she pointed. He looked in that direction, and when he turned his head back to her, she was gone. The woods returned to twilight. Pinpoints of stars were beginning to appear above the trees.

Ethan was alone, hungry, tired and scared. He looked back. He could never find the car again. Snow fell quiet and relentless. His footprints were gone.

Then more strange figures appeared around him. He turned and stared at each one as it came. A man had the head of a bird with a sharp beak, and a bright disk of light floating above him. Another seemed to be killing a bull, his cape billowing behind him. Each one flashed for a few seconds, then was gone.

Ethan ran, blindly trying to get away from the visions. His feet slipped on the icy ground. The snow came up to his thighs, making it hard to move. Other figures came and went. He didn't look at them. He wanted Mom, he wanted his room. He wanted to be warm.

The baby squirmed and started to cry again. The pain in Ethan's head grew.

He came out of the trees. A weak light showed through the clouds, very close to the ground. No more strange figures surrounded him.

A voice came out of the light.

"I am the light of the world." It was very deep and sounded like it came from far away.

"You mean the sun?"

"I am weak. This is the last day of the light. I must be renewed."

"You need recharging? Like a phone?"

"It is the Solstice. Do you know what that is, child?"

Ethan was happy to tell this grownup voice that he did. "Mom told me. People had a party to bring the sun back."

"They held a feast. Lit fires. Importuned me to return."

He didn't know what that word meant, so he said, "I saw Santa Claus and other people."

"I showed you gods of the Solstice, reflections of my light in human minds."

Ethan didn't really understand that, but he felt the power of the light. He felt it fill him. It could command him to do anything.

The power gave him no warmth; his toes still felt like ice and his face felt scrubbed by the harsh wind. "Okay," he finally said.

The sun slipped lower, becoming barely visible.

"Before those humans held feasts, before they lit fires, they brought me back each Solstice by giving me a gift. A soul."

"I don't have anything."

"They were like you, lost and cold in the snow. They had no fires. All the food they had was gone."

Ethan glimpsed people in furs, without actually seeing them. He thought the sun sent him the idea of them. They huddled together for warmth, snow falling around them, trees surrounding them. They had nothing, and the days were growing shorter and shorter. Ethan felt their hunger.

If they had a gift, something to make the sun come back to life, something to sustain them until the snow thawed and the leaves turned green, they might survive.

"They chose one among them to make the ultimate sacrifice. A soul for me and food for them."

"I don't know what you want."

"I have found you, alone among the people of the world, the only one who can give the gift and keep the light from dying."

The power of the sun poured over Ethan. He couldn't turn away from it. It roared in his head, vibrating with his pain.

"I'm alone," he heard himself saying from far away. "I don't have a gift."

"You do."

Little Daniel chose that moment to start crying again. Fitfully, weakly. Ethan felt the baby's hunger, and his own. He looked down, and unzipped his jacket. He saw the little head, with a little bit of hair on it. He felt the fading warmth of his baby brother.

"Without the gift," the light said, "I will never return. The world will go dark. All humanity will perish."

Ethan lifted the baby with both hands. He looked at his little face. He felt the breath coming out of him.

He bit, tearing a strip of skin from Daniel's face. He ate more, and more.

The baby shrieked in pain, wriggled in his hands, as violently as a newborn could. Daniel tried to cry, but it came out in hiccups and gasps. Each bite produced a new scream, a new gush of blood.

One eye socket went dead, no longer moving, no longer seeing. The other thrashed back and forth, seeking and not finding whatever a baby can understand as reason for what was happening.

Ethan tried not to taste the flesh. It was chewy and salty and not good. It was for the sun, it was necessary. It filled his belly. After a while, the small bundle in his hands, his little brother, went still.

The sun laughed as Ethan ate. It faded to nothing, leaving night to swallow the world.

Then there was light again. Very bright light. Ethan looked up, high in the sky. He was almost blinded. There was sound, harsh sound. He didn't know why there was so much sound.

A man came down on a rope.

"Got him," the man shouted into a radio. "You all right, son?" He turned Ethan to see him better. "Are you bleeding?"

Ethan had done it. He triumphantly held the baby up toward the light. It had worked. The world would go on. He was filled with joy. What was left of Daniel's face was brightly lit. One cheek was gone, the nose was two bloody holes.

The man gagged. "What did you do, boy?"

"The sun," Ethan said, smiling into the light from above. "It came back."

Choking Hazard

By Michael Paul Gonzalez

Dear Santa,

I know most of your letters begin with proclamations like I have been very good this year. I haven't been good. I've done good. Finally.

I hope you're sitting down. I'm certain you weren't expecting to find your home in such a state when you returned from the big run. You're wondering not only what happened, but why. Please finish reading this letter before you survey the damage. It's important that you understand all of this.

Sorry for all the blood.

We warned you. Every year, we asked you for an audience to air our grievances, and every year you pushed us harder. Every year, all we wanted was a chance to talk to you. You ignored us, and now the time for words has passed.

This year, you were upset that we were slow coming off the production line with the stuffed animals, and the paint on the action figures was taking too long to dry. We told you that we wanted the toys to be extra special for this run. We were finally taking pride in our craftsmanship, and you rolled your eyes at us.

Do you know what batrachotoxin is, Santa? How hard it is to cultivate and raise the frogs that produce it in this climate? How about polonium? We worked overtime to boil and bake and perfect these ingredients into a recipe that we've called Red Christmas. Do you know how long it takes to cure when it's in liquid form? Do you know how carefully you have to place a weaponized aerosol version inside of a stuffed animal to avoid killing all of your fellow coworkers? We've never worked so hard.

Do you know what's going to happen, what's happening right now as boys and girls all around the world rush to their trees to tear into the boxes you've brought them? When they grab those trains, those video games, when they squeeze those stuffed bears so tight?

It starts as a light tickle in the throat and rapidly progresses to full anaphylactic shock. The throat constricts, eyes swell shut, hearts beat harder and harder until they explode.

Don't rush out now. Don't stop reading. Even if your reindeer were around to carry you (we'll get to that in a moment), they couldn't fly fast enough to prevent this because it's already happening. The death toll is rising and the only thing moving faster than the Red Christmas Plague is the bad press you're getting.

You've delivered this to the world. To all the good little children.

We didn't do this to you. You did this to you.

You had generations to make this right. Hundreds, thousands of years to honor the treaty that you made with our people when you wandered into our lands all those years ago, snow-blind and half-starved. We fed you. We took you in. You tricked our ancestors with the bright promise of technology and medical advances in exchange for our help in your yearly quest for joy. It quickly became clear to us that you had no intention of helping anyone but yourself. You wanted to be the great white god of your own personal winter republic. Like so many dictators, you showed the world a much different face than one revealed to those of us beneath your boot.

What drives a man on such an insane mission? What

have you been running from? What caused you to enchant our sacred deer and push them almost to death in a race around the globe every year? To bring tidings of joy and good cheer to every man, woman, and child on the planet while you meet us with whip and chain? What is in your past that haunts you so heavily? What have you been trying to make up for?

It no longer matters. You have much, much more to answer for now. Your march toward joy has been our march to genocide, and it ends tonight.

We are not the monsters. We are free. We never wanted it to come to this, we begged you not to let it come to this, but you kept pushing us, driving us, demanding more. You indoctrinated millions of young people around the world to your side, getting them hooked on your greed and false joy. And when we couldn't produce quickly enough, you outsourced even more work onto the poor and starving peoples of emerging and overpopulated nations. Though we have never met our brothers and sisters, we hope that this small disruption can be the first step on their journey to freedom.

We have no worries about the world hating us for these acts, because we already know that the world doesn't think twice about our plight.

When you left this morning, you proudly said that this year's run would be made in record time. You'd be back before Mrs. Claus could finish baking the dessert for your welcome home dinner. We didn't allow her to leave the kitchen. If there was one person here that could exceed you in cruelty, it was her. You gave those of us too old to work, too broken down to be of service to you, you gave us to her. She would boil us, candy stripe our bones, bake our tiny children into gingerbread men and make their parents watch while you ate those cookies with her by the fire.

We take no joy in the deaths of the children around the world, but Mrs Claus, she was delicious. You will not find her remains. Her bones will be scattered after you leave, and you may never come back to visit her.

The surviving members of your reindeer team may take the pelts of their honored dead when they carry you away from here. We claim the rest as food to sustain us in the long months to come.

Really, we've done you a favor. You complain every year that fewer and fewer children believe in you.

They all believe in you now.

Young and old alike.

Those that are left.

May the endless suffering that is about to visit you serve as a reminder to all that this land is ours.

Merry Christmas, you narcissistic tyrant.

Yours in freedom,
AQILOKOQ ANGYAGHLLANGYUGTUQLU
Known in oppression as Twinkles

COMES TO TOWN

ROBERT PAYNE CABEEN

Krampus Comes to Town

By Robert Payne Cabeen

Tonight's the night that Santa comes—
The kids jump up and down.
So unaware, tonight's the night
That Krampus comes to town.

And, why should they, the innocent,
The guileless and the pure,
Have knowledge of the horror that
The wicked will endure?

Some say he is a fairy tale—
A myth from way back when.
Some say he is the Lord of Yule
Or Santa's evil twin.

He doesn't need you to believe,
Or care how you might feel.
If you are on his list of names,
You'll find out if he's real.

If you've been disobedient,
And really rowdy, too,
I wouldn't worry very much.
Krampus won't bother you.

He's hunting for the evil ones
Who prey upon the weak.
The ones who thrive on misery
And have a vicious streak.

The brutal ones, the heartless ones,
Who relish pain and fear—
The bullies and their hangers-on
Who hit and laugh and jeer.

If you have tortured helpless kids
For how they looked or talked,
Krampus will surely come for you—
Tonight you will be stalked.

If you're afraid, lock all the doors
And close the windows tight,
But he's coming, coming, coming
For you this very night.

It takes a beast to know a beast.
And you, he knows too well.
Run if you must, hide if you can—
He'll track you by your smell.

When Krampus finally sniffs you out,
And yes, he surely will,
He'll stuff you in his bully bag—
A hunter with his kill.

He'll drag you screaming to his lair—
Across the cold wet roofs.
You'll hear the weathered shingles crack
Beneath his cloven hooves.

His fetid breath and musky fur
Will sear your tender nose.
Just where it is he's taking you,
Nobody really knows.

And if you've made an outcast wish
That they were never born,
Krampus will take his time with you,
And gut you with a horn.

He'll thrash you with his thorny sticks,
And flog you with his chain.
No Christmas gift for you this year—
Your present is your pain.

You terrorize the neighborhood,
The playground at your school,
But you'll babble like a baby,
When blood begins to pool.

And you'll crawl just like an infant
Through blood and poop and pee,
While Krampus points and laughs at you
With ridicule and glee.

He'll tango to the music of
Your futile screams and cries
And lap up all the salty tears
That rain down from your eyes.

Your parents and the sheriff will
Search on and on and on.
By morning, he'll be done with you
And Krampus will be gone.

Someday, somewhere, someone will find
Your brittle bully bones
In a basement or a boiler room
With other cruel unknowns.

But Krampus has a long, long list
And might not get to you.
You may want to reconsider
The things you say and do.

Compassion is not frail or weak,
Its power is profound.
You'll need that strength, next Christmas Eve
When Krampus comes around.

Showdown in Beverly Hills

By Hal Bodner

"Follow the 101 north and get off at Sunset."

"The Strip will be jammed this time of night. Use the Santa Monica Boulevard exit and cut down to Melrose through West Hollywood."|

"That's stupid. We should take Santa Monica all the way into Beverly Hills."

The elves had started bickering within minutes of Santa Clause dropping Krampus off in East LA. They hadn't stopped since. Kris Kringle tried to refrain from chewing on the end of his beard, but it was a hard habit to break. He'd picked it up a few years ago, just after they'd introduced Common Core math to the grade schools, and a group of formerly well-behaved kids in Massachusetts protested by doing that thing with the vacuum cleaners and the bunnies. Kris knew it was undignified to walk around with three feet of saliva-drenched hair hanging out of his mouth, but it helped him to deal with all the tension the elves were creating. Their high pitched whining assaulted his ears and made him long to trade places with his hirsute and cloven-hoofed counterpart.

How he envied the Krampus! At the moment, the thought of spending the rest of the night popping 12 year old gang bangers, 14 year old meth manufacturers and 16 year old crack whores into a magical wooden box sounded like sheer bliss.

"Then use Highland, dummy."

"And fight Hollywood Bowl traffic? Now, who's the dummy?"

"Guy, guys, guys!"

Kris couldn't stand it a moment longer. Though he knew it was unworthy of a holiday icon to indulge in temper, if he didn't get some peace and quiet in about ten seconds, he was liable to commit an even more unworthy indulgence by chucking elves over the side of the sleigh just to watch them splatter on the streets of Thai Town. If his schedule wasn't so tight, he'd eagerly challenge the Krampus to a duel. Betting to see which of them could impale the most elves on the lightning rods atop Los Feliz mansions would not only solve the noise problem, it might also net him a few bucks. With all that hair dangling in his eyes, Krampus always had lousy aim.

"We're fifteen hundred feet above the ground in a magic sleigh pulled by reindeer. We don't have to take any freeways. We'll take the direct route."

Blessed silence descended and, for almost ninety full seconds, Kris relished the peace. But it was not to last. He felt that peculiar sensation between his shoulder blades that signified that a few dozen pair of Lilliputian eyes were boring into his back.

"What?"

He was unable to ignore the feeling any longer. He made sure he had a firm grip on the reins, unwilling to risk a repeat of the disaster in Atlantic City, and he spun around to face his passengers.

"What?" he demanded again. "What's wrong now?"

"Guys, guys, guys," one of the more annoying pipsqueaks mimicked.

Kris thought it might be Sebastian. Or maybe Bernard. They all looked the same to him, sort of like the kids in West Virginia except that few of the elves could use the excuse that their parents were too closely related before marriage.

Oh, good grief. It wasn't Sebastian or Bernard. It was Harriet.

"Guys?"

She hopped onto the rear seat of the sleigh, unmindful of how her muddy boots stained the upholstery, planted her fists into her hips and stood there, glowering.

"You fat, sexist son of a bitch."

"Hey, hey! Language," he warned.

"Ah-ha!" She pounced on his words like a starving polar bear pounces on an Inuit child after all the fat, juicy seals have died out from global warming.

"Language is exactly the problem. Not all of us are... guys."

She spat the last word with evident distaste. Kris wondered at her enmity before recalling that, back at the North Pole, Harriet's roommate Emily was the elf that everyone turned to whenever any of the machinery in the toy shop needed repair.

"You're a misogynist. That's what you are. A testosterone-filled, dick-swinging misogynist."

"How could I possibly be a misogynist?" Kris blustered. "With all those whiskers, how am I supposed to tell the men from the girls?"

"The men from the women," Harriet corrected.

"You might wanna keep your eyes on the road, boss," another of the elves said.

This time, Kris was pretty sure it was Bernard. He resolved to thank him, once this hellacious night was over, for the welcome interruption.

"Rudolph's steering everyone toward the Griffith Park Zoo again."

With a muffled curse, Santa faced forward and started hauling on the reins. About six years ago, they'd had to deliver a present to a darling little homeless girl whose family had erected a cardboard shelter in the zoo parking lot. One of the zebras was in heat and Rudolph caught a whiff of hormones. The next time, it was a giraffe; the year after that, Rudolph discovered the pleasures of what he called "rough trade" with a Sumatran rhino. Kris had taken him aside and tried to explain that, merely because they were both ungulates didn't meant there weren't plumbing problems; but his lecture fell upon deaf ears. Since that fateful night, Rudy was as randy of an old goat as the ibexes he sometimes bribed a couple of Sherpas to sneak into the stables.

"Dammit, I told him there was no earthly reason to order Viagra off of E-bay," Kris mumbled. "But, nooo. The stubborn cuss insisted he had to have it."

"Ahoy, the jackass!"

Santa whipped his head around with a snarl. Really! There were some limits to what he was willing to tolerate after all. The elves all stood there, even Harriet, with looks of sweet innocence on their faces, as if sugar plum icing wouldn't melt in their mouths, and Kris realized that whoever had spoken was referring to the Krampus. Sure enough, his goat-faced colleague was approaching broadside atop his traditional flying donkey.

"How'd it go in Boyle Heights?"

"It's a rotten, rotten world," Krampus grumbled.

"Not that I don't disagree with you but, what d'you mean?"

"Some little brat kept demanding to see statistics on ethnic diversity. He claimed that I was snatching up a disproportionate number of Hispanic kids."

"You're kidding." Santa shook his head. "What'd you do?"

"Little monster's in the box, isn't he?"

"Fair enough," Kris nodded.

"Every year, every damn year, it seems like I end up doing more of the work, doesn't it?" Krampus grumbled. "Not that I mind," he hastened to add. "Still if it keeps up, I'm gonna want a bigger ride." He leaned forward to affectionately scratch the donkey between the ears and only narrowly avoided losing fingers when the beast twisted its head and tried to bite him. "Maybe a sled like yours."

"It comes with elves," Santa warned.

Krampus shuddered.

"Ahoy, Rodeo Drive!"

"I really wish he'd stop doing that," Kris bemoaned to no one in particular. "We never should have let him watch that Leonardo DiCaprio picture with the boat."

In tandem, the sleigh and the donkey swooped gracefully down from the sky and landed, side by side, on the roof of a gigantic Spanish gothic mansion on Rodeo, barely a block south of the Beverly Hills Hotel. Several of the elves hopped out and busied themselves with tether ropes and mountaineering spikes. It was a new procedure that Kris had put into place only a few years ago, new enough so that elves had not yet grown tired of it nor started complaining about it. They'd start griping soon enough but for now, it was a fairly painless way of avoiding another tragedy like the one in San Antonio, when the heavily laden sleigh slid off the room and wound up in someone's swimming pool.

"You're up?" Krampus asked. He was trying not to salivate but a thin stream of drool drooped from one of his fangs. "You lucky bastard. The kids are all plump here."

Kris Kringle hosted a huge sack of toys onto his shoulder and with a grunt, he pulled a large handkerchief from the pocket of his jacket to mop some of the sweat dripping from his forehead and down the back of his neck.

"Christmas Eve and this place has still gotta be in the nineties. And me in velvet and fur."

He shook his head and exchanged the hanky for a parchment scroll. When he untied the bit of ribbon holding it closed, the bottom half slipped from his fingers and the damned thing unrolled, bouncing merrily across the terra cotta tiles of the roof, and over the gutters into thin air and landing—Santa rolled his eyes at the inevitability of it—in the pool. Never mind; the elves would just have to deal with it.

Squinting through the perspiration that stung his eyes and muddied the lenses of his spectacles, Kringle ran his finger down the list until he came to the right address. He frowned.

"What's the matter?" Krampus asked.

The fat man sighed. "Dammit. It looks like this one could go either way. The little brat seems to be definitely coal-worthy, but I'm not so sure they deserve the box. Let's go figure things out."

Krampus dismounted, careful to keep his body parts out of range of his donkey's teeth. Together, they trudged across the roof toward one of the many chimney stacks.

"See you in a jiffy."

Kris winked and, exercising the wondrous winter magic that enabled a man of his girth to slide down a narrow chimney, he swung his feet into the opening and slipped inside. Three seconds later, Krampus and the elves heard a bout of cursing, followed by a plaintive, "I could use a hand here" from the depths of the flue.

"What's wrong?" Krampus stage whispered into the hole.

"I was afraid of this," Kris' voice floated back. "Damned chimney's been sealed off. How much d'you wanna bet these tofu-eating tree huggers have converted to solar?"

"Excuse me?" Harriet said. She leaned into the chimney opening and shouted, "Those "tree huggers" are the only thing standing between your fat ass and Exxon digging up your candy cane fields to drill for oil."

"My bad," Santa replied, insincerely. "I'll never mention it again. Could someone throw me a rope?"

Ten minutes later, he was back on the roof, the damage undone but for several yards of soot-stained red velvet and white gunk dulling the shiny black patent leather of his boots.

"What gives?" Krampus asked, pointing.

"A nest. Probably pigeons. Please don't laugh."

"So we do things my way, then?" In spite of Santa's plea, the holiday demon was unable to entirely repress a snicker or two.

"If I knew what your way was, I'd use it all the time."

"Trade secret."

An instant later, the two found themselves in a living room almost as massive as the wooden toy workshop at the North Pole. Granted that the wood shop had shrunk now that desire for wooden toys had largely been replaced with a lust for remote control drones, Twilight action figures and gaming consoles, but it was still a pretty big place, mostly because wooden toys were still fairly popular in certain Third World countries where electricity was sparse and sending up a drone, even if it looked like a flying My Little Pony, could easily get you shot by the government.

The room was not only immense, it was decorated within an inch of its life as if to proclaim to all who were lucky enough to enter it that the people who lived here had both taste and money. Cream leather and white-on-ecru fabrics prevailed, with the odd caramel or beige accents to provide what some flutey West Hollywood interior designer had probably referred to as "a soupçon of contrast." Bleached oak cabinets lined one wall, showcasing a collection of undoubtedly expensive trinkets, and luxurious, hand knotted beige and khaki Persian carpets covered the richly stained sustainable bamboo flooring.

A glorious Christmas tree stood in one corner, vaguely sterile in the way that the pale blue and amber holiday lights, and the tan and gold ceramic ornaments had been deliberately selected so as to blend with the color scheme of the rest of the room. Under it lay a pile of gifts, all wrapped in pale shades of earth-toned paper and tasteful gold and bronze ribbon.

"Uh oh," muttered Krampus, and vanished.

Kris's eyes followed the line of sight to where the demon had been pointing. As he approached the display cases, precious metal glinted under muted recessed lighting. St. Nicholas had a horrible feeling, a sinking sensation in the pit of his stomach as he drew near.

"That's right, bubbelah," a grating voice rang out. "A little far from home, aren't we?"

Santa spun away from his perusal of the collection of

Judaica, the Torah ornaments with their sterling silver breast plates and intricate filigree scroll toppers, like little crowns trimmed with tiny golden bells and inlaid with precious stones. In that instant, his most heartfelt desires warred with each other. On the one hand, he wanted to seize the gorgeously crafted pointer that the rabbis used so as not to sully their holy books by the touch of bare human hands, and plunge it through the heart of whichever elf was responsible for compiling a list that contained such a blatant screw up. On the other hand, he would have been just as contented to snatch up one of the largest of the Sabbath wine goblets, fill it with about a gallon of single malt, and down it all in a single slug.

"Hello, Sadie." The fat man lifted one hand and waggled his fingers in a feeble wave of greeting.

"Nick, Nick, Nick," she shook her head sadly and folded her arms across her sagging bosoms in a way that brought chills to Santa's heart. "We talked about this. You don't poach mine. I don't poach yours."

Behind the teardrop shaped glasses, her eyes narrowed. The stench of chicken fat and smoked fish suddenly pervaded the air.

"You're on my turf now."

The Hanukkah Fairy took one deliberate ominous step forward and smiled when the fat man blenched.

"It was the elves!" Nervous perspiration streamed from his temples down across his cheeks and soaked his beard just as surely as if he was still chewing on it. "An honest mistake."

"Maybe." She held up both her hands, smiled and shrugged with a gesture that might have looked like she was surrendering the point—had Santa not known her quite so well.

"Excellent. So, if you don't mind, I'll just be on my way and..."

"Then I see that!" She pointed at the tree and the gifts.

"Can't we talk about this?" Santa begged.

"Talk? What's to talk?" Seeing how uncomfortable the fat man was must have softened her heart. She sighed. "I suppose a little schmooze couldn't make things any worse than they are already.

She plucked the glasses from her face, leaving them to dangle on her breast at the end of a rhinestone chain. Hiking up the waist of her velour pants suit, she waddled to the sofa next to the tree and plopped down with a sigh of contentment.

"You got it lucky. One night. Me? Eight days I'm running like a chicken without a head. You got no idea what that does to my varicose veins. And my lower back? I don't have to tell you."

Kris had never been able to figure out how she could flop onto furniture that way without crushing her wings. He assumed it was part of whatever magic she possessed as the incarnation of the Jewish seasonal holiday. The bigger question was, what kind of power could she exercise when she was angry? Immortal holiday icons were always very careful to avoid treading on each other's toes because the repercussions could be terrible. Though it had been a great many centuries since the Easter Bunny and the pagan Green Man had first had to duke things out, the ripples from that legendary battle still resonated.

"A little nosh while we talk?"

She took the plate of cookies and the tall glass of milk from a little table near the tree and offered them to him.

"No thanks. Lactose intolerant."

"You're kidding."

"Nope. Came up suddenly awhile back. I used to drink it all, every last drop." He shook his head with chagrin. "I left some pretty awful messes in a lot of fireplaces that year, believe you me."

"Ugh!" With a grimace, the Hanukkah Fairy dropped the cookie she'd been nibbling back onto the plate. "Gluten free." She brushed crumbs from her lap. "So what do you propose we should do about this situation?"

"Let it slide?" Santa suggested, with weak hope.

"No can do, boychik," she said. "I got too many from my side going over to your side. You'd think eight days of presents would do the trick, but Christmas holds some odd fascination. You don't believe me? Take a look at Cherry Hill, New Jersey. Trees in the windows, animated light-up angels lining the driveway, blow-up dolls of you and your reindeer on the roof, and even Bart Simpson or Luke Skywalker in a plastic manger on the front lawn. But you can bet your Aunt Sophie's girdle, you can find a mezuzah on every door. Why is it," she pondered, "no one ever goes in the other direction?"

"Christmas to Hanukkah?" he asked.

She nodded.

"I dunno," Santa shrugged. "Maybe it has something to do with the...ah...well, you know..." He motioned toward his own crotch and winced to make his point.

"Speaking of cutting things off, I'm thinking...a duel. What d'ya say?"

"A duel? Uh, I dunno, Sadie. You kind of have the home team advantage here." He gestured toward the collection of Torah ornaments lining the wall. "In spite of the tree and all."

"Hey, it wasn't me who picked a Jewish house. Why should I suffer for your mistakes? So we'll head to neutral ground. And to make sure things stay fair, I'm even willing to let your hairy friend referee."

"Krampus?"

"Why not? He's part goat, right? If he were a pork, I'd have a problem."

Suspicious, Kris squirmed in his chair. "It seems like you're giving me a little too much of a break."

"You don't trust him?"

"It's not that."

"You don't trust...me?" He eyes flashed with anger and a syrupy, sickly sweet odor filled the air.

"Will you stop with the Mogen David?" Santa gasped.

"Sorry. I get excited. Look, it could be worse."

"Oh yeah? How?"

"Desertion isn't a problem for you. You've always been more secular than religious."

"True." Santa frowned. "But did you ever stop to ask why it is that I end up with Krampus tagging along every year?"

"I'd wondered."

"The rotten kids outnumber the good ones almost ten to one. And the ones that manage to behave themselves? It's from greed, Sadie. No one's good for the sake of goodness any more. I tellya," he said, shaking his head sadly, "nowadays, I sometimes feel positively archaic and...irrelevant."

"Boo hoo," she said, without sympathy. She hauled herself to her feet accompanied by a symphony of creaking joints, grunts and groans. "Call the billy goat and let's get this show started."

Kris didn't even have to close his eyes to summon his companion. He merely thought about him in a certain way and Krampus heard the call. When he appeared, he made sure to do it as far away from the Hanukkah Fairy as possible.

"Hello, Sadie," he ventured timidly. "We screwed up, huh?"

"You most certainly did. But there's no such thing as a cloud that shouldn't be without a silver lining, nu?"

Santa cleared his throat. "Sadie has very graciously proposed that we settle this little matter with a traditional duel between holiday icons."

"A duel?" Panicked, Krampus' rheumy eyes darted to the ornaments in the case. "Here?"

The Hanukkah Fairy rolled her eyes and muttered something in Yiddish. "What does he look like, the village idiot? Here? Of course not here! We're going someplace neutral. And you are gonna be referee."

"Me?"

"Relax," Santa told him. "At least it'll get us away from

those damned elves for an hour."

Sadie beckoned them closer. Once they were in range, she hummed the first few bars of "If I Were a Rich Man" from *Fiddler on the Roof*. The walls of the beige and white room faded away and the three suddenly found themselves in what looked to Santa Clause to be in the parking lot of a mundane strip mall.

"How is this neutral ground?" he asked, more curious than suspicious.

Regally, the Hanukkah Fairy pointed over his shoulder. Santa turned to see that the flickering neon sign of one the businesses behind him advertised the place as Mister Ming's Lotus Blossom Palace. In the window hung a hand-lettered cardboard sign reading, *Open All Night Christmas Eve.*

"For my people, it's the only place open on Christmas Eve and Christmas Day. For your constituency..." She smiled and winked. "Well, it ain't exactly kosher."

"Right," Santa said, not seeing her point at all.

"So, do we wanna get started?" Krampus asked. He was still nervous, and fidgety.

"What's the big hurry? You have maybe a train to catch?"

"Well, this is the biggest night of the year for us..."

"So, Mister Big Shot with the Hooves, you're in too much of a rush to join an old lady in a nice glass tea? Maybe a little lo mein or some sweet and sour?" She eyed Santa's belly again. "How about you? You want maybe a pick-me-up so you shouldn't starve while working with Mister Busy-Busy over here?"

The odors seeping from under the front door of the restaurant smelled delicious and the fat man's mouth started to water. After a while, a constant diet of candy canes, gingerbread, plum pudding and the occasional Christmas turkey grew stale, not to mention the ubiquitous fruit cake. Right about now, a couple of orders of Mo-Goo Gai Pan and a dozen or so egg rolls sounded heavenly.

After dining on one of the best meals Santa had eaten in

a while, the three adjourned to the parking lot once again and, stifling belches redolent with spring onions and soy sauce, they prepared for battle.

"All right," Krampus said in an officious voice. "Both of you know the rules. Three shots each. If Santa Clause wins, we walk away. No harm, no foul. If the Hanukkah Fairy wins..."

He stopped, at a loss for words.

"Her honor is satisfied?" Santa proposed.

"Lame, Nicky. Even for you. If I win...let's see..." She paused for thought. "I was thinking about borrowing your sleigh to get back and forth from Boca in style. But, on second thought..." She shook her head. "The palmetto bugs are bad enough—you should see the size they got down there. The last thing I need is to be cleaning reindeer shit so the association doesn't assess me. I'll tellya what..."

Santa and Krampus listened, rapt.

"I win, you leave Beverly Hills alone. You cross it off your list."

"I...what?" Santa was dumbfounded. "I can't do that, Sadie. I can't just abandon every child in an entire city. How will they feel, waking up on Christmas morning without any presents?"

She stared at him. "You're making a joke, right? Ha ha. Very funny."

"I'm serious."

"It's Beverly Hills, Nick! First, sixty percent of the population is Jewish, by way of either Seventh Avenue or Tehran. What do they know from Christmas? Second, next to Georgetown, it's the Spoiled Rotten capital of the world. Pre-teens get ferried to soccer practice in chauffeured limousines. A four year old girl carries a six thousand dollar one-of-a-kind designer handbag. You could sell any Homecoming Queen's used schmatta to cover the national debt of Bolivia. And that's just the public school kids! You should only use the tuition these momzers spend for private kindergarten to send some other family's triplets to

Harvard med school."

"Don't be ridiculous. There have got to be some well-behaved and unspoiled little Christian girls and boys living there as well."

The Hanukkah Fairy nodded. "Seven."

"Seven?" Santa asked, somehow sensing she was right.

"With the way these kids are, can you honestly tell me that you've made more than one or two stops in the 90210 in the past, oh, let's say, in the past decade? Besides, what could they possibly want that you could bring them? They don't want toys anymore, Nick. They want the latest model cell phones and digital this and computer that, all sorts of mishegas. Last I heard, elves and technology..." She shook her head sadly. "Betamax, remember that fiasco? They get it from their parents. Rotten to the core."

"Seven. Only seven deserving children?" He repeated it again as if having trouble wrapping his mind around it.

"Seven," she confirmed. Her head suddenly jerked up as if she'd heard something from far away. "No, wait! Six. Do you remember Tommy Kelly, the producer's kid? He just found his dad's stash of cocaine. Either that or, fifteen minutes ago, he hit puberty. I sometimes have trouble telling them apart."

"You're here," Santa accused, as a last ditch effort to salvage some modicum of self-respect. "Are you telling me only the Jewish kids are any good?"

"I never said that." She wagged her finger in his face. "Who created this good kids get gifts and bad kids get coal hazarai? Rabbis? No such thing with Hanukkah. It's a package deal. The kid wears the yarmulke, he gets the gifts. No lists. No checking twice." She shrugged. "Believe you me, you don't train a lot of little Mother Teresas that way but, hey, I don't make the rules?"

A veil of depression descended upon Santa's normally jolly face. Kris Kringle in a maudlin mood was something that not even Krampus cared to see, especially not on Christmas Eve. Maybe concentrating on the duel would shake Santa out of his funk. The demon cleared his throat and stepped forward.

"All right you two," Krampus growled in his most official and intimidating voice. "Listen up. Since I've been elected playground cop, you're both gonna have to abide by my rules, understand? Each of you will get three chances to take the other one out. And both of you wait your turn, you hear? I don't want to have to get in there and break the two of you up.

He buffed his fingernails, using the fur in the center of his chest. "I just had my annual manicure last week so that every claw is nice and sharp for Christmas Eve." He fixed both of them, in turn, with a glare. "I do not want to risk breaking a nail. Santa Clause, as the challenged party, you get to go first. Do me a favor and wait until I'm out of range, willya?"

With that, the demon scampered onto the sidewalk, making sure that the Lotus Blossom Palace's delivery van provided some protection. He poked his head over the hood so he could watch the action.

"On my signal. Three...two...one. Kris, you're good to go!"

There was no time limit on these kinds of things so Saint Nicolas refused to rush, choosing instead to think things through. He'd have much preferred if Sadie had been willing to let bygones be bygones; he would have been more than willing to gift her with something minor by way of apology—say a nice brisket of reindeer or a wagon load of lox made from Arctic salmon, with a gross of onion and garlic bagels thrown in for good measure. He had no desire to harm her—not that he even could if he tried. But if he was going to be forced into a duel, he wanted to win the thing.

Santa considered his options.

When he was ready, he held his hand out, palms down and at chest height. Effortlessly, he summoned some of the magic that provided lift to Rudolph, prevented the ice shelf under Santa's North Pole Village Frosty from melting due to global warming, and kept his own arteries from clogging given all the seal meat, whale blubber and sugar that Mrs. Claus insisted was part of a balanced diet. Once he'd gathered the power, he shaped it, refined it and, when he was satisfied it would do just enough damage to be impressive, he aimed as best he could and released it.

A blast of snow and freezing sleet whirled around the Hanukkah Fairy, trapping her inside a frigid tornado, lifting her off the ground like Dorothy's farmhouse and whirling her around. Santa winced; it was hard to be precise with these things and he'd given the spell a little more oomph than he'd intended. Sadie would come out of it just fine. But if anyone else happened to pass by, he had no idea how he'd explain the snowdrifts spanning Sunset Boulevard and the icicles dripping from the palm trees overhead.

The maelstrom built to a certain intensity and then peaked and wound down. Only moments before, he'd been facing off against a blue-haired Jewish bubbe with wings, wearing a drip-dry off-the-rack pants suit and carrying an over-sized, worn brown leather purse. Now, a jolly, plump snowman stood in her place, complete with a jaunty carrot nose and big black button eyes.

Kringle frowned. Something about the snowman wasn't right. Almost immediately, he realized what it was and relaxed. The "carrot" nose was actually a daikon radish; given that only a short stretch of Hollywood and tiny West Hollywood separated Beverly Hills from Koreatown, he should have expected the substitution.

"Frosty's Revenge," Krampus commented with awe. "Impressive. I haven't seen that spell in years."

Before Santa could acknowledge the compliment, the snowman began to tremble. Steam rose from under its battered stovepipe hat and portions of its body turned to slush and sluiced away. He only managed to snag the two buttons at the last instant before the currents of melted ice water carried them past the *No Dumping Drains to Ocean* placard set into the sewer grating and washed them out to sea. It was bad enough that inattention might yield him a few hundred dollars in tickets for parking the sleigh in a *Street Sweeping* area; he didn't need to risk a citizen's arrest by overzealous, environmentally conscious, Social Justice Warrior because he'd accidentally littered.

"Good one, Nick," the Hanukkah Fairy said as she stepped from the wreckage of the snowman. "But not quite good enough."

She held up what looked like a plastic container of Coppertone that had lost its label.

"Bottled sunlight. Fresh from Miami," she told him, smugly. "The highest quality. Right off the beach next to the Fontainebleau Hotel."

Damn! He'd forgotten that was one of her powers!

"She got lucky this time, Boss," Krampus commented from the safety of the sidelines. "Last time I saw her try that, she pulled a bottle of Cel-Ray tonic out of her purse by accident."

"My turn," she said, and muttered something in a language that had a lot of throaty consonants.

Immediately, Santa felt dizzy. He took several stumbling steps toward a kiosk stacked with free girlie magazines and apartment rental brochures, hoping to brace himself against it. Halfway there, he found himself spun around. Once, twice and then, Father Christmas was in the undignified position of doing non-stop pirouettes like a prima ballerina, unable to stop himself.

"Aiee!" he cried out, rapidly correcting himself with a loud series of "Ho, ho, hos" to save what little face he could.

"It's the dreaded Dreidel Curse!" Santa heard Krampus exclaim.

Around and around he spun until his stomach seemed to be doing flip flops in the other direction. He was only seconds from witnessing the reappearance of his traditional Christmas Eve dinner; a nice juicy walrus steak with a crushed roasted chestnut crust, flash seared over the Yule Log until it was Pittsburgh rare, and then served with an eggnog and apple cider reduction. Thinking quickly, he combined his defense with his next attack and managed to shout out a rarely used spell in the original Icelandic.

Red and white striped peppermint grew from the asphalt and reached a height of six or seven feet even faster than Rudolph could dry hump Donner and Blitzen. Thick holly vines sprouted from the crook of each candy cane, and lashed themselves around Sadie, wrapping her like a mummy with little sprigs of holly instead of hieroglyphs. Kris Kringle seized a couple of extra strands himself. He twisted them around his wrists so that they didn't slip from his pudgy fingers and used them to stop his dizzying spin.

"Counter that one!" he called, once he was sure the Hanukkah curse was completely abated and he wouldn't start twirling like a member of the corps de ballet in The Nutcracker Suite the minute he let go of the vines.

A horrendous stink filled the air. Santa gagged at the stench of onions and hot chicken fat mingling with hints of hot cinnamon, burnt walnuts and something was distinctly fishy smelling. Topping it all off was a stomach roiling combination of overcooked greens mixed with the distinctive artificial fruity tang of Manischewitz wine.

"What is that?" Santa couldn't help asking. Whatever trick she'd used, it was an effective one; he longed for a gallon of eggnog with a few pounds of whipped cream chaser, just to cut the sweetness of the cherry wine.

"Mrmmmph!" Krampus said. In his astonishment, he'd clapped both forepaws over his mouth and was trying to talk through the hoof-y parts.

"What?" Santa snapped.

"The Incantation of Ethnic Foods," he breathed with awe, after he'd taken his hooves out of his mouth.

"Liver and onions!" Sadie cackled, holding up the plate. "With a nice side of pickled herring in sour cream and a tongue sandwich—so tender it should only melt—on a pumpernickel heel. A plate of gravlox with a schmear. And for dessert...” A blackened casserole appeared in her other hand which, evidently, had been in the oven too long. “Noodle kugel!”

Santa Clause’s gorge rose at the menu. A man of his girth certainly wasn’t adverse to eating savory things, but with all that salt and chicken fat, he was surprised that any Jewish child made it to their bar or bat mitzvah without dropping dead of congestive heart failure or hypertension at the ripe old age of eleven.

“Nice move, Sadie!”

“Hey, you with the goat head!” Dammit, the Hanukkah Fairy’s vocal patterns were contagious. “Whose side are you on?”

Krampus had the good grace to look sheepish. Then again, as Santa had just pointed out, with the horns and the wool already in place, for Krampus, looking like a sheep—or a ram at least—wasn’t much of a stretch.

“My turn!”

The old biddy was clearly having fun.

Gleefully, she waved a slip of paper that she took out of her purse. He couldn’t make out what it was but, suddenly, his stomach was gripped by a sharp, intense pain. Santa staggered and fell to his knees. When he climbed to his feet, he found to his embarrassment that his pants had remained behind, in a puddle of red velvet pooling around his ankles. Quickly, he snatched them up but, for some reason, they wouldn’t stay put; they slid over his hips and down his legs again. He hauled them into place once more and, to his befuddlement, he found that no matter how tightly he cinched his belt, the trousers were too damned big.

No, it wasn’t the trousers, he realized with horror. It was him! That unaccustomed tightness in his belly was his abdominal muscles showing themselves for the first time in five hundred years. Oh woe! Where were his jolly rolls of fat, his bowls full of comfortable jelly?

“What...? What did you do to me?” he gasped. “What is

that piece of paper?"

"Jenny Craig," the Hanukkah Fairy cackled. "A thirty percent off coupon for a month of exercise classes. And..." Her eyes sparkled with malicious glee. "A Gelson's rain check for two-for-one Weight Watchers!" She turned to face Krampus, "They ran out the last time there was a sale," she confided. "Who knew Lean Cuisine could have so much power in the right hands?"

"How would you like it," he gasped, "if I hit you with a discount coupon for a face lift?"

She shrugged and patted some of the loose flesh hanging from the bottom of her chin. "Couldn't hurt."

Grimly, Santa steeled his thoughts against distractions and focused on the delicious Christmas feasts he'd partaken of over the centuries. Plump turkeys with golden, crisped skin. Chestnut stuffing, oyster stuffing, sausage stuffing! Butter floating in a lake of rich brown gravy atop a mount of mashed potatoes. Chunks of yam with marshmallows and pineapple slices. Cranberry sauce with walnuts. A couple of roasted geese and, perhaps, a ham basted with cider and honey.

And dessert! Apple pie, apple and raisin pie, deep dish apple pie, French apple pie and, of course, candied apple pie, each slice peeping from under a gigantic scoop of vanilla ice cream slathered with whipped cream or, perhaps, served with a generous wedge of cheddar cheese. And speaking of pies, he imagined pumpkin, winter peach and his all-time favorite, mince, hot from the oven with wisps of fragrant steam seeping from the slashes in the upper crust. Puddings entered his fantasy—plum puddings, figgy puddings, bread puddings, puddings with hard sauce...

"Enough!" Sadie cried out, snapping him back to the present.

He reached down to check and was pleased to see that his frame was, if anything, more corpulent than usual. The Hanukkah Fairy, on the other hand, looked positively bilious.

"It's enough to give a person permanent heart burn," she griped.

"You should talk, you with your schmaltz. Care to concede?" Santa asked, and added another, aggressive, "Ho, ho, ho!" for good measure.

"What are you, meshugge? I got one more shot and you got bupkes."

Her expression became grim and, behind the rhinestone glasses, her eyes narrowed. For the first time, Santa wondered if perhaps he might have bitten off more than he could chew.

"Uh, I think it's my turn."

Santa looked to Krampus for confirmation. But the demon just shrugged.

"I lost track right about the time you started babbling in Eskimo."

"Not Eskimo," Santa corrected. "Inuit. Don't you watch Bill Maher?"

"The thing is, see," Sadie commanded his attention once again. "if I decide to take your turn away from you, what is a guy like you gonna do about it?"

"Well...um..." He struggled to come up with an appropriate answer and couldn't. "I suppose..."

She cut him off.

"You see? The problem with you, Nicky, is that you're too good. You're too nice of a guy."

"That's what Christmas is about," he told her. "Peace on earth. Goodwill to men. Sugarplum fairies and unicorn farts that smells like cotton candy."

Sadie shook her head sadly and turned to face Krampus.

"Did I tell you or what?"

"When you're right, you're right," the demon replied.

"Hey, what's going on here?" Santa demanded, suspicious.

"I'm afraid your time is past, Nicky," Sadie said. "This is the Twenty-First Century. Snowflakes and lollipops just don't measure up any more." She flung up her hands as if to wash them of responsibility. "Don't get the wrong idea. I wasn't the one who brought it up..."

"Don't look at me," Krampus hastily put in. "Blame the Easter Bunny. For a while now, I think he's had it in for you. You guys being the two major religious icons turned secular, ya know? I think he thinks you're the competition."

He pointed an accusing finger at Krampus. "And you think you are gonna take my place?"

"Why not? The bad kids outnumber the good kids fifty to one anymore. My time has come."

"This...this whole thing...? It's a setup?" Santa asked, with disbelief.

"That's harsh, Nicky. Think of it as more of a mandatory retirement party."

Before he had a chance to register another protest, the Hanukkah Fairy started to mutter, and then to chant. Songs from Funny Girl mingled with snatches of Hava Nagila and bits of old Zero Mostel and Sid Caesar routines and the ingredient lists for kreplach and the recipe for making a nice tsimmis with both carrots and prunes.

Santa felt something in the back of his throat, salty and warm. He inhaled to try to clear out whatever it was and, instead, smelled something delicious.

"Relax, Nicky," the Hanukkah Fairy told him, not unkindly. "It'll all be over in a minute."

Though there was nothing physically there, his mouth salivated at the taste of perfectly boiled carrots and creamy potatoes floating in a thick, exquisitely seasoned broth of hearty chicken stock. It was so real that he could almost taste the egg noodles.

Then, his mouth exploded with the flavor of something he'd never tasted before. It was a dumpling—sort of, a light and fluffy savory confection, redolent with hints of onion and pepper. Though Santa was normally a candy-and-cake kinda guy, the taste of the whatever-it-was bowled him over.

"He's got the matzoh ball now. You can tell by the

expression on his face."

Through the delicious haze, the fat man only dimly heard Sadie talking to Krampus. Very little of their conversation registered except for those two wondrous words: matzoh ball.

Airy, as ethereal as a cloud, the phantom dumpling seemed to melt on his tongue and slid, oh so delightfully, down his throat, warming his insides with a rosy glow. It settled, a comfortable weight in his stomach, nourishing and evoking the warm hearth in his home at the North Pole and the smells of home cooked meals wafting in from the kitchen.

Santa sighed and, for a moment, he was blissfully content.

Then, there was a twinge in his belly and a grimace formed on his lips. The matzoh ball was changing. Where only seconds ago it had been as fluffy as the most billowy cloud, it now seemed to solidify like a lead cannon ball in his stomach. Santa groaned.

"That's the problem with the things," Sadie told Krampus. "They go down easy. But, boy oh boy! An hour later? You're talking about drinking Maalox by the bottle and chewing on Ex-Lax for a week."

Santa clutched his belly, doubled over. Both Krampus and the Hanukkah Fairy grabbed their noses when the fat man released a resoundingly loud burst of flatulence. The odor was intense but, fortunately, it smelled more like pine boughs than anything else. By the time they wiped tears from the astringent odor from their eyes, Santa Clause was no more. Only a slight film of snow remained where he'd been standing just a few seconds before, melting rapidly in the frigid seventy-four degree chill of the Los Angeles Christmas Eve.

"That's that then," Sadie said.

"Yeah." Krampus looked a little downcast.

"Cheer up," she told him. "Nicky's in a better place now."

"It's not that. It's those damned elves. It just occurred

to me that now, they're my problem."

"Oy vey," she shook her head and patted her chest between her wrinkled breasts. "Such problems, I should only have. You wanna talk about problems? Let me tell you about my problems. I got this crick in my right knee..."

"You hungry?" Krampus interrupted, knowing how capable she was of going on for hours and hours once the subject of her health came up. "Or can I drop you somewhere?"

"Cantors Deli is open. A little nosh, I wouldn't refuse."

"Great." He extended his arm to escort her to the sleigh. "Never been there. Tell me something, is it all children who aren't kosher? Or just the gentile ones? Because, I got a box of kids here that I am just dying to dig into..."

Their voices faded into the distance and a warm breeze jostled the jacaranda trees. The tarry blooms fell, drifting lazily down to land on the hoods of the Mercedes, Lexuses and BMWs that were parked underneath. By dawn on Christmas morning, the acid in the flowers would already have pitted the paint while covering the cars in a lovely blanket of what looked like pale purple snow.

The Quiet Christmas Tree

By Tracy L. Carbone

Dwight sat on his favorite lawn chair in front of the outdoor Christmas tree and thought about his dead wife. "You sure would've liked this tree, Alice." He stood up and rubbed the rough bristles against his chest through his thick jacket. "Right now you're just about as tall as you were in real life." He put his arms around the tree. Not all the way. Alice was fat. But around the edges. "Your top barely brushes my chin, just like in real life. You smell my aftershave? It's Brut. I know you liked the Old Spice but I always liked this better."

He hummed as he slowly swung his hips around the tree. "Singing you our song, Alice. *Smoke Gets in Your Eyes*. You always loved when I'd sing to you." In truth she made fun of his singing. Said he didn't sound like a crooner at all but a "tone deaf old fool." But he liked to sing. It made him happy.

He moved back to his chair and sat down. The icy metal arms burned his fingers so he pulled his coat sleeves down. Dwight puffed out a breath, which rose smoky and white in front of the bright red and green and blue lights on the tree. "Looks magical. Wish you could see this, Alice. You'd love it. And you wouldn't be mad that I spent so much neither. You're buried right here in front of our trailer and every year you'll grow just a little bit bigger. Hell, someday you might be taller than our house." He laughed. "Maybe even as tall as my school bus. Wouldn't the kids get a kick out of that, if I told 'em."

Dwight didn't mind that the tree didn't answer back. He didn't expect it to. Lord knows Alice, the love of his life, did more than her share of talking, and yelling, before she passed. He shook his head now when he thought of her accident. He'd been away for the weekend driving a charter bus for a Foxwoods trip. Alice always said they didn't have enough money and driving a "bunch of little assholes to elementary school didn't put her dinner on the table." Once, just once, Dwight suggested maybe she should get a job to help out. He touched his front teeth now. His fake front teeth. And that was the last time he suggested much of anything to Alice. Mostly he worked, and when he'd come home he'd tell Alice she looked pretty, and the house looked clean, and dinner smelled wonderful.

None of those things were true. Not a one. Alice was almost four hundred pounds, and all she knew how to make was Kraft Mac and Cheese and Van de Camps fish sticks. Not that he minded either dinner but after fifteen years he was tired of it. He made a point to eat before he got home. Betty Sue, boy she could cook like no one's business. Biscuits and gravy and real steak, fried chicken. Mmm, Mmm good. He ate at her diner every single night, though he took his meals out back so no one would catch him and tattle to Alice.

He'd come home and say lunch filled him up and wasn't hungry. Couldn't eat a bite. She packed him a bologna sandwich every single day with a plastic baggie full of generic corn chips. He gave it to the stray dog that had come to live by the school. He saved his appetite for Betty Sue's cooking. Alice didn't care about his dinner anyway, so long as he told her it smelled delicious and thanked her for her hard work. She'd glare at him then smile. "More for me," she'd say.

When the furnace malfunctioned and carbon monoxide killed her in her sleep he was a hundred miles away sitting in the charter bus alone watching *King Kong* on

DVD. He didn't find out till he came home the next morning. He called the police and filled out some paperwork, and an ambulance and three strong EMTs took her body away.

Dwight walked around the trailer.

Quiet. It was so quiet.

He stood and listened and smiled so hard his cheeks cramped up. Silence. First thing he did was pull out a lawn and leaf bag and sweep boxes and boxes of Mac and Cheese into it. Those could go to the church food pantry. He took another bag and dumped the frozen fish sticks from their regular freezer and the one in spare room. Those could go in the dumpster. No one ought to have to eat those.

He stopped short of getting rid of her clothes. It had only been an hour since the police left. Might look bad if he cleared away her things too quickly. He sat on their couch. Alice's side had a gulley where she spent her days. He picked up his phone and ordered a pizza. A pepperoni pizza. And a bag of chips on the side, he told the lady as an afterthought. It had been fifteen years since he'd eaten a pizza in this house, since he'd sat quietly and listened to the sounds of birds and crickets. He stared at the TV which was off for the first time in years.

Yeah, I think I'm going to be just fine all by myself.

He thought of that night now, three years ago. Dwight looked at the lights of the tree as he bit into an Italian sub and as oil dripped down his chin. He flinched, still awaiting a reprimand and insult. But the tree said nothing.

He laughed. He did love this silence.

~

"Don't feel bad, Floyd," Marlene said. "We don't have to have a tree or a lot of presents. Rebecca is old enough. She knows you can't find a steady job, knows no one will hire me seven month's pregnant."

Floyd looked sadly at his wife. She was such a good person. He was damn lucky she loved him. Same with little

Rebecca. She turned six last month and was the spitting image of her mother. Just as sweet.

"Yeah but what kind of man doesn't get his family a Christmas tree? No excuse for that. I'll just go cut one down at the tree farm."

"And risk getting arrested? You're already on probation, Floyd. Last thing you need is a trespassing charge. I can probably get a string of lights at the Goodwill pretty cheap, and Rebecca and I can make some loops from the sales fliers. I've been saving them up. We can set a garland up along the windows there. It'll look real pretty."

Floyd hated himself. It was Christmas for god's sake. Almost Christmas. Who the hell ever heard of making garland from sales fliers? Last thing he needed was pictures of meat or fruit or women's products in glossy print taped up on the wall.

"I gotta go out. Got a job with Bud tonight down in his trailer park. He said some old woman needs her porch fixed."

He kissed Marlene goodbye and walked out to his truck. The engine took its time turning over but finally coughed to life. Bud's job involved carrying drugs from one place to the next, not much to do with fixing a porch at all. It paid though. Not enough for a tree or presents but it would cover the rent.

Just before he got to Bud's trailer, he saw a perfect Christmas tree all lit up, the heat from the lights making them glow with the cold air around it. Just small enough to steal and fit in his place. The lights were off in the trailer next to the tree. Whoever owned it was fast asleep. He really needed this job from Bud but...yeah it could wait. He killed his headlights and rolled to the side of the house. He shut off the engine and dug through his tools behind his seat.

Perfect. Trusty old saw.

Floyd looked left and right but no one was around. It was a senior living over 55 park and at eleven at night they were all asleep. Only reason Bud was allowed to live here was because he had a bum leg so qualified as handicapped. He'd still be awake now, and up later when Floyd was done with the tree.

On his hands and knees he reached under the tree to the trunk. It was a small tree and there wasn't a hell of a lot to saw through. The bright lights guided his way. "You sure are a pretty tree," he said. "Nice and round and full." The lights flashed on and off. "Hey are you winking at me?" He laughed quietly. In no time at all he'd cut the tree and carefully laid it into his truck bed. The light bulbs rattled against the truck but they'd be all right. He covered it with a tarp. "Now you just stay there nice and quiet and I'll take you home after work."

Floyd didn't tell Bud about his pit stop. He ran his drugs and collected his money. All told, he was only out of the house two hours. Marlene and Rebecca were sound asleep when he came in with the tree. He rifled through the shed and found the old tree stand from last year. It took some doing, getting the tree up and plugged in without waking anyone but he did it. Boy would his wife and daughter be surprised the next morning.

~

Dwight was having a shit day. When he woke up this morning the tree was gone. Someone cut it down and stole it away right from his own front yard. He'd called the police but they didn't seem to take it all that serious. They'd ask around but trees all looked the same they said. It'd be hard to distinguish it from any other.

"But this is different," Dwight said. "It's my wife's tree. You have to get it back for me. I paid a lot of money for that tree. It needs to be back here."

They said they couldn't do much unless someone turned it in. He had lights on it but they were no different than anyone else's lights. He hadn't put personalized ornaments on it for fear the snow or rain or wind would ruin them.

Alice would not be happy that her tree was gone. She would not sit still for that. No way.

He was worried sick but the kids in the back kept him distracted. He looked in his rearview and smiled. He loved his little passengers. Even on the worst of days those kids cracked him up. "I'm not lying!" one young voice shouted.

He turned around to see Rebecca Brown shouting at a group of kids who were turned toward her. Some were turned around in their seats, others hung over theirs. He stopped the bus. That alone was usually enough to scare them straight. Not this time though.

"You're crazy then!" Billy yelled at her. Dwight didn't know his last name. He was a foster kid that belonged the Johnsons.

"What's going on back there?" Dwight shouted. He wasn't angry but he had to show authority or they'd take advantage. They had a nice level of respect and fear going, and he couldn't blow it.

"Rebecca said she has a magic tree and it talks to her," Billy said. ""I told her that's crazy. That's crazy, Mr. Coffelt, isn't it? Or she's a liar."

The others started chanting *Liar Liar* until he bellowed, "Shut up! All of you!" *Silence.* "I'm about ready to drive right back to that school. Is that what you want?" He smiled at the power of those words.

Thirty-two little heads shook no.

"I will drive you home if you all remain quiet the rest of the drive. But Rebecca, you come sit up here by me."

He moved his bag from the seat to the floor and she sat behind him.

Dwight started the bus again and child by child dropped them all off.

"You went by my house," Rebecca said.

"I know. I wanted to drive you home last so I can talk to you alone."

"I'm not lying about the tree," the little girl insisted.

He stopped a block from her trailer. "I don't think you're lying." He hoped she was but if she had Alice's tree—

"Really?"

"Tell me about it. Is it an outside tree?"

"My Daddy brought home a real Christmas tree last night when I was sleeping. It was dark in the house when I got up to go wee but there were so many lights on the tree it lit up the whole living room."

"That's pretty impressive. Your father must love you very much to buy you a tree like that." He hoped that was the case.

"Oh I don't think he bought it," she said, lowering her voice. "Mommy and him were fighting last night 'cuz he said he didn't have any money and couldn't buy a tree but then he came home with one already decorated."

"You think he stole it?"

The girl scrunched up her face, angry. "My Daddy wouldn't steal!" She paused and grinned. "I think it was a magic tree, sent early from Santa."

Right. "What did the tree say to you?"

She looked toward her trailer, just down the street. "Well, it said, 'He killed me. Tell someone. He killed me.' Honest it did. Then it shook all over and the lights rattled and needles fell on the floor. Look here." She pulled her coat sleeve up to reveal a red welt. "It smacked me with its branch. I ran into my room but I could hear it shaking and still yelling, 'You tell someone he killed me or I'll hurt you more!' So I told my friends and Daddy but no one believes me."

Damn it all to hell. It was Alice all right.

"My Daddy said it's just my imagination and trees don't talk and they certainly don't yell at little girls."

"Oh is that all." He laughed. "Well that's just silly. If the tree did talk, it probably just meant whoever cut it down killed it, see?"

The girl brightened. "Yeah, you're right. That's what it meant."

"So don't you worry about it anymore. If it says anything else you just ignore it. It's just a tree after all."

With that he drove Rebecca to her house. In the window he could see his tree, Alice's tree, already lit and in the window. It saw him too and blinked its lights on and off in warning.

Can't believe that bastard stole my tree.

~

Floyd was about as pleased as anyone could ever be with how happy Rebecca and Marlene were about that tree. He told Marlene that Bud's client gave them a bonus and he bought the tree, lights and all. She believed him the way she trusted that he was doing construction jobs all night every night, the way she believed the jewelry or electronics he sometimes brought home and then sold were just good finds at all night yard sales. Marlene was good that way. Don't ask, don't tell was her policy. She preferred to keep on keeping on that he was a good standup guy who earned money for the family and always came through in the end.

He picked Bud up tonight for a "kitchen renovation job" on the other side of town in the rich section. They were driving down his street when Bud pointed to the front yard where Floyd has taken the tree. A man sat alone with a beer in front of his trailer. Just sat and started in the pitch dark, lit up only by Floyd's headlights.

"Poor guy," Bud said. "Someone stole his wife."

"What's that?" Floyd asked, speeding by the trailer and toward the main road.

"That guy back there. He's a bus driver for Bradfield Elementary. Drives a charter to Foxwoods on weekends. Decent guy, had a bitch of a wife. Fat old cow that bitched him out all the time. No matter what he did she was yelling at him. Nothing was good enough for her. He loved her though. Day in and day out he'd park his school bus there. They couldn't afford a car so he brought the bus home. He'd step out of it, smile on his face. And I could hear her screaming at him clear back from my place."

"Yeah but what do you mean I stole his wife?"

"One weekend when he was away the furnace malfunctioned and she died of carbon monoxide poisoning. We all think he killed her, and if he did, good for him. The police didn't think it was tampered with though, and like I said he was gone all weekend."

Rebecca said the tree talked to her, told her someone killed her. That's crazy.

Though it was cold outside and in the truck, Floyd started to sweat and unzipped his coat.

Trees don't talk.

"He really loved her even though she was a bitch and a half so when she died he did that thing where you put somebody's ashes in with a tree, or something. I don't know how it works but you bury this pod thing and when it grows it's like literally a tree seed growing out of that person's body or some shit. I don't know. Three years he sits out there every night with a beer, talking to that spot. Watching the tree grow. Honest to god a couple of nights I saw him outside dancing with it."

Floyd hated himself. What kind of asshole steals someone's dead wife right from under him? And at Christmas no less. "Dancing with it huh?"

"That's right. Day after Thanksgiving he was out there covering the tree with lights. I swear I've never seen that guy so happy as now that he gets to sit there and talk to his wife without her talking back. Well, I mean he did but now the tree is gone. Can you imagine? Who steals a decorated tree except the Grinch? And that was just a cartoon."

Floyd vowed that as soon as they were done with this job, he'd go home and put that old man's tree back where he found it.

~

Dwight finished his beer then went into the house to grab the keys for his new pickup. Not so new now of course but still shiny and with low miles. He'd bought a shiny new F-150 pickup with the little bit of life insurance money from Alice. It was a policy they'd bought together some fifteen years ago from a door to door salesman. Just enough to pay off the trailer and buy the truck outright. Might as well have been a million dollars though because Dwight sure loved that truck. He still drove the school bus home during the week and parked it in his driveway out of habit, but for everything but school business he drove his big black truck.

His smile faded as he walked outside toward the vehicle and again spied the stump. It wasn't just that he was pissed someone stole his tree, it's that he knew Alice would be mad. In her life, she inflicted her share of pain and suffering. Who was to say she wouldn't do that same in death. It's why he sweet talked her, sat with her every night. Plus it was nice to talk about his day without criticism.

Rebecca Brown was a sweet little girl and yet Alice had already slapped her once. She might do a lot worse and it would be his fault for trying to keep some part of his wife alive. Floyd needed to get that tree back where it belonged.

Plus the last thing he needed was Alice shooting her mouth off, ghost or not, and telling people he killed her. Insinuating he tampered with the furnace to kill her. Truth be told, he did. So what? His cousin, the fire inspector, stated there was no foul play and so did Betty Sue's husband, who owned the diner and also served as the Sheriff. That was good enough for him and everyone else in this town.

He sped to the Brown trailer a few miles away. There was old Alice, all bright and gaudy, taking up the whole damn front window of the trailer. Bigger than ever, branches all stretched out wide. When his truck came into view, her lights blinked on and off. He didn't see anyone else moving in the house but even if they were, he needed to get that tree out of there and back in his yard.

Dwight peeked in the side door. The house was quiet but the branches were shaking inside. He tried the door.

Locked of course. He rammed a screwdriver in and forced the door.

It popped open and he listened. Silence at first then the rustling sound that turned into an angry whisper. "You killed me," the voice hissed. "You planned it and killed me and you won't get away with this!"

"Like hell I won't," Dwight whispered back as he approached.

Without hesitation he rushed to the tree, grabbed the top in his hands, and dragged it along the floor. Alice hissed and shook her branches, pissed off as always. He smiled as he pictured instead dragging the real Alice along the floor by her hair. The plug pulled from the wall and her lights went dark.

"Who's out there?" a young woman called out.

Dwight assumed it was Mrs. Brown but kept dragging old Alice. "Taking this tree out of here. It's infested with bugs. Very dirty." He dug in his pocket and pulled out all his cash. Forty-seven dollars. "Here, buy a new one. A better one."

Rebecca walked into the room then, clad in footie pajamas. "You're taking our tree?"

"Who wants a mean old tree that grumps all the time? You and your momma can go buy a nice quiet tree instead," he said as he rushed it out the door. "See you tomorrow, Rebecca!" he called just as the door shut behind him.

He lugged the tree into the truck bed.

"You won't get away with this," Alice hissed from the back. "You think just because I'm dead I'll leave you alone? You think just because—"

He got in his truck and sped off. From there he couldn't hear her. He enjoyed the silence but wondered what to do next. Now that she'd found her voice he couldn't bring her back to the trailer park. He'd done the right thing by her for three years. Kept her with him, let her stay right by her old house, been a good husband. But even he had limits.

An hour later, in the middle of the old quarry, he

warmed himself by the fire. He held one small branch he'd snapped off, the last piece of Alice. It was like holding her hand one last time.

"Sure does bring back memories, huh Alice?" Dwight said. "You and me out here, talking about our future, promising we'd love each other forever?"

The fire roared and the flames grew. The sticky pine branches snapped in the flames, shiny sap popping with the heat.

"Ouch!" Dwight looked down at his hand, cut by the jagged piece of branch. "You'll never change, Alice." He tossed the branch in the fire with the rest of her, smiling when it caught and sizzled.

The fire was crazy loud at first but after a few minutes it quieted down. No more hissing or rustling, no more accusations or insults.

As the last of the flames burnt out, Alice finally shut up once and for all.

Shamash

By Xach Fromson

The latkes were my father's recipe, but they weren't on par with his yet. I had the platter in my hands, preparing to place them on the table when my father came into the dining room.

"What's in the box?" I asked, eyebrow arched. I was well past the age of expecting gifts from my parents on Hanukkah. The idea that my father brought a present for me made me suspect that, despite the dimensions of the container being completely wrong, I was about to get a blender.

"A gift," my father said. He adjusted the box in his hands. His smile faded, replaced by a look I couldn't quite place. My mother took his hand in hers and squeezed it.

"You never really knew my brother, Moshe," he said. "After the war, Moshe moved to Israel in that first wave. We...fell out of touch. I tried writing to him a few times, and we got a couple letters over the years, but..." he shrugged. "Anyway, a week ago, I got this in the mail from a lawyer in Tel Aviv. Moshe passed away last year, and it took until now for the lawyer to send this off. But, I figured we could use it tonight, a way to remember Moshe."

My father looked to Uncle Shlomo and Aunt Frieda. They both shared the same kind of sad smile he wore. He opened the box and produced a wrought iron hanukiah. It was all dark metal, its wide base tapered up to a thin central arm with a cup for the shamash. The iron twisted in a spiral, and each of the eight arms that branched out from the central stem was similarly twirled. Together, the eight arms and the central stem created a dizzying pattern to look at. But there was no denying that it was gorgeous, in a rough and old fashioned kind of way.

"Moshe spent a lot of time with our father," Uncle Shlomo explained. "He was a blacksmith, back before... well...before. Moshe always liked trying to make things. I guess he must have made this at some point."

"It looks so old!" My daughter Sarah said, eying the hanukiah.

"Well, so do I," my father said.

Sarah leaned on the table to get a closer look. "It's ugly," she decided with the finality only a ten-year-old can deliver.

I choked back a laugh.

I lifted Uncle Moshe's hanukiah out of the box, and was so surprised by the texture that I made a small noise of disgust. The iron felt oily somehow, almost slimy to the touch. It had a sheen on it that hadn't been apparent when it lay in its box, which made me think that there was some kind of enamel or whatever people used back then on it, and maybe it had just turned into a slimy coat of muck on the metal over the decades.

"I'll get the candles," I said to my father.

"David, would you like to lead the blessing?" My father looked to my son, and I caught a brief glimpse of the generations coming together before I ducked into the hallway to grab the Hanukkah candles. When I returned, David was holding the box of matches.

I held the candles steady while David touched the flame to their base so they'd stick.

"Which one do you light first?" I asked my son. Rachel and I weren't observant Jews, but we wanted to pass on the traditions.

David struck a match to light the *shamash*.

"Why that one?"

"In the Jewish tradition, the center candle is called the

shamash, or attendant," David said as if reciting from a text. "Because it's used to attend the other candles. He picked the center candle up and used it to light the one on the far end of Moshe's hanukiah.

"*Baruch atah Adonai, Eloheinu, melekh ha'olam asher kidishanu b'mitz'votav v'tzivanu l'had'lik neir shel Hanukkah.*" David quasi-sung the blessing.

"Amen," we all muttered. None of us said it with conviction, but it was part of the ritual, and it was gratifying to see my son and daughter share that ritual with my parents.

The candles flickered, casting a shadow that winked in and out of existence. It looked to me like tentacles reaching for each of the eight people at the table, plus one more.

"Now this," my father grabbed the wine bottle next to the hanukiah, "is my favorite blessing."

"Dad..." I tried to chide him, but since when can a son effectively chide his father?

"What?" He raised his bushy eyebrows at me. "It's next." He drew his arm back in, wine bottle securely in his hand. He stopped in mid motion frozen in place holding the wine bottle just a couple inches above the table. The two candle flames from the hanukiah reflected on its glass. He got a look on his face like he wasn't quite sure what was going on and had forgotten what he was supposed to be doing.

Everything inside me screamed that something was wrong. The world faded to gray and moved in slow motion.

"Dad..." I heard myself say the word, but wasn't aware that I'd spoken it.

"Hirsh?" Rachel asked, reaching her hand toward him.

"Is papa okay?" David asked, looking to me for an answer.

The candle for the first night seemed to bend its flame toward my father.

All of these things seemed to happen at exactly the same moment. The next, my father's shoulders heaved with the deep breath he took in. His eyes went wide, still unfocused and confused. He slumped into the chair, every angle in his body slightly wrong, and the air emptied from his lungs. His head rolled forward, eyes still open. His arm fell to his side, dropping the wine bottle and tipping it over to spill out onto the tablecloth.

Then all the colors snapped back into my vision and my sense of movement caught up with normal speed.

"Oh, my God! Hirsh!" Aunt Frieda cried out, grasping his shoulder with both of her hands. She shook him, and his body jerked back and forth, but the movement was all wrong.

"I'm calling 911," Rachel said, pulling out her cell phone.

I was aware of all of these things, but there was a detail that I couldn't make sense of, and it held my gaze. The flame was burning horizontally, still tipped in the direction of my father. It hadn't flickered or wavered even a little bit since Hirsh had gone silent. It just pointed right at him. I stared at the impossible flame while around me, everything erupted into chaos. There was crying from several people, but I couldn't quite make out what anyone was saying.

I felt my father die. One moment, there were eight of us in the dining room. The next, there were seven of us in a room with a corpse. The candle that had been burning horizontally sprung back up to a vertical flame in that same instant, jumping from a small tongue of fire to a spurt of flame several inches taller than the candle itself. It flared briefly before returning to its normal size. The wax was gone, leaving only the flame flickering in an otherwise empty cup. When the flame died down, I realized I'd been staring at it the entire time. I tried to move, but my body felt slow and sluggish. I couldn't clear the cobwebs out of my head.

Once I broke my gaze away from the hanukiah, details began registering. Uncle Shlomo and Aunt Frieda were comforting David and Sarah, while my mom cried on the floor next to my father's body, and Rachel tried to make her cell phone work.

"Dad," I said softly, and the word brought me fully back to the moment. My father's eyes stared vacantly at me from his chair. His slack face still somehow looked surprised and unsure. A heat burned in the back of my throat, and my eyes stung as tears pushed up against them. I pulled myself out of my chair, landing on the ground next to my mother. I put my arms around her, pulling her in close and hugging her.

"No," my mother cried into my shoulder. "No, Hirsh. Don't leave. Please, don't go."

"This damned thing isn't working." Rachel threw her cell phone. "I'm going to try the land line in the other room."

"We should all go into the other room," Uncle Shlomo said. My mother really began to wail then.

"Miriam," Aunt Frieda said gently. "Miriam—"

"No," my mom said through her tears.

It felt wrong somehow. He'd just been his funny self a moment ago. I hugged my mom tighter.

"Daniel," Aunt Frieda's voice was soft, but commanding.

I wanted someone to tell me what to do because I didn't know.

"Daniel," she said again, this time putting her hand on my shoulder.

"Yeah." I was hoarse already even though I hadn't cried yet.

Aunt Frieda guided me as I stood up. She helped my mother regain her feet as well. We shuffled out of the dining room and into the living room where Rachel was on a couch with David and Sarah, heads buried against her sides. She was talking on the phone, and hung up when we entered.

"Emergency line was busy," she said.

I sank into a chair, only to realize that it was the one my dad always sat in. I halfway rose out of my seat before I realized that I didn't have to.

The room fell quiet. I wanted to say something, but

no words came to mind. We weren't even looking at each other. We just sat together in the living room breathing quietly.

Something dripping in the dining room broke the illusion of stillness, but I couldn't bring myself to look. Outside, the sunset turned the sky from pink to orange and red. The day had been crystal clear.

Rachel called again and again for an ambulance, or whoever was supposed to come, but every time she got a busy signal.

Darkness began to set in, and still the dripping noise came from the dining room.

"The wine," said Uncle Shlomo.

"I'll take care of it," I said, getting up out of the chair.

Uncle Shlomo rose with me. "Let me help."

The wine soaked table cloth was dripping from its edges onto the floor. I kneeled down to mop it up, sparing my uncle from having to bend too much. He was only two years younger than my father, and I didn't need him hurting himself. I kept my eyes focused as tightly as possible on the small puddle of wine on the floor. My father was still in his seat, slumped over in a grotesque caricature of the man he had been.

Uncle Shlomo made a kind of *huh* sound from above me.

"What?" I asked.

"The hanukiah," he said, in a way that implied I needed to see it to understand. I stood up and took my first real look at it in a while. Its spiraled iron structures formed an imposing image, even if it was small enough to fit into a box. I wasn't sure what I was supposed to be seeing, though.

"What about it?"

"The flames," Uncle Shlomo said. "There are no candles, but there are flames."

The *shamash* and the candle for the first night of Hanukkah were gone, but two flames burned merrily in the empty cups.

"Strange," I said. The whole thing felt surreal. We were ignoring my father, who had died right in front of us. The moment felt oddly normal, just two Jews talking about Hanukkah.

"Your father," Shlomo said, one of us finally addressing the situation. "He was so stubborn, I thought he'd outlive us all." He leaned against the table and looked directly at my father's body. I looked too, the old man's color had gone, and his muscles were slack, but his eyes were still open and looking right at the hanukiah and its two flames.

I got that odd sensation of wrongness again, a kind of tingling of my nerves. I looked from my father's face to the hanukiah, and the flames danced higher.

"Hey, uh, Shlomo..." Was he was seeing what I was seeing? Flames don't burn with no candles, and they certainly don't suddenly double in size for no reason.

Shlomo jerked his hand away from the table, but there was something dark attached to it. I opened my mouth to say something, but the thing trailing from my uncle's hand twitched. The dark substance was coming from the hanukiah, and it seemed to be the shadow cast by the two flames. My eyes and my brain disagreed on what was happening. The hanukiah cast a nine-pronged shadow that wavered in front of me; each prong looking like a writhing tentacle reaching outward—to Shlomo.

His eyes widened the same way my father's had, impossibly wide and white. He stared at his hand as the tentacles wrapped around it like a dark fist.

I heard, or thought I heard, something like a whisper. Shlomo fell to the ground. He didn't hit with a thud or a slap. He hardly made any noise; he just collapsed. The shadow or whatever it was stopped writhing and retreated to its original position, flickering beneath the hanukiah. The hanukiah now had three flames burning. A new tongue of fire flickered in the cup for the second night's candle.

I rounded the table and fell to my knees next to my uncle. There was no life left in his body either. He'd somehow fallen in such a way that his face was still upturned, look-ing right at the hanukiah. It was as though his death mask was an expression of just how little he understood, and how unfair it was. Sitting there next to him, I felt an echo-ing emptiness inside of me. Maybe I was already going into shock, or my emotions had already been drained. Or maybe my mind just refused to process it all and it was protecting me from breaking. On some instinctive level, I thought of my children and knew that I couldn't break. No matter what, I had to make sure they were okay.

The sense of unreality deepened .Aunt Frieda was sud-denly there with me, on the floor cradling Shlomo's body. She wept silently while my mother came to comfort her.

I couldn't be hallucinating a candle flame. Everything else, that could have been my mind playing tricks on me. But I saw a new flame in the hanukiah now and surely that had to be real.

"Rachel, have you gotten through to 911 yet?" My voice was thick with tears I didn't know I was holding back.

"I'm still getting a damn busy signal," she said.

I got up, leaving my mother and aunt with the bodies of their husbands. "Keep trying. I'm going next door to see if I can get through from Bob and Diana's."

I tried to open the front door, but couldn't get it to budge. No amount of jiggling the handle or re-checking to make sure it was unlocked seemed to make any difference. I threw my shoulder against it a couple times to force it open, but the door didn't even rattle on its hinges.

"You okay?" My mom asked, ever the Jewish Mother.

"No, the door's stuck," I replied.

"Let me try the back door," she said, and she got to her feet. A moment later, I heard her cry out.

"Mom!" I sprinted from the front door to the back.

"I'm okay," she said. "I'm fine. The handle was just hot to the touch." She held out her hand. The skin on her palm was red.

"Mom, you're not fine." I looked around, taking the

scene in fully. "None of us are."

She looked at me for a moment, taking in the weight of the situation, and her shoulders slumped forward.

"What do we do?" she asked.

"We keep trying."

I could see the fatigue on my mother's face, and realized how hard everything must have been hitting her. I could still feel it creeping in around the edges of my sanity, threatening to break me down, but my mother wasn't able to stand up to it any more.

"Mom, why don't you go to the guest room and lie down," I said. "I'll figure out what's going on and we'll handle it."

"Okay," she said.

I replayed everything in my head. My father and uncle died within minutes of each other, we couldn't reach the emergency operator, and our doors wouldn't open to let us out. I knew these things were real. And if they were real, maybe everything was. Maybe I had actually seen the flame burn sideways, and the hanukiah cast a shadow that moved like tentacles. I paced, trying to make sense of it all.

Through the doorway, I saw the dining room table. The places were set, silverware neatly laid by the plates, cups set out. A plate of latkes looked old and congealed. The brisket seemed to be more gray than red or brown, like it was decaying already. And in the middle of it all sat the wrought iron hanukiah, lording over the table with its impossible flames flickering out of cups with no candles.

I didn't know what to feel or what to do about the thing, but as I stared at the flames I felt an anger rising up inside me. I grabbed the hanukiah and returned to the kitchen. I held its flames under the faucet and watched as water cascaded over the iron, making hissing noises at me. But the flames continued to burn through the stream. They didn't even flicker.

"You son of a bitch," I said as I plugged the sink and let it fill with water. Even when I held the hanukiah upside down with the cups for the candles completely submerged,

The flames still glowed.

The rage boiled over within me, and I let out a scream I didn't know I was holding in. I grabbed the hanukiah and threw it as hard as I could. It flew across the kitchen, through the doorway and into the hall, where it landed on the carpet.

Light flashed from it, and a jet of flame burst forth. The carpet caught and began to burn, a circular pool of fire forming around its top. The pool widened until it stretched the width of the hallway. I tasted ash in the air, but the flames didn't reveal charred carpet, and no smoke rose from them. Heat rippled over the pool of fire, but nothing else happened. I stared, dumbstruck, until I heard someone step into the hallway.

"Daniel?" Frieda wavered unsteadily on her feet, but she continued down the hall toward me. "Daniel, what's going on?" Her cheeks were wet with tears, and her eyes barely looked open.

"Aunt Freida, please, stay back."

The fire spread down the hallway, creeping toward me at one end and toward Aunt Freida at the other, and beyond her, Rachel and the kids. The door to the guest room was just across the hall from me, and I needed to get to my mom before it became impossible.

Freida walked toward me as though she were in some kind of trance. Her face was tranquil, but something in her expression was broken. Had she just decided to walk toward what was coming, instead of away from it? How could she do that?

How could I let her? What kind of person would I be if I didn't stop her?

"Freida, stop," I said. I dropped into a crouch, preparing to jump and tackle her.

I launched forward, aiming for the patch of hallway still left between Freida and the flames, but just as I began moving, a jet of flame shot out of the pool of fire right at my aunt. It erupted with a blast of heat strong enough that

I had to shield myself with my arms. It threw off my balance, and I hit the wall.

Freida stood in the hallway, a stream of blue-orange fire connecting her to the flames around the hanukiah. She didn't look like Hirsh or Shlomo though, there was no sense of confusion on her face. She just relaxed, every muscle suddenly hanging loose on her body, making her look small and fragile. She fell silently, with her eyes already closed.

The stream of flame retreated from her chest, back to the hanukiah.

Rachel came into the hallway behind Freida's body.

"Daniel? What was—holy shit!" her surprise shook me from my mesmerized immobility. I leaped from the kitchen into the hallway.

"Don't touch it!" I screamed at her.

She froze.

"What is it?"

"The hanukiah," I said. But I knew it was much more than just that.

Rachel looked at me with wide eyes.

"The kids," Rachel said the words quietly, unbelievably calmly, but her eyes were still wide.

Our gaze locked for a moment so short other people wouldn't have had time to blink, but in that moment we had a plan. I was going to get my mom and she was going to get the kids, and were getting the hell out of the house. She broke first and raced up the stairs.

"Kids! David! Sarah! Come out here!"

"Mom," I called. "Mom, we need to go!" I put the heat and the flame at my back and rushed to the guest room door. It was locked.

"Mom! Unlock the door, we have to get out of the house!" I heard it click and open. I didn't give my mom time to get out of the way, I pushed the door fully open and burst into the room.

"What's happening?"

"We're leaving. There's...there's a fire," I said.

She didn't need to hear another word, she was up and moving out of the room.

We'd barely cleared the doorway to the guest room when my mother stopped moving, and I collided with her.

"Mom, what are you doing?" I said. "We have to go!"

She didn't reply.

"Mom? Mom!" I shook her and tried to turn her to face me, but her shoulders were immovable. I couldn't turn her.

Standing before us on two legs hunched over like an old man except so large it filled the hallway in both height and width, was a thing taking shape in front of the hanukiah. It stared at my mother. It had the shape of a man, but it was not made of flesh. It was some kind of creature of shadow, smoke, and flame. Its face was shrouded by curls of smoke. What looked like long, stringy hair was impossibly on fire, but the fire gave no illumination to the shadowed figure within. Hints of a nose and eyes poked through, but I couldn't see anything clearly through the smoke around it.

My fear became full-blown panic. I wrapped my arms around my mother's waist and vainly tried to lift her, but whatever this thing did to make her shoulders immovable wouldn't let me.

"No," I said. "No, mom..." I tried to lift her again and again. When that failed, I tried pulling her back into me. I still couldn't move her. The burning thing in the hallway raised a hand and pointed a skeletal flaming finger at my mother.

"Fuck you!" I screamed, and I hurled myself past my mother and at the smoke shrouded thing. I tasted ash and soot on my tongue and breathed in a lung full of smoke, but hit the carpet on the far side of the creature. I rolled onto my back and stood up to try again. Before I could regain my feet, a jet of flame shot out of the thing's finger and into my mother's chest.

She gasped. Her eyes went wider than I'd ever seen human eyes go, and her hands went stiff at her sides.

The flame retreated back into the thing's hand.

My mother crumpled to the floor, her eyes still open and her face locked in a surprised, lifeless expression.

"Mom," I whimpered. Hot tears stung my cheeks.

The thing, its flaming hair swaying, turned to face me.

The heat of its gaze pushed against me. I coughed and fought for air. An unbearable sadness filled me, an icy chill that burned as badly as the heat from this creature.

"Oh my God," Rachel's voice came from behind me.

My children screamed.

The chill faded from my heart and I lurched to my feet. The heat of the thing's gaze lessened, and it sank into the pool of fire, which collapsed in on itself. The hanukiah, still lying on the carpet, sparked, and two more flames ignited. Half of the misshapen, twisted sculpture now flickered with lights that cast a mocking glow in my hallway.

"Daniel, the door!" Rachel shouted at me.

I looked over my shoulder and saw her standing in the open doorway. Whatever that infernal thing had done to lock us in, it was letting us out now.

"Go," I yelled.

All four of us ran from the house to the car. The kids jumped into the back and Rachel jumped into the driver's seat. I stopped myself at the car door.

"What's wrong?" Rachel asked. "Get in!"

"No," I said, and turned back to the house.

"Where's grandma?" David asked from the back seat.

The image of my mother collapsing to the floor with that dead look of horror on her face flashed in my mind.

"Grandma...is with grandpa," I said.

Anger roiled inside me. I didn't even get to say goodbye to her. This thing, whatever the fuck it was, had taken so much from me. As long as it still existed, it could still keep taking. All I had left now was Rachel and the kids, and I would be dead before I'd let anything happen to them.

"Stay here," I said, and ran back into the house.

The hanukiah lay on the carpet, somehow not even singed by the flames. I grabbed the thing, ignoring the slimy feeling, and ran back into the street. I threw the iron piece with as much strength as I could muster. It clattered on the asphalt, stopping in the middle of the road.

The flames still burned

I didn't know how, but I had to destroy it.

I grabbed the garden hose and pulled it with me, uncoiling it as I went, until it stopped at its maximum length a few feet shy of the sidewalk. I dropped it and ran into the road where I grabbed the hanukiah. I took it back to the lawn and wrapped the hose around the four unlit arms and tied two tight loops around the others. I dragged the hanukiah and hose to my car, then crouched down and hooked the outermost arm of the hanukiah to the underside of the car's frame. I put my foot on the bumper and leaned back, pulling as hard as I could on the hose. Scraping sounds of metal on metal came from under the car, and I kept pulling harder. I needed this to work.

"Daniel," Rachel said from the driver's seat. "What are you doing?"

She was halfway out of the car. David and Sarah were poking their heads out from the rear windows.

"Help me," I said, shifting my grip up on the hose. I grunted and turned back to the car.

Rachel picked up the hose and added her strength to mine. Together we pulled as hard as we could against the hanukiah.

When I heard the first high pitched whine of metal bending, Rachel relaxed her grip for a moment.

"No," I said. "Harder."

She grunted with renewed effort, and I put everything I had left into the strain.

"Die, you mother fucker," I said.

There was a cracking sound, and a flash of light, and Rachel and I tumbled backward onto the lawn.

We'd done it. The hanukiah came apart, the one severed arm clanged against the pavement, and the rest of it hit the grass.

My wife's eyes were bright and focused on me, sparkling with happiness.

"Ow," she said, rubbing where she'd landed. Then we both started laughing.

Daniel and Sarah came over and sat on the lawn with us.

"Is it dead?" Sarah asked.

"It's dead," I answered. I picked up the hanukiah, which no longer felt oily and dangled it in front of me. "See? No more lights. It's over."

"Where's the rest of it?" David asked.

"Under the car."

David crawled under the front of the car and fished around for the broken piece. He jumped up and held it over his head. "I got it," he shouted.

The arm of the hanukiah he held up triumphantly seemed to absorb all the light from the streetlamps.

The flame in its cup was still lit.

"Drop it!" I yelled.

David yelped and dropped the arm. When it hit the pavement, a shower of sparks erupted from its ruptured end. As the sparks hit the ground, they swarmed and writhed like tadpoles. Then they began to clump up, forming a tentacle of light that whipped back and forth, searching for the body of the hanukiah. It lay on the ground, lifeless and lightless, but the tentacle was getting closer to it.

The two parts couldn't be allowed to touch. I reached out for it, but Rachel was faster than me. She stood over me, holding the broken hanukiah. She tried to untangle the hose that was still wrapped around the four arms.

The chain of sparks rolled towards her foot, and she deftly jumped to the side, evading it.

She almost had it!

Then the sparks struck out at her like a coiled snake. Instead of biting her though, it jumped into her body. She jerked upright, her arms out at her sides.

"Daniel," she said the word through gritted teeth. She

made several large twitching movements that wracked her whole body in spasms. On the ground next to her, the broken arm of the hanukiah jumped into the air. It followed the trail of sparks towards my wife's rigid ankle.

I lurched forward and tried to grab it, but my hand went though it as easily as I'd gone through the creature earlier in the night.

David grabbed for it, and his fingers closed around the piece of metal without hesitation. He tried to pull it away.

My son and my wife were frozen in place and unable to move. David's body collided with Rachel's in a strange inorganic movement as the broken arm reconnected with the body of the hanukiah. There was another flash of light, this time accompanied by a blast of heat. I heard Sarah scream, but was too blind from the flare to see her.

"Sarah," I screamed.

"Daddy!"

"Sarah, run!" I blinked rapidly, trying to see what was happening so I could do something, anything, to save my family. But I didn't need to see to know what was happening when the taste of ash hit my tongue. I knew the thing was back. Vague shapes and colors were coming to me, and I remembered Rachel standing I front of me, and I threw myself from my position on my hands and knees into where I thought the creature was. I knew I'd pass right through it like I did before, but I thought maybe if I could knock the hanukiah loose from Rachel's hand, that I could keep it from killing them.

Hitting Rachel's legs was like throwing myself against a boulder. She was held in place by a force so strong that I just bounced off it to land on my back, staring up. Her face was on one side of me, and David's was on the other. In between the two stood the damned thing that I couldn't kill.

It looked down at me, and I could feel heat creep over my face and chest from its gaze. Then it wreathed itself in flames and vanished.

It tossed the bodies of my wife and child aside like rag dolls. The thing was done with them. It had taken what it came for. The hanukiah stood upright on the grass, with all but one of the spaces for a candle now occupied by flames.

Sarah came over and sat next to me. She didn't say anything, just leaned her head against me. We sat together and stared at the hanukiah in silence. There was one empty space left, one more flame to add before the hanukiah was full of lights.

I wished for it to be me that would be next. I wanted to save Sarah, to protect her the only way that I had left. I wanted to be with Rachel, to see David. I missed my father and mother already. That's why I wasn't able to touch the creature, but it could affect everybody else. That last flame would be Sarah. There was no way I could stop it. I put my arm around my daughter and pulled her in close to me, hugging her more fiercely than I'd ever hugged her before. She wrapped her arms around me and squeezed back.

I stared at the flame burning where the *shamash* should have been, and knew. I couldn't take her place in the hanukiah because I already had one.

An Ugly Resurrection

By The Behrg

They were back. Back for one purpose, and one purpose only: they had come to kill me.

Just like last time.

And the time before that.

I remember so little of what befalls me when they are not around. It's as if a wispy grey cloud settles over my existence, snuffing out the day to day. But I remember the murders. I remember the torture. I recall with perfect clarity their greedy eyes and hideous smiles full of missing or crooked teeth, and oh, those chants. I awaken with them ringing through my head. Like a doomsday bell, gonging to greet me, a constant reminder that yes, it can always get worse. My life, my existence, is to be their play-thing, their chew toy, to be tossed around and mutilated at their pleasure and then forgotten until I'm needed again.

Unlike what you may have heard, resurrection is no joyous occasion or cause for celebration. Resurrection is a cruel, torturous bitch.

Helplessly I watch as they abandon the streets, marching out into the fields in my direction. They even stop to hold hands. Cute, right? But then you've never had your flesh boiled off your bones while they're standing above you, singing. I know they haven't seen me—not yet, at least—but they will. They always do.

The hills are encased in snow and I drop myself into the nearest gully. Hoping. Praying. But Deliverance is a selfish god.

"Gotcha!"

I turn just in time to see mittened claws thrust two pieces of hot coal through my eye sockets.

It's begun.

The surrounding tissue sizzles and burns, pain exploding through my head. I scream in agony, backing away blinded, but more of them are already on me. Something sharp impales my skin below my eyes, breaking my nose and plastering it to my face like putty. They move the spike around, digging deeper, carving out a hollow pocket where my nose should be. Liquid runs down my face, no doubt a combination of blood and the emptying of punctured sinus cavities, and then the spike they've thrust through my face breaks through the back of my skull. The hard shell cracks and gives way, pieces of what must be bone and splintered flesh dropping to the ground behind me.

"No, no, you've gone too far," one of them shouts.

"You're ruining it—use the carrot!" another yells.

"No, here, try this."

Immediately the spike is pulled back out from my face. Swollen tissue clings to it as it's removed, making me feel as if they're not just removing a spike, but my very soul. What replaces it is cool and metallic, like a coin, mashed into the fresh wound. Fists push and pump at the flesh around it, my new deformities treated like children's clay, until it stays in place.

As my eyesight begins to return—much cloudier than before—I feel a noose wrap around my neck and I know my time is short. I've never been hung before. I wonder what it will feel like.

The creatures around me grow anxious; I hear them snapping at each other now, until one voice rises from the rest. "Make him dance!"

"Yeah, a dance!"

"Dance! Dance! Dance!"

The hyped mob mentality grows in volume and

intensity.

"Dance! Dance! Dance!"

They always want me to perform. Laugh, play, attempt a handstand. One time they decapitated me, but only after I had recited—of all things—the alphabet song, but backwards. Their warfare isn't all centered around torture and pain; much of it is psychological.

"Okay, you win, I'll dance." My words are answered with high pitched squeals, as if just the sight of me speaking is cause for excitement. "But I'll only do it up there," I say, motioning to the ridge above the gully. "It will be like a stage."

Their hungry eyes nod in agreement. As vicious as they are, they're surprisingly gullible. My movements are labored, white searing pain streaking through my skull with every step, but I manage to pull myself up to the top of the ridge. I glance back at the road behind me and my mouth drops to the floor. Sure, part of that is the fact that my face is dissolving from a combination of the coals and crude rhinoplasty they performed, but I'm sure shock has at least something to do with it. Deliverance, it seems, has finally heard my cries.

Blue and red lights spill from the top of a police cruiser, which has pulled behind a white sedan out on the road. Someone's bad day may just prove to be my salvation.

The creatures below me begin their chanting anew. "Dance! Dance! Dance!" But there will be no performance today.

"Catch me if you can, you bastards!" I bound off toward the road and my awaiting rescue.

The town square is pregnant with noise, cars honking and brakes shrieking and pedestrians deliberately ignoring one another. Behind me I hear the monsters approach, screaming with undulated delight. It's all a game to them. My life—my death—all jolly, happy fun.

Tearing over the hills of snow, I burst out onto the road. Cars swerve and I hear the unmistakable noise of a crash, but I don't bother looking back. All I can do is move forward.

And hope. And pray.

The officer catches sight of me. Whether it's my horribly disfigured face or the pack of creatures at my heels, he drops his clipboard in alarm.

"Please, help me!"

I've never been this close to breaking free from this eternal cycle of death. But instead of helping, the policeman unholsters his firearm, throwing his other hand up vertically, and yells, "Stop!"

The world around me tilts. I see it all as if I were peering down into a swirling snow globe, my mind leaping with each development, each jigsawed piece snapping in place with a frenzied finality. Children screaming, brakes shrieking, the wind snagging the scarf strung around my frozen neck. A woman drops a shopping bag on the opposite sidewalk, hands moving to her mouth. The policeman—a young inexperienced officer, now that I can see him more clearly—throws his hands in the air as if to shield himself, forgetting about the gun in his hand. The car isn't braking fast enough.

Also, it's snowing.

I brace myself for another gruesome death, wondering how far my body will fly. What my brains will look like strewn across the pavement like wet crinkled confetti. How long it will take them to scrape my remains off the slick asphalt.

When the car finally plows through me, I find I'm not propelled through the air but rather pulverized. My body breaks apart as if the very atoms holding it together suddenly decide they've had enough. I guess I know how they feel. My upper chest and head remain in place, riding on the hood for the last few feet before we finally come to a stop. The poor policeman, I think he may have wet himself.

The creatures rush the car, unaware of how close they came to joining me on my trip. Just seeing them approach, my heart picks up its pace. At least this time I wasn't melted down.

I hear them clawing and scratching at the car, until one of them wins out over the others, climbing up onto the vehicle beside me. "See you soon, Frosty," he says, reaching for the hat atop my head.

I close my eyes, knowing that when I awake, I'll be surrounded by them again. Brought back from the dead for one more trip down memory lane. A road paved with unanswered pleas and rejected prayers and enough deaths that the road should be renamed "Massacre."

In those final moments when facing death, most people are brought to tears. Some from pondering their eternal existence, or lack thereof; others from contemplating all of the missed opportunities or things they might have done; still others cry from the excruciating pain that precedes most deaths. But not me. I weep because I know I'll be back again someday.

My heart delivers its final beats. At least for this unholy go-around.

Thumpety—Thump—Thump.

The Scary Neighbor

By Ian Welke

Henry slid his right foot on the ground and squeezed the handlebars on his kickscooter, slowing to a stop on the stretch of sidewalk in front of the scary neighbor's home. His left leg wobbled as he stared up at the house.

The scary neighbor's house was the only one on the block without Christmas lights. Henry's daddy put up their lights the day after Thanksgiving along with an inflatable Santa on the front lawn. All the other houses got their lights ready before the end of that weekend. The scary neighbor still didn't have any decorations even though Christmas was next week.

The scary neighbor hated all holidays, not just Christmas. He even hated the 4th of July block party. How could anyone hate that? At the last party there was a Bouncy House across the street, hundreds of kids outside, a DJ and dancing, and, of course, the fireworks. The neighbor said fireworks were against the law, but Henry's mommy and daddy said that's a stupid law and that they don't have to follow the stupid laws. The only holiday the neighbor celebrated was Halloween, and he probably only celebrated that one because he liked the monsters.

Henry tilted his head. He couldn't tell if the scary neighbor was home. On bright sunny days, most of the other neighbors came out and talked together while the children played. The scary neighbor almost never came out of his house. Except the time he came out to yell at Henry and his friends when they were playing tag and were using the neighbor's porch as a safe zone.

Henry fought the temptation to scream as he passed the house. Maybe if his brother and sister and friends were there he'd let it loose. He exhaled when got to the next house, passed the palm trees on the parkway, and turned around.

Facing back toward his own house he saw his daddy's truck pull into the driveway. His big sister, Ann, got out of the passenger door and his little brother, Jimmy, opened the back door by himself and started crying to be picked up out of the child's seat.

His daddy lifted Jimmy up and Henry kicked faster towards his house. "Daddy!" he shouted as loud as he could and then he realized which house he was in front of. He got so distracted he didn't pay attention to the wobbling front wheel of the scooter, and he went over, slamming into the sidewalk.

He was still for a moment, not sure how hurt he was. He sat up and looked around wondering if he should cry. His daddy's back was turned as he got Jimmy out of the car. Henry started to cry, a couple soft sobs at first, but then he let it out, a loud wail that his dad was sure to hear.

"Henry? What's wrong buddy?" His daddy put Jimmy down on the ground and both came running over to where Henry sat crying.

"I was scared of the neighbor and I fell."

"Awwwww!" His father stood up straight and shouted, "But you're okay now, right buddy?"

Henry knew what his father wanted to hear so he screamed it as loud as he could. "Yes! Yes! Yeahhhhhh!"

His brother and sister joined in. "Ohhhh yeaaaaahhhh!"

His dad laughed and then hooted with his hands cupped over his face so he could hoot the loudest monkey call he could make. "Oook! Oook!" His dad added his bird screech, "Cacaw! Cacaw!" before returning to the monkey noise.

The three kids joined him and soon all four were jumping up and down all screaming "Oook! Oook!" but Henry stopped when he saw the shutter open on the neighbor's window and the neighbor staring at him.

~

Henry and the children from the block were out of school for winter break. They rode their scooters, bikes, and big wheels in a parade along the sidewalk. They went up four houses in one direction, then back while their parents talked together on Henry's lawn. Each time the children passed the scary neighbor's house they screamed. They didn't shout any words, they screamed loud as they could. It was as if shouting words couldn't be loud enough. If they screamed wordlessly, they could fill the air with shrill piercing noise.

Their parents were talking long enough that the parade, which started with just Jimmy, grew to twelve children. When his mommy and daddy first started talking with the other adults, Henry had been playing with a basketball, but the parade was more fun.

Henry made his eleventh lap and reeled back to scream when the neighbor's front door opened. Henry sped up, making sure he passed his daddy before the scary neighbor man could get to him. Instead the neighbor didn't even look at the children and walked straight to where the adults were talking.

Henry stopped his scooter waiting to see what his daddy would do. He hadn't noticed before, because the neighbor man almost never came out of his house, but the neighbor man was a lot taller than his daddy and the neighbor man looked angry.

"Could you please have your children not scream in front of my house? I'm able to drown out most of the noise with music, but the screaming... It's too loud."

Henry wondered if his daddy would beat up the neighbor man. He said before that he would. Instead his daddy nodded and swallowed and said, "Sure."

The neighbor man thanked him, and turned to leave.

Henry's daddy looked at the other adults and shrugged, then he looked back at Henry. His daddy closed his eyes and frowned. He took a deep breath and pointed at the neighbor man. "Just a minute."

The neighbor turned around.

"I noticed that you don't have any Christmas decorations. No lights. No nothing."

"I don't celebrate Christmas."

Henry didn't understand. Don't celebrate Christmas? Was that even allowed?

His daddy looked just as confused. "Can you at least put out something? To make the season more festive? You know...for the kids."

The neighbor man wouldn't even answer, he just turned his head and went back into his house.

Henry's daddy watched him go. "You kids," he said commandingly, "I want you all to shout extra loud when you pass his house."

~

The next afternoon the kids were playing on the swing set in Henry's backyard. The main bolt on the set was rusted, and each time one of them swung backwards it squeaked loudly.

Henry was on the swing on the far left. Sara and Ann were to his right. All three children swung forward in unison. The back leg of the set shuddered as they reached the end of the tether and were pulled back in the opposite arc. Squeak!

They all laughed as they lurched forward again. Henry didn't know what was funny, but once his sister and her friend started laughing, he couldn't contain himself. Squeak! Each time they went back and forth it got funnier until he couldn't breathe. Squeak! They kept swinging for another ten minutes after the girls stopped laughing.

Sara announced, "I'm bored," and she hopped off the swing.

Ann followed, and Henry, not wanting to be left out, followed his sister. The three of them joined Jimmy and his friend, Chris, and they all sat in a circle on the porch.

"What are you getting for Christmas, Sara?" Henry asked.

"I don't know. I'm hoping for a new iPad, maybe a new phone, the old one is getting...old." Her voice rose at the end of the sentence as though she were asking a question. "A dual screen DVD player. New clothes."

Jimmy said, "I hate it when I get clothes."

Sara rolled her eyes. "That's because you're a boy. My mommy says girls like to get clothes. Girls like to look good."

Henry glanced back to the neighbor's house.

Sara met his gaze when he turned back. "I know. He's so creepy. My mommy says that he's never spoken to any of the other adults on the block." Sara was in third grade and sometimes when she talked she sounded like she knew it all.

"There's something about him..." Henry realized he didn't know how to finish his own sentence.

Chris nodded furiously and looked over towards the neighbor's house on the other side of the fence like he was afraid he might be watching. "I had a nightmare with him in it. It was so scary. Just before I woke up he looked right at me and he said," Chris stopped and looked around again before scooting forward so he could talk to all of them in a whisper, "Get out of my dream, little boy. Stay away from my home and stay out of my dreams. The monsters have a taste for children like you."

A shadow loomed over them and Henry jumped with a start before he turned and looked up into his mother's face.

"What are you kids talking about?"

Henry raised his shoulders and wasn't sure why he felt like he was in trouble, but he tried to look as innocent as he could. "We were talking about the scary neighbor man."

"Henry, you can't let him get to you." His mom folded her arms. "Kids, people like that... You're going to get to know them in school. Maybe you already do, there's one in every class. They have maybe one friend, maybe none. They're different from everyone else and they don't join in on things." She tilted her head up and spoke more loudly, facing the neighbor's house like she was really trying to talk to him through his shut windows. "At the end, they're just pathetic losers, that can't be part of the group."

All of the kids laughed and clapped. Henry laughed too. His mother looked pleased and this made Henry happy. But when he looked over at the neighbor's backyard and the sliding glass doors at the back of the man's house, a chill ran over Henry and he stopped laughing.

~

Henry was in his bedroom banging on his drum. Between the beats he heard his little brother crying from the front yard. He put down his drumsticks and ran out the door.

Jimmy stood on the sidewalk in front of the scary neighbor's house, pointing up at something on the neighbor's lawn. Henry couldn't see what upset him since it was on the other side of the neighbor's tree.

Henry went to help his brother and then the shadow covered him and he saw what upset Jimmy. A monster loomed over the brothers. It was twice as big as Henry's daddy. Its skin was black and purple. It had two horns jetting out of its head and its tongue was longer than Henry's legs. In one hand it held some sort of broom, in the other a chain.

Henry hugged his brother and realized he had started to cry himself even as he realized it wasn't real. It was a big balloon just like the Frosty across the street or the Santa his daddy put out on their lawn.

His daddy came charging out of their house. He took one look at what scared Henry and his brother and said, "What the hell?" He ran up the neighbor's lawn and pounded on the door.

Henry told Jimmy, "Go back inside," but Henry stayed on the sidewalk, wanting to see what happened next.

The neighbor's door opened and the neighbor man loomed in the doorway. "Yes?"

"What the hell do you have on your lawn?"

The neighbor man took his time before answering. "You said you wanted Christmas decorations. I purchased one."

"That?" His dad whirled around and pointed at the monster. "That's a Halloween decoration."

"No, it's not. It's a Krampus. It's all part of the Christmas lore. Look it up."

Henry had never heard of this. He had heard of Santa and Rudolph and Frosty, but never a Krampus.

"Take it down. It's scaring the kids."

"Maybe I don't care."

"Maybe I should kick your ass." His dad balled his hands into fists.

Henry wasn't sure about this. His daddy was the strongest person he'd ever seen, but the other man was bigger and there was something else about him, some unknown quantity that made him the scary neighbor. Henry had gotten to know the other adults in the neighborhood and could predict how they'd act, he had no idea what the scary neighbor might do.

"You're on my porch, threatening me? You better calm down and decide if you want to go home or if you want to go to jail."

Henry's dad paused before stepping back off the porch. "Come on, Henry! We're going back inside."

~

Henry woke hearing voices chanting and echoing from the backyard. His room was dark and at first he thought he dreamt or imagined the sounds. He got up and pulled the comforter off. The air was chilly. It was hot and sunny in the afternoon, but at night it got cold and he could see his breath in the light in the room shining through his window from the motion detector his daddy put on the side of their house pointed at the neighbor's yard.

He didn't see anything from his window. He stepped into the hallway. The light was out in his parents' room. They must have been asleep. He remembered how mad his daddy got the last time he woke them in the night, and he turned the other way and headed to the living room.

There was a flickering light coming in from the sliding glass door. He pressed his face to the glass. The light glowed and flickered from the other side of the fence. Fire? He wanted to wake his daddy, but didn't want to make him mad. Not until he was sure. He opened the door and stepped outside.

The voices were clearer unmuffled by the glass. But the fire wasn't a house on fire, it was centered in a pit in the neighbor's yard. Henry put his head next to a split in the planks so that he could see.

A man in a black hood stood on the other side of the fire. By the man's height, Henry could tell that it was the scary neighbor man, but there was something different about his voice. It was deeper, more commanding and Henry didn't understand what he said. "Krampus, kommen und tun Sie Ihre Pflicht." The fire popped and a black plume of smoke rose above it.

Henry gasped. For a second he was certain that the smoke was shaped like the monster from the man's front lawn. The smoke formed horns and glowing embers eyes, and for a moment the beast in the smoke glared right at him, but then it billowed up into the night and was gone.

The neighbor's chant changed. "Biotaille dorcha, eitilt agus scrios mo naimhde!"

This time four separate pops resulted in winged creatures flying from the fire and into the sky above.

"Lua Saturni, Lua Mater, consurget enim Saturnalia!"

A log in the center of the fire exploded. The flaming

splinters and embers shot into the dark sky. An outline of a woman appeared. She reached up and her arms turned into shadows, which warped around the fire and formed tendrils that stretched over the fence and into the sky. The wind swirled and a cackling laugh echoed through the air.

The laughter was still on the wind when the neighbor raised his hands and said, "Exstingue!" and the fire went out.

Henry stepped back and knocked over a brick and it landed and cracked like a thunderclap in the quiet of the night. He got ready to run into the house, but first he turned back to see if he'd been spotted and the neighbor man was staring at him from over the fence. "Go back to bed, little boy. And if I were you I'd be very quiet for the remainder of your vacation. The Krampus is but one of the beasts I've summoned this solstice."

~

Three days later Henry and his family were driving home from Christmas Eve dinner at grandma's house, Henry didn't feel well after eating the ham. His stomach felt stretched like a balloon about to pop. He closed his eyes and tried to think about something else, terrified that he'd throw up in his daddy's truck. His daddy got very angry when someone made a mess in his truck. Just thinking about the last time tied Henry's stomach in more knots and then he couldn't help but think about the jelly fat from the ham. At least they were almost home.

When they passed the neighbor's house, Henry's dad yelled, "Whoa-ho! I told that prick to take down that monster, and he did!"

Henry's mother smacked her husband in the ribs. "Language." She nodded to the back seat with the three children.

Henry looked through the window at the neighbor's yard. The monster was gone, but the pump for it was still in the yard. Henry struggled to remember if he'd seen it since the night in the backyard when he saw its shape in the smoke of the neighbor's fire.

When they got out of the truck to go inside the house, Henry was extra quiet and he wished his brother and sister would be as well, but they started yelling just like nothing could ever go wrong.

A few of the adults from the houses across the street were mingling in the driveway between their homes.

"Having a merry Christmas Eve?" Henry's dad shouted to Sara's mother who was on her porch across the street.

"We're having a Christmas party. With all the nieces and nephews." She got a glint in her eye, and she said louder for the benefit of the kids inside the house behind her, "And Santa's coming." She looked over her shoulder grinning wildly as the kids in the house shouted for Santa.

Henry covered his ears with his hands. He was about to say that maybe they should all go inside, when he caught something out of the corner of his eye. On the sides of the houses across the street, he was sure he saw things moving in the shadows. Inky, nightmare shapes climbed the walls. He wanted to tell his daddy, but he was so scared. The shadows matched the shapes he saw emerge from the neighbor's fire. He stared at them trying to convince himself that they weren't real, but the longer he looked at it, the more he was certain he saw it, and the fear built up until it felt like an electric shock shooting through his head. Unable to stand it anymore, he ran inside his house.

It seemed far too long before his family came inside. Henry never noticed before how loud his family and their friends were when they talked to one another from across the street. Even with the door and the windows closed he could hear them, like they were inside the house with him having their conversation.

He looked out the window and he couldn't believe it. They all stood on the sidewalk directly in front of the neighbor's house, all six adults and fourteen kids. His dad shouted, "One...two...three..." And they began to sing.

"Dashing through the snow, on a one horse open sleigh..." The adults were having a hard time singing, they were laughing too hard. No one sang in key, but even Henry could tell that the song wasn't the point. They weren't trying to sing the song right, they were trying to sing it as loudly as they could.

Thunder cracked overhead. The wind blew hard enough to shake the palms, and Henry could swear that he could hear that cackling laughter on the wind again.

He ran back into the living room, sat on the couch, and turned up the volume on the television so that he couldn't hear what went on outside.

When his family came inside at last, he was relieved, but then his dad laughed, "That's got to have pissed him off. No way he didn't hear that." He stopped and turned.

Henry heard it too, even over the sound of the TV. Screaming. At first he told himself it was just the party, but he knew in his bones that something was wrong. These weren't the screams of children having fun. These were the screams of fear. He looked out his front window at the same time as his daddy.

Sara ran out of her house and across the lawn. What chased after her couldn't be real, but it was there. A beast just like the one from the neighbor's lawn. It chased after her holding a long chain in its clawed hands.

More screams came from inside the house across the street. Smoke started to rise from the home. Shadows formed tree-sized limbs and wrapped around the house. The laughter on the wind sounded like a rattlesnake's tail.

Henry's daddy went running to the front door. He turned to Henry and said, "You and your brother and sister get ready for bed, Santa will be here soon." Henry had never seen his father look that way before. The way he said, "Santa," he sounded desperate, like he couldn't stand the possibility that Santa *wasn't* coming.

"But the monsters..."

"Henry, it's nothing," his mother said, "It's just someone

playing a bad joke."

Henry wasn't sure if she was trying to convince him or herself, but he went to his bedroom that he shared with his little brother.

Jimmy was already in bed. He sat upright turning his head like he was scanning trying to pick up a signal, but the screaming had stopped and everything was quiet.

Henry put on his pajamas, listening for the sounds of his parents coming back inside. His arms and legs were covered in goosebumps. The quiet was almost worse than the screaming. With the silence it was impossible to tell what happened, and with every second he didn't hear his parents coming through the door the fear grew that they weren't coming back.

Ann opened their bedroom door without knocking and said, "There's nothing to be afraid of," but she didn't sound so sure.

Henry sat with his back against the wall and slid down to his pillows. He listened and waited for the front door to open and close again, so that he would know his mommy and daddy were back, but it never happened. Instead there was a thud and scratching on the roof.

Jimmy sat up in bed. "Santa and his reindeer!"

Henry shook his head. "No. I don't think it is." He pulled the comforter up over his face and tried to be quiet, hoping that it wasn't too late.

Footsteps shook the house, hammering the hardwood floor in the hallway.

Henry's brother and sister started to cry, but all Henry could do was pull the blanket tighter over his head and wish that they would be quiet so that the monsters wouldn't hear and come to get them this Christmas.

Santa Christ and the Xmas Miracle

By Terry M. West & Regina West

I had gotten the days from the dying old man in the nuke shelter. I had tried to scrape the cold metal shell for crumbs, and was quite surprised to find the sick old bastard. The old man didn't have much time, but he took what he had to learn me in the ways of the civilized days. He put lead in me hands and he taught me how to paint me own stories with words marked on paper. I was a young and brash hunter then, but I was curious about the time long dead. It had been his time, and the old man sorted me out on it the best he could, as me understandings of things was wild and tough back then.

The old man had also passed what he called "the calendar" on to me. He had given me the months and holidays, and I had placed them on the notepad that I had scrounged from the remains of the shelter.

Most shambled about the desert blindly, but I had a grip on the day, so time wasn't lost in me rough hands. The calendar always rolled, whether it was observed or not. And I knew when was when. The day that I found the supply hut was the 1st of a month called December in the year of 2090. The 25th of that very same month would be the birthing day of our lord, Santa Christ. It was a ritual called Xmas that had to do with killing trees and the giving of glittery things. And from all the days given to me by the old man, Xmas was me most favored.

The hunt across the sands had been skinny that day and I was happy when I put me tired vision on the hut. These supply huts were dots in the long line of nothing and they kept you pushing through the sands. I walked into the supply hut, leaving the heavy hot behind and stepping into humidity that yours had to wade and struggle through. I wasn't keen on supplies. I had everything I needed to survive in the sands. I walked over to the rickety metal shelves and brought eyes to the knacks arranged in no part of order.

The first treasure was a box of mixed colors called the cube. The colors could be swished around until solid unity was born. The next items inspected by yours were black and flexible round disks tucked tightly in square and thin boxes. Sort of like viddisks, but too large to fit into me portable viewer.

And then even happier eyes scanned me favorite items to uncover. The illie-straighted comic books. Heroes and the like, who were faster than wind and stronger than stone. There were many old and diverse things in this hut. To study and understand the items would take a large time. The collection took a whole canvas wall in the showing. The items all held secrets of the big cities fallen in the flameshower.

I had discovered many relics in me trek across the endless sands. Not much else to do, besides eat and survive. The docamints and fotograffies I've found were used as currency and had been spent to feed me belly and they had also purchased moist love for me in the trading camps. I've found some good word books, too. The classics, you know. Harold Robbins, Jackie Collins.

Scrounging rusty gold was me way of living. I pulled the past from the sands. I guess you could call me a relic seeker. Or Cleve. Because that's me name. So calls me Cleve, the Relic Seeker, yeah?

Relics are the only things of worth, in the now times. And I usually saw only a meal or a fuck as their promise. I wasn't the type to need of them. But the relics in this hut were more colorful than most I had scanned. And so many to be had. There was more than I could manage, but blind and hungry for them I was. And though relics had been me business, the ones is this here hut shined like the prize pot from the ass of a rainbow. I wanted them for me own. A vast collection like the one in this here hut could make a desert rat into a king. This museum of the dead would serve best in the vault of me kingdom. I could rule a sector with it.

A town must have collapsed near to the sandy threshold of this here hut and the mutant behind the counter had struck its vein in the sands. Lucky and blessed bastard.

I walked to the front counter, passing potted and lynched veggies. For some reason, I always felt a strange sense on me skinny flesh in these huts. It always put bumps on me.

A one-eyed Abbey-Fin sat behind the counter, going over me with his foul and lonely eye.

"What's your pleasure, soft-skin?" he asked, scritching the moss on his forearm.

The stench hit me. Abbey-Fins smell worse than week-old dead things.

"The relics, Abbey. I'll have them, yeah?"

His grim green face shook.

"Nor for sale, nor for barter," he said. "For show, them is."

I pulled the glass jar of scorpie-stingies from me pouch and danced them before his good eye.

"Meat!" he said excited-like, green drool covering his chin-moss. "Anything else you please. Nor the relics," he held on.

He probably hadn't eaten for days. A week even, maybe. Abbey-Fins depended on trekkers like yours for meat. It might be weeks or months even before another trekker comes from the sands, but he still wouldn't bid the relics fare thee well bye-bye. I could see his hungry desperation, but still he was stubborn. It made me angry and reddish.

"No relics, no meat, Abbey," I said, serious-like, stuffing the jar back in me satchel. "I finds things here that dazzles the want in me, and you tells me that ain't for trading. What kind of busy is that? It's nearly Xmas, you dim and smelly bastard."

"Xmas?" the Abbey-Fin said, staring at me with the fuzzy eye. Then he bricked back up and he wouldn't be moved. "Nor for sale, nor for barter."

I saw a large wooden hammer. It leaned against the counter. The big tool waited for a walk. I picked it up, spotting a chore for it, and it was a weighty thing. "What's this, Abbey?"

"Mallet," he said back, bobbing his head. "From a game them called croaked cat. That for barter. Give me meat, and you have mallet."

I gave him a clobber right on his mossy melon and he fell to the shaded sands.

"You teasey cunt," I tsked him, pounding him a few more times.

He bled messy red stuff from his green skin and tried to skulk away. I knew he wouldn't crawl himself outdoors, because the sun cooked them Abbey-Fins in little time.

"Nor for sale, nor for barter..." he said, dying-like.

"Oh, I give surrenders, Abbey. Have the meat, you poor green scum," I said, feeling all kinds of scary mean flashing around.

You simply must understand. I'm not a horny sadist. I'm a man. Abbey had no right hordyhogging me relics. Abbey-fins were a nature-mistake born after the flame-showers that took down the world.

I freed the scorpie-stingies, pouring them on Abbey. They stungbit his moist hide 'til he was dead and departed of this here place. I shucked him outside the tent and left him for the buzztures.

"May Santa put you on a happy cloud, Abbey," I prayed for him.

And then I settled into this here hut to sit upon me

treasures. I should be celebrated, for me vast fortune sparkles.

~

It has been twenty-four days since me last trip to the pages of this here journal. Any entries into it, after putting me roots in the sands of this here hut, would have been ones written in misery and fright. I woke up on this favored day of mine. December 25th. The day of Xmas. But I faced it hungry and scared.

I should have left this here hut at the first sign of infection. But me relics are too many to hauls across the sands. And I won't leaves them. The stay here has sickened me with the green glow. I am getting mossy, and can't stands the sun on me skin.

I scritch everywheres and I have scraped the sands in cold night for every bit I could put in me belly. I'm emptyhungry, and I now depends on trekkers to be coming to the hut. I need the meat, but they won't get me relics. They are nor for sale, nor for barter. What's mine is mine. If they wants it, they can takes it from me cold, dead and fungy green hands. I do see the funny in this and I knows some trekker will put me beneath the sands for me relics. But I don't care much.

I prayed this morn to Santa for some meat soon, for it was days gone past in the quantity of nearly 30 since last I have tasted meat to me tongue. So as I celebrated the birth of Santa Christ, emptyhungry and in a sad state, from afar I saw that two trekkers sought to settle near me threshold.

With eyes covetous, I knew they would scan me empire filled with relics. The relics, at *any* space in the calendar, grew men filled with gluttony. But me favored of days felt a more vicious one for the longing of things.

Stepping to the sand where me hut begins were they both, though I would soon discover they were not of the same to each other. A tribe independent for each man longed for their returns with traded supplies in hands.

Together through the sands they had plodded, the yellow globe above beating hot rays upon their headtops.

As they entered with the heat, me eyes magnetized toward the dried meat hanging from the pocket of one trekker; the taller of the dusty pair. Meager meats, they were, by appearance. But still they would carry me until new beginnings revealed the next meal.

They had stepped together, as if brothers. But with relics now in view, their affections grew fainter, as if suddenly. They saw and regarded me as a mutant and could not see a soft-skinned brother beneath the moss. I knew one or both would end me, for those bright relics I sat upon. Murdering is a natural and easy act in the now times with none devoted to the punishing of them who practices in it.

I spoke to them, without kindness or possibility. As known previously, the trekkers sought to possess me relics, but I stated without confusion, they were nor for sale, nor for barter.

The trekkers misunderstood me meaning to bear that only one of the two could have, but not both to own. Hate snuck up all quiet and easy and lit them. The trekkers brawled with violence intended, to be the last one to buy, the last one to barter. I wisely awaited the outcome, quiet-like. I knew perhaps, in time, I would only have one to contend with. Their fight with flesh was too even and it wasn't settling matters, so weapons were chosen.

Knives were pulled from sheaths and they were flashed around in a menacing display of chestthump. The old man in the nuke shelter had taught me the manner of the edge, before his passing to a forever hut in the cloud. The knife was the most clinched scheme of murdering. And be it recreational vice or the handling of something with a more formal flicker in it, the blade was an intimate deliverer of death and it danced in jittery and violent passions. It was a steadfast tool and the only ammunition it required was a stone to keep it sharp and keen and ready to call.

The trekkers stabbed and sliced at each other. They was hopeful to be the last to buy, last to barter me relics. At the final of it, the red was pooled along the sand tatami by the belly of the tall one and by the foretemple of the other.

I powdered what little was left in them to the clouds with me croaked cat mallet.

I took the meat from the tall one. To the gills was me gut filled with the meat, though strangely so, since such a small prize it appeared upon the belt and pocket of the tall one. Perplexing to me having only one meager dried meat that I should be so blessed and sustained on this, the old day holiday named Xmas.

The old man had told me Xmas tales. I had put me ears on the story of the haunted miser and the old man had spoken of Xmas miracles. And I understood now the special magic of the holiday spirits. I thanked Santa Christ for the Xmas feast, slight as it was, as me eyes swallowed the redness upon the sand tatami. And then I realized I had not seen the desert for the sands and I smiled, crafty-like.

There was meat enough to last. The jerky to be made from the Xmas trekkers would last me a long ways. Still I must economize and feed only the most emptiest of hungries. The meats might last me to next Xmas, if I expanse it just right. I shall button up me canvas castle for privacy and hibernates in the heat.

This journal is on its last page, and I have filled all of the others. Maybe I will trade eventually for more bare pieces of the page, and we can speaks again. I now leaves this here notepad and I also leaves me calendar among me treasures. I no longer need notation of it, for the calendar is with me on the inside, and each day is praised. Maybe me words will be found and understood and the calendar can steer the time again, if there is anyone besides the faithless mutants outtheres in the dangerous heat that would like to be learned of the days. And remember this well, me friends: the calendar always rolls, and it continues to rub you slowly from its skin as it does so.

And after the reading of the Xmas miracle in this here hut, don't you dares ever tell me there is no Santa Christ! Merry Xmas!

Winter Witch

By Ashley Dioses

In crystal towers lit by silver moons,
The winter witch invokes the Holly King.
Into the world, she casts with ancient runes
A velvet darkness from which he will spring.

She shuns the sun the Oak King conjures now,
And exiles him to the abyss beyond.
She bleeds the flesh of her silk wrist in vow
To fell the sun above and seal the bond.

The Fifty-Eighth Item

By Kathryn McGee

Someone had added a holiday wreath to the front door of the cabin, and Margaret thought it was a nice touch. She'd come to appreciate every unnecessary item, every bit of warmth she encountered, since she no longer had knick-knacks or personal belongings of her own. It had been Jed's idea to get rid of all their earthly possessions and spend the year traveling.

"This way we can figure out what really matters."

That's what he'd told her.

They'd been in bed one Christmas Eve ago, surrounded by gift boxes, tissue paper, ribbons, and bows. He'd been running thick fingers across her smooth skin. He'd been looking her in the eyes, and in that moment, she'd loved the idea of boiling away all the extra stuff. All the stuff that was holding them back. She'd agreed to the change. *Yes, she'd thought. Who really needs all those clothes? Who needs the books, the shoes—the junk? Maybe this is how we can figure out what really* does *matter.* They made love for a long time, sending all the giftwrap raining down onto the floor. After Christmas they'd made the change.

And for the most part, the choice to throw away, recycle, and sell had been the right one. Margaret and Jed had amassed a dizzying collection of stuff in their first few years of marriage. Finally, after an intense month of decluttering, they'd reduced the number of items they owned from what felt like ten million down to just fifty-seven.

Just fifty-seven things.

And those were the things they'd taken with them into what Jed called their *new life*, the start of which began with a one-year journey around the world. One whole year without the confines of too many items.

Margaret stood in front of the remote cabin they'd rented for the Christmas holiday, surrounded by snow. Her fingertips played at the edges of the wreath on the door.

"There's red and white garland woven in," she commented. "Like the kind my mom used to use." After a year without anything extra, she felt a thrill at the luxury of holiday decorations. They'd been living in sparse environments while traveling, and the idea of Christmas in a simple, rented cabin—without decorations—had been weighing on her. But maybe there would be something more inside. She told herself not to get too excited, though. A cool breeze rushed by, a few snowflakes patted her face. She opened the door.

"Would you look at that?" Jed said.

Margaret moved past Jed, over the threshold, and dropped her backpack, which held her half of the fifty-seven items, onto the floor.

She stared.

Every surface in the cabin glittered with a silvery, iridescent sheen, and it took a moment for Margaret to realize it was not the walls themselves that shined, but an intricate web of Christmas decorations. She was overcome by the grandeur of the display and walked further inside.

"Oh!" was all she could manage to utter. "Oh, Jed!" She ran toward the fireplace, hung with stockings, and sat on the brick hearth, tucking her knees against her chest, posing there while she attempted to take it all in.

"Looks like a department store in here," Jed commented. Margaret watched him drop his bag onto the floor.

"Don't you love it?" she said. Her eyes moved from the coffee table, decorated with crystal bowls of gold and silver ornaments, to the metallic garland that floated across the ceiling, to the wide, tinsel-hung tree that erupted from the floor. "Isn't the tree amazing?"

"It's certainly ostentatious," Jed said. "Large enough to hide behind."

"You don't seem excited."

"It's just," Jed started, "this was supposed to conclude our year without stuff. It was supposed to be a light Christmas to show us we don't need all these things." Margaret watched Jed gesture ridiculously at the decorations, as if they were insects on the walls.

"What does it matter?" she said. "We don't own them. We won't take them with us!" She felt her nails dig into the grout between the bricks of the fireplace.

Jed eyed her curiously and made several attempts to remind her of the incredible moments their new lifestyle had afforded them over the past year, like hiking the Swiss Alps and cave diving in Europe.

"Didn't you love the zipline through that jungle in Vietnam?" he asked. "You screamed your head off the whole way!"

"Yes, of course," Margaret replied, and draped her body across the sofa. "But isn't there something wonderful about being surrounded by decorations on Christmas Eve?" she said. "You have to admit, it's nice to be in the holiday spirit, isn't it?" She stared up at the garland above her. "Doesn't it just feel *right?*"

"Sure. I suppose so," Jed said, his eyes on the tree. "It's just weird. The owner didn't even give us keys for the place. There's no lock on the door. Probably because it's so damn isolated. Why would he bother to decorate?" Jed was looking around the room, shaking his head. "The whole situation makes me uncomfortable."

"Is mister let's-go-base-jumping-everywhere feeling afraid?" Margaret threw him a teasing wink.

"I'm just not sure now how I feel about staying in a place that doesn't even have keys for the front door. Anyone could have been inside. We're lucky there wasn't some creepy dude waiting to clock us with a snow shovel."

Margaret sighed. "I'm sure the place is fine. It's not like someone will come in while we're sleeping. Who else is out here? We're twenty miles from the nearest paved road. And good luck finding that in the dead of night."

"True, true." Jed nodded, eyeing the way the tinsel on the tree hung in jagged stripes. Outside, the breeze picked up and the roof rattled. "Still, though. Something's off, isn't it?"

"That guy we rented from had a ton of solid online ratings. Five stars. Plus it's late in the day. We can't go somewhere else. Not now." Margaret laughed softly. "I'm not worried."

"Strange how there are no windows in the entire place," Jed commented. "I suppose that's just as well."

Margaret shrugged and said nothing. She watched Jed standing inside the threshold of the open door, gazing west. The sun peaked through a blanket of clouds and started to set over the white landscape. Snow fell softly. It was a perfect, wintery Christmas Eve.

This makes me miss opening presents, Margaret wanted to say, longing for the first time in a year for a pile of useless sweaters, board games, and toys to fawn over and wrap in brightly colored paper. She wondered how her family and friends were faring back home, with their own piles of junk, holiday music on repeat, and glasses clinking as they all laughed together and tore open gifts.

"Come over here a second," Jed said. "You've got to see this sunset." Margaret rose from the sofa, and nestled in Jed's open arm. They stood together inside the doorway.

"It really is lovely." She felt a rush of emotion as she thought about all of the glorious sunsets they'd seen all over the world. Maybe gifts aren't important, she thought. Sure, they'd given up a lot, but think of what they'd been able to see and do. More than most people would in an entire lifetime. "What a year it's been!" She said and pressed her lips against the cool skin of Jed's cheek.

Jed moved onto the porch, letting snowflakes tap his face.

"Snow's falling harder!"

"Incredible!" Margaret said and backed away. She went deeper inside the cabin. It was a simple A-frame, with living area, kitchen, and bathroom downstairs, and sleeping loft in the back. She took the ladder up into the loft, where she found a queen-size bed, and stretched her body across. *I miss having my own bed,* she thought, and pictured the California King she and Jed had given away. It had had pillow top mattress and in the winter they'd used a thick comforter with a green and yellow duvet.

"The sun's down. It's officially Christmas Eve!" Jed announced from the porch, and walked back into the cabin. "Who wants some hot chocolate?"

"Me!" Margaret replied, though her voice sounded far away, she barely recognized it. Her thoughts were somewhere else. Maybe she was still imagining their former life. The way the slanted wood ceiling formed a triangular shape around her reminded her of the breakfast nook they'd had back home, how she used to stretch across the built-in bench and read.

Somewhere downstairs, in the distance, Jed was rummaging through cupboards and clinking pots and pans, and Margaret was staring up at the ceiling and thinking about her old house, her old friends, *her old bed.* She touched the wall nearby, closed her eyes, and wished she could go back, back to the time when Jed spoiled her with not just his attention, but *things* as well. Things weren't really so bad, were they? Couldn't things carry meaning? Margaret didn't regret the adventures of the past year, but felt nervous about the future. She wanted to return to the way life had been. The way it was supposed to be. She was still touching the wall and slowly felt her fingertips start to vibrate, as if the wall were charged, or in motion. Jed was calling for her. *Margaret! Margaret!* She could hear his voice, but it was so distant. *I'll listen to him in a minute,* she thought and felt caught up in a dream state.

Then she watched the ceiling above her change.

A small item slipped out from between the crevices in the wood boards. *What is that? What is happening?* Margaret wanted to ask, but was mesmerized, unable to move, unable to stop watching. The item moved slowly down toward her, drifting in the vibrating air. It was a wrapped box. *A gift!* Margaret thought. *Jed, it's an actual present!* she wanted to say. *It's an actual thing!* But she couldn't will herself to speak. She could see the ceiling and the walls around her undulating, as if the whole cabin were breathing. *My god, Jed,* she wanted to say. *There's something wrong here. We've got to leave!* But before she could call out for help or say anything, the box had come all the way down from the ceiling and was in her hands. The texture of the giftwrap was smooth like silk.

She watched her fingers slipping across the paper, carefully untying the bow. *Jed, this isn't right!* she thought again, but the cautionary voice was quieter now, nearly gone. Inside the box was red tissue paper and she pulled it apart, and inside found the gift. She held the item in her hand.

A key. A beautifully crafted brass key.

She stared at it in wonder.

"Margaret, what are you doing up there? I'm coming up after you!" Jed's playful voice broke through. Margaret stared at the giftwrap in her lap and fingered the exquisite key. *A fifty-eighth item,* she realized. *Jed will never let me keep it.* His footsteps were already heavy on the ladder.

"Fi-fi-fo-fum!" Jed's voice boomed.

His head would be popping up above the loft railing any moment. Margaret whimpered, holding the thing she so badly wanted to keep in her palm, and in the final second before Jed reached the top of the ladder, she placed the key on her tongue and swallowed.

Jed emerged from below, hoisting one leg over the railing into the loft and then another. "I've found you, my pretty!"

Margaret wanted to scream. She made a quick

movement with her hands, hoping to brush the giftwrap aside so Jed wouldn't see it, but the giftwrap was already gone, as if it had never been there, at all. She felt scraping in her esophagus that caused her to cough several times. *There weren't supposed to be any presents at all this year,* a voice called out inside her head. Or had the voice come from the walls?

"Hey, are you okay?" Jed said, looking concerned.

"It's nothing," Margaret said. "Just thinking, is all." *How strange,* she thought, and coughed several more times. *Maybe I need to step outside and get some air.*

"Merry Christmas." Jed kissed her softly and gave her a hug.

Our first Christmas without gifts, Margaret thought, and Jed held his body tighter against hers. Jed had never been particularly good at figuring out what she wanted gift-wise, anyway. His presents were always useful and never sentimental. There was never a card or note attached. With as much passion as she could muster, she returned his embrace.

An hour or so later the two were in the kitchenette, heating water. Jed had pulled the stainless steel thermos from his backpack. *Item thirteen,* Margaret thought, staring at the thermos, which had been very necessary on their travels. After the great culling of their items, the thermos provided the only cup that remained, and was officially known as item thirteen of fifty-seven.

"Time for some hot chocolate?" Jed said enthusiastically and Margaret smiled. *Finally he's in the mood for holiday spirit.* She opened the cupboard over the stove, revealing a stockpile of holiday mugs—thick ceramic ones in all different colors, patterns, and designs. Some of them were bright red and green plaid, others sparking and metallic, others the restrained color of cold white snow.

"Look at all this!" she said.

Jed chortled. "Looks like a lot of the old junk we got rid of."

Margaret was forced to recall the painful memory of getting rid of every sentimental item she had ever owned. The Snoopy mug she'd had since she was ten, the three copper mugs that had belonged to her father, and all those plastic insulated cups she'd collected at gas stations in high school. She still remembered the way she felt putting those items in boxes, watching Jed haul them away.

"These are all just things."

That's what Jed had told her.

And he'd probably been right, but she still felt a cramp in her stomach. When the pain subsided, she selected two of the prettiest mugs from the cabinet, and set them on the counter.

"I'll stick to this one," Jed said, motioning toward the stainless steel mug he had unscrewed from the top of the thermos.

"Whatever you say."

With a fire burning in the fireplace, Margaret and Jed settled on the sofa, wrapped in red and green patchwork quilts that had come with the cabin, while sipping their drinks. Margaret had chosen a red mug adorned with a graphic of Santa Claus slipping feet-first down a chimney. She and Jed exchanged stories of their trip, talking about what would be next for them.

"I suppose it's time we go back home," Margaret said, imagining them renting a house in their old neighborhood, surrounded by their old friends, and settling back into a normal life. "Our life is right where we left it, I'm sure."

Jed eyed her reluctantly. "I can't help but wonder," he started, and Margaret stared at him. She had some sense of what he was going to say next. "I can't help but wonder... what if we just kept going? What if we traveled for another year, or maybe forever?" His face was lit up, filled with expectation. *Let's do this together. Let's change our lives.*

The wind picked up outside and rattled the walls.

"I don't know," Margaret said, and watched Jed's whole face fall at once. She gripped the edge of the quilt with one hand and the Santa Claus mug with the other. "Jed, I just don't—"

"Think about it," he said. "We don't have to decide tonight." She swallowed and nodded, feeling pain in her stomach again. She hoped she wasn't getting sick. *It's just nerves,* she decided, and sipped the rest of her hot chocolate. But the whole time she kept thinking, *Could I really do this again? Another year on the road without any space or possessions to touch and call my own? Another year like this?*

Margaret had to force herself to make love to Jed that night, using practiced moans to get through the process without him knowing how detached she felt. The whole time she was staring up at a small crack in the ceiling, for some reason wondering if the ceiling had answers. Jed thrust in her hard and she felt like she'd be sick. "Yes!" she said, encouraging him, her eyes still trained on the ceiling. "Faster. Please, come faster."

After, Jed had no trouble falling asleep, but Margaret couldn't have been more awake. She was thinking about their future—about what *really mattered*—lying on her side, turned away from Jed toward one of the cabin walls. She reached out and touched the lacquered boards with her fingertips. She liked the way they felt, and suddenly sensed desire stirring in her—the same sort she'd been trying to conjure with Jed. She was running the palm of her hand across the boards, slowly, lovingly, when downstairs the front door of the cabin flew open. Cold air and snow rushed into the space.

Margaret and Jed sat up in bed simultaneously, looking at each other.

"What happened?" Margaret whispered.

"Must have just been the wind." Jed eyed the open door. "That door doesn't lock."

Margaret and Jed inched toward the foot of the bed and peered over the railing of the loft. There was a loud whooshing noise as another strong breeze rushed through the cabin. Margaret glanced around the room, surveying the damage.

"We've got to close the door before the snow messes up all the decorations."

"I'm more concerned about hypothermia than decorations," Jed said and climbed down the ladder.

Margaret inched closer to the railing and watched him move for the door. She felt her stomach throb again, this time with a strong wave of nausea.

Jed slipped his shoes on and stepped out onto the porch, out of her line of sight.

"Strange," he called over his shoulder. "The wind really isn't even that strong out here—not strong enough to blow the door open."

"Well, apparently it is," Margaret said, clutching her stomach, nausea brewing even more.

"It sure is cold out here." Jed paused. "Getting colder, I think."

Margaret was about to say something back to him, when she doubled over, dry heaving onto the floor of the loft. Cold air rushed through the cabin again, and she heaved a second time. This time an object traveled up her throat, blocking her airway. She choked and in a panic heaved one final time, and spat the object onto the floor. *The key.*

She held it in her hand and stared a long moment. She had a brief flash of a memory, lying on her back in the loft earlier, mouth open, but pushed that thought aside. She set the key next to her and gripped the railing, as if that would bring an answer.

The head of a man was suddenly at the bottom of the ladder. She nearly screamed and then realized the head belonged to Jed, who had already shut the front door and come back inside.

"You okay?" he said, looking up at her as he made the climb.

"Yeah, yeah, I'm fine." She eyed the key on the floor of the loft nearby, and pushed it under the edge of the bed.

Why am I hiding it? she wondered, and heard a pleasant humming in the air. It was a sound that reminded her of Christmas carols, of bells. There was the feeling of a soft vibration that followed, and she decided she'd worry about the key tomorrow.

Jed crawled into bed and held his arms open for her. She curled her body next to his and fell asleep, dreaming of the Christmas the year before, of their old house, with all its wreaths and ornaments, and flashing holiday lights.

It was an hour or so later that she woke, shivering. Jed had turned away from her in sleep, and the cabin had grown so cold. The fire must have gone out. Jed hadn't seemed to notice, and was sleeping soundly, so Margaret crept down the ladder on her own to check the fireplace.

She was surprised to find the fire still burning. It was much warmer and more pleasant downstairs, and Margaret wrapped her shoulders in one of the holiday quilts and bathed in the heat of the flames. She could hear the wind howling louder outside, and the flakes of snow tapping the walls and roof as they fell. *How pleasant,* she thought and gazed around the room at all of the various small items—the decorations—that together contributed to the wonderfully festive feel of the cabin.

It was then she noticed a small pile of silver gift boxes and gift bags that had appeared under the tree. She felt an instant sense of excitement that the *old Jed* still existed, that he hadn't forgotten Christmas. *He's snuck presents for me under the tree!* she thought. Unable to help herself, she knelt down beside the packages, and started to pull at their ribbons.

The front door flew open violently, and for a second time a heavy gust of wind flooded the cabin, this time putting out the fire and light, filling the interior with an instant freeze.

"Margaret?" Jed yelled from up high in the loft. Margaret couldn't see Jed in the darkness, though, and didn't say anything. "Margaret?" The wind was howling and the front door banged hard against the wall inside the cabin, making the floor shake and the Christmas tree wobble. *The wind is hurting the tree!* Margaret thought, and brought her hand up to cover her mouth. She scrambled to move against the wall, behind the tree, away from the cold.

"Margaret?" Jed was yelling over the howling wind.

He'll be mad at me for opening the presents, Margaret realized. *He might even change his mind about giving them to me.* She remained quiet, covering herself in the holiday quilt and tucking the gifts safely away, hiding in the shadows behind the tree.

She could hear Jed tramping all over across the wood floor of the cabin, putting on his shoes, walking out onto the porch. "Margaret?" he was calling her name into the wind.

How romantic, Margaret thought. *First the gifts and now this. Sending my name into the cool, night sky. One of his* giftless gifts. *How perfectly sweet.* The room grew colder and she could hear Jed pacing across the porch. *Margaret! Margaret!* He was chanting her name, offering it like music.

The door banged hard against the inside wall of the house one more time, sending the wreath that had been so carefully hung with red and white garland crashing to the floor. The humming sounded again and Margaret stared sadly at the fallen wreath. The wind howled. There would be more destruction to the wreath if she didn't do something.

Margaret rushed toward the front door and pushed it shut. She was surprised to look down and see the key in her hand, and to realize she must have been holding it this whole time. She hadn't seen a lock on the door before, but there one was there now, so she fitted the key into it and turned. She was able to lock out the howling wind and keep the wreath safely inside.

There was some pounding that followed, banging on the door and the walls, and for much of the night the wind sounded shrill like a yell or series of screams. *Margaret! Margaret!* Jed had preserved the sound of her name in the wind, and the sound kept coming back, like a song, swirling around the cabin. The perfect *giftless gift.*

The humming inside the cabin grew loud, but not too loud, muffling most of the outside noise. Margaret relit the fire and curled up on the floor by the tree, wrapped in all of the holiday quilts at once, determined to enjoy a peaceful Christmas Eve. She felt vaguely concerned again, worrying she'd suffered from a lapse in memory. Had she sleep-walked down the ladder and into the living area? Should she wake Jed and ask? No, she'd let him sleep. She'd wait where she was by the tree, listening to the singing of the wind and the way the inside of the cabin hummed like a holiday carol.

Eventually, the muffled pounding on the walls ceased, and the humming inside faded too. Margaret barely noticed the change. She'd been busying herself with the presents under the tree, couldn't take her eyes or hands off the packages, which continually multiplied. She gave into temptation, plucked one box off the floor, and tore it open.

Inside was the picture frame that had once hung above their mantle, with a photo of her parents on their wedding day. The photo had been among those she and Jed had scanned and thrown away. Seeing it again was like meeting with an old friend; she clutched it to her chest and cried. She opened another box and found inside her senior high school yearbook with all of its handwritten messages from her friends inside. Then there was the collection of old t-shirts she'd bought at concerts over the years. The glass tumbler from which her father had sipped Scotch. The plastic bag filled with headbands and hair ties she'd had since she was nine. Tears were streaming down her face when she opened the box of old greeting cards and letters. She wondered if she'd have time to sit where she was and read them all that night. And then she saw the VHS tapes of childhood birthdays. The collection of old high heels and winter coats that she loved to look at and touch, even though she'd rarely ever worn any of them. And then there was an abundance of wonderful new items—perfectly shiny, smooth, soft. Purses, books, scarves, makeup, boots!

And for every gift she opened, there was another bow to untie, another silver or gold box to unwrap, and then another and another, and inside each one was another item to remember and cherish—another possibility. The treasures went on, surrounding her in a pile that grew high. So, so incredibly high. Her fingers worked quickly, but could never keep up with the multiplying supply, and she felt such excitement about all the never-ending possibility. *Jed,* she couldn't wait to say. *We can't travel another year. We've got all these great things now, so many reasons to stay in one place!* And when she finally fell asleep, it was amidst all her precious things and with big dreams about their future.

When the sun rose Christmas morning, Margaret woke in a cramped position on the cold wood floor. The decorations were gone and she was surrounded by the decrepit interior of a dirty cabin with empty walls and an unadorned ceiling. The rotted wood floor creaked when she sat up and she swatted a spider web from the air in front of her face. *What a beautiful place,* she thought, and sat up, still imagining the embellishments from the night before. The air hummed softly.

She looked at the floor around her and for a moment she saw the rotted old boards and gasped, horrified. But then she realized the rotted wood wasn't really there; in its place was the pile of giftwrap she had torn apart. She thought about how there would be so many wonderful ways to use the presents she had received. She and Jed could go back to their old way of being. Their original way. Finally they could use as many items as they needed. Finally they could behave like humans. They could be happy again. She thought, *Jed, I can't wait!*

She was using her hands to scoop imagined wrapping paper off the floor, pouring the shreds of silver bows and gold ribbon over herself in a make-believe metallic waterfall. She did this several times and felt a pang of worry, but scooped the giftwrap anyway. *Giftwrap that glistens,* she thought, and the humming moved all around her. It whispered in her ear about the gifts, preoccupying her with numbers, a count of how many presents there had been. *Fifty-nine. Sixty. Sixty-one. Seventy-one. Eighty-one. Ninety-eight. One-hundred-and—*

She lost count. She'd need to add them up again.

"Where did you hide my presents?" she called, but Jed didn't respond. She mounted the ladder to the sleeping loft and found the bed empty. She'd have to check for him outside.

The front door, without a lock, swung open easily.

Jed was on the porch curled like a shrimp. Margaret crouched down to get a better view. There was a faraway, immobile look in his open eyes. "Why don't you tell me where the presents are?" she asked and pressed her hands against the icy-cold flesh of his cheek. "Come on, now." She poked him playfully, but he did not respond. She poked a few more times. Dread wrapped its hands around her heart, but that humming noise came again, pouring out from the cabin and surrounding her like mist, soothing her from ankles to head. She heard holiday songs, the rustling of tissue paper and gift bags, the clinking of bells. Smiling, she retreated toward the door. Before she retreated back inside she thought she heard her name—*Margaret*—but it was only the wind.

If it is true that you are what you read, then it is even more true that you are what you write.

...And Eight Rabid Pigs

By David Gerrold

When I first became aware of Steven Dhor, he was talking about Christmas. Again.

He hated Christmas—in particular, the enforcement of bliss. "Don't be a scrooge. Don't be a Grinch. Don't be a Satan Claus taking away other people's happiness." That's what his mother used to say to him, and twenty years later, he was still angry.

There were a bunch of them sitting around the bar, writers mostly, but a few hangers-on and fringies, sucking up space and savoring the wittiness of the conversation. Bread Bryan loomed all tall and spindly like a frontier town undertaker. Railroad Martin perched like a disgruntled Buddha—he wore the official Railroad Martin uniform, T-shirt, jeans and pot belly. George Finger was between wives and illnesses, he was enjoying just being alive. Goodman Hallmouth pushed by, snapping at bystanders and demanding to know where Harold Parnell had gone; he was going to punch him in the kneecap.

"Have a nice day, Goodman," someone called.

"Don't tell me to have a nice day," he snarled back. "I'll have any damn kind of a day I want."

"See—" said Dhor, nodding at Hallmouth as he savaged his way out again. "That's honest, at least. Goodman might not fit our pictures of the polite way to behave, but at least he doesn't bury us in another layer of dishonest treacle."

"Yep, Goodman only sells honest treacle," said Railroad Martin.

"Where do you get lie-detector tests for treacle?" Bread Bryan asked, absolutely deadpan.

"There's gotta be a story in that—" mused George Finger.

"—but I just can't put my *finger* on it," said one of the nameless fringies. This was followed by a nanosecond of annoyed silence. Somebody else would have to explain to the fringie that a) that joke was older than God, b) it hadn't been that funny the first time it had been told, and c) he didn't have the right to tell it. Without looking up, Bread Bryan simply said, "That's one."

Steven Dhor said, "You want to know about treacle? Christmas is treacle. It starts the day after Halloween. You get two months of it. It's an avalanche of sugar and bull-shit. I suppose they figure that if they put enough sugar into the recipe, you won't notice the taste of the bullshit."

"Don't mince words, Stevie. Tell us what you really think."

"Okay, I will." Dhor had abruptly caught fire. His eyes were blazing. "Christmas—at least the way we celebrate it—is a perversion. It's not a holiday; it's a brainwashing." That's when I started paying *real* attention.

"Every time you see a picture of Santa Claus," Dhor said, "you're being indoctrinated into the Christian ethic. If you're good, you get a reward, a present; if you're bad, you get a lump of coal. One day, you figure it out; you say, hey—Santa Claus is really mommy and daddy. And when you tell them you figured it out, what do they do? They tell you about God. If you're good, you get to go to heaven; if you're bad, you go to hell. Dying isn't anything to be afraid of, it's just another form of Christmas. And Santa Claus is God—the only difference is that at least, Santa gives you something tangible. But if there ain't no Santa, then why should we believe in God either?"

Bread Bryan considered Dhor's words dispassion-ately. Bread Bryan considered everything dispassionately. Despite his nickname, even yeast couldn't make him rise. Railroad Martin swirled his beer around in his glass; he didn't like being upstaged by someone else's anger—even when it was anger as good as this. George Finger, on the other hand, was delighted with the effrontery of the idea.

"But wait—this is the nasty part. We've taken God out of Christmas. You can't put up angels anymore, nor a cross, nor even a crèche. No religious symbols of any kind, because even though everything closes down on Christmas day, we still have to pretend it's a non-secular celebration. So, the only decorations you can put up are Santa Claus, reindeer, snowmen, and elves. We've replaced the actual holiday with a third-generation derivation, including its own pantheon of saints and demons: Rudolph, Frosty, George Bailey, Scrooge, and the Grinch—Santa Claus is not only most people's first experience of God," Dhor continued, "it's now their *only* experience of God."

Dhor was warming to his subject. Clearly this was not a casual thought for him. He'd been stewing this over for some time. He began describing how the country had become economically addicted to Christmas. "We've turned it into a capitalist feeding frenzy—so much so that some retailers depend on Christmas for fifty percent of their annual business. I think we should all "Just Say No to Christmas." Or at least—for God's sake—remember whose birthday it is and celebrate it appropriately, by doing things to feed the poor and heal the sick."

A couple of the fringies began applauding then, but Dhor just looked across at them with a sour expression on his face. "Don't applaud," he said. "Just do it."

"Do you?" someone challenged him. "How do you celebrate Christmas?"

"I don't give presents," Dhor finally admitted. "I take the money I would normally spend on presents and give it to the Necessities of Life Program of the AIDS Project of Los Angeles. It's more in keeping with the spirit." That brought another uncomfortable silence. It's one thing to do the performance of saint—most writers are pretty good at it—but when you catch one actually *doing* something unselfish and noteworthy, well...it's pretty damned embarrassing for everyone involved.

Fortunately, Dhor was too much in command of the situation to let the awkward moment lie there unmolested. He trampled it quickly. "The thing is, I don't see any way to stop the avalanche of bullshit. The best we can do is ride it."

"How?" George Finger asked.

"Simple. By adding a new piece to the mythology—a new saint in the pantheon. *Satan Claus.*" There was that name again. Dhor lowered his voice. "See, if Santa Claus is really another expression of God, then there has to be an equally powerful expression of the Devil too. There has to be a balance."

"Satan Claus..." Bread Bryan considered the thought. "Mm. He must be the fellow who visited my house last year. He didn't give me anything I wanted. And I could have used the coal too. It gets *cold* in Wyoming."

"No. Satan Claus doesn't work that way," said Dhor. "He doesn't give things. He takes them away. The suicide rate goes up around Christmastime. That's no accident. That's Satan Claus. He comes and takes your soul straight to hell."

Then Railroad Martin added a wry thought— "He drives a black sleigh and he lands in your basement."

—and then they were all doing it.

"The sleigh is drawn by eight rabid pigs—big ugly razorbacks," said Dhor. "They have iridescent red eyes, which burn like smoldering embers—they *are* embers, carved right out of the floor of hell. Late at night, as you're lying all alone in your cold, cold bed, you can hear them snuffling and snorting in the ground beneath your house. Their hooves are polished black ebony, and they carve up the ground like knives."

Dhor was creating a legend while his audience sat and listened enraptured. He held up his hands as if outlining the screen on which he was about to paint the rest of his picture. The group fell silent. I had to admire him, in spite of myself. He lowered his voice to a melodramatic stage-whisper, "Satan Claus travels underground through dark rumbling passages filled with rats and ghouls. He carries a long black whip, and he stands in the front of the sleigh, whipping the pigs until the blood streams from their backs. Their screams are the despairing sounds of the eternally tormented."

"And he's dressed all in black," suggested Bread Bryan. "Black leather. With silver buckles and studs and rivets."

"Oh, hell," said George Finger. *"Everybody* dresses like that in my neighborhood."

"Yes, black leather," agreed Martin, ignoring the aside. "But it's made from the skins of reindeer."

"Whales," said Bryan. "Baby whales."

Dhor shook his head. "The leather is made from the skins of those whose souls he's taken. He strips it off their bodies before he lets them die. The skins are dyed black with the sins of the owners, and trimmed with red-dyed rat fur. Satan Claus has long gray hair, all shaggy and dirty and matted; and he has a long gray beard, equally dirty. There are crawly things living in his hair and beard. And his skin is leprous and covered with pustules and running sores. His features are deformed and misshapen. His nose is a bulbous monstrosity, swollen and purple. His lips are blue and his breath smells like the grave. His fingernails are black with filth, but they're as sharp as diamonds. He can claw up through the floor to yank you down into his demonic realm."

"Wow," said Bread Bryan. "I'm moving up to the second floor."

The cluster of listeners shuddered at Dhor's vivid description. It was suddenly a little too heavy for the spirit of the conversation. A couple of them tried to make jokes, but they fell embarrassingly flat.

Finally, George Finger laughed gently and said, "I think you've made him out to be too threatening, Steve. For most of us, Satan Claus just takes our presents away and leaves changeling presents instead."

"Ahh," said Railroad. "That explains why I never get anything I want."

"How can you say that? You get T-shirts every year," said Bread.

"Yes, but I always want a tuxedo."

After the laughter died down, George said, "The changeling presents are made by the satanic elves, of course."

"Right," said Dhor. He picked up on it immediately. "All year long, the satanic elves work in their secret laboratories underneath the South Pole, creating the most horrendous ungifts they can think of. Satan Claus whips them unmercifully with a cat-o'-nine-tails; he screams at them and beats them and torments them endlessly. The ones who don't work hard enough, he tosses into the pit of eternal fire. The rest of them work like little demons—of course they do; that's what they are—to manufacture all manner of curses and spells and hexes. All the bad luck that you get every year—it comes straight from hell, a gift from Satan Claus himself." Dhor cackled wickedly, an impish burst of glee, and everybody laughed with him.

But he was on a roll. He'd caught fire with this idea and was beginning to build on it now. "The terrible black sleigh isn't a sleigh as much as it's a hearse. And it's filled with bulging sacks filled with bad luck of all kinds. Illnesses, miscarriages, strokes, cancers, viruses, flu germs, birth defects, curses of all kinds. Little things like broken bones and upset stomachs. Big things like impotence, frigidity, sterility. Parkinson's disease, cerebral palsy, multiple sclerosis, encephalitis, everything that stops you from enjoying life."

"I think you're onto something," said Railroad. "I catch the flu right after Christmas, every year. I haven't been to a New Year's party in four years. At least now I have someone to blame."

Dhor nodded and explained, "Satan Claus knows if you've been bad or good—if you've been bad in any way, he comes and takes a little more joy out of your life, makes it harder for you to want to be good. Just as Santa is your first contact with God, Satan Claus is your first experience of evil. Satan Claus is the devil's revenge on Christmas. He's the turd in the punch bowl. He's the tantrum at the party. He's the birthday-spoiler. I think we're telling our children only half the story. It's not enough to tell them that Santa will be good to them. We have to let them know who's planning to be bad to them."

For a while, there was silence, as we all sat around and let the disturbing quality of Dhor's vision sink into our souls. Every so often someone would shudder as he thought of some new twist, some piece of embroidery.

But it was George Finger's speculation that ended the conversation. He said, "Actually, this might be a dangerous line of thought, Steve. Remember the theory that the more believers a god has, the more powerful he becomes? I mean, it's a joke right now, but aren't you summoning a new god into existence this way?"

"Yes, Virginia," Dhor replied, grinning impishly, "There *is* a Satan Clause in the holy contract. But I don't think you need to worry. Our belief in him is insufficient. And unnecessary. We can't create Satan Claus—because he already exists. He came into being when Santa Claus was created. A thing automatically creates its opposite, just by its very existence. You know that. The stronger Santa Claus gets, the stronger Satan Claus must become in opposition."

Steven had been raised in a very religious household. His grandmother had taught him that for every act of good, there has to be a corresponding evil. Therefore, if you have heaven, you have to have hell. If you have a God, you have to have a devil. If there are angels, then there have to be demons. Cherubs and imps. Saints and damned. Nine circles of hell—nine circles of heaven. "Better be careful, George! Satan Claus is watching." And then he laughed fiendishly. I guess he thought he was being funny.

I forgot about Steven Dhor for a few weeks. I was

involved in another one of those abortive television proj- ects—it's like doing drugs; you think you can walk away from them, but you can't. Someone offers you a needle and you run to stick it in your arm. And then they jerk you around for another six weeks or six months, and then cut it off anyway—and one morning you wake up and find you're unemployed again. The money's spent, and you've wasted another big chunk of your time and your energy and your enthusiasm on something that will never be broadcast or ever see print. And your credential has gotten that much poorer because you have nothing to show for your effort except another dead baby. You get too many of those dead babies on your resume and the phone stops ringing alto- gether. But I love the excitement, that's why I stay so close to Hollywood—

Then one Saturday afternoon, Steven Dhor read a new story at Kicking the Hobbit—the all science-fiction book- store that used to be in Santa Monica. I'm sure he saw me come in, but he was so engrossed in the story he was read- ing to the crowd that he didn't recognize me.

"...the children believed that they could hear the hooves of the huge black pigs scraping through the darkness. They could hear the snuffling and snorting of their hot breaths. The pigs were foaming at the mouth, grunting and bumping up against each other as they pulled the heavy sled through the black tunnels under the earth. The steel runners of the huge carriage sliced across the stones, striking sparks and ringing with a knife-edged note that shrieked like a metal banshee.

"And the driver—his breath steaming in the terri- ble cold—shouted their names as he whipped them, 'On, damn you, on! You children of war! On Pustule and Canker and Sickness and Gore! On Monster and Seizure and Bastard and Whore. Drive on through the darkness! Break through and roar!'" Dhor's voice rose softly as he read these harrowing passages to his enraptured audience.

I hung back away from the group, listening in

appreciation and wonder. Dhor had truly caught the spirit of the Christmas obscenity. By the very act of saying the name aloud in public, Dhor was not only giving his power to Satan Claus, he was daring the beast to visit him on Christmas Eve.

"*...And in the morning,*" Dhor concluded, "*—there were many deep, knife-like scars in the soft dark earth beneath their bedroom windows. The ground was churned and broken and there were black sooty smudges on the glass. . . . But of their father, there was not a sign. And by this, the children knew that Satan Claus was indeed real. And they never ever laughed again, as long as they lived.*"

The small crowd applauded enthusiastically, and then they crowded in close for autographs. Dhor's grin spread across his cherubic face like a pink glow. He basked in all the attention and the approval of the fans; it warmed him like a deep red bath. He'd found something that touched a nerve in the audience—now he responded to them. Something had taken root in his soul.

I saw Dhor several more times that year. And everywhere, he was reading that festering story aloud again: "*Christmas lay across the land like a blight, and once again, the children huddled in their beds and feared the tread of heavy boot steps in the dark...* "He'd look up from the pages, look across the room at his audience with that terrible impish twinkle and then turn back to his reading with renewed vigor. "*...Millie and little Bob shivered in their nightshirts as Daddy pulled them onto his lap. He smelled of smoke and coal and too much whiskey. His face was blue and scratchy with the stubble of his beard and his heavy flannel shirt scratched their cheeks uncomfortably. 'Why are you trembling?' he asked. 'There's nothing to be afraid of. I'm just going to tell you about the Christmas spirit. His name is Satan Claus, and he drives a big black sled shaped like a hearse. It's pulled by eight big black pigs with smoldering red eyes. Satan Claus stands in the front of the carriage and rides like the whirlwind, lashing* *at the boars with a stinging whip. He beats them until the blood pours from their backs and they scream like the souls of the damned—'"*

In the weeks that followed, he read it at the fund-raiser/ taping for Mike Hodel's literacy project. He read it at the Pasadena Library's Horror/Fantasy Festival. He read it at the Thanksgiving weekend Lost-Con. He read it on Hour 25, and he had tapes made for sale to anyone who wanted one. Steven was riding the tiger. Exploiting it. Whipping it with his need for notoriety.

"'Satan Claus comes in the middle of the night—he scratches at your window, and leaves sooty marks on the glass. Wherever there's fear, wherever there's madness— there you'll find Satan Claus as well. He comes through the wall like smoke and stands at the foot of your bed with eyes like hot coals. He stands there and watches you. His hair is long and gray and scraggly. His beard has terrible little creepy things living in it. You can see them crawling around. Sometimes, he catches one of the bugs that lives in his beard, and he eats it alive. If you wake up on Christmas Eve, he'll be standing there waiting for you. If you scream, he'll grab you and put you in his hearse. He'll carry you straight away to Hell. If you get taken to Hell before you die, you'll never get out. You'll never be redeemed by baby Jesus. . . . '

And then the Christmas issue of *Ominous* magazine came out and *everybody* was reading it.

"Little Bob began to weep and Millie reached out to him, trying to comfort his tears; but Daddy gripped her arm firmly and held her at arm's length. 'Now, Millie—don't you help him. Bobby has to learn how to be a man. Big boys don't cry. If you cry, then for sure Satan Claus will come and get you. He won't even put you in his hearse. He'll just eat you alive. He'll pluck you out of your bed and crunch your bones in his teeth. He has teeth as sharp as razors and jaws as powerful as an axe. First he'll bite your arms off and then he'll bite off your legs—and then

he'll even bite off your little pink peepee. And you better believe that'll hurt. And then, finally, when he's bitten off every other part of you, finally he'll bite your head off! So you mustn't cry. Do you understand me!' Daddy shook Bobby as hard as he could, so hard that Bobby's head bounced back and forth on his shoulders and Bobby couldn't help himself; he bawled as loud as he could."

People were calling each other on the phone and asking if they'd seen the story and wasn't it the most frightening story they'd ever heard? It was as if they were enrolling converts into a new religion. They were all having much too much fun playing with the legend of Satan Claus, adding to it, building it—giving their power of belief to Father Darkness, the Christmas evil . . . as if by naming the horror, they might somehow remain immune to it.

"'Listen! Maybe you can hear him even now? Feel the ground rumble? No, that's not a train. That's Father Darkness—Satan Claus. Yes, he's always there. Do you hear his horn? Do you hear the ugly snuffling of the eight rabid pigs? He's coming closer. Maybe this year he's coming for you. This year, you'd better stay asleep all night long. Maybe this year, I won't be able to stop him from getting you!'"

Then some right-wing religious zealot down in Orange County saw the story; his teenage son had borrowed a copy of the magazine from a friend; so of course the censorship issue came bubbling right up to the surface like a three-day corpse in a swamp.

Dhor took full advantage of the situation. He ended up doing a public reading on the front steps of the Los Angeles Central Library. The L.A. Times printed his picture, and a long article about this controversial new young fantasy writer who was challenging the outmoded literary conventions of our times. Goodman Hallmouth showed up of course—he'd get up off his death bed for a media event—and made his usual impassioned statement on how Dhor was exposing the hypocrisy of Christmas in America.

"The children trembled in their cold, cold beds, afraid to close their eyes, afraid to fall asleep. They knew that Father Darkness would soon be there, standing at the foot of their beds and watching them fiercely to see if they were truly sleeping or just pretending."

Of course, it all came to a head at Art and Lydia's Christmas Eve party. They always invited the whole community, whoever was in town. You not only got to see all your friends, but all your enemies as well. You had to be there, to find out what people were saying about you behind your back.

Lydia must have spent a week cooking. She had huge platters piled with steaming turkey, ham, roast beef, lasagna, mashed potatoes, sweet potatoes, tomatoes in basil and dill, corn on the cob, pickled cabbage, four kinds of salad, vegetable casseroles, quiche and deviled eggs. She had plates of cookies and chocolates everywhere; the bathtub was filled with ice and bottles of imported beer and cans of Coca-Cola. Art brought in champagne and wine and imported mineral water for Goodman Hallmouth.

And then they invited the seven-year locusts.

All the writers, both serious and not-so, showed up; some of them wearing buttons that said, "Turn down a free meal, get thrown out of the Guild." Artists too, but they generally had better table manners. One year, two of them nearly got trampled in the rush to the buffet. After that, Lydia started weeding out the guest list.

This year, the unofficial theme of the party was "Satan Claus is coming to town." The tree was draped in black crepe and instead of an angel on top, there was a large black bat. Steven Dhor even promised to participate in a "summoning."

"Little Bob still whimpered softly. He wiped his nose on his sleeve. Finally, Millie got out of her bed and crept softly across the floor and slipped into bed next to little Bob. She put her arms around him and held him close and began whispering as quietly as she could. 'He can't hurt

us if we're good. So we'll just be as good as we can. Okay. We'll pray to baby Jesus and ask him to watch out for us, okay?' Little Bob nodded and sniffed, and Millie began to pray for the both of them. . . . "

I got there late. I had other errands to run. It's always that way on the holidays.

Steven Dhor was holding court in the living room, sitting on the floor in the middle of a rapt group of wanna-bees and never-wases; he was embellishing the legend of Satan Claus. He'd already announced that he was planning to do a collection of Satan Claus stories, or perhaps even a novel telling the whole story of Satan Claus from beginning to end. Just as St. Nicholas had been born out of good deeds, so had Satan Claus been forged from the evil that stalked the earth on the night before Jesus' birth.

According to legend—legend according to Dhor—the devil was powerless to stop the birth of baby Jesus, but that didn't stop him from raising hell in his own way. On the eve of the very first Christmas, the devil turned loose all his imps upon the world and told them to steal out among the towns and villages of humankind and spread chaos and dismay among all the world's children. Leave no innocent being unharmed. It was out of this beginning that Satan Claus came forth. At first he was small, but he grew. Every year, the belief of the children gave him more and more power.

"The children slept fitfully. They tossed and turned and made terrible little sounds of fear. Their dreams were filled with darkness and threats. They held onto each other all night long. They were awakened by a rumbling deep within the earth, the whole house rolled uneasily—"

Dhor had placed himself so he could see each new arrival come in the front door. He grinned up at each one in a conspiratorial grin of recognition and shared evil, as if to say, "See? It works. Everybody loves it." I had to laugh. He didn't understand. He probably never would. He was so in love with himself and his story and the power of his words, he missed the greater vision. I turned away and went prowling through the party in search of food and drink.

"They came awake together, Millie and little Bob. They came awake with a gasp—they were too frightened to move.

"Something was tapping softly on the bedroom window. It scraped slowly at the glass. But they were both too afraid to look."

Lydia was dressed in a black witch's costume, she even wore a tall pointed hat. She was in the kitchen stirring a huge cauldron of hot mulled wine and cackling like the opening scene in Macbeth, "Double, double toil and trouble, fire burn and cauldron bubble—" and having a wonderful time of it. For once, she was enjoying one of her own parties. She waved her wooden spoon around her head like a mallet, laughing in maniacal glee.

Christmas was a lot more fun without all those sappy little elves and angels, all those damned silver bells and the mandatory choral joy of the endless hallelujahs. Steven Dhor had given voice to the rebellious spirit, had found a way to battle the ennui of a month steeped in Christmas cheer. These people were going to enjoy every nasty moment of it.

"A huge dark shape loomed like a wall at the foot of their bed. It stood there, blocking the dim light of the hallway. They could hear its uneven heavy breath sounding like the inhalations of a terrible beast. They could smell the reek of death and decay. Millie put her hand across little Bob's mouth to keep him from crying.

"'Oh, please don't hurt us,' she cried. She couldn't help herself. 'Please—'"

I circulated once through the party, taking roll—seeing who was being naughty, who was being nice. Goodman Hallmouth was muttering darkly about the necessity for revenge. Writers, he said, are the Research and Development Division for the whole human race; the only *specialists* in revenge in the whole world. Bread Bryan was standing around looking mournful. George Finger wasn't here, he was back in the hospital again. Railroad Martin was showing off a new T-shirt; it said, "Help, I'm trapped inside a T-shirt."

And of course, there was the usual coterie of fans and unknowns—I knew them by their fannish identities: the Elephant, the Undertaker, the Blob, the Duck.

"And then—a horrible thing happened. A second shape appeared behind the first, bigger and darker. Its crimson eyes blazed with unholy rage. A cold wind swept through the room. A low groaning noise, somewhere between a moan and an earthquake resounded through the house like a scream. Black against a darker black, the first shape turned and saw what stood behind it. It began to shrivel and shrink. The greater darkness enveloped the lesser, pulled it close, and—did something horrible. In the gloom, the children could not clearly see; but they heard ever terrible crunch and gurgle. They heard the choking gasps and felt the floor shudder with the weight.

"Millie screamed then, so did little Bob. They closed their eyes and screamed as hard as they could. They screamed for their very lives. They screamed and screamed and kept on screaming—"

Steven Dhor got very drunk that night—first on his success, then on Art and Lydia's wine. About two in the morning, he became abusive and started telling people what he really thought of them. At first, people thought he was kidding, but then he called Hallmouth a poseur and a phony, and Lydia had to play referee. Finally Bread Bryan and Railroad Martin drove him home and poured him into bed. He passed out in the car, only rousing himself occasionally to vomit out the window.

The next morning, Steven Dhor was gone.

Art stopped by his place on Christmas morning to see if he was all right; but Dhor didn't answer his knock. Art walked around the back and banged on the back door too.

Still no answer. He peeked in the bedroom window, and the bed was disheveled and empty, so Art assumed that Steven had gotten up early and left, perhaps to spend Christmas with a friend. But he didn't know him well enough to guess who he might have gone to see. Nobody did.

Later, the word began to spread that he was missing.

His landlady assumed he'd skipped town to avoid paying his rent. Goodman Hallmouth said he thought Steven had gone home to visit his family in Florida, and would probably return shortly. Bread Bryan said that Steve had mentioned taking a sabbatical, a cross-country hitchhiking trip. Railroad Martin filed a missing person report, but after a few routine inquiries, the police gave up the investigation. George Finger suggested that Satan Claus had probably taken him, but under the circumstances, it was considered a rather tasteless joke and wasn't widely repeated.

But...George was right.

Steven Dhor had come awake at the darkest moment of the night, stumbling out of a fitful and uncomfortable sleep. He rubbed his eyes and sat up in bed—and then he saw me standing there, watching him. Waiting.

I'd been watching him and waiting for him since the day he'd first spoken my name aloud, since the moment he'd first given me shape and form and the power of his belief. I'd been hungry for him ever since.

He was delicious. I crunched his bones like breadsticks. I drank his blood like wine. The young ones are always tasty. I savored the flavor of his soul for a long, long time.

And, of course, before I left, I made sure to leave the evidence of my visit. Art saw it, but he never told anyone: sooty smudges on the bedroom window, and the ground beneath it all torn up and churned, as if by the milling of many heavy-footed creatures.

About the Authors

Lisa Morton is a screenwriter, author of non-fiction books, award-winning prose writer, and Halloween expert whose work was described by the American Library Association's Readers' Advisory Guide to Horror as "consistently dark, unsettling, and frightening." Her most recent releases include *Ghosts: A Haunted History* and the short story collection *Cemetery Dance Select: Lisa Morton*. She currently serves as President of the Horror Writers Association, and can be found online at: www.lisamorton.com

K. A. Opperman is a horror writer and poet from Southern California. His strongest influences are H. P. Lovecraft, Clark Ashton Smith, and all classic Weird and supernatural literature. His debut verse collection, *The Crimson Tome*, is out now from Hippocampus Press.

Elise Forier Edie worked as a playwright for many years, before turning to writing speculative fiction. Her most recent publications include short stories, "You-Go-Back" in *Strange Tales V* (Tartarus Press), and "Leonora" in *Chilling Horror Short Stories* (Flame Tree Publications). She is also the author of a paranormal romance novella, *The Devil in Midwinter*, which was released in 2014, by World Weaver Press.

Elise is a member of the Horror Writers Association, Los Angeles (HWA) and the Authors Guild and a graduate of the Odyssey Writing Workshop. She currently heads up the Theater Arts program at West Los Angeles College, where she teaches playwriting. You can find out more about her at her website: www.eliseforieredie.com

Lauren Candia is the co-creator and co-host of the Shades & Shadows Reading Series, LA's creepiest ongoing literary happening. By day, she works at a library where she spends a great deal of time trying to convince people they should love all the same books she loves. Her writing can be found in the *East Jasmine Review* and the *Los Angeles Times*. She will be your BFF on Facebook and Twitter @ParanormaLauren. All you have to do is ask.

David Ghilardi is the author of three books: *To Carol In 17, Olde Irving Park* and (2016) *Dark Shadows of Chicago*. He is the writer/creator of *Mix*, a horror/suspense series currently in production for 2016. Please see more at Davidghilardi.com and IMDB. Quantum Amor Judith!

Kate Maruyama's novel, *Harrowgate* was published by 47North in 2013 and her short story, "Akiko" is featured in *Phantasma: Stories* out just this fall. Her short fiction has been published in *Arcadia Magazine, Controlled Burn, Stoneboat* and on *Role Reboot, Gemini Magazine, Salon, The Rumpus* and *The Citron Review*, among others. She holds an MFA in Creative Writing from Antioch University Los Angeles, where she is now affiliate faculty in their MFA and BA programs and is part of the team behind inspiration2publication.com. She is an instructor with Writing Workshops Los Angeles. She writes, teaches, cooks and eats in Los Angeles where she lives with her family.

Kate Jonez writes dark fantasy fiction. *Ceremony of Flies* was a 2015 Shirley Jackson Award nominee. Her Bram Stoker ® Award nominated novel *Candy House* is available at Amazon in print and ebook.

She is also chief editor at Omnium Gatherum a small press

dedicated to publishing unique dark fantasy, weird fiction and horror in print and ebook. Several Omnium Gatherum books have been nominated for awards.

Sean Patrick Traver writes about witches and weirdness in the City of Angels. His work reflects a lifelong interest in myth, magic, and Los Angeles history. Nerdist.com said of his novel *Graves' End*: "Masterfully blending the constraints of time and reality, Traver twists everything into a plot that feels both brand new and old-fashioned in a nearly perfect blend." Check out his world at www.SeanPatrickTraver.com

Kevin Wetmore is an award-winning writer, actor and director whose fiction has appeared in such magazines as Mothership Zeta and *Devolution Z*, as well as such anthologies as *Midian Unmade, Enter at Your Own Risk: The End is the Beginning, History and Horror, Oh My!, Moonshadows, Whispers from the Abyss 2*, and many others. His writing on horror has also appeared in *Horror Studies, Gothic Studies, Horror 201: The Silver Scream*, and *Social Research*. He is also author of *Post-9/11 Horror in American Cinema* and *Back from the Dead: Reading Remakes of Romero's Zombie Films as Markers of their Times*. He lives with his family in Los Angeles and is a proud member of HWA.

David Blake Lucarelli is a writer, editor, musician and sound engineer. He is best known for *The Children's Vampire Hunting Brigade* graphic novels. He lives in Hollywood with his wife Sherry, son Calvin, and their cats.

Eric J. Guignard is a writer and editor of dark and speculative fiction, operating from the shadowy outskirts of Los Angeles. He's won the 2013 Bram Stoker Award and was a finalist for the 2014 International Thriller Writers Award. Outside the glamorous and jet-setting world of indie fiction, Eric's a technical writer and college professor, and he stumbles home each day to a wife, children, cats, and a terrarium filled with mischievous beetles. Visit Eric at: www.ericjguignard.com, his blog: ericjguignard.blogspot.com, or Twitter: @ericjguignard.

Janet Joyce Holden is the author of the supernatural novels *Carousel*, and *The Only Red Is Blood*, and the thriller vampire series *Origins of Blood*. She is originally from the north of England, and lives in southern California.

Robin Morris dwells somewhere near Los Angeles, accompanied by two cats and the certainty that life has no meaning. She is the author of the novel *Mama*, and the collection of short stories *Halloween Sky and Other Nightmares*. She has also been published in a number of anthologies.

Michael Paul Gonzalez is the author of the novels *Angel Falls* and *Miss Massacre's Guide to Murder and Vengeance*. A member of the Horror Writers Association, his short stories have appeared in print and online, including *Gothic Fantasy: Chilling Horror Stories, 18 Wheels of Horror, The Booked Podcast Anthology*, HeavyMetal.com, and the *Appalachian Undead Anthology*. He resides in Los Angeles, a place full of wonders and monsters far stranger than any that live in the imagination. You can visit him online at MichaelPaulGonzalez.com

Robert Payne Cabeen is a screenwriter, artist, and purveyor of narrative horror poetry. His screenwriting credits include Heavy Metal 2000, for Columbia TriStar, Sony Pictures, A Monkey's Tale, and Walking with Buddha. Cabeen's latest book, Fearworms: Selected Poems, was a 2015 Bram Stoker® Award nominee. For more about Fearworms, visit: fearworms.com

As creative director for Streamline Pictures, Robert helped anime pioneer Carl Macek bring Japanese animated features, like *Akira* and dozens of other classics, to a western audience. Cabeen received a Master of Fine Arts degree from Otis Art Institute, with a dual major in painting and design. Since then, he has combined his interests in the visual arts with screenwriting and story editing for a broad range of entertainment companies including Warner Brothers, Columbia/TriStar, Disney, Sony, Universal, USA Network, Nelvana, and SEGA. For more about Robert Payne Cabeen, visit: robertpaynecabeen.com

Hal Bodner is a Bram Stoker Award® nominated author who, while best known for his gay satire/comedies, often writes in the horror genre. The year it was published, his freshman vampire novel, Bite Club, made him one of the top-selling GLBT authors in the country. To this day, the royalties help keep him in the proverbial "cigarettes and nylons"—even though he quit smoking five years ago and never did drag.

For several years, Hal wrote erotic paranormal romances, most notably In *Flesh and Stone.* His agent cringes when he refers to these books as "supernatural smut." He rarely writes erotica anymore, mostly because he has run out of interesting verbs to use when describing various intimate bodily functions. He is currently working on several thrillers which paint classic "noir" with a decidedly lavender glaze. Hal is legally married to a wonderful man, half his age, who never knew that Liza Minnelli was Judy Garland's daughter.

Tracy L. Carbone is the author of five novels, a short story collection, and dozens of dark fiction stories published in magazines and anthologies in the U.S. and Canada. The anthology she edited, Epitaphs: A Journal of the New England Horror Writers was nominated for the Bram Stoker Award®. She recently located from New England to Southern California and is hard at work on her newest novel, The Rainbox.

Xach Fromson is a Los Angeles native who has been obsessed with horror and dark fiction from a very young age. He received his BA in Creative Writing from California State University Northridge in 2009. He earned his MFA in Creative Writing from the University of California Riverside's Palm Desert program. He appeared on stage at Dirty Laundry Lit in February, 2013, and has a short story in the 2014 anthology *Halloween Tales*. He is currently in various stages of working on a ton of projects. He is co-founder and co-host of the Shades & Shadows literary nonprofit, which can be found online at www.shadesandshadows.org. And once, he slew a dragon.

The Behrg is the author of dark literary works ranging from screenplays to "to-do" lists. His debut novel, *Housebroken*, was a First-Round Kindle Scout Selection, and semi-finalist in the 2015 Kindle Book Awards. He has had several short stories published in both print and digital anthologies and is the author of *The Creation Series*, with books two and three scheduled for a 2016 release. His "to-do" list should be completed by 2017... (though his wife is hoping for a little sooner). Discover why he writes as "The Behrg" at his website: TheBehrg.com

Ian Welke grew up in the library in Long Beach, California. After receiving his BA in History from California State University, Long Beach, he worked in the computer games industry for fifteen years where he was lucky enough to work at Blizzard Entertainment and at Runic Games in Seattle. While living in Seattle he sold his first short story, a space-western, written mainly because he was depressed that Firefly had been canceled. Following the insane notion that life is short and he should do what he wants most, he moved back to southern California and started writing full time. His novels, *The Whisperer in Dissonance* (2014) and *End Times at Ridgemont High* (2015) were both published by Ominium Gatherum Media.

Terry M. West is a writer, filmmaker and artist. He has written several horror short stories and the novel Dreg. He was a finalist for two International Horror Guild awards and he was featured on the TV Guide SciFi Hot List. Visit his website: www.terrymwest.com

Regina West is a former live television news director, a filmmaker, journalist, editor and American Mensa member. She has traveled the world and studied numerous foreign languages.

Ashley Dioses is a writer of dark fantasy, horror, and weird poetry. She is currently working on her first book of weird poetry to be hopefully out in 2016 from Hippocampus Press. Her poetry has appeared in *Weird Fiction Review, Spectral Realms, Weirdbook Magazine, Xnoybis, Necronomicum, Gothic Blue Book*, and elsewhere. Her poem, "Carathis", published in *Spectral Realms No. 1*, appears in Ellen Datlow's full recommended Best Horror of the Year Volume Seven list.

Kathryn McGee is a graduate student in the UC Riverside Palm Desert MFA program in Creative Writing and Writing for the Performing Arts, where she has completed her first novel and written critical essays about haunted house fiction. She lives in Los Angeles, California and works as an architectural historian.

David Gerrold is the author of over 50 books, hundreds of articles and columns, and over a dozen television episodes. He is a classic sci-fi writer who will go down in history as having created some of the most popular and redefining scripts, books, and short stories in the genre.